VANITY FAIR
A NOVEL WITHOUT A HERO

PART II (CONT.)
PART III

WILLIAM MAKEPEACE THACKERAY

VANITY FAIR

A NOVEL WITHOUT A HERO

PART II (CONT.)
PART III

GARDEN CITY PUBLISHING COMPANY, INC.
Garden City, New York

DE LUXE EDITION

1937
GARDEN CITY PUBLISHING CO., INC.

CONTENTS

CONTENTS

VANITY FAIR
A NOVEL WITHOUT A HERO

PART II (CONT.)
PART III

CHAPTER XVIII

STRUGGLES AND TRIALS

OUR friends at Brompton were meanwhile passing their Christmas after their fashion, and in a manner by no means too cheerful.

Out of the hundred pounds a year, which was about the amount of her income, the widow Osborne had been in the habit of giving up nearly three-fourths to her father and mother, for the expenses of herself and her little boy. With £120 more, supplied by Jos, this family of four people, attended by a single Irish servant who also did for Clapp and his wife, might manage to live in decent comfort through the year, and hold up their heads yet, and be able to give a friend a dish of tea still, after the storms and disappointments of their early life. Sedley still maintained his ascendancy over the family of Mr. Clapp, his ex-clerk. Clapp remembered the time when, sitting on the edge of the chair, he tossed off a bumper to the health of "Mrs. S——, Miss Emmy, and Mr. Joseph in India," at the merchant's rich table in Russell Square. Time magnified the splendour of those recollections in the honest clerk's bosom. Whenever he came up from the kitchen-parlour to the drawing-room, and partook of tea or gin-and-water with Mr. Sedley, he would say, "This was not what you was accustomed to once, sir," and as gravely and reverentially drink the health of the ladies as he had done in the days of their utmost prosperity. He thought Miss 'Melia's playing the divinest music ever performed, and her the finest lady. He never would sit down before Sedley at the club even, nor would he have that gentleman's character abused by any member of the society. He had seen the first men in London shaking hands with Mr. S——; he said, " He'd known him in times when Rothschild might be seen on 'Change with him any day, and he owed him personally everythink."

Clapp, with the best of characters and hand-writings, had been able very soon after his master's disaster to find other employment for himself. " Such a little fish as me can swim in any bucket," he used to remark, and a member of the house from which old Sedley had seceded was very glad to make use of Mr. Clapp's services, and to reward them with a comfortable salary. In fine, all Sedley's wealthy friends had dropped off one by one, and this poor ex-dependent still remained faithfully attached to him.

Out of the small residue of her income, which Amelia kept back for herself, the widow had need of all the thrift and care possible in order to enable her to keep her darling boy dressed in such a manner as became George Osborne's son, and to defray the expenses of the little school to which, after much misgiving and reluctance, and many secret pangs and fears on her own part, she had been induced to send the lad. She had sate up of nights conning lessons and spelling over crabbed grammars and geography books in order to teach them to Georgy. She had worked even at the Latin accidence, fondly hoping that she might be capable of instructing him in that language. To part with him all day: to send him out to the mercy of a schoolmaster's cane and his schoolfellows' roughness, was almost like weaning him over again, to that weak mother, so tremulous and full of sensibility. He, for his part, rushed off to

the school with the utmost happiness. He was longing
for the change. That childish gladness wounded his
mother, who was herself so grieved to part with him.
She would rather have had him more sorry, she thought:
and then was deeply repentant within herself, for daring
to be so selfish as to wish her own son to be unhappy.

Georgy made great progress in the school, which was
kept by a friend of his mother's constant admirer, the
Rev. Mr. Binny. He brought home numberless prizes
and testimonials of ability. He told his mother countless stories every night about his school-companions:
and what a fine fellow Lyons was, and what a sneak
Sniffin was; and how Steel's father actually supplied
the meat for the establishment, whereas Golding's mother
came in a carriage to fetch him every Saturday; and how
Neat had straps to his trousers — might he have straps?
— and how Bull Major was so strong (though only in
Eutropius) that it was believed he could lick the Usher,
Mr. Ward, himself. So Amelia learned to know every
one of the boys in that school as well as Georgy himself: and of nights she used to help him in his exercises
and puzzle her little head over his lessons as eagerly as
if she was herself going in the morning into the presence
of the master. Once, after a certain combat with Master
Smith, George came home to his mother with a black
eye, and bragged prodigiously to his parent and his
delighted old grandfather about his valour in the fight,
in which, if the truth was known, he did not behave
with particular heroism, and in which he decidedly had
the worst. But Amelia has never forgiven that Smith
to this day, though he is now a peaceful apothecary
near Leicester Square.

In these quiet labours and harmless cares the gentle
widow's life was passing away, a silver hair or two marking the progress of time on her head, and a line deepen-

ing ever so little on her fair forehead. She used to smile at these marks of time. "What matters it," she asked, "for an old woman like me?" All she hoped for was to live to see her son great, famous, and glorious, as he deserved to be. She kept his copy-books, his drawings, and compositions, and showed them about in her little circle, as if they were miracles of genius. She confided some of these specimens to Miss Dobbin; to show them to Miss Osborne, George's aunt, to show them to Mr. Osborne himself—to make that old man repent of his cruelty and ill-feeling towards him who was gone. All her husband's faults and foibles she had buried in the grave with him: she only remembered the lover, who had married her at all sacrifices; the noble husband so brave and beautiful, in whose arms she had hung on the morning when he had gone away to fight, and die gloriously for his king. From heaven the hero must be smiling down upon that paragon of a boy whom he had left to comfort and console her.

We have seen how one of George's grandfathers (Mr. Osborne), in his easy chair in Russell Square, daily grew more violent and moody, and how his daughter, with her fine carriage, and her fine horses, and her name on half the public charity-lists of the town, was a lonely, miserable, persecuted old maid. She thought again and again of the beautiful little boy, her brother's son, whom she had seen. She longed to be allowed to drive in the fine carriage to the house in which he lived; and she used to look out day after day as she took her solitary drive in the Park, in hopes that she might see him. Her sister, the banker's lady, occasionally condescended to pay her old home and companion a visit in Russell Square. She brought a couple of sickly children attended by a prim nurse, and in a faint genteel giggling tone cackled to her sister about her fine acquaint-

ance, and how her little Frederick was the image of
Lord Claud Lollypop, and her sweet Maria had been
noticed by the Baroness as they were driving in their
donkey-chaise at Roehampton. She urged her to make
her papa do something for the darlings. Frederick she
had determined should go into the Guards; and if they
made an elder son of him (and Mr. Bullock was positively ruining and pinching himself to death to buy
land), how was the darling girl to be provided for? " I
expect *you*, dear," Mrs. Bullock would say, " for of
course my share of our Papa's property must go to the
head of the house, you know. Dear Rhoda McMull
will disengage the whole of the Castletoddy property
as soon as poor dear Lord Castletoddy dies, who is
quite epileptic; and little Macduff McMull will be Viscount Castletoddy. Both the Mr. Bludyers of Mincing
Lane have settled their fortunes on Fanny Bludyer's little
boy. My darling Frederick must positively be an eldest
son ; and — and do ask Papa to bring us back his account
in Lombard Street, will you, dear? It does n't look well,
his going to Stumpy and Rowdy's." After which kind
of speeches, in which fashion and the main chance were
blended together, and after a kiss, which was like the
contact of an oyster —Mrs. Frederick Bullock would
gather her starched nurslings, and simper back into her
carriage.

Every visit which this leader of *ton* paid to her family
was more unlucky for her. Her father paid more money
into Stumpy and Rowdy's. Her patronage became
more and more insufferable. The poor widow in the
little cottage at Brompton, guarding her treasure there,
little knew how eagerly some people coveted it.

On that night when Jane Osborne had told her father
that she had seen his grandson, the old man had made
her no reply: but he had shown no anger — and had

bade her good night on going himself to his room in rather a kindly voice. And he must have meditated on what she said, and have made some inquiries of the Dobbin family regarding her visit; for a fortnight after it took place, he asked her where was her little French watch and chain she used to wear?

"I bought it with my money, sir," she said in a great fright.

"Go and order another like it, or a better if you can get it," said the old gentleman, and lapsed again into silence.

Of late the Misses Dobbin more than once repeated their entreaties to Amelia, to allow George to visit them. His aunt had shown her inclination; perhaps his grandfather himself, they hinted, might be disposed to be reconciled to him. Surely, Amelia could not refuse such advantageous chances for the boy. Nor could she: but she acceded to their overtures with a very heavy and suspicious heart, was always uneasy during the child's absence from her, and welcomed him back as if he was rescued out of some danger. He brought back money and toys, at which the widow looked with alarm and jealousy: she asked him always if he had seen any gentleman — "Only old Sir William, who drove him about in the four-wheeled chaise, and Mr. Dobbin, who arrived on the beautiful bay horse in the afternoon — in the green coat and pink neck-cloth, with the gold-headed whip, who promised to show him the Tower of London, and take him out with the Surrey hounds." At last, he said "There *was* an old gentleman, with thick eye-brows and a broad hat, and large chain and seals." He came one day as the coachman was lunging Georgy round the lawn on the gray pony. "He looked at me very much. He shook very much. I said 'My name is

Norval' after dinner. My aunt began to cry. She is always crying." Such was George's report on that night.

Then Amelia knew that the boy had seen his grandfather: and looked out feverishly for a proposal which she was sure would follow, and which came, in fact, in a few days afterwards. Mr. Osborne formally offered to take the boy, and make him heir to the fortune which he had intended that his father should inherit. He would make Mrs. George Osborne an allowance, such as to assure her a decent competency. If Mrs. George Osborne proposed to marry again, as Mr. O. heard was her intention, he would not withdraw that allowance. But it must be understood, that the child would live entirely with his grandfather in Russell Square, or at whatever other place Mr. O. should select; and that he would be occasionally permitted to see Mrs. George Osborne at her own residence. This message was brought or read to her in a letter one day, when her mother was from home, and her father absent as usual, in the City.

She was never seen angry but twice or thrice in her life, and it was in one of these moods that Mr. Osborne's attorney had the fortune to behold her. She rose up trembling and flushing very much as soon as, after reading the letter, Mr. Poe handed it to her, and she tore the paper into a hundred fragments, which she trod on. "I marry again! — I take money to part from my child! Who dares insult me by proposing such a thing? Tell Mr. Osborne it is a cowardly letter, sir — a cowardly letter — I will not answer it. I wish you good morning, sir — and she bowed me out of the room like a tragedy Queen," said the lawyer who told the story.

Her parents never remarked her agitation on that day, and she never told them of the interview. They had their own affairs to interest them, affairs which deeply interested this innocent and unconscious lady. The old gentleman, her father, was always dabbling in speculation. We have seen how the Wine Company and the Coal Company had failed him. But, prowling about the City always eagerly and restlessly still, he lighted upon some other scheme, of which he thought so well that he embarked in it in spite of the remonstrances of Mr. Clapp, to whom indeed he never dared to tell how far he had engaged himself in it. And as it was always Mr. Sedley's maxim not to talk about money matters before women, they had no inkling of the misfortunes that were in store for them until the unhappy old gentleman was forced to make gradual confessions.

The bills of the little household, which had been settled weekly, first fell into arrear. The remittances had not arrived from India, Mr. Sedley told his wife with a disturbed face. As she had paid her bills very regularly hitherto, one or two of the tradesmen to whom the poor lady was obliged to go round asking for time were very angry at a delay to which they were perfectly used from more irregular customers. Emmy's contribution, paid over cheerfully without any questions, kept the little company in half rations however. And the first six months passed away pretty easily: old Sedley still keeping up with the notion that his shares must rise and that all would be well.

No sixty pounds, however, came to help the household at the end of the half year; and it fell deeper and deeper into trouble — Mrs. Sedley, who was growing infirm and was much shaken, remained silent or wept a great deal with Mrs. Clapp in the kitchen. The butcher was particularly surly: the grocer insolent: once or twice little Georgy had grumbled about the dinners: and Amelia, who still would have been satisfied with a slice of bread for her own dinner, could not but perceive that her son was neglected, and purchased little things out of her private purse to keep the boy in health.

At last they told her, or told her such a garbled story as people in difficulties tell. One day, her own money having been received, and Amelia about to pay it over: she who had kept an account of the moneys expended by her, proposed to keep a certain portion back out of her dividend, having contracted engagements for a new suit for Georgy.

Then it came out that Jos's remittances were not paid; that the house was in difficulties, which Amelia ought to have seen before, her mother said, but she cared for nothing or nobody except Georgy. At this she passed all her money across the table, without a word, to her mother, and returned to her room to cry her eyes out. She had a great access of sensibility too that day, when obliged to go and countermand the clothes, the darling clothes on which she had set her heart for Christmas Day, and the cut and fashion of which she had arranged in many conversations with a small milliner, her friend.

Hardest of all, she had to break the matter to Georgy, who made a loud outcry. Everybody had new clothes at Christmas. The others would laugh at him. He *would* have new clothes. She had promised them to him. The poor widow had only kisses to give him. She darned the old suit in tears. She cast about among her little ornaments to see if she could sell anything to procure the desired novelties. There was her India shawl that Dobbin had sent her. She remembered in former days going with her mother to a fine India shop on Ludgate Hill, where the ladies had all sorts of dealings and bargains in these articles. Her cheeks flushed and her eyes shone with pleasure as she thought of this resource, and she kissed away George to school in the morning, smiling brightly after him. The boy felt that there was good news in her look.

Packing up her shawl in a handkerchief, (another of the gifts of the good Major), she hid them under her cloak, and walked flushed and eager all the way to Ludgate Hill, tripping along by the Park wall, and running over the crossings, so that many a man turned as she hurried by him, and looked after her rosy pretty face. She calculated how she should spend the proceeds of her shawl: how, besides the clothes, she would buy the books that he longed for, and pay his half-year's schooling; and how she would buy a cloak for her father instead of that old great-coat which he wore. She was not mistaken as to the value of the Major's gift. It was a very fine and beautiful web: and the merchant made a very good bargain when he gave her twenty guineas for her shawl.

She ran on amazed and flurried with her riches to Darton's shop in St. Paul's Churchyard, and there purchased the " Parents' Assistant," and the " Sanford and Merton " Georgy longed for, and got into the coach there with her parcel, and went home exulting. And she pleased herself by writing in the fly-leaf in her neatest little hand " George Osborne, A Christmas gift from his affectionate mother." The books are extant to this day, with the fair delicate superscription.

She was going from her own room with the books in her hand to place them on George's table, where he might find them on his return from school; when in the passage, she and her mother met. The gilt bindings of the seven handsome little volumes caught the old lady's eye.

" What are those? " she said.

"Some books for Georgy," Amelia replied — "I — I promised them to him at Christmas."

"Books!" cried the elder lady, indignantly, "Books, when the whole house wants bread! Books, when to keep you and your son in luxury, and your dear father out of gaol, I've sold every trinket I had, the India shawl from my back — even down to the very spoons, that our tradesmen might n't insult us, and that Mr. Clapp, which indeed he is justly entitled, being not a hard landlord, and a civil man, and a father, might have his rent. O Amelia! you break my heart with your books and that boy of yours, whom you are ruining, though part with him you will not. O Amelia, may God send you a more dutiful child than I have had! There's Jos deserts his father in his old age: and there's George, who might be provided for, and who might be rich, going to school like a lord, with a gold watch and chain round his neck — while my dear, dear old man is without a sh — shilling." Hysteric sobs and cries ended Mrs. Sedley's speech — it echoed through every room in the small house, whereof the other female inmates heard every word of the colloquy.

"O mother, mother!" cried poor Amelia in reply. "You told me nothing — I — I promised him the books. I — I only sold my shawl this morning. Take the money — take everything" — and with quivering hands she took out her silver, and her sovereigns, — her precious golden sovereigns, which she thrust into the hands of her mother, whence they overflowed and tumbled, rolling down the stairs.

And then she went into her room, and sank down in despair and utter misery. She saw it all now. Her selfishness was sacrificing the boy. But for her he might have wealth, station, education, and his father's place, which the elder George had forfeited for her sake. She had but to speak the words, and her father was restored to competency: and the boy raised to fortune. O what a conviction it was to that tender and stricken heart!

CHAPTER XIX

GAUNT HOUSE

ALL the world knows that Lord Steyne's town palace stands in Gaunt Square, out of which Great Gaunt Street leads, whither we first conducted Rebecca, in the time of the departed Sir Pitt Crawley. Peering over the railings and through the black trees into the garden of the Square, you see a few miserable governesses with wan-faced pupils wandering round and round it, and round the dreary grassplot in the centre of which rises the statue of Lord Gaunt, who fought at Minden, in a three-tailed wig, and otherwise habited like a Roman Emperor. Gaunt House occupies nearly a side of the Square. The remaining three sides are composed of mansions that have passed away into dowagerism; tall, dark houses, with window-frames of stone, or picked out of a lighter red. Little light seems to be behind those lean, comfortless casements now: and hospitality to have passed away from those doors as much as the laced lacqueys and link-boys of old times, who used to put out their torches in the blank iron extinguishers that still flank the lamps over the steps. Brass plates have penetrated into the Square — Doctors, the Diddlesex Bank Western Branch — the English and European Reunion, &c. — it has a dreary look — nor is my Lord Steyne's palace less dreary. All I have ever seen of it is the

vast wall in front, with the rustic columns at the great
gate, through which an old porter peers sometimes with
a fat and gloomy red face — and over the wall the garret and bed-room windows, and the chimneys, out of
which there seldom comes any smoke now. For the
present Lord Steyne lives at Naples, preferring the
view of the Bay and Capri and Vesuvius, to the dreary
aspect of the wall in Gaunt Square.

A few score yards down New Gaunt Street, and leading into Gaunt Mews indeed, is a little modest back
door, which you would not remark from that of any of
the other stables. But many a little close carriage has
stopped at that door, as my informant (little Tom
Eaves, who knows everything, and who showed me the
place) told me. "The Prince and Perdita have been
in and out of that door, sir," he has often told me;
" Marianne Clarke has entered it with the Duke of ——.
It conducts to the famous *petits appartements* of Lord
Steyne — one, sir, fitted up all in ivory and white satin,
another in ebony and black velvet; there is a little ban-
queting-room taken from Sallust's house at Pompeii,
and painted by Cosway — a little private kitchen, in
which every saucepan was silver, and all the spits were
gold. It was there that Egalité Orleans roasted part-
ridges on the night when he and the Marquis of Steyne
won a hundred thousand from a great personage at
ombre. Half of the money went to the French Revolution, half to purchase Lord Gaunt's Marquisate and
Garter — and the remainder — " but it forms no part
of our scheme to tell what became of the remainder,
for every shilling of which, and a great deal more, little
Tom Eaves, who knows everybody's affairs, is ready to
account.

Besides his town palace, the Marquis had castles and
palaces in various quarters of the three kingdoms,

whereof the descriptions may be found in the road-
books — Castle Strongbow, with its woods, on the Shan-
non shore; Gaunt Castle, in Carmarthenshire, where
Richard II. was taken prisoner — Gauntly Hall in Yorkshire, where I have been informed there were two hundred silver teapots for the breakfasts of the guests of
the house, with everything to correspond in splendour;
and Stillbrook in Hampshire, which was my lord's farm,
an humble place of residence, of which we all remember the wonderful furniture which was sold at my lord's
demise by a late celebrated auctioneer.

The Marchioness of Steyne was of the renowned
and ancient family of the Caerlyons, Marquises of Camelot, who have preserved the old faith ever since the
conversion of the venerable Druid, their first ancestor,
and whose pedigree goes far beyond the date of the
arrival of King Brute in these islands. Pendragon is the
title of the eldest son of the house. The sons have
been called Arthurs, Uthers, and Caradocs, from imme-
morial time. Their heads have fallen in many a loyal
conspiracy. Elizabeth chopped off the head of the
Arthur of her day, who had been Chamberlain to Philip
and Mary, and carried letters between the Queen of
Scots and her uncles the Guises. A cadet of the house
was an officer of the great Duke, and distinguished in
the famous Saint Bartholomew conspiracy. During the
whole of Mary's confinement, the house of Camelot
conspired in her behalf. It was as much injured by its
charges in fitting out an armament against the Span-
iards, during the time of the Armada, as by the fines
and confiscations levied on it by Elizabeth for harbour-
ing of priests, obstinate recusancy, and Popish misdoings. A recreant of James's time was momentarily
perverted from his religion by the arguments of that
great theologian, and the fortunes of the family some-

what restored by his timely weakness. But the Earl of
Camelot, of the reign of Charles, returned to the old
creed of his family, and they continued to fight for it,
and ruin themselves for it, as long as there was a Stuart
left to head or to instigate a rebellion.

Lady Mary Caerlyon was brought up at a Parisian
convent; the Dauphiness Marie Antoinette was her
godmother. In the pride of her beauty she had been
married — sold, it was said — to Lord Gaunt, then at
Paris, who won vast sums from the lady's brother at
some of Philip of Orleans's banquets. The Earl of
Gaunt's famous duel with the Count de la Marche, of
the Grey Musqueteers, was attributed by common report to the pretensions of that officer (who had been a
page, and remained a favourite of the Queen) to the
hand of the beautiful Lady Mary Caerlyon. She was
married to Lord Gaunt while the Count lay ill of his
wound, and came to dwell at Gaunt House, and to figure
for a short time in the splendid Court of the Prince of
Wales. Fox had toasted her. Morris and Sheridan
had written songs about her. Malmesbury had made
her his best bow; Walpole had pronounced her charming; Devonshire had been almost jealous of her; but
she was scared by the wild pleasures and gaieties of
the society into which she was flung, and after she had
borne a couple of sons, shrank away into a life of devout seclusion. No wonder that my Lord Steyne, who
liked pleasure and cheerfulness, was not often seen after
their marriage, by the side of this trembling, silent,
superstitious, unhappy lady.

The before-mentioned Tom Eaves (who has no part
in this history, except that he knew all the great folks
in London, and the stories and mysteries of each
family), had further information regarding my Lady
Steyne, which may or may not be true. "The humili-

ations," Tom used to say, " which that woman has been made to undergo, in her own house, have been frightful; Lord Steyne has made her sit down to table with women with whom I would rather die than allow Mrs. Eaves to associate — with Lady Crackenbury, with Mrs. Chippenham, with Madame de la Cruchecassée, the French secretary's wife," (from every one of which ladies Tom Eaves — who would have sacrificed his wife for knowing them — was too glad to get a bow or a dinner), " with the *reigning favourite*, in a word. And do you suppose that that woman, of that family, who are as proud as the Bourbons, and to whom the Steynes are but lacqueys, mushrooms of yesterday (for after all, they are *not* of the Old Gaunts, but of a minor and doubtful branch of the house); do you suppose, I say," (the reader must bear in mind that it is always Tom Eaves who speaks), " that the Marchioness of Steyne, the haughtiest woman in England, would bend down to her husband so submissively, if there were not some cause? Pooh! I tell you there are *secret reasons*. I tell you, that in the emigration, the Abbé de la Marche who was here and was employed in the Quiberoon business with Puisaye and Tinteniac, was the same Colonel of Mousquetaires Gris with whom Steyne fought in the year '86 — that he and the Marchioness met again: that it was after the Reverend Colonel was shot in Brittany, that Lady Steyne took to those extreme practices of devotion which she carries on now; for she is closeted with her director every day — she is at service at Spanish Place, every morning, I've watched her there — that is, I've happened to be passing there — and depend on it, there's a mystery in her case. People are not so unhappy unless they have something to repent of," added Tom Eaves with a knowing wag of his head; " and depend on it, that woman would not be so submissive as she is, if the Marquis had not some sword to hold over her."

So, if Mr. Eaves's information be correct, it is very likely that this lady, in her high station, had to submit to many a private indignity, and to hide many secret griefs under a calm face. And let us, my brethren who have not our names in the Red Book, console ourselves by thinking comfortably how miserable our betters may be, and that Damocles, who sits on satin cushions, and is served on gold plate, has an awful sword hanging over his head in the shape of a bailiff, or an hereditary disease, or a family secret, which peeps out every now and then from the embroidered arras in a ghastly manner, and will be sure to drop one day or the other in the right place.

In comparing, too, the poor man's situation with that of the great, there is (always according to Mr. Eaves) another source of comfort for the former. You who have little or no patrimony to bequeath or to inherit, may be on good terms with your father or your son, whereas the heir of a great prince, such as my Lord Steyne, must naturally be angry at being kept out of his kingdom, and eye the occupant of it with no very agreeable glances. "Take it as a rule," this sardonic old Eaves would say, "the fathers and elder sons of all great families hate each other. The Crown Prince is always in opposition to the crown or hankering after it. Shakspeare knew the world, my good sir, and when he describes Prince Hal (from whose family the Gaunts pretend to be descended, though they are no more related to John of Gaunt than you are,) trying on his father's coronet, he gives you a natural description of all heirs-apparent. If you were heir to a dukedom and a thousand pounds a day, do you mean to say you would not wish for possession? Pooh! And it stands to reason that every great man, having experienced this feeling towards his father, must be aware that his son entertains it towards himself; and so they can't but be suspicious and hostile.

" Then again, as to the feeling of elder towards younger sons. My dear sir, you ought to know that every elder brother looks upon the cadets of the house as his natural enemies, who deprive him of so much ready money which ought to be his by right. I have often heard George Mac Turk, Lord Bajazet's eldest son, say that if he had his will when he came to the title, he would do what the sultans do, and clear the estate by chopping off all his younger brothers' heads at once; and so the case is, more or less, with them all. I tell you they are all Turks in their hearts. Pooh! sir, they know the world." And here, haply, a great man coming up, Tom Eaves's hat would drop off his head, and he would rush forward with a bow and a grin, which showed that he knew the world too — in the Tomeavesian way, that is. And having laid out every shilling of his fortune on an annuity, Tom could afford to bear no malice to his nephews and nieces, and to have no other feeling with regard to his betters, but a constant and generous desire to dine with them.

Between the Marchioness and the natural and tender regard of mother for children, there was that cruel barrier placed of difference of faith. The very love which she might feel for her sons, only served to render the timid and pious lady more fearful and unhappy. The gulf which separated them was fatal and impassable. She could not stretch her weak arms across it, or draw her children over to that side away from which her belief told her there was no safety. During the youth of his sons, Lord Steyne, who was a good scholar and amateur casuist, had no better sport in the evening

after dinner in the country than in setting the boys'
tutor, the Reverend Mr. Trail (now my Lord Bishop
of Ealing,) on her ladyship's director, Father Mole, over
their wine, and in pitting Oxford against St. Acheul.
He cried " Bravo, Latimer! Well said, Loyola! " alter-
nately; he promised Mole a bishopric if he would come
over; and vowed he would use all his influence to get
Trail a cardinal's hat if he would secede. Neither
divine allowed himself to be conquered; and though
the fond mother hoped that her youngest and favourite
son would be reconciled to her church — his mother
church — a sad and awful disappointment awaited the
devout lady — a disappointment which seemed to be a
judgment upon her for the sin of her marriage.

My Lord Gaunt married, as every person who frequents the Peerage knows, the Lady Blanche Thistlewood, a daughter of the noble house of Bareacres,
before mentioned in this veracious history. A wing of
Gaunt House was assigned to this couple; for the head
of the family chose to govern it, and while he reigned
to reign supreme: his son and heir, however, living little
at home, disagreeing with his wife, and borrowing upon
post-obits such moneys as he required beyond the very
moderate sums which his father was disposed to allow
him. The Marquis knew every shilling of his son's
debts. At his lamented demise, he was found himself
to be possessor of many of his heir's bonds, purchased
for their benefit, and devised by his Lordship to the
children of his younger son.

As, to my Lord Gaunt's dismay, and the chuckling
delight of his natural enemy and father, the Lady Gaunt
had no children — the Lord George Gaunt was desired
to return from Vienna, where he was engaged in waltzing
and diplomacy, and to contract a matrimonial alliance
with the Honourable Joan, only daughter of John

Johnes, First Baron Helvellyn, and head of the firm of
Jones, Brown, and Robinson, of Threadneedle Street,
Bankers; from which union sprang several sons and
daughters, whose doings do not appertain to this story.

The marriage at first was a happy and prosperous one.
My Lord George Gaunt could not only read, but write
pretty correctly. He spoke French with considerable
fluency; and was one of the finest waltzers in Europe.
With these talents, and his interest at home, there was
little doubt that his lordship would rise to the highest
dignities in his profession. The lady, his wife, felt that
courts were her sphere; and her wealth enabled her to
receive splendidly in those continental towns whither her
husband's diplomatic duties led him. There was talk of
appointing him minister, and bets were laid at the Travellers' that he would be ambassador ere long, when of a
sudden, rumours arrived of the secretary's extraordinary
behaviour. At a grand diplomatic dinner given by his
chief, he had started up, and declared that a *pâté de foie
gras* was poisoned. He went to a ball at the hotel of
the Bavarian envoy, the Count de Springbock-Hohen-
laufen, with his head shaved, and dressed as a Capuchin
friar. It was not a masked ball, as some folks wanted to
persuade you. It was something queer, people whispered. His grandfather was so. It was in the family.

His wife and family returned to this country, and took
up their abode at Gaunt House. Lord George gave up
his post on the European continent, and was gazetted
to Brazil. But people knew better; he never returned
from that Brazil expedition — never died there — never
lived there — never was there at all. He was nowhere:
he was gone out altogether. "Brazil," said one gossip
to another, with a grin — "Brazil is St. John's Wood.
Rio Janeiro is a cottage surrounded by four walls; and
George Gaunt is accredited to a keeper, who has in-

vested him with the order of the Strait-Waistcoat."
These are the kinds of epitaphs which men pass over
one another in Vanity Fair.

Twice or thrice in a week, in the earliest morning, the
poor mother went for her sins and saw the poor invalid.
Sometimes he laughed at her (and his laughter was more
pitiful than to hear him cry); sometimes she found the
brilliant dandy diplomatist of the Congress of Vienna
dragging about a child's toy, or nursing the keeper's
baby's doll. Sometimes he knew her and Father Mole,
her director and companion: oftener he forgot her, as
he had done wife, children, love, ambition, vanity. But
he remembered his dinner-hour, and used to cry if his
wine-and-water was not strong enough.

It was the mysterious taint of the blood: the poor
mother had brought it from her own ancient race. The
evil had broken out once or twice in the father's family,
long before Lady Steyne's sins had begun, or her fasts
and tears and penances had been offered in their expia-
tion. The pride of the race was struck down as the
first-born of Pharaoh. The dark mark of fate and
doom was on the threshold, — the tall old threshold sur-
mounted by coronets and carved heraldry.

The absent lord's children meanwhile prattled and
grew on quite unconscious that the doom was over them
too. First they talked of their father, and devised plans
against his return. Then the name of the living dead
man was less frequently in their mouth — then not mentioned at all. But the stricken old grandmother trembled
to think that these too were the inheritors of their father's
shame as well as of his honours: and watched sickening
for the day when the awful ancestral curse should come
down on them.

This dark presentiment also haunted Lord Steyne.
He tried to lay the horrid bed-side ghost in Red Seas

of wine and jollity, and lost sight of it sometimes in the crowd and rout of his pleasures. But it always came back to him when alone, and seemed to grow more threatening with years. "I have taken your son," it said, "why not you? I may shut you up in a prison some day like your son George. I may tap you on the head to-morrow, and away go pleasure and honours, feasts and beauty, friends, flatterers, French cooks, fine horses and houses — in exchange for a prison, a keeper, and a straw mattress like George Gaunt's." And then my lord would defy the ghost which threatened him: for he knew of a remedy by which he could baulk his enemy.

So there was splendour and wealth, but no great happiness perchance, behind the tall carved portals of Gaunt House with its smoky coronets and ciphers. The feasts there were of the grandest in London, but there was not over-much content therewith, except among the guests who sate at my lord's table. Had he not been so great a Prince very few possibly would have visited him: but in Vanity Fair the sins of very great personages are looked at indulgently. "*Nous regardons à deux fois*" (as the French lady said) before we condemn a person of my lord's undoubted quality. Some notorious carpers and squeamish moralists might be sulky with Lord Steyne, but they were glad enough to come when he asked them.

"Lord Steyne is really too bad," Lady Slingstone said, "but everybody goes, and of course I shall see that my girls come to no harm." "His lordship is a man to whom I owe much, everything in life," said the Right Reverend Doctor Trail, thinking that the Archbishop was rather shaky; and Mrs. Trail and the young ladies would as soon have missed going to church as to one of his lordship's parties. "His morals are bad," said little Lord Southdown to his sister, who meekly expostulated, having heard terrific legends from her mamma with respect to the doings at Gaunt House; "but hang it, he's got the best dry Sillery in Europe!" And as for Sir Pitt Crawley, Bart. — Sir Pitt that pattern of decorum, Sir Pitt who had led off at missionary meetings, — he never for one moment thought of not going too. "Where you see such persons as the Bishop of Ealing and the Countess of Slingstone, you may be pretty sure, Jane," the Baronet would say, "that *we* cannot be wrong. The great rank and station of Lord Steyne put him in a position to command people in our station in life. The Lord Lieutenant of a County, my dear, is a respectable man. Besides George Gaunt and I were intimate in early life: he was my junior when we were attachés at Pumpernickel together."

In a word everybody went to wait upon this great man — everybody who was asked: as you the reader (do not say nay) or I the writer hereof would go if we had an invitation.

CHAPTER XX

IN WHICH THE READER IS INTRODUCED TO THE VERY BEST OF COMPANY

AT last Becky's kindness and attention to the chief of her husband's family, were destined to meet with an exceeding great reward; a reward which, though certainly somewhat unsubstantial, the little woman coveted with greater eagerness than more positive benefits. If she did not wish to lead a virtuous life, at least she desired to enjoy a character for virtue, and we know that no lady in the genteel world can possess this desideratum, until she has put on a train and feathers, and has been presented to her Sovereign at Court. From that august interview they come out stamped as honest women. The Lord Chamberlain gives them a certificate of virtue. And as dubious goods or letters are passed through an oven at quarantine, sprinkled with aromatic vinegar, and then pronounced clean — many a lady whose reputation would be doubtful otherwise and liable to give infection, passes through the wholesome ordeal of the Royal presence, and issues from it free from all taint.

It might be very well for my Lady Bareacres, my Lady Tufto, Mrs. Bute Crawley in the country, and other ladies who had come into contact with Mrs. Rawdon Crawley, to cry fie at the idea of the odious little adventuress making her curtsey before the Sovereign, and to declare, that if dear good Queen Charlotte had

been alive, *she* never would have admitted such an extremely ill-regulated personage into Her chaste drawing-
room. But when we consider, that it was the First
Gentleman in Europe in whose high presence Mrs.
Rawdon passed her examination, and as it were, took
her degree in reputation, it surely must be flat disloyalty
to doubt any more about her virtue. I, for my part,
look back with love and awe to that Great Character in
history. Ah, what a high and noble appreciation of
Gentlewomanhood there must have been in Vanity Fair,
when that revered and august being was invested, by
the universal acclaim of the refined and educated portion of this empire, with the title of Premier Gentil-
homme of his Kingdom. Do you remember, dear
M——, oh friend of my youth, how one blissful night
five-and-twenty years since, the "Hypocrite" being
acted, Elliston being manager, Dowton and Liston performers, two boys had leave from their loyal masters to
go out from Slaughter House School where they were
educated, and to appear on Drury Lane stage, amongst
a crowd which assembled there to greet the king. THE
KING? There he was. Beef-eaters were before the
august box: the Marquis of Steyne (Lord of the Powder Closet) and other great officers of state were behind
the chair on which he sate, *He* sate — florid of face,
portly of person, covered with orders, and in a rich
curling head of hair — How we sang God save him!
How the house rocked and shouted with that magnificent music. How they cheered, and cried, and waved
handkerchiefs. Ladies wept: mothers clasped their
children: some fainted with emotion. People were suf-
focated in the pit, shrieks and groans rising up amidst
the writhing and shouting mass there of his people who
were, and indeed showed themselves almost to be, ready
to die for him. Yes, we saw him. Fate cannot deprive

us of *that*. Others have seen Napoleon. Some few still exist who have beheld Frederick the Great, Doctor Johnson, Marie Antoinette, &c. — be it our reasonable boast to our children, that we saw George the Good, the Magnificent, the Great.

Well, there came a happy day in Mrs. Rawdon Crawley's existence when this angel was admitted into the paradise of a Court which she coveted; her sister-in-law acting as her god-mother. On the appointed day, Sir Pitt and his lady, in their great family carriage (just newly built, and ready for the Baronet's assumption of the office of High Sheriff of his county), drove up to the little house in Curzon Street, to the edification of Raggles, who was watching from his green-grocer's shop, and saw fine plumes within, and enormous bunches of flowers in the breasts of the new livery-coats of the footmen.

Sir Pitt, in a glittering uniform, descended and went into Curzon Street, his sword between his legs. Little Rawdon stood with his face against the parlour window-panes, smiling and nodding with all his might to his aunt in the carriage within; and presently Sir Pitt issued forth from the house again, leading forth a lady with grand feathers, covered in a white shawl, and holding up daintily a train of magnificent brocade. She stepped into the vehicle as if she were a princess and accustomed all her life to go to Court, smiling graciously on the footman at the door, and on Sir Pitt, who followed her into the carriage.

Then Rawdon followed in his old Guards' uniform, which had grown wofully shabby, and was much too tight. He was to have followed the procession, and waited upon his sovereign in a cab; but that his good-natured sister-in-law insisted that they should be a family party. The coach was large, the ladies not very big, they would hold their trains in their laps — finally, the four went fraternally together; and their carriage presently joined the line of loyal equipages which was making its way down Piccadilly and St. James's Street, towards the old brick palace where the Star of Brunswick was in waiting to receive his nobles and gentlefolks.

Becky felt as if she could bless the people out of the carriage windows, so elated was she in spirit, and so strong a sense had she of the dignified position which she had at last attained in life. Even our Becky had her weaknesses, and as one often sees how men pride themselves upon excellences which others are slow to perceive: how, for instance, Comus firmly believes that he is the greatest tragic actor in England; how Brown, the famous novelist, longs to be considered, not a man of genius, but a man of fashion; while Robinson, the great lawyer, does not in the least care about his reputation in Westminster Hall, but believes himself incomparable across country, and at a five-barred gate — so to be, and to be thought, a respectable woman was Becky's aim in life, and she got up the genteel with amazing assiduity, readiness, and success. We have said, there were times when she believed herself to be a fine lady, and forgot that there was no money in the chest at home — duns round the gate, tradesmen to coax and wheedle — no ground to walk upon, in a word. And as she went to Court in the carriage, the family carriage, she adopted a demeanour so grand, self-satisfied, deliberate, and imposing, that it made even Lady Jane laugh. She walked into the royal apartments with a toss of the head which would have befitted an empress, and I have no doubt had she been one, she would have become the character perfectly.

We are authorised to state that Mrs. Rawdon Crawley's

costume de cour on the occasion of her presentation to the Sovereign was of the most elegant and brilliant description. Some ladies we may have seen — we who wear stars and cordons, and attend the St. James's assemblies, or we, who, in muddy boots, dawdle up and down Pall Mall, and peep into the coaches as they drive up with the great folks in their feathers — some ladies of fashion, I say, we may have seen, about two o'clock of the forenoon of a levee day, as the laced-jacketed band of the Life Guards are blowing triumphal marches seated on those prancing music-stools, their cream-coloured chargers — who are by no means lovely and enticing objects at that early period of noon. A stout countess of sixty, *décolletée*, painted, wrinkled with rouge up to her drooping eyelids, and diamonds twinkling in her wig, is a wholesome and edifying, but not a pleasant sight. She has the faded look of a St. James's Street illumination, as it may be seen of an early morning, when half the lamps are out, and the others are blinking wanly, as if they were about to vanish like ghosts before the dawn. Such charms as those of which we catch glimpses while her ladyship's carriage passes, should appear abroad at night alone. If even Cynthia looks haggard of an afternoon, as we may see her sometimes in the present winter season, with Phœbus staring her out of countenance from the opposite side of the heavens, how much more can old Lady Castlemouldy keep her head up when the sun is shining full upon it through the chariot windows, and showing all the chinks and crannies with which time has marked her face? No. Drawing-rooms should be announced for November, or the first foggy day: or the elderly sultanas of our Vanity Fair should drive up in closed litters, descend in a covered way, and make their curtsey to the Sovereign under the protection of lamplight.

Our beloved Rebecca had no need, however, of any such a friendly halo to set off her beauty. Her complexion could bear any sunshine as yet; and her dress, though if you were to see it now, any present lady of Vanity Fair would pronounce it to be the most foolish and preposterous attire ever worn, was as handsome in her eyes and those of the public, some five-and-twenty years since, as the most brilliant costume of the most famous beauty of the present season. A score of years hence that too, that milliner's wonder, will have passed into the domain of the absurd, along with all previous vanities. But we are wandering too much. Mrs. Rawdon's dress was pronounced to be charmante on the eventful day of her presentation. Even good little Lady Jane was forced to acknowledge this effect, as she looked at her kinswoman; and owned sorrowfully to herself that she was quite inferior in taste to Mrs. Becky.

She did not know how much care, thought, and genius Mrs. Rawdon had bestowed upon that garment. Rebecca had as good taste as any milliner in Europe, and such a clever way of doing things as Lady Jane little understood. The latter quickly spied out the magnificence of the brocade of Becky's train, and the splendour of the lace on her dress.

The brocade was an old remnant, Becky said; and as for the lace, it was a great bargain. She had had it these hundred years.

"My dear Mrs. Crawley, it must have cost a little fortune," Lady Jane said, looking down at her own lace, which was not nearly so good; and then examining the quality of the ancient brocade which formed the material of Mrs. Rawdon's Court dress, she felt inclined to say that she could not afford such fine clothing, but checked that speech, with an effort, as one uncharitable to her kinswoman.

And yet, if Lady Jane had known all, I think even her kindly temper would have failed her. The fact is, when she was putting Sir Pitt's house in order, Mrs. Rawdon had found the lace and the brocade in old wardrobes, the property of the former ladies of the house, and had quietly carried the goods home, and had suited them to her own little person. Briggs saw her take them, asked no questions, told no stories; but I believe quite sympathised with her on this matter, and so would many another honest woman.

And the diamonds — "Where the doose did you get the diamonds, Becky?" said her husband, admiring some jewels which he had never seen before, and which sparkled in her ears and on her neck with brilliance and profusion.

Becky blushed a little, and looked at him hard for a moment. Pitt Crawley blushed a little too, and looked out of window. The fact is, he had given her a very small portion of the brilliants; a pretty diamond clasp, which confined a pearl necklace which she wore; and the Baronet had omitted to mention the circumstance to his lady.

Becky looked at her husband, and then at Sir Pitt, with an air of saucy triumph — as much as to say, "Shall I betray you?"

"Guess!" she said to her husband. "Why, you silly man," she continued, "where do you suppose I got them? — all except the little clasp, which a dear friend of mine gave me long ago. I hired them, to be sure. I hired them at Mr. Polonius's, in Coventry Street. You don't suppose that all the diamonds which go to Court belong to the owners; like those beautiful stones which Lady Jane has, and which are much handsomer than any which I have, I am certain."

"They are family jewels," said Sir Pitt, again looking uneasy. And in this family conversation the carriage

[301]

rolled down the street, until its cargo was finally discharged at the gates of the palace where the Sovereign was sitting in state.

The diamonds, which had created Rawdon's admiration, never went back to Mr. Polonius, of Coventry Street, and that gentleman never applied for their restoration; but they retired into a little private repository, in an old desk, which Amelia Sedley had given her years and years ago, and in which Becky kept a number of useful and, perhaps, valuable things, about which her husband knew nothing. To know nothing, or little, is in the nature of some husbands. To hide, in the nature of how many women? O ladies! how many of you have surreptitious milliners' bills? How many of you have gowns and bracelets, which you dare n't show, or which you wear trembling? — trembling, and coaxing with smiles the husband by your side, who does not know the new velvet gown from the old one, or the new bracelet from last year's, or has any notion that the ragged-looking yellow lace scarf cost forty guineas, and that Madame Bobinot is writing dunning letters every week for the money!

Thus Rawdon knew nothing about the brilliant diamond ear-rings, or the supurb brilliant ornament which decorated the fair bosom of his lady; but Lord Steyne, who was in his place at court, as Lord of the Powder Closet, and one of the great dignitaries and illustrious defences of the throne of England, and came up with all his stars, garters, collars, and cordons, and paid particular attention to the little woman, knew whence the jewels came, and who paid for them.

As he bowed over her he smiled, and quoted the hackneyed and beautiful lines, from the "Rape of the Lock," about Belinda's diamonds, "which Jews might kiss and infidels adore."

" But I hope your lordship is orthodox," said the little lady, with a toss of her head. And many ladies round about whispered and talked, and many gentlemen nodded and whispered, as they saw what marked attention the great nobleman was paying to the little adventuress.

What were the circumstances of the interview between Rebecca Crawley, née Sharp, and her Imperial Master, it does not become such a feeble and inexperienced pen as mine to attempt to relate. The dazzled eyes close before that Magnificent Idea. Loyal respect and decency tell even the imagination not to look too keenly and audaciously about the sacred audience-chamber, but to back away rapidly, silently, and respectfully, making profound bows out of the August Presence.

This may be said, that in all London there was no more loyal heart than Becky's after this interview. The name of her king was always on her lips, and he was proclaimed by her to be the most charming of men. She went to Colnaghi's and ordered the finest portrait of him that art had produced, and credit could supply. She chose that famous one in which the best of monarchs is represented in a frock-coat with a fur collar, and breeches and silk stockings, simpering on a sofa from under his curly brown wig. She had him painted in a brooch and wore it — indeed she amused and somewhat pestered her acquaintance with her perpetual talk about his urbanity and beauty. Who knows? Perhaps the little woman thought she might play the part of a Maintenon or a Pompadour.

But the finest sport of all after her presentation was to hear her talk virtuously. She had a few female acquaintances, not, it must be owned, of the very highest reputation in Vanity Fair. But being made an honest woman of, so to speak, Becky would not consort any longer with these dubious ones, and cut Lady Crackenbury when the latter nodded to her from her opera-box; and gave Mrs. Washington White the go-by in the Ring. "One must, my dear, show one is somebody," she said. "One mustn't be seen with doubtful people. I pity Lady Crackenbury from my heart; and Mrs. Washington White may be a very good-natured person. *You* may go and dine with them, as you like your rubber. But *I* mustn't, and won't; and you will have the goodness to tell Smith to say I am not at home when either of them calls."

The particulars of Becky's costume were in the newspapers — feathers, lappets, superb diamonds, and all the rest. Lady Crackenbury read the paragraph in bitterness of spirit, and discoursed to her followers about the airs which that woman was giving herself. Mrs. Bute Crawley and her young ladies in the country had a copy of the *Morning Post* from town; and gave a vent to their honest indignation. "If you had been sandy-haired, green-eyed, and a French rope-dancer's daughter," Mrs. Bute said to her eldest girl (who, on the contrary, was a very swarthy, short, and snub-nosed young lady), "you might have had superb diamonds forsooth, and have been presented at Court, by your cousin, the Lady Jane. But you're only a gentlewoman, my poor dear child. You have only some of the best blood in England in your veins, and good principles and piety for your portion. I, myself, the wife of a Baronet's younger brother, too, never thought of such a thing as going to Court — nor would other people, if good Queen Charlotte had been alive." In this way the worthy Rectoress consoled herself: and her daughters sighed, and sate over the Peerage all night.

A few days after the famous presentation, another great and exceeding honour was vouchsafed to the virtuous Becky. Lady Steyne's carriage drove up to Mr. Rawdon Crawley's door, and the footman, instead of driving down the front of the house, as by his tremendous knocking he appeared to be inclined to do, relented, and only delivered in a couple of cards, on which were engraven the names of the Marchioness of Steyne and the Countess of Gaunt. If these bits of pasteboard had been beautiful pictures, or had had a hundred yards of Malines lace rolled round them, worth twice the number of guineas, Becky could not have regarded them with more pleasure. You may be sure they occupied a conspicuous place in the china bowl on the drawing-room table, where Becky kept the cards of her visitors. Lord! lord! how poor Mrs. Washington White's card and Lady Crackenbury's card, which our little friend had been glad enough to get a few months back, and of which the silly little creature was rather proud once —Lord! lord! I say, how soon at the appearance of these grand court cards, did those poor little neglected deuces sink down to the bottom of the pack. Steyne! Bareacres, Johnes of Helvellyn! and Caerlyon of Camelot! we may be sure that Becky and Briggs looked out those august names in the Peerage, and followed the noble races up through all the ramifications of the family tree.

My Lord Steyne coming to call a couple of hours afterwards, and looking about him, and observing everything as was his wont, found his ladies' cards already ranged as the trumps of Becky's hand, and grinned, as this old cynic always did at any naïve display of human weakness. Becky came down to him presently: whenever the dear girl expected his lordship, her toilette was prepared, her hair in perfect order, her mouchoirs, aprons, scarfs, little morocco slippers, and other female gimcracks arranged, and she seated in some artless and agreeable posture ready to receive him

—whenever she was surprised, of course she had to fly to her apartment to take a rapid survey of matters in the glass, and to trip down again to wait upon the great peer.

She found him grinning over the bowl. She was discovered, and she blushed a little. "Thank you, Monseigneur," she said. "You see your ladies have been here. How good of you! I could n't come before — I was in the kitchen making a pudding."

"I know you were, I saw you through the area-railings as I drove up," replied the old gentleman.

"You see everything," she replied.

"A few things, but not that, my pretty lady," he said good-naturedly. "You silly little fibster! I heard you in the room over head, where I have no doubt you were putting a little rouge on; you must give some of yours to my Lady Gaunt, whose complexion is quite preposterous; and I heard the bed-room door open, and then you came downstairs."

"Is it a crime to try and look my best when *you* come here?" answered Mrs. Rawdon plaintively, and she rubbed her cheek with her handkerchief as if to show there was no rouge at all, only genuine blushes and modesty in her case. About this who can tell? I know there is some rouge that won't come off on a pocket-handkerchief; and some so good that even tears will not disturb it.

"Well," said the old gentleman, twiddling round his wife's card, "you are bent on becoming a fine lady. You pester my poor old life out to get you into the world. You won't be able to hold your own there, you silly little fool. You 've got no money."

"You will get us a place," interposed Becky, as quick as possible.

"You 've got no money, and you want to compete

with those who have. You poor little earthenware pip-
kin, you want to swim down the stream along with the
great copper kettles. All women are alike. Everybody is striving for what is not worth the having! Gad!
I dined with the King yesterday, and we had neck of
mutton and turnips. A dinner of herbs is better than a
stalled ox very often. You will go to Gaunt House.
You give an old fellow no rest until you get there. It's
not half so nice as here. You'll be bored there. I am.
My wife is as gay as Lady Macbeth, and my daughters
as cheerful as Regan and Goneril. I dare n't sleep in
what they call my bed-room. The bed is like the balda-
quin of St. Peter's, and the pictures frighten me. I have
a little brass bed in a dressing-room: and a little hair
mattress like an anchorite. I am an anchorite. Ho!
ho! You'll be asked to dinner next week. And *gare
aux femmes*, look out and hold your own! How the
women will bully you!" This was a very long speech
for a man of few words like my Lord Steyne; nor was it
the first which he uttered for Becky's benefit on that
day.

Briggs looked up from the work-table at which she
was seated in the farther room, and gave a deep sigh as
she heard the great Marquis speak so lightly of her sex.

"If you don't turn off that abominable sheep-dog,"
said Lord Steyne, with a savage look over his shoulder
at her, " I will have her poisoned."

"I always give my dog dinner from my own plate,"
said Rebecca, laughing mischievously; and having enjoyed for some time the discomfiture of my lord, who
hated poor Briggs for interrupting his tête-à-tête with
the fair Colonel's wife, Mrs. Rawdon at length had pity
upon her admirer, and calling to Briggs, praised the fine-
ness of the weather to her, and bade her to take out
the child for a walk.

" I can't send her away," Becky said presently, after a pause, and in a very sad voice. Her eyes filled with tears as she spoke, and she turned away her head.

"You owe her her wages, I suppose?" said the Peer.

"Worse than that," said Becky, still casting down her eyes, "I have ruined her."

" Ruined her?—then why don't you turn her out?" the gentleman asked.

" Men do that," Becky answered bitterly. "Women are not so bad as you. Last year when we were reduced to our last guinea, she gave us everything. She shall never leave me, until we are ruined utterly ourselves, which does not seem far off, or until I can pay her the utmost farthing."

" —— it, how much is it?" said the Peer, with an oath. And Becky, reflecting on the largeness of his means, mentioned not only the sum which she had borrowed from Miss Briggs, but one of nearly double the amount.

This caused the Lord Steyne to break out in another brief and energetic expression of anger, at which Rebecca held down her head the more, and cried bitterly. " I could not help it. It was my only chance. I dare not tell my husband. He would kill me if I told him what I have done. I have kept it a secret from everybody but you — and you forced it from me. Ah, what shall I do, Lord Steyne? for I am very, very unhappy!"

Lord Steyne made no reply except by beating the devil's tattoo, and biting his nails. At last he clapped his hat on his head, and flung out of the room. Rebecca did not rise from her attitude of misery until the door slammed upon him, and his carriage whirled away. Then she rose up with the queerest expression of victorious mischief glittering in her green eyes. She burst out laughing once or twice to herself, as she sate at work: and sitting down to the piano, she rattled away

a triumphant voluntary on the keys, which made the
people pause under her window to listen to her brilliant
music.

That night, there came two notes from Gaunt House
for the little woman, the one containing a card of invitation from Lord and Lady Steyne to a dinner at Gaunt
House next Friday: while the other enclosed a slip of
gray paper bearing Lord Steyne's signature and the address of Messrs. Jones, Brown, and Robinson, Lombard
Street.

Rawdon heard Becky laughing in the night once or
twice. It was only her delight at going to Gaunt House
and facing the ladies there, she said, which amused her
so. But the truth was, that she was occupied with a
great number of other thoughts. Should she pay off
old Briggs and give her her *congé?* Should she
astonish Raggles by settling his account? She turned
over all these thoughts on her pillow, and on the next
day, when Rawdon went out to pay his morning visit to
the Club, Mrs. Crawley (in a modest dress with a veil
on) whipped off in a hackney-coach to the City: and
being landed at Messrs. Jones and Robinson's bank,
presented a document there to the authority at the desk,
who, in reply, asked her "How she would take it?"

She gently said "she would take a hundred and fifty
pounds in small notes and the remainder in one note:"
and passing through St. Paul's Churchyard stopped
there and bought the handsomest black silk gown for
Briggs which money could buy; and which, with a kiss
and the kindest speeches, she presented to the simple
old spinster.

Then she walked to Mr. Raggles, inquired about his
children affectionately, and gave him fifty pounds on
account. Then she went to the livery-man from whom
she jobbed her carriages and gratified him with a similar

sum. "And I hope this will be a lesson to you, Spavin," she said, "and that on the next Drawing-room day my brother, Sir Pitt, will not be inconvenienced by being obliged to take four of us in his carriage to wait upon His Majesty, because my *own* carriage is not forthcoming." It appears there had been a difference on the last drawing-room day. Hence the degradation which the Colonel had almost suffered, of being obliged to enter the presence of his Sovereign in a hack cab.

These arrangements concluded, Becky paid a visit upstairs to the before-mentioned desk, which Amelia Sedley had given her years and years ago, and which contained a number of useful and valuable little things: in which private museum she placed the one note which Messrs. Jones and Robinson's cashier had given her.

CHAPTER XXI

IN WHICH WE ENJOY THREE COURSES AND A DESSERT

WHEN the ladies of Gaunt House were at breakfast that morning, Lord Steyne (who took his chocolate in private, and seldom disturbed the females of his household, or saw them except upon public days, or when they crossed each other in the hall, or when from his pit-box at the Opera he surveyed them in their box on the grand tier) — His lordship, we say, appeared among the ladies and the children who were assembled over the tea and toast, and a battle royal ensued apropos of Rebecca.

"My Lady Steyne," he said, "I want to see the list for your dinner on Friday; and I want you, if you please, to write a card for Colonel and Mrs. Crawley."

"Blanche writes them," Lady Steyne said in a flutter. "Lady Gaunt writes them."

"I will not write to that person," Lady Gaunt said, a tall and stately lady, who looked up for an instant and then down again after she had spoken. It was not good to meet Lord Steyne's eyes for those who had offended him.

"Send the children out of the room, Go!" said he, pulling at the bell-rope. The urchins, always frightened before him, retired: their mother would have followed too. "Not you," he said. "You stop."

"My Lady Steyne," he said, "once more will you have the goodness to go to the desk, and write that card for your dinner on Friday?"

[311]

"My Lord, I will not be present at it," Lady Gaunt said; "I will go home."

"I wish you would, and stay there. You will find the bailiffs at Bareacres very pleasant company, and I shall be freed from lending money to your relations, and from your own damned tragedy airs. Who are you to give orders here? You have no money. You've got no brains. You were here to have children, and you have not had any. Gaunt's tired of you; and George's wife is the only person in the family who doesn't wish you were dead. Gaunt would marry again if you were."

"I wish I were," her Ladyship answered, with tears and rage in her eyes.

"You, forsooth, must give yourself airs of virtue; while my wife, who is an immaculate saint, as everybody knows, and never did wrong in her life, has no objection to meet my young friend Mrs. Crawley. My Lady Steyne knows that appearances are sometimes against the best of women; that lies are often told about the most innocent of them. Pray, Madam, shall I tell you some little anecdotes about my Lady Bareacres, your mamma?"

"You may strike me if you like, sir, or hit any cruel blow," Lady Gaunt said. To see his wife and daughter suffering always put his Lordship into a good humour.

"My sweet Blanche," he said, "I am a gentleman, and never lay my hand upon a woman, save in the way of kindness. I only wish to correct little faults in your character. You women are too proud, and sadly lack humility, as Father Mole, I'm sure, would tell my Lady Steyne if he were here. You mustn't give yourselves airs: you must be meek and humble, my blessings. For all Lady Steyne knows, this calumniated, simple, good-humoured Mrs. Crawley is quite innocent — even more innocent than herself. Her husband's character is not good, but it is as good as Bareacres', who has played a little and not paid a great deal, who cheated you out of the only legacy you ever had, and left you a pauper on my hands. And Mrs. Crawley is not very well born; but she is not worse than Fanny's illustrious ancestor, the first de la Jones."

"The money which I brought into the family, sir," Lady George cried out—

"You purchased a contingent reversion with it," the Marquis said, darkly. "If Gaunt dies, your husband may come to his honours; your little boys may inherit them, and who knows what besides? In the meanwhile, ladies, be as proud and virtuous as you like abroad, but don't give *me* any airs. As for Mrs. Crawley's character, I shan't demean myself or that most spotless and perfectly irreproachable lady, by even hinting that it requires a defence. You will be pleased to receive her with the utmost cordiality, as you will receive all persons whom I present in this house. This house?" He broke out with a laugh. "Who is the master of it? and what is it? This Temple of Virtue belongs to me. And if I invite all Newgate or all Bedlam here, by —— they shall be welcome."

After this vigorous allocution, to one of which sort Lord Steyne treated his "Hareem," whenever symptoms of insubordination appeared in his household, the crestfallen women had nothing for it but to obey. Lady Gaunt wrote the invitation which his Lordship required, and she and her mother-in-law drove in person, and with bitter and humiliated hearts, to leave the cards on Mrs. Rawdon, the reception of which caused that innocent woman so much pleasure.

There were families in London who would have sacrificed a year's income to receive such an honour at the hands of those great ladies. Mrs. Frederick Bullock, for instance, would have gone on her knees from Mayfair to Lombard Street, if Lady Steyne and Lady Gaunt had been waiting in the City to raise her up, and say, "Come to us next Friday," not to one of the great crushes and grand balls of Gaunt House, whither everybody went, but to the sacred, unapproachable, mysterious, delicious entertainments, to be admitted to one of which was a privilege, and an honour, and a blessing indeed.

Severe, spotless, and beautiful, Lady Gaunt held the very highest rank in Vanity Fair. The distinguished courtesy with which Lord Steyne treated her, charmed everybody who witnessed his behaviour, caused the severest critics to admit how perfect a gentleman he was, and to own that his lordship's heart at least was in the right place.

The ladies of Gaunt House called Lady Bareacres in to their aid, in order to repulse the common enemy. One of Lady Gaunt's carriages went to Hill Street for her Ladyship's mother, all whose equipages were in the hands of the bailiffs, whose very jewels and wardrobe, it was said, had been seized by those inexorable Israelites. Bareacres Castle was theirs, too, with all its costly pictures, furniture, and articles of vertu — the magnificent Vandykes; the noble Reynolds pictures; the Lawrence portraits, tawdry and beautiful, and, thirty years ago, deemed as precious as works of real genius; the matchless Dancing Nymph of Canova, for which Lady Bareacres had sate in her youth — Lady Bareacres splendid then, and radiant in wealth, rank, and beauty — a toothless, bald, old woman now — a mere rag of a former robe of state. Her lord, painted at the same time by Lawrence, as waving his sabre in front of Bareacres Castle, and clothed in his uniform as Colonel of the Thistlewood Yeomanry, was a withered, old, lean man

in a great-coat and a Brutus wig: slinking about Gray's
Inn of mornings chiefly, and dining alone at clubs. He
did not like to dine with Steyne now. They had run
races of pleasure together in youth when Bareacres was
the winner. But Steyne had more bottom than he, and
had lasted him out. The Marquis was ten times a greater
man now than the young Lord Gaunt of '85; and Bareacres nowhere in the race — old, beaten, bankrupt, and
broken down. He had borrowed too much money of
Steyne to find it pleasant to meet his old comrade often.
The latter, whenever he wished to be merry, used jeer-
ingly to ask Lady Gaunt, why her father had not come
to see her? "He has not been here for four months,"
Lord Steyne would say. "I can always tell by my
cheque-book afterwards, when I get a visit from Bareacres. What a comfort it is, my ladies, I bank with
one of my sons' fathers-in-law, and the other banks with
me!"

Of the other illustrious persons whom Becky had the
honour to encounter on this her first presentation to the
grand world, it does not become the present historian
to say much. There was his Excellency the Prince of
Peterwaradin, with his Princess; a nobleman tightly
girthed, with a large military chest, on which the *plaque*
of his order shone magnificently, and wearing the red
collar of the Golden Fleece round his neck. He was
the owner of countless flocks. "Look at his face. I
think he must be descended from a sheep," Becky whispered to Lord Steyne. Indeed, his Excellency's countenance, long, solemn, and white, with the ornament round
his neck, bore some resemblance to that of a venerable
bell-wether.

There was Mr. John Paul Jefferson Jones, titularly
attached to the American Embassy, and correspondent
of the *New York Demagogue;* who, by way of making

himself agreeable to the company, asked Lady Steyne, during a pause in the conversation at dinner, how his dear friend, George Gaunt, liked the Brazils? — He and George had been most intimate at Naples, and had gone up Vesuvius together. Mr. Jones wrote a full and particular account of the dinner, which appeared duly in the *Demagogue*. He mentioned the names and titles of all the guests, giving biographical sketches of the principal people. He described the persons of the ladies with great eloquence; the service of the table; the size and costume of the servants; enumerated the dishes and wines served; the ornaments of the sideboard, and the probable value of the plate. Such a dinner he calculated could not be dished up under fifteen or eighteen dollars per head. And he was in the habit, until very lately, of sending over *protégés*, with letters of recommendation to the present Marquis of Steyne, encouraged to do so by the intimate terms on which he had lived with his dear friend, the late lord. He was most indignant that a young and insignificant aristocrat, the Earl of Southdown, should have taken the *pas* of him in their procession to the dining-room. "Just as I was stepping up to offer my hand to a very pleasing and witty fashionable, the brilliant and exclusive Mrs. Rawdon Crawley," — he wrote — "the young patrician interposed between me and the lady, and whisked my Helen off without a word of apology. I was fain to bring up the rear with the Colonel, the lady's husband, a stout red-faced warrior who distinguished himself at Waterloo, where he had better luck than befell some of his brother red-coats at New Orleans."

The Colonel's countenance on coming into this polite society wore as many blushes as the face of a boy of sixteen assumes when he is confronted with his sister's schoolfellows. It has been told before that honest Rawdon had not been much used at any period of his life to ladies' company. With the men at the Club or the Mess-room, he was well enough; and could ride, bet, smoke, or play at billiards with the boldest of them. He had had his time for female friendships too: but that was twenty years ago, and the ladies were of the rank of those with whom Young Marlow in the comedy is represented as having been familiar before he became abashed in the presence of Miss Hardcastle. The times are such that one scarcely dares to allude to that kind of company which thousands of our young men in Vanity Fair are frequenting every day, which nightly fills casinos and dancing-rooms, which is known to exist as well as the Ring in Hyde Park or the Congregation at St. James's —but which the most squeamish if not the most moral of societies is determined to ignore. In a word, although Colonel Crawley was now five-and-forty years of age, it had not been his lot in life to meet with a half-dozen good women, besides his paragon of a wife. All except her and his kind sister Lady Jane, whose gentle nature had tamed and won him, scared the worthy Colonel; and on occasion of his first dinner at Gaunt House he was not heard to make a single remark except to state that the weather was very hot. Indeed Becky would have left him at home, but that virtue ordained that her husband should be by her side to protect the timid and fluttering little creature on her first appearance in polite society.

On her first appearance Lord Steyne stepped forward, taking her hand, and greeting her with great courtesy, and presenting her to Lady Steyne, and their ladyships, her daughters. Their ladyships made three stately curtsies, and the elder lady to be sure gave her hand to the new comer, but it was as cold and lifeless as marble.

Becky took it, however, with grateful humility; and performing a reverence which would have done credit to the best dancing master, put herself at Lady Steyne's feet, as it were, by saying that his Lordship had been her father's earliest friend and patron, and that she, Becky, had learned to honour and respect the Steyne family from the days of her childhood. The fact is, that Lord Steyne had once purchased a couple of pictures of the late Sharp, and the affectionate orphan could never forget her gratitude for that favour.

The Lady Bareacres then came under Becky's cognisance — to whom the Colonel's lady made also a most respectful obeisance: it was returned with severe dignity by the exalted person in question.

"I had the pleasure of making your Ladyship's acquaintance at Brussels, ten years ago," Becky said, in the most winning manner. "I had the good fortune to meet Lady Bareacres, at the Duchess of Richmond's ball, the night before the battle of Waterloo. And I recollect your Ladyship, and my Lady Blanche, your daughter, sitting in the carriage in the porte-cochère at the Inn, waiting for horses. I hope your Ladyship's diamonds are safe."

Everybody's eyes looked into their neighbour's. The famous diamonds had undergone a famous seizure, it appears, about which Becky, of course, knew nothing. Rawdon Crawley retreated with Lord Southdown into a window, where the latter was heard to laugh immoderately, as Rawdon told him the story of Lady Bareacres wanting horses, and "knuckling down by Jove," to Mrs. Crawley. "I think I need n't be afraid of *that* woman," Becky thought. Indeed, Lady Bareacres exchanged terrified and angry looks with her daughter, and retreated to a table, where she began to look at pictures with great energy.

When the potentate from the Danube made his appearance, the conversation was carried on in the French language, and the Lady Bareacres and the younger ladies found, to their farther mortification, that Mrs. Crawley was much better acquainted with that tongue, and spoke it with a much better accent than they. Becky had met other Hungarian magnates with the army in France, in 1816–17. She asked after her friends with great interest. The foreign personages thought that she was a lady of great distinction; and the Prince and the Princess asked severally of Lord Steyne and the Marchioness, whom they conducted to dinner, who was that petite dame who spoke so well?

Finally, the procession being formed in the order described by the American diplomatist, they marched into the apartment where the banquet was served: and which, as I have promised the reader he shall enjoy it, he shall have the liberty of ordering himself so as to suit his fancy.

But it was when the ladies were alone that Becky knew the tug of war would come. And then indeed the little woman found herself in such a situation, as made her acknowledge the correctness of Lord Steyne's caution to her to beware of the society of ladies above her own sphere. As they say the persons who hate Irishmen most are Irishmen; so, assuredly, the greatest tyrants over women are women. When poor little Becky, alone with the ladies, went up to the fire-place whither the great ladies had repaired, the great ladies marched away and took possession of a table of drawings. When Becky followed them to the table of drawings, they dropped off one by one to the fire again. She tried to speak to one of the children (of whom she was commonly fond in public places), but Master George Gaunt was called away by his mamma; and the

[319]

stranger was treated with such cruelty finally, that even Lady Steyne herself pitied her, and went up to speak to the friendless little woman.

"Lord Steyne," said her Ladyship, as her wan cheeks glowed with a blush, "says you sing and play very beautifully, Mrs. Crawley — I wish you would do me the kindness to sing to me."

"I will do anything that may give pleasure to my Lord Steyne or to you," said Rebecca, sincerely grateful, and seating herself at the piano, began to sing.

She sang religious songs of Mozart, which had been early favourites of Lady Steyne, and with such sweetness and tenderness that the lady, lingering round the piano, sate down by its side, and listened until the tears rolled down her eyes. It is true that the opposition ladies at the other end of the room kept up a loud and ceaseless buzzing and talking: but the Lady Steyne did not hear those rumours. She was a child again — and had wandered back through a forty years' wilderness to her Convent Garden. The chapel organ had pealed the same tones, the organist, the sister whom she loved best of the community, had taught them to her in those early happy days. She was a girl once more, and the brief period of her happiness bloomed out again for an hour — she started when the jarring doors were flung open, and with a loud laugh from Lord Steyne, the men of the party entered full of gaiety.

He saw at a glance what had happened in his absence: and was grateful to his wife for once. He went and spoke to her, and called her by her Christian name, so as again to bring blushes to her pale face — "My wife says you have been singing like an angel," he said to Becky. Now there are angels of two kinds, and. both sorts, it is said, are charming in their way.

Whatever the previous portion of the evening had been, the rest of that night was a great triumph for Becky. She sang her very best, and it was so good that every one of the men came and crowded round the piano. The women, her enemies, were left quite alone. And Mr. Paul Jefferson Jones thought he had made a conquest of Lady Gaunt by going up to her Ladyship, and praising her delightful friend's first-rate singing.

CHAPTER XXII

CONTAINS A VULGAR INCIDENT

THE Muse, whoever she be, who presides over this Comic History, must now descend from the genteel heights in which she has been soaring, and have the goodness to drop down upon the lowly roof of John Sedley at Brompton, and describe what events are taking place there. Here, too, in this humble tenement, live care, and distrust, and dismay. Mrs. Clapp in the kitchen is grumbling in secret to her husband about the rent, and urging the good fellow to rebel against his old friend and patron and his present lodger. Mrs. Sedley has ceased to visit her landlady in the lower regions now, and indeed is in a position to patronise Mrs. Clapp no longer. How can one be condescending to a lady to whom one owes a matter of forty pounds, and who is perpetually throwing out hints for the money? The Irish maidservant has not altered in the least in her kind and respectful behaviour; but Mrs. Sedley fancies that she is growing insolent and ungrateful, and, as the guilty thief who fears each bush an officer, sees threatening inuendoes and hints of capture in all the girl's speeches and answers. Miss Clapp, grown quite a young woman now, is declared by the soured old lady to be an unbearable and impudent little minx. Why Amelia can be so fond of her, or have her in her room so much, or walk out with her so constantly, Mrs. Sedley cannot conceive. The bitterness of poverty has poisoned the life of the once cheerful and kindly woman. She is thankless for Amelia's constant and gentle bearing towards her; carps at her for her efforts at kindness or service: rails at her for her silly pride in her child, and her neglect of her parents. Georgy's house is not a very lively one since Uncle Jos's annuity has been withdrawn, and the little family are almost upon famine diet.

Amelia thinks, and thinks, and racks her brain, to find some means of increasing the small pittance upon which the household is starving. Can she give lessons in anything? paint card-racks? do fine work? She finds that women are working hard, and better than she can, for twopence a-day. She buys a couple of begilt Bristol boards at the Fancy Stationer's, and paints her very best upon them — a shepherd with a red waistcoat on one, and a pink face smiling in the midst of a pencil landscape — a shepherdess on the other, crossing a little bridge, with a little dog, nicely shaded. The man of the Fancy Repository and Brompton Emporium of Fine Arts (of whom she bought the screens, vainly hoping that he would re-purchase them when ornamented by her hand), can hardly hide the sneer with which he examines these feeble works of art. He looks askance at the lady who waits in the shop, and ties up the cards again in their envelope of whitey-brown paper, and hands them to the poor widow and Miss Clapp, who had never seen such beautiful things in her life, and had been quite confident that the man must give at least two guineas for the screens. They try at other shops in the interior of London, with faint sickening hopes. "Don't want 'em," says one. "Be off," says another fiercely. Three-and-sixpence have been spent in vain — the screens

retire to Miss Clapp's bed-room, who persists in thinking them lovely.

She writes out a little card in her neatest hand, and
after long thought and labour of composition; in which
the public is informed that " A Lady who has some
time at her disposal, wishes to undertake the education
of some little girls, whom she would instruct in English,
in French, in Geography, in History, and in Music —
address A. O., at Mr. Brown's; " and she confides the
card to the gentleman of the Fine Art Repository, who
consents to allow it to lie upon the counter, where it
grows dingy and flyblown. Amelia passes the door
wistfully many a time, in hopes that Mr. Brown will
have some news to give her; but he never beckons her
in. When she goes to make little purchases, there is
no news for her. Poor simple lady, tender and weak
— how are you to battle with the struggling violent
world?

She grows daily more care-worn and sad : fixing
upon her child alarmed eyes, whereof the little boy
cannot interpret the expression. She starts up of a
night and peeps into his room stealthily, to see that he
is sleeping and not stolen away. She sleeps but little
now. A constant thought and terror is haunting her.
How she weeps and prays in the long silent nights —
how she tries to hide from herself the thought which
will return to her, that she ought to part with the boy,
that she is the only barrier between him and prosperity.
She can't, she can't. Not now, at least. Some other
day. Oh! it is too hard to think of and to bear.

A thought comes over her which makes her blush
and turn from herself, — her parents might keep the
annuity — the curate would marry her and give a home
to her and the boy. But George's picture and dearest
memory are there to rebuke her. Shame and love say

no to the sacrifice. She shrinks from it as from something unholy; and such thoughts never found a resting-
place in that pure and gentle bosom.

The combat, which we describe in a sentence or two,
lasted for many weeks in poor Amelia's heart: during
which she had no confidante: indeed, she could never
have one: as she would not allow to herself the possibility of yielding: though she was giving way daily
before the enemy with whom she had to battle. One
truth after another was marshalling itself silently against
her, and keeping its ground. Poverty and misery for
all, want and degradation for her parents, injustice to
the boy — one by one the outworks of the little citadel
were taken, in which the poor soul passionately guarded
her only love and treasure.

At the beginning of the struggle, she had written off
a letter of tender supplication to her brother at Calcutta, imploring him not to withdraw the support which
he had granted to their parents, and painting in terms
of artless pathos their lonely and hapless condition.
She did not know the truth of the matter. The payment of Jos's annuity was still regular: but it was a
money-lender in the City who was receiving it: old
Sedley had sold it for a sum of money wherewith to
prosecute his bootless schemes. Emmy was calculating
eagerly the time that would elapse before the letter
would arrive and be answered. She had written down
the date in her pocket-book of the day when she despatched it. To her son's guardian, the good Major
at Madras, she had not communicated any of her griefs
and perplexities. She had not written to him since
she wrote to congratulate him on his approaching
marriage. She thought with sickening despondency,
that that friend, — the only one, the one who had felt
such a regard for her, — was fallen away.

[325]

One day, when things had come to a very bad pass — when the creditors were pressing, the mother in hysteric grief, the father in more than usual gloom, the inmates of the family avoiding each other, each secretly oppressed with his private unhappiness and notion of wrong — the father and daughter happened to be left alone together; and Amelia thought to comfort her father, by telling him what she had done. She had written to Joseph — an answer must come in three or four months. He was always generous, though careless. He could not refuse, when he knew how straitened were the circumstances of his parents.

Then the poor old gentleman revealed the whole truth to her — that his son was still paying the annuity, which his own imprudence had flung away. He had not dared to tell it sooner. He thought Amelia's ghastly and terrified look, when, with a trembling, miserable voice he made the confession, conveyed reproaches to him for his concealment. "Ah!" said he, with quivering lips and turning away, "you despise your old father now!"

"O papa! it is not that," Amelia cried out, falling on his neck, and kissing him many times. "You are always good and kind. You did it for the best. It is not for the money — it is — O my God! my God! have mercy upon me, and give me strength to bear this trial;" and she kissed him again wildly, and went away.

Still the father did not know what that explanation meant, and the burst of anguish with which the poor girl left him. It was that she was conquered. The sentence was passed. The child must go from her — to others — to forget her. Her heart and her treasure — her joy, hope, love, worship — her God, almost! She must give him up; and then — and then she would go to George: and they would watch over the child, and wait for him until he came to them in Heaven.

She put on her bonnet, scarcely knowing what she did, and went out to walk in the lanes by which George used to come back from school, and where she was in the habit of going on his return to meet the boy. It was May, a half-holiday. The leaves were all coming out, the weather was brilliant: the boy came running to her flushed with health, singing, his bundle of school-books hanging by a thong. There he was. Both her arms were round him. No, it was impossible. They could not be going to part. "What is the matter, mother?" said he; "you look very pale."

"Nothing, my child," she said, and stooped down and kissed him.

That night Amelia made the boy read the story of Samuel to her, and how Hannah, his mother, having weaned him, brought him to Eli the High Priest to minister before the Lord. And he read the song of gratitude which Hannah sang: and which says, who it is who maketh poor and maketh rich, and bringeth low and exalteth — how the poor shall be raised up out of the dust, and how, in his own might, no man shall be strong. Then he read how Samuel's mother made him a little coat, and brought it to him from year to year when she came up to offer the yearly sacrifice. And then, in her sweet simple way, George's mother made commentaries to the boy upon this affecting story. How Hannah, though she loved her son so much, yet gave him up because of her vow. And how she must always have thought of him as she sat at home, far away, making the little coat; and Samuel, she was sure, never forgot his mother: and how happy she must have been as the time came (and the years pass away very quick) when she should see her boy, and how good and

wise he had grown. This little sermon she spoke with
a gentle solemn voice, and dry eyes, until she came to
the account of their meeting — then the discourse broke
off suddenly, the tender heart overflowed, and taking
the boy to her breast, she rocked him in her arms, and
wept silently over him in a sainted agony of tears.

Her mind being made up, the widow began to take such
measures as seemed right to her for advancing the end
which she proposed. One day, Miss Osborne, in Russell Square (Amelia had not written the name or number of the house for ten years — her youth, her early
story came back to her as she wrote the superscription)
— one day Miss Osborne got a letter from Amelia,
which made her blush very much and look towards her
father, sitting glooming in his place at the other end of
the table.

In simple terms, Amelia told her the reasons which
had induced her to change her mind respecting her boy.
Her father had met with fresh misfortunes which had
entirely ruined him. Her own pittance was so small
that it would barely enable her to support her parents,
and would not suffice to give George the advantages
which were his due. Great as her sufferings would be
at parting with him she would, by God's help, endure
them for the boy's sake. She knew that those to whom
he was going, would do all in their power to make him
happy. She described his disposition, such as she
fancied it; quick and impatient of control or harshness;
easily to be moved by love and kindness. In a postscript, she stipulated that she should have a written
agreement, that she should see the child as often as she
wished, — she could not part with him under any other
terms.

"What? Mrs. Pride has come down, has she?" old

Osborne said, when with a tremulous eager voice Miss Osborne read him the letter — "Reg'lar starved out, hey? ha, ha! I knew she would." He tried to keep his dignity and to read his paper as usual, — but he could not follow it. He chuckled and swore to himself behind the sheet.

At last he flung it down: and scowling at his daughter, as his wont was, went out of the room into his study adjoining, from whence he presently returned with a key. He flung it to Miss Osborne.

"Get the room over mine — his room that was — ready," he said. "Yes, sir," his daughter replied in a tremble. It was George's room. It had not been opened for more than ten years. Some of his clothes, papers, handkerchiefs, whips and caps, fishing-rods and sporting gear, were still there. An army list of 1814, with his name written on the cover; a little dictionary he was wont to use in writing; and the Bible his mother had given him, were on the mantel-piece; with a pair of spurs, and a dried inkstand covered with the dust of ten years. Ah! since that ink was wet, what days and people had passed away! The writing-book still on the table, was blotted with his hand.

Miss Osborne was much affected when she first entered this room with the servants under her. She sank quite pale on the little bed. "This is blessed news, mam — indeed, mam," the housekeeper said; "and the good old times is returning, mam. The dear little feller, to be sure, mam; how happy he will be! But some folks in May Fair, mam, will owe him a grudge, mam;" and she clicked back the bolt which held the window-sash, and let the air into the chamber.

"You had better send that woman some money," Mr. Osborne said, before he went out. "She shan't want for nothing. Send her a hundred pound."

"And I 'll go and see her to-morrow?" Miss Osborne asked.

"That's your look out. She don't come in here, mind. No, by —, not for all the money in London. But she must n't want now. So look out, and get things right." With which brief speeches Mr. Osborne took leave of his daughter, and went on his accustomed way into the City.

"Here, Papa, is some money," Amelia said that night, kissing the old man, her father, and putting a bill for a hundred pounds into his hands. "And — and, Mamma, don't be harsh with Georgy. He — he is not going to stop with us long." She could say nothing more, and walked away silently to her room. Let us close it upon her prayers and her sorrow. I think we had best speak little about so much love and grief.

Miss Osborne came the next day, according to the promise contained in her note, and saw Amelia. The meeting between them was friendly. A look and a few words from Miss Osborne showed the poor widow that, with regard to this woman at least, there need be no fea. lest she should take the first place in her son's affec. tion. She was cold, sensible, not unkind. The mothei had not been so well pleased, perhaps, had the rival been better looking, younger, more affectionate, warmer-hearted. Miss Osborne, on the other hand, thought of old times and memories, and could not but be touched with the poor mother's pitiful situation. She was con-quered, and laying down her arms, as it were, she humbly submitted. That day they arranged together the preliminaries of the treaty of capitulation.

George was kept from school the next day, and saw his aunt. Amelia left them alone together, and went to her room. She was trying the separation: — as that poor gentle Lady Jane Grey felt the edge of the axe

that was to come down and sever her slender life.
Days were passed in parleys, visits, preparations. The
widow broke the matter to Georgy with great caution;
she looked to see him very much affected by the intelligence. He was rather elated than otherwise, and the
poor woman turned sadly away. He bragged about the
news that day to the boys at school; told them how he
was going to live with his grandpapa, his father's father,
not the one who comes here sometimes; and that he
would be very rich, and have a carriage, and a pony,
and go to a much finer school, and when he was rich
he would buy Leader's pencil-case, and pay the tart
woman. The boy was the image of his father, as his
fond mother thought.

Indeed I have no heart, on account of our dear
Amelia's sake, to go through the story of George's last
days at home.

At last the day came, the carriage drove up, the
little humble packets containing tokens of love and
remembrance were ready and disposed in the hall long
since — George was in his new suit, for which the tailor
had come previously to measure him. He had sprung
up with the sun and put on the new clothes; his mother
hearing him from the room close by, in which she had
been lying, in speechless grief and watching. Days
before she had been making preparations for the
end; purchasing little stores for the boy's use; marking
his books and linen; talking with him and preparing
him for the change — fondly fancying that he needed
preparation.

So that he had change, what cared he? He was
longing for it. By a thousand eager declarations as to
what he would do, when he went to live with his grandfather, he had shown the poor widow how little the idea
of parting had cast him down. " He would come and

see his mamma often on the pony," he said: " he would come and fetch her in the carriage; they would drive in the Park, and she should have everything she wanted." The poor mother was fain to content herself with these selfish demonstrations of attachment, and tried to convince herself how sincerely her son loved her. He must love her. All children were so: a little anxious for novelty, and — no, not selfish, but self-willed. Her child must have his enjoyments and ambition in the world. She herself, by her own selfishness and imprudent love for him, had denied him his just rights and pleasures hitherto.

I know few things more affecting than that timorous debasement and self-humiliation of a woman. How she owns that it is she and not the man who is guilty: how she takes all the faults on her side: how she courts in a manner punishment for the wrongs which she has not committed, and persists in shielding the real culprit! It is those who injure women who get the most kindness from them — they are born timid and tyrants, and maltreat those who are humblest before them.

So poor Amelia had been getting ready in silent misery for her son's departure, and had passed many and many a long solitary hour in making preparations for the end. George stood by his mother, watching her arrangements without the least concern. Tears had fallen into his boxes; passages had been scored in his favourite books; old toys, relics, treasures had been hoarded away for him, and packed with strange neatness and care, — and of all these things the boy took no note. The child goes away smiling as the mother breaks her heart. By heavens it is pitiful, the bootless love of women for children in Vanity Fair.

A few days are past: and the great event of Amelia's life is consummated. No angel has intervened. The child is sacrificed and offered up to fate; and the widow is quite alone.

The boy comes to see her often, to be sure. He rides on a pony with the coachman behind him, to the delight of his old grandfather, Sedley, who walks proudly down the lane by his side. She sees him, but he is not her boy any more. Why, he rides to see the boys at the little school, too, and to show off before them his new wealth and splendour. In two days he has adopted a slightly imperious air and patronising manner. He was born to command, his mother thinks, as his father was before him.

It is fine weather now. Of evenings on the days when he does not come, she takes a long walk into London — yes, as far as Russell Square, and rests on the stone by the railing of the garden opposite Mr. Osborne's house. It is so pleasant and cool. She can look up and see the drawing-room windows illuminated, and, at about nine o'clock, the chamber in the upper story where Georgy sleeps. She knows — He has told her. She prays there as the light goes out, prays with an humble humble heart, and walks home shrinking and silent. She is very tired when she comes home. Perhaps she will sleep the better for that long weary walk; and she may dream about Georgy.

One Sunday she happened to be walking in Russell Square, at some distance from Mr. Osborne's house (she could see it from a distance though) when all the bells of Sabbath were ringing, and George and his aunt came out to go to church; a little sweep asked for charity, and the footman, who carried the books, tried to drive him away; but Georgy stopped and gave him money. May God's blessing be on the boy! Emmy ran round the square, and coming up to the sweep, gave him her mite too. All the bells of Sabbath were ringing, and she followed them until she came to the Foundling Church, into which she went. There she sat in a place whence she could see the head of the boy under his father's tombstone. Many hundred fresh children's voices rose up there and sang hymns to the Father Beneficent; and little George's soul thrilled with delight at the burst of glorious psalmody. His mother could not see him for awhile, through the mist that dimmed her eyes.

CHAPTER XXIII

IN WHICH A CHARADE IS ACTED WHICH MAY OR
MAY NOT PUZZLE THE READER

AFTER Becky's appearance at my Lord Steyne's private and select parties, the claims of that estimable woman as regards fashion were settled; and some of the very greatest and tallest doors in the metropolis were speedily opened to her — doors so great and tall that the beloved reader and writer hereof may hope in vain to enter at them. Dear brethren, let us tremble before those august portals. I fancy them guarded by grooms of the chamber with flaming silver forks with which they prong all those who have not the right of the *entrée*. They say the honest newspaper-fellow who sits in the hall and takes down the names of the great ones who are admitted to the feasts, dies after a little time. He can't survive the glare of fashion long. It scorches him up, as the presence of Jupiter in full dress wasted that poor imprudent Semele — a giddy moth of a creature who ruined herself by venturing out of her natural atmosphere. Her myth ought to be taken to heart amongst the Tyburnians, the Belgravians, — her story, and perhaps Becky's too. Ah, ladies! — ask the Reverend Mr. Thurifer if Belgravia is not a sounding brass, and Tyburnia a tinkling cymbal. These are vanities. Even these will pass away. And some day or other (but it will be after our time, thank goodness,) Hyde Park Gardens will be no better known than the celebrated horticultural outskirts of Babylon; and Belgrave Square will be as desolate as Baker Street, or Tadmor in the wilderness.

Ladies, are you aware that the great Pitt lived in Baker Street? What would not your grandmothers have given to be asked to Lady Hester's parties in that now decayed mansion? I have dined in it — *moi qui vous parle.* I peopled the chamber with ghosts of the mighty dead. As we sate soberly drinking claret there with men of to-day, the spirits of the departed came in and took their places round the darksome board. The pilot who weathered the storm tossed off great bumpers of spiritual port: the shade of Dundas did not leave the ghost of a heeltap.—Addington sate bowing and smirking in a ghastly manner, and would not be behindhand when the noiseless bottle went round; Scott, from under bushy eyebrows, winked at the apparition of a beeswing; Wilberforce's eyes went up to the ceiling, so that he did not seem to know how his glass went up full to his mouth and came down empty; — up to the ceiling which was above us only yesterday, and which the great of the past days have all looked at. They let the house as a furnished lodging now. Yes, Lady Hester once lived in Baker Street, and lies asleep in the wilderness. Eothen saw her there — not in Baker Street: but in the other solitude.

It is all vanity to be sure: but who will not own to liking a little of it? I should like to know what well-constituted mind, merely because it is transitory, dislikes roast-beef? That is a vanity; but may every man who reads this, have a wholesome portion of it through life, I beg: aye, though my readers were five hundred thousand. Sit down, gentlemen, and fall to, with a good hearty appetite; the fat, the lean, the gravy, the horse-radish as you like it — don't spare it. Another glass of

wine, Jones, my boy — a little bit of the Sunday side.
Yes, let us eat our fill of the vain thing, and be thankful
therefor. And let us make the best of Becky's aristocratic pleasures likewise — for these too, like all other
mortal delights, were but transitory.

The upshot of her visit to Lord Steyne was, that His
Highness the Prince of Peterwaradin took occasion to
renew his acquaintance with Colonel Crawley, when
they met on the next day at the Club, and to compliment Mrs. Crawley in the Ring of Hyde Park with a
profound salute of the hat. She and her husband were
invited immediately to one of the Prince's small parties
at Levant House, then occupied by His Highness during
the temporary absence from England of its noble proprietor. She sang after dinner to a very little *comité*.
The Marquis of Steyne was present, paternally superintending the progress of his pupil.

At Levant House Becky met one of the finest gentlemen and greatest ministers that Europe has produced
— the Duc de la Jabotière, then Ambassador from the
Most Christian King, and subsequently Minister to that
monarch. I declare I swell with pride as these august
names are transcribed by my pen; and I think in what
brilliant company my dear Becky is moving. She became a constant guest at the French Embassy, where
no party was considered to be complete without the
presence of the charming Madame Ravdonn Cravley.

Messieurs de Truffigny (of the Périgord family) and
Champignac, both attachés of the Embassy, were
straightway smitten by the charms of the fair Colonel's
wife: and both declared, according to the wont of their
nation, (for who ever yet met a Frenchman, come out of
England, that has not left half a dozen families miserable,
and brought away as many hearts in his pocket-book?)

both, I say, declared that they were *aux mieux* with the charming Madame Ravdonn.

But I doubt the correctness of the assertion. Champignac was very fond of écarté, and made many *parties* with the Colonel of evenings, while Becky was singing to Lord Steyne in the other room ; and as for Truffigny, it is a well-known fact that he dared not go to the Travellers', where he owed money to the waiters, and if he had not had the Embassy as a dining-place, the worthy young gentleman must have starved. I doubt, I say, that Becky would have selected either of these young men as a person on whom she would bestow her special regard. They ran of her messages, purchased her gloves and flowers, went in debt for opera-boxes for her, and made themselves amiable in a thousand ways. And they talked English with adorable simplicity, and to the constant amusement of Becky and my Lord Steyne, she would mimic one or other to his face, and compliment him on his advance in the English language with a gravity which never failed to tickle the Marquis, her sardonic old patron. Truffigny gave Briggs a shawl by way of winning over Becky's confidante, and asked her to take charge of a letter which the simple spinster handed over in public to the person to whom it was addressed ; and the composition of which amused everybody who read it greatly. Lord Steyne read it : everybody but honest Rawdon ; to whom it was not necessary to tell everything that passed in the little house in May Fair.

Here, before long, Becky received not only " the best " foreigners (as the phrase is in our noble and admirable society slang), but some of the best English people too. I don't mean the most virtuous, or indeed the least virtuous, or the cleverest, or the stupidest, or the richest, or the best born, but " the best," — in a word, people about whom there is no question — such as the great Lady Fitz-Willis, that Patron Saint of Almack's, the great Lady Slowbore, the great Lady Grizzel Macbeth (she was Lady G. Glowry, daughter of Lord Grey of Glowry,) and the like. When the Countess of Fitz-Willis (her ladyship is of the Kingstreet family, see Debrett and Burke) takes up a person, he or she is safe. There is no question about them any more. Not that my Lady Fitz-Willis is any better than anybody else, being, on the contrary, a faded person, fifty-seven years of age, and neither handsome, nor wealthy, nor entertaining; but it is agreed on all sides that she is of the " best people." Those who go to her are of the best: and from an old grudge probably to Lady Steyne (for whose coronet her ladyship, then the youthful Georgina Frederica, daughter of the Prince of Wales's favourite, the Earl of Portansherry, had once tried), this great and famous leader of the fashion chose to acknowledge Mrs. Rawdon Crawley: made her a most marked curtsey at the assembly over which she presided: and not only encouraged her son, St. Kitts (his lordship got his place through Lord Steyne's interest), to frequent Mrs. Crawley's house, but asked her to her own mansion, and spoke to her twice in the most public and condescending manner during dinner. The important fact was known all over London that night. People who had been crying fie about Mrs. Crawley were silent. Wenham, the wit and lawyer, Lord Steyne's right-hand man, went about everywhere praising her: some who had hesitated, came forward at once and welcomed her: little Tom Toady, who had warned Southdown about visiting such an abandoned woman, now besought to be introduced to her. In a word, she was admitted to be among the " best" people. Ah, my beloved readers and brethren, do not envy poor Becky prematurely — glory like this is said to be fugitive. It is currently reported that even in the very inmost circles, they are no happier than the poor wanderers outside the zone; and Becky, who penetrated into the very centre of fashion, and saw the great George IV. face to face, has owned since that there too was Vanity.

We must be brief in descanting upon this part of her career. As I cannot describe the mysteries of free-masonry, although I have a shrewd idea that it is a hum-bug: so an uninitiated man cannot take upon himself to pourtray the great world accurately, and had best keep his opinions to himself whatever they are.

Becky has often spoken in subsequent years of this season of her life, when she moved among the very greatest circles of the London fashion. Her success excited, elated, and then bored her. At first no occu-pation was more pleasant than to invent and procure (the latter a work of no small trouble and ingenuity, by the way, in a person of Mrs. Rawdon Crawley's very narrow means) — to procure, we say, the prettiest new dresses and ornaments; to drive to fine dinner parties, where she was welcomed by great people; and from the fine dinner parties to fine assemblies, whither the same people came with whom she had been dining, whom she had met the night before, and would see on the morrow — the young men faultlessly appointed, hand-somely cravatted with the neatest glossy boots and white gloves — the elders portly, brass-buttoned, noble-look-ing, polite, and prosy — the young ladies blonde, timid, and in pink — the mothers grand, beautiful, sumptuous, solemn, and in diamonds. They talked in English, not in bad French, as they do in the novels. They talked about each others' houses, and characters, and families: just as the Joneses do about the Smiths. Becky's former acquaintances hated and envied her: the poor woman herself was yawning in spirit. "I wish I were out of it,"

she said to herself. " I would rather be a parson's wife,
and teach a Sunday School than this; or a sergeant's
lady and ride in the regimental waggon; or, O how
much gayer it would be to wear spangles and trousers,
and dance before a booth at a fair."

" You would do it very well," said Lord Steyne, laughing. She used to tell the great man her *ennuis* and
perplexities in her artless way — they amused him.

" Rawdon would make a very good Ecuyer — Master
of the Ceremonies — what do you call him — the man in
the large boots and the uniform, who goes round the ring
cracking the whip? He is large, heavy, and of a military figure. I recollect," Becky continued, pensively,
" my father took me to see a show at Brookgreen Fair
when I was a child; and when we came home I made
myself a pair of stilts, and danced in the studio to the
wonder of all the pupils."

" I should have liked to see it," said Lord Steyne.

" I should like to do it now," Becky continued.
" How Lady Blinkey would open her eyes, and Lady
Grizzel Macbeth would stare! Hush! silence! there is
Pasta beginning to sing." Becky always made a point
of being conspicuously polite to the professional ladies
and gentlemen who attended at these aristocratic
parties — of following them into the corners where
they sate in silence, and shaking hands with them, and
smiling in the view of all persons. She was an artist
herself, as she said very truly: there was a frankness
and humility in the manner in which she acknowledged
her origin, which provoked, or disarmed, or amused
lookers-on, as the case might be. " How cool that
woman is," said one; " what airs of independence she
assumes, where she ought to sit still and be thankful
if anybody speaks to her." " What an honest and
good-natured soul she is," said another. " What an

artful little minx," said a third. They were all right very likely; but Becky went her own way, and so fascinated the professional personages, that they would leave off their sore throats in order to sing at her parties, and give her lessons for nothing.

Yes, she gave parties in the little house in Curzon Street. Many scores of carriages, with blazing lamps, blocked up the street, to the disgust of No. 100, who could not rest for the thunder of the knocking, and of 102, who could not sleep for envy. The gigantic footmen who accompanied the vehicles, were too big to be contained in Becky's little hall, and were billeted off in the neighbouring public-houses, whence, when they were wanted, call-boys summoned them from their beer. Scores of the great dandies of London squeezed and trod on each other on the little stairs, laughing to find themselves there; and many spotless and severe ladies of *ton* were seated in the little drawing-room, listening to the professional singers, who were singing according to their wont, and as if they wished to blow the windows down. And the day after, there appeared among the fashionable *réunions* in the *Morning Post*, a paragraph to the following effect:—

"Yesterday, Colonel and Mrs. Crawley entertained a select party at dinner at their house in May Fair. Their Excellencies the Prince and Princess of Peterwaradin, H. E. Papoosh Pasha, the Turkish Ambassador (attended by Kibob Bey, dragoman of the mission), the Marquess of Steyne, Earl of Southdown, Sir Pitt and Lady Jane Crawley, Mr. Wagg, &c. After dinner Mrs. Crawley had an assembly which was attended by the Duchess (Dowager) of Stilton, Duc de la Gruyère, Marchioness of Cheshire, Marchese Alessandro Strachino, Comte de Brie, Baron Schapzuger, Chevalier Tosti, Countess of Slingstone, and Lady F. Macadam, Major-

General and Lady G. Macbeth, and (2) Miss Macbeths;
Viscount Paddington, Sir Horace Fogey, Hon. Sands
Bedwin, Bobbachy Bahawder," and an &c. which the
reader may fill at his pleasure through a dozen close
lines of small type.

And in her commerce with the great our dear friend
showed the same frankness which distinguished her
transactions with the lowly in station. On one occasion,
when out at a very fine house, Rebecca was (perhaps
rather ostentatiously) holding a conversation in the
French language with a celebrated tenor singer of that
nation, while the Lady Grizzel Macbeth looked over her
shoulder scowling at the pair.

" How very well you speak French," Lady Grizzel
said, who herself spoke the tongue in an Edinburgh
accent most remarkable to hear.

" I ought to know it," Becky modestly said, casting
down her eyes. " I taught it in a school, and my
mother was a Frenchwoman."

Lady Grizzel was won by her humility, and was
mollified towards the little woman. She deplored the
fatal levelling tendencies of the age, which admitted
persons of all classes into the society of their superiors;
but her ladyship owned, that this one at least was well
behaved and never forgot her place in life. She was a
very good woman: good to the poor: stupid, blameless,
unsuspicious. — It is not her ladyship's fault that she
fancies herself better than you and me. The skirts of
her ancestors' garments have been kissed for centuries:
it is a thousand years, they say, since the tartans of the
head of the family were embraced by the defunct
Duncan's lords and councillors, when the great ancestor
of the House became King of Scotland.

Lady Steyne, after the music scene, succumbed before
Becky, and perhaps was not disinclined to her. The

younger ladies of the house of Gaunt were also compelled into submission. Once or twice they set people
at her, but they failed. The brilliant Lady Stunnington
tried a passage of arms with her, but was routed with
great slaughter by the intrepid little Becky. When
attacked sometimes, Becky had a knack of adopting a
demure *ingénue* air, under which she was most dangerous. She said the wickedest things with the most
simple unaffected air when in this mood, and would
take care artlessly to apologise for her blunders, so that
all the world should know that she had made them.

Mr. Wagg, the celebrated wit, and a led captain and
trencher-man of my Lord Steyne, was caused by the
ladies to charge her; and the worthy fellow, leering at
his patronesses, and giving them a wink, as much as to
say, "Now look out for sport," — one evening began an
assault upon Becky, who was unsuspiciously eating her
dinner. The little woman, attacked on a sudden, but
never without arms, lighted up in an instant, parried
and riposted with a home-thrust, which made Wagg's
face tingle with shame; then she returned to her soup
with the most perfect calm and a quiet smile on her
face. Wagg's great patron, who gave him dinners and
lent him a little money sometimes, and whose election,
newspaper, and other jobs Wagg did, gave the luckless
fellow such a savage glance with the eyes as almost
made him sink under the table and burst into tears.
He looked piteously at my lord, who never spoke to
him during dinner, and at the ladies, who disowned him.
At last Becky herself took compassion upon him, and
tried to engage him in talk. He was not asked to
dinner again for six weeks; and Fiche, my lord's confidential man, to whom Wagg naturally paid a good
deal of court, was instructed to tell him that if he ever
dared to say a rude thing to Mrs. Crawley again, or

make her the butt of his stupid jokes, Milor would put every one of his notes of hand into his lawyer's hands, and sell him up without mercy. Wagg wept before Fiche, and implored his dear friend to intercede for him. He wrote a poem in favour of Mrs. R. C., which appeared in the very next number of the "Harum-scarum Magazine," which he conducted. He implored her good will at parties where he met her. He cringed and coaxed Rawdon at the club. He was allowed to come back to Gaunt House after a while. Becky was always good to him, always amused, never angry.

His lordship's vizier and chief confidential servant (with a seat in parliament and at the dinner table), Mr. Wenham, was much more prudent in his behaviour and opinions than Mr. Wagg. However much he might be disposed to hate all parvenus (Mr. Wenham himself was a staunch old True Blue Tory, and his father a small coal-merchant in the north of England), this aide-de-camp of the Marquis never showed any sort of hostility to the new favourite; but pursued her with stealthy kindnesses, and a sly and deferential politeness, which somehow made Becky more uneasy than other people's overt hostilities.

How the Crawleys got the money which was spent upon the entertainments with which they treated the polite world, was a mystery which gave rise to some conversation at the time, and probably added zest to these little festivities. Some persons averred that Sir Pitt Crawley gave his brother a handsome allowance: if he did, Becky's power over the Baronet must have been extraordinary indeed, and his character greatly changed in his advanced age. Other parties hinted that it was Becky's habit to levy contributions on all her husband's friends: going to this one in tears with an account that there was an execution in the house;

falling on her knees to that one, and declaring that the whole family must go to gaol or commit suicide unless such and such a bill could be paid. Lord Southdown, it was said, had been induced to give many hundreds through these pathetic representations. Young Feltham, of the —th Dragoons (and son of the firm of Tiler and Feltham, hatters and army accoutrement makers), and whom the Crawleys introduced into fashionable life, was also cited as one of Becky's victims in the pecuniary way. People declared that she got money from various simply disposed persons, under pretence of getting them confidential appointments under government. Who knows what stories were or were not told of our dear and innocent friend? Certain it is, that if she had had all the money which she was said to have begged or borrowed or stolen, she might have capitalised and been honest for life, whereas, — but this is advancing matters.

The truth is, that by economy and good management — by a sparing use of ready money and by paying scarcely anybody, — people can manage, for a time at least, to make a great show with very little means: and it is our belief that Becky's much-talked-of parties, which were not, after all was said, very numerous, cost this lady very little more than the wax candles which lighted the walls. Stillbrook and Queen's Crawley supplied her with game and fruit in abundance. Lord Steyne's cellars were at her disposal, and that excellent nobleman's famous cooks presided over her little kitchen, or sent by my lord's order the rarest delicacies from their own. I protest it is quite shameful in the world to abuse a simple creature, as people of her time abuse Becky, and I warn the public against believing one-tenth of the stories against her. If every person is to be banished from society who runs into debt and cannot pay — if we are to be peering into everybody's private life, speculating upon their income, and cutting them if we don't approve of their expenditure — why, what a howling wilderness and intolerable dwelling Vanity Fair would be. Every man's hand would be against his neighbour in this case, my dear sir, and the benefits of civilisation would be done away with. We should be quarrelling, abusing, avoiding one another. Our houses would become caverns : and we should go in rags because we cared for nobody. Rents would go down. Parties would n't be given any more. All the tradesmen of the town would be bankrupt. Wine, wax-lights, comestibles, rouge, crinoline-petticoats, diamonds, wigs, Louis-Quatorze gimcracks, and old china, park hacks, and splendid high-stepping carriage-horses — all the delights of life, I say, — would go to the deuce, if people did but act upon their silly principles, and avoid those whom they dislike and abuse. Whereas, by a little charity and mutual forbearance, things are made to go on pleasantly enough : we may abuse a man as much as we like, and call him the greatest rascal unhung — but do we wish to hang him therefore ? No. We shake hands when we meet. If his cook is good we forgive him, and go and dine with him ; and we expect he will do the same by us. Thus trade flourishes — civilisation advances : peace is kept ; new dresses are wanted for new assemblies every week ; and the last year's vintage of La-fitte, will remunerate the honest proprietor who reared it.

At the time whereof we are writing, though the Great George was on the throne and ladies wore *gigots* and large combs like tortoise-shell shovels in their hair, instead of the simple sleeves and lovely wreaths which are actually in fashion, the manners of the very polite world were not, I take it, essentially different from those of the present day : and their amusements pretty similar. To us, from the outside, gazing over the policeman's shoulders at the bewildering beauties as they pass into Court or ball, they may seem beings of unearthly splendour, and in the enjoyment of an exquisite happiness by us unattainable. It is to console some of these dissatisfied beings, that we are narrating our dear Becky's struggles, and triumphs, and disappointments, of all of which, indeed, as is the case with all persons of merit, she had her share.

At this time the amiable amusement of acting charades had come among us from France: and was considerably in vogue in this country, enabling the many ladies amongst us who had beauty to display their charms, and the fewer number who had cleverness, to exhibit their wit. My Lord Steyne was incited by Becky, who perhaps believed herself endowed with both the above qualifications, to give an entertainment at Gaunt House, which should include some of these little dramas — and we must take leave to introduce the reader to this brilliant *réunion*, and, with a melancholy welcome too, for it will be among the very last of the fashionable entertainments to which it will be our fortune to conduct him.

A portion of that splendid room, the picture gallery of Gaunt House, was arranged as the charade theatre. It had been so used when George III. was king; and a picture of the Marquis of Gaunt is still extant, with his hair in powder and a pink ribbon, in a Roman shape, as it was called, enacting the part of Cato in Mr. Addison's tragedy of that name, performed before their Royal Highnesses the Prince of Wales, the Bishop of Osnaburgh, and Prince William Henry, then children like the actor. One or two of the old properties were drawn out of the garrets, where they had lain ever since, and furbished up anew for the present festivities.

Young Bedwin Sands, then an elegant dandy and
Eastern traveller, was manager of the revels. An Eastern traveller was somebody in those days, and the ad-
venturous Bedwin, who had published his quarto, and
passed some months under the tents in the desert, was
a personage of no small importance. — In his volume
there were several pictures of Sands in various oriental
costumes; and he travelled about with a black attendant of most unprepossessing appearance, just like
another Brian de Bois Guilbert. Bedwin, his costumes,
and black man, were hailed at Gaunt House as very
valuable acquisitions.

He led off the first charade. A Turkish officer with
an immense plume of feathers (the Janizaries were
supposed to be still in existence, and the tarboosh had
not as yet displaced the ancient and majestic head-dress
of the true believers), was seen couched on a divan,
and making believe to puff at a narghile, in which,
however, for the sake of the ladies, only a fragrant
pastille was allowed to smoke. The Turkish dignitary
yawns and expresses signs of weariness and idleness.
He claps his hands and Mesrour the Nubian appears,
with bare arms, bangles, yataghans, and every eastern
ornament — gaunt, tall, and hideous. He makes a
salaam before my lord the Aga.

A thrill of terror and delight runs through the assembly. The ladies whisper to one another. The
black slave was given to Bedwin Sands by an Egyptian
Pasha in exchange for three dozen of Maraschino. He
has sewn up ever so many odalisques in sacks and
tilted them into the Nile.

"Bid the slave-merchant enter," says the Turkish
voluptuary with a wave of his hand. Mesrour conducts
the slave-merchant into my lord's presence: he brings
a veiled female with him. He removes the veil. A

thrill of applause bursts through the house. It is Mrs. Winkworth (she was a Miss Absolom) with the beautiful eyes and hair. She is in a gorgeous oriental costume; the black braided locks are twined with innumerable jewels; her dress is covered over with gold piastres. The odious Mahometan expresses himself charmed by her beauty. She falls down on her knees, and entreats him to restore her to the mountains where she was born, and where her Circassian lover is still deploring the absence of his Zuleikah. No entreaties will move the obdurate Hassan. He laughs at the notion of the Circassian bridegroom. Zuleikah covers her face with her hands, and drops down in an attitude of the most beautiful despair. There seems to be no hope for her when — when the Kislar Aga appears.

The Kislar Aga brings a letter from the Sultan. Hassan receives and places on his head the dread firman. A ghastly terror seizes him, while on the negro's face (it is Mesrour again in another costume) appears a ghastly joy. "Mercy! mercy!" cries the Pasha: while the Kislar Aga, grinning horribly, pulls out — a *bow-string*.

The curtain draws just as he is going to use that awful weapon. Hassan from within bawls out, "First two syllables" — and Mrs. Rawdon Crawley, who is going to act in the charade, comes forward and compliments Mrs. Winkworth on the admirable taste and beauty of her costume.

The second part of the charade takes place. It is still an eastern scene. Hassan, in another dress, is in an attitude by Zuleikah, who is perfectly reconciled to him. The Kislar Aga has become a peaceful black slave. It is sunrise on the desert, and the Turks turn their heads eastwards and bow to the sand. As there are no dromedaries at hand, the band facetiously plays

"The Camels are coming." An enormous Egyptian head figures in the scene. It is a musical one, — and, to the surprise of the oriental travellers, sings a comic song, composed by Mr. Wagg. The eastern voyagers go off dancing, like Papageno and the Moorish King, in the "Magic Flute." "Last two syllables" roars the head.

The last act opens. It is a Grecian tent this time. A tall and stalwart man reposes on a couch there. Above him hang his helmet and shield. There is no need for them now. Ilium is down. Iphigenia is slain. Cassandra is a prisoner in his outer halls. The king of men (it is Colonel Crawley, who, indeed, has no notion about the sack of Ilium or the conquest of Cassandra), the anax andrôn is asleep in his chamber at Argos. A lamp casts the broad shadow of the sleeping warrior flickering on the wall — the sword and shield of Troy glitter in its light. The band plays the awful music of Don Juan, before the statue enters.

Ægisthus steals in pale and on tiptoe. What is that ghastly face looking out balefully after him from behind the arras? He raises his dagger to strike the sleeper, who turns in his bed, and opens his broad chest as if for the blow. He cannot strike the noble slumbering chieftain. Clytemnestra glides swiftly into the room like an apparition — her arms are bare and white, — her tawny hair floats down her shoulders, — her face is deadly pale, — and her eyes are lighted up with a smile so ghastly, that people quake as they look at her.

A tremor ran through the room. "Good God!" somebody said, "it's Mrs. Rawdon Crawley."

Scornfully she snatches the dagger out of Ægisthus's hand, and advances to the bed. You see it shining over her head in the glimmer of the lamp, and — and the lamp goes out, with a groan, and all is dark.

[351]

The darkness and the scene frightened people. Rebecca performed her part so well, and with such ghastly truth, that the spectators were all dumb, until, with a burst, all the lamps of the hall blazed out again, when everybody began to shout applause. " Brava! brava! " old Steyne's strident voice was heard roaring over all the rest. " By —, she'd do it too," he said between his teeth. The performers were called by the whole house, which sounded with cries of " Manager! Clytemnestra! " AGAMEMNON could not be got to show in his classical tunic, but stood in the background with Ægisthus and others of the performers of the little play. Mr. Bedwin Sands led on Zuleikah and Clytemnestra. A great personage insisted on being presented to the charming Clytemnestra. " Heigh ha? Run him through the body. Marry somebody else, hay?" was the apposite remark made by his Royal Highness.

" Mrs. Rawdon Crawley was quite killing in the part," said Lord Steyne. Becky laughed; gay, and saucy looking, and swept the prettiest little curtsey ever seen.

Servants brought in salvers covered with numerous cool dainties, and the performers disappeared to get ready for the second charade-tableau.

The three syllables of this charade were to be depicted in pantomime, and the performance took place in the following wise: —

First syllable. Colonel Rawdon Crawley, C.B., with a slouched hat and a staff, a great coat, and a lantern borrowed from the stables, passed across the stage bawling out, as if warning the inhabitants of the hour. In the lower window are seen two bagmen playing apparently at the game of cribbage, over which they yawn much. To them enters one looking like Boots, (the Honourable G. Ringwood) which character the young gentleman performed to perfection, and divests them of their lower coverings; and presently Chambermaid (the Right Honourable Lord Southdown) with two candlesticks, and a warming-pan. She ascends to the upper apartment, and warms the bed. She uses the warming-pan as a weapon wherewith she wards off the attention of the bagmen. She exits. They put on their night-caps, and pull down the blinds. Boots comes out and closes the shutters of the ground-floor chamber. You hear him bolting and chaining the door within. All the lights go out. The music plays *Dormez, dormez, chers Amours*. A voice from behind the curtain says, "First syllable."

Second syllable. The lamps are lighted up all of a sudden. The music plays the old air from John of Paris, *Ah quel plaisir d'être en voyage*. It is the same scene. Between the first and second floors of the house represented, you behold a sign on which the Steyne arms are painted. All the bells are ringing all over the house. In the lower apartment you see a man with a long slip of paper presenting it to another, who shakes his fist, threatens and vows that it is monstrous. "Ostler, bring round my gig," cries another at the door. He chucks Chambermaid (the Right Honourable Lord Southdown) under the chin; she seems to deplore his absence, as Calypso did that of that other eminent traveller Ulysses. Boots (the Honourable G. Ringwood) passes with a wooden box, containing silver flagons, and cries "Pots" with such exquisite humour and naturalness, that the whole house rings with applause, and a bouquet is thrown to him. Crack, crack, crack, go the whips. Landlord, chambermaid, waiter rush to the door; but just as some distinguished guest is arriving, the curtains close, and the invisible theatrical manager cries out "Second syllable."

"I think it must be 'Hotel,'" says Captain Grigg of the Life Guards; there is a general laugh at the Captain's cleverness. He is not very far from the mark.

While the third syllable is in preparation, the band begins a nautical medley — "All in the Downs," "Cease Rude Boreas," "Rule Britannia," "In the Bay of Biscay O!"—some maritime event is about to take place. A bell is heard ringing as the curtain draws aside. "Now, gents, for the shore!" a voice exclaims. People take leave of each other. They point anxiously as if towards the clouds, which are represented by a dark curtain, and they nod their heads in fear. Lady Squeams (the Right Honourable Lord Southdown), her lap-dog, her bags, reticules, and husband sit down, and cling hold of some ropes. It is evidently a ship.

The Captain (Colonel Crawley, C.B.), with a cocked hat and a telescope, comes in, holding his hat on his head, and looks out; his coat tails fly about as if in the wind. When he leaves go of his hat to use his telescope, his hat flies off, with immense applause. It is blowing fresh. The music rises and whistles louder and louder; the mariners go across the stage staggering, as if the ship was in severe motion. The Steward (the Honourable G. Ringwood) passes reeling by, holding six basins. He puts one rapidly by Lord Squeams — Lady Squeams, giving a pinch to her dog, which begins to howl piteously, puts her pocket-handkerchief to her face, and rushes away as for the cabin. The music rises up to the wildest pitch of stormy excitement, and the third syllable is concluded.

There was a little ballet, Le Rossignol, in which Montessu and Noblet used to be famous in those days, and which Mr. Wagg transferred to the English stage as an opera, putting his verse, of which he was a skilful writer, to the pretty airs of the ballet. It was dressed in the old French costume, and little Lord Southdown now appeared admirably attired in the disguise of an old woman hobbling about the stage with a faultless crooked stick.

Trills of melody were heard behind the scenes, and gurgling from a sweet pasteboard cottage covered with roses and trellis work. " Philomèle, Philomèle," cries the old woman, and Philomèle comes out.

More applause — it is Mrs. Rawdon Crawley in powder and patches, the most *ravissante* little Marquise in the world.

She comes in laughing, humming, and frisks about the stage with all the innocence of theatrical youth — she makes a .curtsey. Mamma says "Why, child, you are always laughing and singing," and away she goes, with —

THE ROSE UPON MY BALCONY.

The rose upon my balcony the morning air perfuming,
Was leafless all the winter time and pining for the spring;
You ask me why her breath is sweet and why her cheek is
    blooming,
It is because the sun is out and birds begin to sing.

The nightingale, whose melody is through the greenwood ringing,
Was silent when the boughs were bare and winds were blowing
    keen :
And if, Mamma, you ask of me the reason of his singing :
It is because the sun is out and all the leaves are green.

Thus each performs his part, Mamma, the birds have found their
    voices,
The blowing rose a flush, Mamma, her bonny cheek to dye;
And there 's sunshine in my heart, Mamma, which wakens and
    rejoices,
And so I sing and blush, Mamma, and that 's the reason why.

During the intervals of the stanzas of this ditty, the good-natured personage addressed as mamma by the singer, and whose large whiskers appeared under her cap, seemed very anxious to exhibit her maternal affection by embracing the innocent creature who performed the daughter's part. Every caress was received with loud acclamations of laughter by the sympathising audience. At its conclusion (while the music was performing a symphony as if ever so many birds were warbling) the whole house was unanimous for an *encore:* and applause and bouquets without end were showered upon the NIGHTINGALE of the evening. Lord Steyne's voice of applause was loudest of all. Becky, the nightingale, took the flowers which he threw to her, and pressed them to her heart with the air of a consummate comedian. Lord Steyne was frantic with delight. His guests' enthusiasm harmonised with his own. Where was the beautiful black-eyed Houri whose appearance in the first charade had caused such delight? She was twice as handsome as Becky, but the brilliancy of the latter had quite eclipsed her. All voices were for her. Stephens, Caradori, Ronzi de Begnis, people compared her to one or the other, and agreed with good reason, very likely, that had she been an actress none on the stage could have surpassed her. She had reached her culmination : her voice rose trilling and bright over the storm of applause : and soared as high and joyful as her triumph. There was a ball after the dramatic entertainments, and everybody pressed round Becky as the great point of attraction of the evening. The Royal Personage declared with an oath, that she was perfection, and engaged her again and again in conversation. Little Becky's soul swelled with pride and delight at these honours; she saw fortune, fame, fashion before her. Lord Steyne was her slave; followed her everywhere, and scarcely spoke to any one in the room beside; and paid her the most marked compliments and attention.

She still appeared in her Marquise costume, and danced a minuet with Monsieur de Truffigny, Monsieur Le Duc de la Jabotière's attaché; and the Duke, who had all the traditions of the ancient court, pronounced that Madame Crawley was worthy to have been a pupil of Vestris, or to have figured at Versailles. Only a feeling of dignity, the gout, and the strongest sense of duty and personal sacrifice, prevented his Excellency from dancing with her himself; and he declared in public, that a lady who could talk and dance like Mrs. Rawdon, was fit to be ambassadress at any court in Europe. He was only consoled when he heard that she was half a French-woman by birth. "None but a compatriot," his Excellency declared, "could have performed that majestic dance in such a way."

Then she figured in a waltz with Monsieur de Kling-enspohr, the Prince of Peterwaradin's cousin and attaché. The delighted Prince, having less *retenue* than his French diplomatic colleague, insisted upon taking a turn with the charming creature, and twirled round the ball-room with her, scattering the diamonds out of his boot-tassels and hussar jacket until his highness was fairly cut of breath. Papoosh Pasha himself would have liked to dance with her if that amusement had been the custom of his country. The company made a circle round her, and applauded as wildly as if she had been a Noblet or a Taglioni. Everybody was in ecstacy; and Becky too, you may be sure. She passed by Lady Stunnington with a look of scorn. She patronised Lady Gaunt and her astonished and mortified sister-in-law — she *écraséd* all rival charmers. As for poor Mrs. Wink-worth, and her long hair and great eyes, which had made such an effect at the commencement of the even-ing; where was she now? Nowhere in the race. She might tear her long hair and cry her great eyes out;

but there was not a person to heed or to deplore the discomfiture.

The greatest triumph of all was at supper time. She was placed at the grand exclusive table with his Royal Highness the exalted personage before mentioned, and the rest of the great guests. She was served on gold plate. She might have had pearls melted into her champagne if she liked — another Cleopatra; and the potentate of Peterwaradin would have given half the brilliants off his jacket for a kind glance from those dazzling eyes. Jabotière wrote home about her to his government. The ladies at the other tables, who supped off mere silver, and marked Lord Steyne's constant attention to her, vowed it was a monstrous infatuation, a gross insult to ladies of rank. If sarcasm could have killed, Lady Stunnington would have slain her on the spot.

Rawdon Crawley was scared at these triumphs. They seemed to separate his wife farther than ever from him somehow. He thought with a feeling very like pain how immeasurably she was his superior.

When the hour of departure came, a crowd of young men followed her to her carriage, for which the people without bawled, the cry being caught up by the linkmen who were stationed outside the tall gates of Gaunt House, congratulating each person who issued from the gate and hoping his Lordship had enjoyed this noble party.

Mrs. Rawdon Crawley's carriage, coming up to the gate after due shouting, rattled into the illuminated court-yard, and drove up to the covered way. Rawdon put his wife into the carriage, which drove off. Mr. Wenham had proposed to him to walk home, and offered the Colonel the refreshment of a cigar.

They lighted their cigars by the lamp of one of the many link-boys outside, and Rawdon walked on with his friend Wenham. Two persons separated from the crowd and followed the two gentlemen; and when they had walked down Gaunt Square a few score of paces, one of the men came up, and touching Rawdon on the shoulder, said, "Beg your pardon, Colonel, I wish to speak to you most particular." This gentleman's acquaintance gave a loud whistle as the latter spoke, at which signal a cab came clattering up from those stationed at the gate of Gaunt House — and the aide-de-camp ran round and placed himself in front of Colonel Crawley.

That gallant officer at once knew what had befallen him. He was in the hands of the bailiffs. He started back, falling against the man who had first touched him.

"We're three on us — it's no use bolting," the man behind said.

"It's you, Moss, is it?" said the Colonel, who appeared to know his interlocutor. "How much is it?"

"Only a small thing," whispered Mr. Moss, of Cursitor Street, Chancery Lane, and assistant officer to the Sheriff of Middlesex — "One hundred and sixty-six, six and eightpence, at the suit of Mr. Nathan."

"Lend me a hundred, Wenham, for God's sake," poor Rawdon said — "I've got seventy at home."

"I've not got ten pounds in the world," said poor Mr. Wenham — "Good night, my dear fellow."

"Good night," said Rawdon ruefully. And Wenham walked away — and Rawdon Crawley finished his cigar as the cab drove under Temple Bar.

CHAPTER XXIV

IN WHICH LORD STEYNE SHOWS HIMSELF IN A MOST AMIABLE LIGHT

WHEN Lord Steyne was benevolently disposed, he did nothing by halves, and his kindness towards the Crawley family did the greatest honour to his benevolent discrimination. His lordship extended his good-will to little Rawdon: he pointed out to the boy's parents the necessity of sending him to a public school; that he was of an age now when emulation, the first principles of the Latin language, pugilistic exercises, and the society of his fellow-boys would be of the greatest benefit to the boy. His father objected that he was not rich enough to send the child to a good public school; his mother, that Briggs was a capital mistress for him, and had brought him on (as indeed was the fact) famously in English, the Latin rudiments, and in general learning: but all these objections disappeared before the generous perseverence of the Marquis of Steyne. His lordship was one of the governors of that famous old collegiate institution called the Whitefriars. It had been a Cistercian Convent in old days, when the Smithfield, which is contiguous to it, was a tournament ground. Obstinate heretics used to be brought thither convenient for burning hard by. Henry VIII., the Defender of the Faith, seized upon the monastery and its possessions, and hanged and tortured some of the monks who could not accommodate themselves to the pace of his reform. Finally, a great merchant bought the house and land adjoining, in which, and with the help of other wealthy endowments of land and money, he established a famous foundation hospital for old men and children. An extern school grew round the old almost monastic foundation, which subsists still with its middle-age costume and usages; and all Cistercians pray that it may long flourish.

Of this famous house, some of the greatest noblemen, prelates, and dignitaries in England are governors: and as the boys are very comfortably lodged, fed, and educated, and subsequently inducted to good scholarships at the University and livings in the Church, many little gentlemen are devoted to the ecclesiastical profession from their tenderest years, and there is considerable emulation to procure nominations for the foundation. It was originally intended for the sons of poor and deserving clerics and laics; but many of the noble governors of the Institution, with an enlarged and rather capricious benevolence, selected all sorts of objects for their bounty. To get an education for nothing, and a future livelihood and profession assured, was so excellent a scheme that some of the richest people did not disdain it; and not only great men's relations, but great men themselves, sent their sons to profit by the chance — Right Rev. Prelates sent their own kinsmen or the sons of their clergy, while, on the other hand, some great noblemen did not disdain to patronise the children of their confidential servants, — so that a lad entering this establishment had every variety of youthful society wherewith to mingle.

Rawdon Crawley, though the only book which he studied was the Racing Calendar, and though his chief recollections of polite learning were connected with the floggings which he received at Eton in his early youth, had that decent and honest reverence for classical learning which all English gentlemen feel, and was glad to think that his son was to have a provision for life, perhaps, and a certain opportunity of becoming a scholar. And although his boy was his chief solace and companion, and endeared to him by a thousand small ties, about which he did not care to speak to his wife, who had all along shown the utmost indifference to their son, yet Rawdon agreed at once to part with him, and to give up his own greatest comfort and benefit for the sake of the welfare of the little lad. He did not know how fond he was of the child until it became necessary to let him go away. When he was gone, he felt more sad and downcast than he cared to own — far sadder than the boy himself, who was happy enough to enter a new career, and find companions of his own age. Becky burst out laughing once or twice, when the Colonel, in his clumsy, incoherent way, tried to express his sentimental sorrows at the boy's departure. The poor fellow felt that his dearest pleasure and closest friend was taken from him. He looked often and wistfully at the little vacant bed in his dressing-room, where the child used to sleep. He missed him sadly of mornings, and tried in vain to walk in the Park without him. He did not know how solitary he was until little Rawdon was gone. He liked the people who were fond of him; and would go and sit for long hours with his good-natured sister Lady Jane, and talk to her about the virtues, and good looks, and hundred good qualities of the child.

Young Rawdon's aunt, we have said, was very fond of him, as was her little girl, who wept copiously when the time for her cousin's departure came. The elder Rawdon was thankful for the fondness of mother and daughter. The very best and honestest feelings of the man came out in these artless outpourings of paternal feeling in which he indulged in their presence, and encouraged

by their sympathy. He secured not only Lady Jane's
kindness, but her sincere regard, by the feelings which
he manifested, and which he could not show to his own
wife. The two kinswomen met as seldom as possible.
Becky laughed bitterly at Jane's feelings and softness;
the other's kindly and gentle nature could not but
revolt at her sister's callous behaviour.

It estranged Rawdon from his wife more than he
knew or acknowledged to himself. She did not care for
the estrangement. Indeed, she did not miss him or
anybody. She looked upon him as her errand-man and
humble slave. He might be ever so depressed or sulky,
and she did not mark his demeanour, or only treated it
with a sneer. She was busy thinking about her position,
or her pleasures, or her advancement in society; she
ought to have held a great place in it, that is certain.

It was honest Briggs who made up the little kit for
the boy which he was to take to school. Molly, the
housemaid, blubbered in the passage when he went
away — Molly kind and faithful in spite of a long arrear
of unpaid wages. Mrs. Becky could not let her husband have the carriage to take the boy to school. Take
the horses into the City! — such a thing was never
heard of. Let a cab be brought. She did not offer to
kiss him when he went: nor did the child propose to
embrace her: but gave a kiss to old Briggs (whom, in
general, he was very shy of caressing), and consoled
her by pointing out that he was to come home on
Saturdays, when she would have the benefit of seeing
him. As the cab rolled towards the City, Becky's carriage rattled off to the Park. She was chattering and
laughing with a score of young dandies by the Serpentine, as the father and son entered at the old gates of
the school — where Rawdon left the child, and came
away with a sadder purer feeling in his heart than per-

haps that poor battered fellow had ever known since he himself came out of the nursery.

He walked all the way home very dismally, and dined alone with Briggs. He was very kind to her, and grateful for her love and watchfulness over the boy. His conscience smote him that he had borrowed Briggs's money and aided in deceiving her. They talked about little Rawdon a long time, for Becky only came home to dress and go out to dinner — and then he went off uneasily to drink tea with Lady Jane, and tell her of what had happened, and how little Rawdon went off like a trump, and how he was to wear a gown and little knee-breeches, and how young Blackball, Jack Blackball's son, of the old regiment, had taken him in charge and promised to be kind to him.

In the course of a week, young Blackball had constituted little Rawdon his fag, shoe-black, and breakfast toaster; initiated him into the mysteries of the Latin Grammar, and thrashed him three or four times; but not severely. The little chap's good-natured honest face won his way for him. He only got that degree of beating which was, no doubt, good for him; and as for blacking shoes, toasting bread, and fagging in general, were these offices not deemed to be necessary parts of every young English gentleman's education?

Our business does not lie with the second generation and Master Rawdon's life at school, otherwise the present tale might be carried to any indefinite length. The Colonel went to see his son a short time afterwards, and found the lad sufficiently well and happy, grinning and laughing in his little black gown and little breeches.

His father sagaciously tipped Blackball, his master, a sovereign, and secured that young gentleman's good will towards his fag. As a *protégé* of the great Lord Steyne, the nephew of a County member, and son of a Colonel and C.B., whose name appeared in some of the most fashionable parties in the *Morning Post*, perhaps the school authorities were disposed not to look unkindly on the child. He had plenty of pocket-money, which he spent in treating his comrades royally to raspberry tarts, and he was often allowed to come home on Saturdays to his father, who always made a jubilee of that day. When free, Rawdon would take him to the play, or send him thither with the footman; and on Sundays he went to church with Briggs and Lady Jane and his cousins. Rawdon marvelled over his stories about school, and fights, and fagging. Before long, he knew the names of all the masters and the principal boys as well as little Rawdon himself. He invited little Rawdon's crony from school, and made both the children sick with pastry, and oysters, and porter after the play. He tried to look knowing over the Latin grammar when little Rawdon showed him what part of that work he was "in." "Stick to it, my boy," he said to him with much gravity, "there's nothing like a good classical education! nothing!"

Becky's contempt for her husband grew greater every day. "Do what you like, — dine where you please, — go and have ginger-beer and sawdust at Astley's, or psalm-singing with Lady Jane, — only don't expect *me* to busy myself with the boy. I have your interests to attend to, as you can't attend to them yourself. I should like to know where you would have been now, and in what sort of a position in society, if I had not looked after you?" Indeed, nobody wanted poor old Rawdon at the parties whither Becky used to go. She was often asked without him now. She talked about great people as if she had the fee-simple of May Fair; and when the Court went into mourning, she always wore black.

Little Rawdon being disposed of, Lord Steyne, who took such a parental interest in the affairs of this amiable poor family, thought that their expenses might be very advantageously curtailed by the departure of Miss Briggs; and that Becky was quite clever enough to take the management of her own house. It has been narrated in a former chapter, how the benevolent nobleman had given his *protégé* money to pay off her little debt to Miss Briggs, who however still remained behind with her friends; whence my lord came to the painful conclusion that Mrs. Crawley had made some other use of the money confided to her than that for which her generous patron had given the loan. However, Lord Steyne was not so rude as to impart his suspicions upon this head to Mrs. Becky, whose feelings might be hurt by any controversy on the money-question, and who might have a thousand painful reasons for disposing otherwise of his lordship's generous loan. But he determined to satisfy himself of the real state of the case: and instituted the necessary inquiries in a most cautious and delicate manner.

In the first place he took an early opportunity of pumping Miss Briggs. That was not a difficult operation. A very little encouragement would set that worthy woman to talk volubly, and pour out all within her. And one day when Mrs. Rawdon had gone out to drive (as Mr. Fiche, his Lordship's confidential servant, easily learned at the livery stables where the Crawleys kept their carriage and horses, or rather, where the livery-man kept a carriage and horses for Mr. and Mrs. Crawley) — my lord dropped in upon the Curzon Street house — asked Briggs for a cup of coffee — told her that he had good accounts of the little boy at school — and in five minutes found out from her that Mrs. Rawdon had given her nothing except a black silk gown, for which Miss Briggs was immensely grateful.

He laughed within himself at this artless story. For the truth is, our dear friend Rebecca had given him a most circumstantial narration of Briggs's delight at receiving her money — eleven hundred and twenty-five pounds — and in what securities she had invested it; and what a pang Becky herself felt in being obliged to pay away such a delightful sum of money. "Who knows," the dear woman may have thought within herself, "perhaps he may give me a little more?" My lord, however, made no such proposal to the little schemer — very likely thinking that he had been sufficiently generous already.

He had the curiosity, then, to ask Miss Briggs about the state of her private affairs — and she told his Lordship candidly what her position was — how Miss Crawley had left her a legacy — how her relatives had had part of it — how Colonel Crawley had put out another portion, for which she had the best security and interest — and how Mr. and Mrs. Rawdon had kindly busied themselves with Sir Pitt, who was to dispose of the remainder most advantageously for her, when he had time. My lord asked how much the Colonel had already invested for her, and Miss Briggs at once and truly told him that the sum was six hundred and odd pounds.

But as soon as she had told her story, the voluble Briggs repented of her frankness, and besought my lord not to tell Mr. Crawley of the confessions which she had made. "The Colonel was so kind — Mr. Crawley might be offended and pay back the money, for which she could get no such good interest anywhere else." Lord Steyne, laughing, promised he never would divulge their conversation, and when he and Miss Briggs parted he laughed still more.

"What an accomplished little devil it is!" thought
he. "What a splendid actress and manager! She had
almost got a second supply out of me the other day,
with her coaxing ways. She beats all the women I
have ever seen in the course of all my well-spent life.
They are babies compared to her. I am a green-horn
myself, and a fool in her hands — an old fool. She is
unsurpassable in lies." His lordship's admiration for
Becky rose immeasurably at this proof of her cleverness. Getting the money was nothing — but getting
double the sum she wanted, and paying nobody — it was
a magnificent stroke. And Crawley, my lord thought
— Crawley is not such a fool as he looks and seems.
He has managed the matter cleverly enough on his
side. Nobody would ever have supposed from his face
and demeanour that he knew anything about this money
business; and yet he put her up to it, and has spent the
money, no doubt. In this opinion my lord, we know,
was mistaken; but it influenced a good deal his behaviour towards Colonel Crawley, whom he began to
treat with even less than that semblance of respect
which he had formerly shown towards that gentleman.
It never entered into the head of Mrs. Crawley's patron
that the little lady might be making a purse for herself;
and, perhaps, if the truth must be told, he judged of
Colonel Crawley by his experience of other husbands,
whom he had known in the course of the long and well-
spent life which had made him acquainted with a great
deal of the weakness of mankind. My lord had bought
so many men during his life, that he was surely to be
pardoned for supposing that he had found the price of
this one.

He taxed Becky upon the point on the very first
occasion when he met her alone, and he complimented
her, good-humouredly, on her cleverness in getting

more than the money which she required. Becky was only a little taken aback. It was not the habit of this dear creature to tell falsehoods, except when necessity compelled, but in these great emergencies it was her practice to lie very freely; and in an instant she was ready with another neat plausible circumstantial story which she administered to her patron. The previous statement which she had made to him was a falsehood — a wicked falsehood: she owned it; but who had made her tell it? "Ah, my Lord," she said, "you don't know all I have to suffer and bear in silence: you see me gay and happy before you — you little know what I have to endure when there is no protector near me. It was my husband, by threats and the most savage treatment, forced me to ask for that sum about which I deceived you. It was he, who, foreseeing that questions might be asked regarding the disposal of the money, forced me to account for it as I did. He took the money. He told me he had paid Miss Briggs; I did not want, I did not dare to doubt him. Pardon the wrong which a desperate man is forced to commit, and pity a miserable, miserable woman." She burst into tears as she spoke. Persecuted virtue never looked more bewitchingly wretched.

They had a long conversation, driving round and round the Regent's Park in Mrs. Crawley's carriage together, a conversation of which it is not necessary to repeat the details: but the upshot of it was, that, when Becky came home, she flew to her dear Briggs with a smiling face, and announced that she had some very good news for her. Lord Steyne had acted in the noblest and most generous manner. He was always thinking how and when he could do good. Now that little Rawdon was gone to school, a dear companion and friend was no longer necessary to her. She was

grieved beyond measure to part with Briggs; but her
means required that she should practise every retrench-
ment, and her sorrow was mitigated by the idea that her
dear Briggs would be far better provided for by her
generous patron than in her humble home. Mrs. Pilkington, the housekeeper at Gauntly Hall, was growing
exceedingly old, feeble, and rheumatic: she was not
equal to the work of superintending that vast mansion,
and must be on the look out for a successor. It was a
splendid position. The family did not go to Gauntly
once in two years. At other times the housekeeper
was the mistress of the magnificent mansion — had four
covers daily for her table; was visited by the clergy
and the most respectable people of the county — was
the lady of Gauntly, in fact; and the two last house-
keepers before Mrs. Pilkington had married rectors of
Gauntly: but Mrs. P. could not, being the aunt of the
present Rector. The place was not to be hers yet;
but she might go down on a visit to Mrs. Pilkington,
and see whether she would like to succeed her.

What words can paint the ecstatic gratitude of Briggs!
All she stipulated for was that little Rawdon should be
allowed to come down and see her at the Hall. Becky
promised this — anything. She ran up to her husband
when he came home, and told him the joyful news.
Rawdon was glad, deuced glad; the weight was off his
conscience about poor Briggs's money. She was provided for, at any rate, but — but his mind was disquiet.
He did not seem to be all right somehow. He told
little Southdown what Lord Steyne had done, and the
young man eyed Crawley with an air which surprised
the latter.

He told Lady Jane of this second proof of Steyne's
bounty, and she, too, looked odd and alarmed; so did
Sir Pitt. "She is too clever and — and gay to be al-

lowed to go from party to party without a companion,"
both said. "You must go with her, Rawdon, wherever
she goes, and you *must* have somebody with her — one
of the girls from Queen's Crawley, perhaps, though they
were rather giddy guardians for her."

Somebody Becky should have. But in the meantime
it was clear that honest Briggs must not lose her chance
of settlement for life; and so she and her bags were
packed, and she set off on her journey. And so two of
Rawdon's out-sentinels were in the hands of the enemy.

Sir Pitt went and expostulated with his sister-in-law
upon the subject of the dismissal of Briggs, and other
matters of delicate family interest. In vain she pointed
out to him how necessary was the protection of Lord
Steyne for her poor husband; how cruel it would be on
their part to deprive Briggs of the position offered to
her. Cajolements, coaxings, smiles, tears could not
satisfy Sir Pitt, and he had something very like a
quarrel with his once admired Becky. He spoke of
the honour of the family: the unsullied reputation of
the Crawleys; expressed himself in indignant tones
about her receiving those young Frenchmen — those
wild young men of fashion, my Lord Steyne himself,
whose carriage was always at her door, who passed
hours daily in her company, and whose constant presence made the world talk about her. As the head of
the house he implored her to be more prudent. Society
was already speaking lightly of her. Lord Steyne,
though a nobleman of the greatest station and talents, was a man whose attentions would compromise
any woman; he besought, he implored, he commanded
his sister-in-law to be watchful in her intercourse with
that nobleman.

Becky promised anything and everything Pitt wanted;
but Lord Steyne came to her house as often as ever,

and Sir Pitt's anger increased. I wonder was Lady Jane angry or pleased that her husband at last found fault with his favourite Rebecca? Lord Steyne's visits continuing, his own ceased; and his wife was for refusing all further intercourse with that nobleman, and declining the invitation to the Charade-night which the Marchioness sent to her; but Sir Pitt thought it was necessary to accept it, as his Royal Highness would be there.

Although he went to the party in question, Sir Pitt quitted it very early, and his wife, too, was very glad to come away. Becky hardly so much as spoke to him or noticed her sister-in-law. Pitt Crawley declared her behaviour was monstrously indecorous, reprobated in strong terms the habit of play-acting and fancy dressing, as highly unbecoming a British female; and after the charades were over, took his brother Rawdon severely to task for appearing himself, and allowing his wife to join in such improper exhibitions.

Rawdon said she should not join in any more such amusement; but indeed, and perhaps from hints from his elder brother and sister, he had already become a very watchful and exemplary domestic character. He left off his clubs and billiards. He never left home. He took Becky out to drive: he went laboriously with her to all her parties. Whenever my Lord Steyne called, he was sure to find the Colonel. And when Becky proposed to go out without her husband, or received invitations for herself, he peremptorily ordered her to refuse them; and there was that in the gentleman's manner which enforced obedience. Little Becky, to do her justice, was charmed with Rawdon's gallantry. If he was surly, she never was. Whether friends were present or absent, she had always a kind smile for him, and was attentive to his pleasure and comfort. It was the early days of their marriage over again: the same good humor, *prévenances*, merriment, and artless confidence and regard. "How much pleasanter it is," she would say, " to have you by my side in the carriage than that foolish old Briggs! Let us always go on so, dear Rawdon. How nice it would be, and how happy we should always be, if we had but the money!" He fell asleep after dinner in his chair; he did not see the face opposite to him, haggard, weary, and terrible; it lighted up with fresh candid smiles when he woke. It kissed him gaily. He wondered that he had ever had suspicions. No, he never had suspicions; all those dumb doubts and surly misgivings which had been gathering on his mind were mere idle jealousies. She was fond of him; she always had been. As for her shining in society it was no fault of hers; she was formed to shine there. Was there any woman who could talk, or sing, or do anything like her? If she would but like the boy! Rawdon thought. But the mother and son never could be brought together.

And it was while Rawdon's mind was agitated with these doubts and perplexities that the incident occurred which was mentioned in the last chapter; and the unfortunate Colonel found himself a prisoner away from home.

CHAPTER XXV

A RESCUE AND A CATASTROPHE

FRIEND RAWDON drove on then to Mr. Moss's mansion in Cursitor Street, and was duly inducted into that dismal place of hospitality. Morning was breaking over the cheerful house-tops of Chancery Lane as the rattling cab woke up the echoes there. A little pink-eyed Jew-boy, with a head as ruddy as the rising morn, let the party into the house, and Rawdon was welcomed to the ground-floor apartments by Mr. Moss, his travelling companion and host, who cheerfully asked him if he would like a glass of something warm after his drive.

The Colonel was not so depressed as some mortals would be, who, quitting a palace and a *placens uxor*, find themselves barred into a spunging-house, for, if the truth must be told, he had been a lodger at Mr. Moss's establishment once or twice before. We have not thought it necessary in the previous course of this narrative to mention these trivial little domestic incidents: but the reader may be assured that they can't unfrequently occur in the life of a man who lives on nothing a-year.

Upon his first visit to Mr. Moss, the Colonel, then a bachelor, had been liberated by the generosity of his Aunt; on the second mishap, little Becky, with the greatest spirit and kindness, had borrowed a sum of money from Lord Southdown, and had coaxed her hus-

band's creditor (who was her shawl, velvet-gown, lace
pocket-handkerchief, trinket, and gim-crack purveyor,
indeed) to take a portion of the sum claimed, and Rawdon's promissory note for the remainder: so on both
these occasions the capture and release had been conducted with the utmost gallantry on all sides, and Moss
and the Colonel were therefore on the very best of terms.

"You'll find your old bed, Colonel, and everything
comfortable," that gentleman said, "as I may honestly
say. You may be pretty sure its kep aired, and by the
best of company, too. It was slep in the night afore
last by the Honorable Capting Famish, of the Fiftieth
Dragoons, whose Mar took him out, after a fortnight,
jest to punish him, she said. But, Law bless you, I
promise you, he punished my champagne, and had a
party ere every night — reglar tip-top swells, down from
the clubs and the West End — Capting Ragg, the Honorable Deuceace, who lives in the Temple, and some fellers
as knows a good glass of wine, I warrant you. I've got
a Doctor of Diwinity upstairs, five gents in the Coffee-
room, and Mrs. Moss has a tably-dy-hoty at half-past
five, and a little cards or music afterwards, when we shall
be most happy to see you."

"I'll ring when I want anything," said Rawdon, and
went quietly to his bed-room. He was an old soldier, we
have said, and not to be disturbed by any little shocks of
fate. A weaker man would have sent off a letter to his
wife on the instant of his capture. "But what is the use
of disturbing her night's rest?" thought Rawdon. "She
won't know whether I am in my room or not. It will be
time enough to write to her when she has had her sleep
out, and I have had mine. It's only a hundred-and-
seventy, and the deuce is in it if we can't raise that."
And so, thinking about little Rawdon (whom he would
not have know that he was in such a queer place), the

Colonel turned into the bed lately occupied by Captain
Famish, and fell asleep. It was ten o'clock when he
woke up, and the ruddy-headed youth brought him,
with conscious pride, a fine silver dressing-case, wherewith he might perform the operation of shaving. Indeed Mr. Moss's house, though somewhat dirty, was
splendid throughout. There were dirty trays, and wine-
coolers *en permanence* on the side-board, huge dirty gilt
cornices, with dingy yellow satin hangings to the barred
windows which looked into Cursitor Street — vast and
dirty gilt picture-frames surrounding pieces sporting
and sacred, all of which works were by the greatest
masters; and fetched the greatest prices, too, in the bill
transactions, in the course of which they were sold and
bought over and over again. The Colonel's breakfast
was served to him in the same dingy and gorgeous plated
ware. Miss Moss, a dark-eyed maid in curl papers, appeared with the teapot, and, smiling, asked the Colonel
how he had slep? and she brought him in the *Morning
Post*, with the names of all the great people who had
figured at Lord Steyne's entertainment the night before.
It contained a brilliant account of the festivities, and of
the beautiful and accomplished Mrs. Rawdon Crawley's
admirable personifications.

After a lively chat with this lady (who sat on the
edge of the breakfast table in an easy attitude displaying the drapery of her stocking and an ex-white satin
shoe, which was down at heel), Colonel Crawley called
for pens and ink, and paper; and being asked how many
sheets, chose one which was brought to him between
Miss Moss's own finger and thumb. Many a sheet
had that dark-eyed damsel brought in; many a poor
fellow had scrawled and blotted hurried lines of entreaty, and paced up and down that awful room until
his messenger brought back the reply. Poor men

always use messengers instead of the post. Who
has not had their letters, with the wafers wet, and
the announcement that a person is waiting in the
hall?

Now on the score of his application, Rawdon had not
many misgivings.

"DEAR BECKY," (Rawdon wrote,)

"*I hope you slept well.* Don't be *frightened* if I don't bring
you in your *coffy.* Last night as I was coming home smoaking,
I met with an *accadent.* I was *nabbed* by Moss of Cursitor
Street — from whose *gilt and splendid parler* I write this — the
same that had me this time two years. Miss Moss brought in
my tea — she is grown very *fat,* and, as usual, had *her stockens
down at heal.*

"It's Nathan's business — a hundred-and-fifty — with costs,
hundred-and-seventy. Please send me my desk and some
cloths — I'm in pumps and a white tye (something like Miss
M.'s stockings) — I've seventy in it. And as soon as you
get this, Drive to Nathan's — offer him seventy-five down,
and ask *him to renew* — say I'll take wine — we may as
well have some dinner sherry; but not *picturs,* they're too
dear.

"If he won't stand it. Take my ticker and such of your
things as you can *spare,* and send them to Balls — we must, of
coarse, have the sum to-night. It won't do to let it stand
over, as to-morrow's Sunday; the beds here are not very *clean,*
and there may be other things out against me — I'm glad it
an't Rawdon's Saturday for coming home. God bless you.

"Yours in haste,
"R. C.

"P.S. Make haste and come."

This letter, sealed with a wafer, was despatched by
one of the messengers who are always hanging about
Mr. Moss's establishment; and Rawdon, having seen

him depart, went out in the court-yard, and smoked his cigar with a tolerably easy mind — in spite of the bars overhead; for Mr. Moss's court-yard is railed in like a cage, lest the gentlemen who are boarding with him should take a fancy to escape from his hospitality.

Three hours, he calculated, would be the utmost time required, before Becky should arrive and open his prison doors: and he passed these pretty cheer-fully in smoking, in reading the paper, and in the coffee-room with an acquaintance, Captain Walker, who happened to be there, and with whom he cut for sixpences for some hours, with pretty equal luck on either side.

But the day passed away and no messenger returned, — no Becky. Mr. Moss's tably-dy-hoty was served at the appointed hour of half-past five, when such of the gentlemen lodging in the house as could afford to pay for the banquet, came and partook of it in the splendid front parlour before described, and with which Mr. Crawley's temporary lodging communicated, when Miss M. (Miss Hem, as her papa called her,) appeared with-out the curl-papers of the morning, and Mrs. Hem did the honours of a prime boiled leg of mutton and turnips, of which the Colonel ate with a very faint appetite. Asked whether he would " stand " a bottle of cham-pagne for the company, he consented, and the ladies drank to his 'ealth, and Mr. Moss, in the most polite manner " looked towards him."

In the midst of this repast, however, the door-bell was heard, — young Moss of the ruddy hair, rose up with the keys and answered the summons, and coming back, told the Colonel that the messenger had returned with a bag, a desk and a letter, which he gave him. " No ceremony, Colonel, I beg," said Mrs. Moss with a wave

of her hand, and he opened the letter rather tremu-
lously. — It was a beautiful letter, highly scented, on a
pink paper, and with a light green seal.

" MON PAUVRE CHER PETIT," (Mrs. Crawley wrote).

" I could not sleep *one wink* for thinking of what had
become of *my odious old monstre :* and only got to rest in the
morning after sending for Mr. Blench (for I was in a fever),
who gave me a composing draught and left orders with Finette
that I should be disturbed *on no account.* So that my poor
old man's messenger, who had *bien mauvaise mine* Finette
says, and *sentoit le Genièvre,* remained in the hall for some
hours waiting my bell. You may fancy my state when I read
your poor dear old ill-spelt letter.

" Ill as I was, I instantly called for the carriage, and as soon
as I was dressed (though I could n't drink a drop of chocolate
— I assure you I could n't without my *monstre* to bring it to
me), I drove *ventre à terre* to Nathan's. I saw him — I wept
— I cried — I fell at his odious knees. Nothing would mol-
lify the horrid man. He would have all the money, he said,
or keep my poor monstre in prison. I drove home with the
intention of paying that *triste visite chez mon oncle* (when every
trinket I have should be at your disposal though they would
not fetch a hundred pounds, for some, you know, are with *ce
cher oncle* already), and found Milor there with the Bulgarian
old sheep-faced monster, who had come to compliment me
upon last night's performances. Paddington came in, too,
drawling and lisping and twiddling his hair ; so did Champignac, and his chef — everybody with *foison* of compliments and
pretty speeches — plaguing poor me, who longed to be rid of
them, and was thinking *every moment of the time* of *mon pauvre
prisonnier.*

" When they were gone, I went down on my knees to Milor ;
told him we were going to pawn everything, and begged and
prayed him to give me two hundred pounds. He pish'd and
psha'd in a fury — told me not to be such a fool as to pawn —
and said he would see whether he could lend me the money.

[379]

At last he went away, promising that he would send it me in the morning: when I will bring it to my poor old monster with a kiss from his affectionate

" Becky.

" I am writing in bed. Oh I have such a headache and such a heartache ! "

When Rawdon read over this letter, he turned so red and looked so savage, that the company at the table d'hote easily perceived that bad news had reached him. All his suspicions, which he had been trying to banish, returned upon him. She could not even go out and sell her trinkets to free him. She could laugh and talk about compliments paid to her, whilst he was in prison. Who had put him there? Wenham had walked with him. Was there . . . . He could hardly bear to think of what he suspected. Leaving the room hurriedly, he ran into his own — opened his desk, wrote two hurried lines, which he directed to Sir Pitt or Lady Crawley, and bade the messenger carry them at once to Gaunt Street, bidding him to take a cab, and promising him a guinea if he was back in an hour.

In the note he besought his dear brother and sister, for the sake of God; for the sake of his dear child and his honour; to come to him and relieve him from his difficulty. He was in prison: he wanted a hundred pounds to set him free — he entreated them to come to him.

He went back to the dining-room after despatching his messenger, and called for more wine. He laughed and talked with a strange boisterousness, as the people thought. Sometimes he laughed madly at his own fears, and went on drinking for an hour; listening all the while for the carriage which was to bring his fate back.

At the expiration of that time, wheels were heard whirling up to the gate — the young Janitor went out with his gate-keys. It was a lady whom he let in at the bailiff's door.

"Colonel Crawley," she said, trembling very much. He, with a knowing look, locked the outer door upon her — then unlocked and opened the inner one, and calling out, "Colonel, you're wanted," led her into the back parlour, which he occupied.

Rawdon came in from the dining-parlour where all those people were carousing, into his back room; a flare of coarse light following him into the apartment where the lady stood, still very nervous.

"It is I, Rawdon," she said, in a timid voice, which she strove to render cheerful. "It is Jane." Rawdon was quite overcome by that kind voice and presence. He ran up to her — caught her in his arms — gasped out some inarticulate words of thanks, and fairly sobbed on her shoulder. She did not know the cause of his emotion.

The bills of Mr. Moss were quickly settled, perhaps to the disappointment of that gentleman, who had counted on having the Colonel as his guest over Sunday at least; and Jane, with beaming smiles and happiness in her eyes, carried away Rawdon from the bailiff's house, and they went homewards in the cab in which she had hastened to his release. "Pitt was gone to a parliamentary dinner," she said, "when Rawdon's note came, and so, dear Rawdon, I — I came myself;" and she put her kind hand in his. Perhaps it was well for Rawdon Crawley that Pitt was away at that dinner. Rawdon thanked his sister a hundred times, and with an ardour of gratitude which touched and almost alarmed that soft-hearted woman. "Oh," said he, in his rude, artless way, "you — you don't know how I'm changed since I've known you, and — and little Rawdy. I — I'd like to change somehow. You see I want — I want —

to be —." — He did not finish the sentence, but she could interpret it. And that night after he left her, and as she sate by her own little boy's bed, she prayed humbly for that poor wayworn sinner.

Rawdon left her and walked home rapidly. It was nine o'clock at night. He ran across the streets, and the great squares of Vanity Fair, and at length came up breathless opposite his own house. He started back and fell against the railings, trembling as he looked up. The drawing-room windows were blazing with light. She had said that she was in bed and ill. He stood there for some time, the light from the rooms on his pale face.

He took out his door-key and let himself into the house. He could hear laughter in the upper rooms. He was in the ball-dress in which he had been captured the night before. He went silently up the stairs; leaning against the banisters at the stair-head. — Nobody was stirring in the house besides — all the servants had been sent away. Rawdon heard laughter within — laughter and singing. Becky was singing a snatch of the song of the night before; a hoarse voice shouted " Brava! Brava! " — it was Lord Steyne's.

Rawdon opened the door and went in. A little table with a dinner was laid out — and wine and plate. Steyne was hanging over the sofa on which Becky sate. The wretched woman was in a brilliant full toilette, her arms and all her fingers sparkling with bracelets and rings; and the brilliants on her breast which Steyne had given her. He had her hand in his, and was bowing over it to kiss it, when Becky started up with a faint scream as she caught sight of Rawdon's white face. At the next instant she tried a smile, a horrid smile, as if to welcome her husband: and

Steyne rose up, grinding his teeth, pale, and with fury in his looks.

He, too, attempted a laugh — and came forward holding out his hand. "What, come back! How d'ye do, Crawley?" he said, the nerves of his mouth twitching as he tried to grin at the intruder.

There was that in Rawdon's face which caused Becky to fling herself before him. "I am innocent, Rawdon," she said; "before God, I am innocent." She clung hold of his coat, of his hands; her own were all covered with serpents, and rings, and baubles. "I am innocent. — Say I am innocent," she said to Lord Steyne.

He thought a trap had been laid for him, and was as furious with the wife as with the husband. "You innocent! Damn you," he screamed out. "You innocent! Why every trinket you have on your body is paid for by me. I have given you thousands of pounds which this fellow has spent, and for which he has sold you. Innocent, by ——! You're as innocent as your mother, the ballet-girl, and your husband the bully. Don't think to frighten me as you have done others. Make way, sir, and let me pass;" and Lord Steyne seized up his hat, and, with flame in his eyes, and looking his enemy fiercely in the face, marched upon him, never for a moment doubting that the other would give way.

But Rawdon Crawley springing out, seized him by the neck-cloth, until Steyne, almost strangled, writhed, and bent under his arm. "You lie, you dog!" said Rawdon. "You lie, you coward and villain!" And he struck the Peer twice over the face with his open hand, and flung him bleeding to the ground. It was all done before Rebecca could interpose. She stood there trembling before him. She admired her husband, strong, brave, and victorious.

"Come here," he said. — She came up at once.

"Take off those things." — She began, trembling, pulling the jewels from her arms, and the rings from her shaking fingers, and held them all in a heap, quivering and looking up at him. "Throw them down," he said, and she dropped them. He tore the diamond ornament out of her breast, and flung it at Lord Steyne. It cut him on his bald forehead. Steyne wore the scar to his dying day.

"Come upstairs," Rawdon said to his wife. "Don't kill me, Rawdon," she said. He laughed savagely. — "I want to see if that man lies about the money as he has about me. Has he given you any?"

"No," said Rebecca, "that is ——"

"Give me your keys," Rawdon answered, and they went out together.

Rebecca gave him all the keys but one: and she was in hopes that he would not have remarked the absence of that. It belonged to the little desk which Amelia had given her in early days, and which she kept in a secret place. But Rawdon flung open boxes and wardrobes, throwing the multifarious trumpery of their contents here and there, and at last he found the desk. The woman was forced to open it. It contained papers, love-letters many years old — all sorts of small trinkets and woman's memoranda. And it contained a pocket-book with bank notes. Some of these were dated ten years back, too, and one was quite a fresh one — a note for a thousand pounds which Lord Steyne had given her.

"Did he give you this?" Rawdon said.

"Yes;" Rebecca answered.

"I 'll send it to him to-day," Rawdon said (for day had dawned again, and many hours had passed in this search), "and I will pay Briggs, who was kind to the

boy, and some of the debts. You will let me know
where I shall send the rest to you. You might have
spared me a hundred pounds, Becky, out of all this — I
have always shared with you."

"I am innocent," said Becky. And he left her without another word.

What were her thoughts when he left her? She remained for hours after he was gone, the sunshine pouring into the room, and Rebecca sitting alone on the
bed's edge. The drawers were all opened and their
contents scattered about, — dresses and feathers, scarfs
and trinkets, a heap of tumbled vanities lying in a
wreck. Her hair was falling over her shoulders; her
gown was torn where Rawdon had wrenched the brilliants out of it. She heard him go downstairs a few
minutes after he left her, and the door slamming and
closing on him. She knew he would never come back.
He was gone for ever. Would he kill himself? — she
thought — not until after he had met Lord Steyne. She
thought of her long past life, and all the dismal incidents of it. Ah, how dreary it seemed, how miserable,
lonely and profitless! Should she take laudanum, and
end it, too — have done with all hopes, schemes, debts,
and triumphs? The French maid found her in this
position — sitting in the midst of her miserable ruins
with clasped hands and dry eyes. The woman was her
accomplice and in Steyne's pay. " Mon Dieu, Madame,
what has happened?" she asked.

What *had* happened? Was she guilty or not? She
said not; but who could tell what was truth which came
from those lips; or if that corrupt heart was in this case
pure? All her lies and her schemes, all her selfishness
and her wiles, all her wit and genius had come to this
bankruptcy. The woman closed the curtains, and with

some entreaty and show of kindness, persuaded her
mistress to lie down on the bed. Then she went below
and gathered up the trinkets which had been lying on
the floor since Rebecca dropped them there at her husband's orders, and Lord Steyne went away.

CHAPTER XXVI

SUNDAY AFTER THE BATTLE

THE mansion of Sir Pitt Crawley in Great Gaunt Street, was just beginning to dress itself for the day, as Rawdon, in his evening costume, which he had now worn two days, passed by the scared female who was scouring the steps, and entered into his brother's study. Lady Jane in her morning-gown, was up and above stairs in the nursery, superintending the toilettes of her children, and listening to the morning prayers which the little creatures performed at her knee. Every morning she and they performed this duty privately, and before the public ceremonial at which Sir Pitt presided, and at which all the people of the household were expected to assemble. Rawdon sate down in the study before the baronet's table, set out with the orderly blue books and the letters, the neatly docketed bills and symmetrical pamphlets; the locked account-books, desks, and despatch boxes, the Bible, the *Quarterly Review* and the *Court Guide*, which all stood as if on parade awaiting the inspection of their chief.

A book of family sermons, one of which Sir Pitt was in the habit of administering to his family on Sunday mornings, lay ready on the study table, and awaiting his judicious selection. And by the sermon-book was the *Observer* newspaper, damp and neatly folded, and for Sir Pitt's own private use. His gentleman alone took the opportunity of perusing the newspaper before he laid it by his master's desk. Before he had brought it into the study that morning, he had read in the journal a flaming account of "Festivities at Gaunt House," with the names of all the distinguished personages invited by the Marquis of Steyne to meet his Royal Highness. Having made comments upon this entertainment to the housekeeper and her niece as they were taking early tea and hot buttered toast in the former lady's apartment, and wondered how the Rawding Crawleys could git on, the valet had damped and folded the paper once more, so that it looked quite fresh and innocent against the arrival of the master of the house.

Poor Rawdon took up the paper and began to try and read it until his brother should arrive. But the print fell blank upon his eyes; and he did not know in the least what he was reading. The Government news and appointments (which Sir Pitt as a public man was bound to peruse, otherwise he would by no means permit the introduction of Sunday papers into his household), the theatrical criticisms, the fight for a hundred pounds a-side between the Barking Butcher and the Tutbury Pet, the Gaunt House chronicle itself, which contained a most complimentary though guarded account of the famous charades of which Mrs. Becky had been the heroine — all these passed as in a haze before Rawdon, as he sat waiting the arrival of the chief of the family.

Punctually, as the shrill-toned bell of the black marble study clock began to chime nine, Sir Pitt made his appearance, fresh, neat, smugly shaved, with a waxy clean face, and stiff shirt collar, his scanty hair combed and oiled, trimming his nails as he descended the stairs majestically, in a starched cravat and a gray flannel dressing-gown, — a real old English gentleman, in a word, — a model of neatness and every propriety. He started when he saw poor Rawdon in his study in tumbled clothes, with blood-shot eyes, and his hair over his face. He thought his brother was not sober, and had been out all night on some orgy. " Good gracious, Rawdon," he said, with a blank face, " what brings you here at this time of the morning? Why ain't you at home?"

" Home," said Rawdon, with a wild laugh. " Don't be frightened, Pitt. I'm not drunk. Shut the door; I want to speak to you."

Pitt closed the door and came up to the table, where he sate down in the other arm-chair, — that one placed for the reception of the steward, agent, or confidential visitor who came to transact business with the Baronet, — and trimmed his nails more vehemently than ever.

" Pitt, it's all over with me," the Colonel said, after a pause. " I'm done."

" I always said it would come to this," the Baronet cried, peevishly, and beating a tune with his clean-trimmed nails. " I warned you a thousand times. I can't help you any more. Every shilling of my money is tied up. Even the hundred pounds that Jane took you last night were promised to my lawyer to-morrow morning; and the want of it will put me to great inconvenience. I don't mean to say that I won't assist you ultimately. But as for paying your creditors in full, I might as well hope to pay the National Debt. It is madness, sheer madness, to think of such a thing. You must come to a compromise. It's a painful thing for the family; but everybody does it. There was George Kitely, Lord Ragland's son, went through the Court last week, and was what they call white-washed, I believe. Lord Ragland would not pay a shilling for him, and —— "

" It's not money I want," Rawdon broke in. " I'm

not come to you about myself. Never mind what happens to me —— "

" What is the matter, then? " said Pitt, somewhat relieved.

" It's the boy," said Rawdon, in a husky voice. " I want you to promise me that you will take charge of him when I 'm gone. That dear good wife of yours has always been good to him; and he's fonder of her than he is of his. . . . — Damn it. Look here, Pitt — you know that I was to have had Miss Crawley's money. I was n't brought up like a younger brother: but was always encouraged to be extravagant and kep idle. But for this I might have been quite a different man. I did n't do my duty with the regiment so bad. You know how I was thrown over about the money, and who got it."

" After the sacrifices I have made, and the manner in which I have stood by you, I think this sort of reproach is useless," Sir Pitt said. " Your marriage was your own doing, not mine."

" That 's over now," said Rawdon. — " That 's over now." And the words were wrenched from him with a groan, which made his brother start.

" Good God! is she dead? " Sir Pitt said, with a voice of genuine alarm and commiseration.

" I wish *I* was," Rawdon replied. " If it was n't for little Rawdon I 'd have cut my throat this morning — and that damned villain's too."

Sir Pitt instantly guessed the truth, and surmised that Lord Steyne was the person whose life Rawdon wished to take. The Colonel told his senior briefly, and in broken accents, the circumstances of the case. " It was a regular plan between that scoundrel and her," he said. " The bailiffs were put upon me: I was taken as I was going out of his house: when I wrote to her for money, she said she was ill in bed, and put me off to another day. And when I got home I found her in diamonds and sitting with that villain alone." He then went on to describe hurriedly the personal conflict with Lord Steyne. To an affair of that nature, of course, he said, there was but one issue: and after his conference with his brother, he was going away to make the necessary arrangements for the meeting which must ensue. "And as it may end fatally with me," Rawdon said with a broken voice, "and as the boy has no mother, I must leave him to you and Jane, Pitt — only it will be a comfort to me if you will promise me to be his friend."

The elder brother was much affected, and shook Rawdon's hand with a cordiality seldom exhibited by him. Rawdon passed his hand over his shaggy eyebrows. "Thank you brother," said he. "I know I can trust your word."

"I will, upon my honour," the Baronet said. And thus, and almost mutely, this bargain was struck between them.

Then Rawdon took out of his pocket the little pocketbook which he had discovered in Becky's desk: and from which he drew a bundle of the notes which it contained. "Here's six hundred," he said — "you didn't know I was so rich. I want you to give the money to Briggs, who lent it to us — and who was kind to the boy — and I've always felt ashamed of having taken the poor old woman's money. And here's some more — I've only kept back a few pounds — which Becky may as well have, to get on with." As he spoke he took hold of the other notes to give to his brother: but his hands shook, and he was so agitated that the pocket-book fell from him, and out of it the thousand pound note which had been the last of the unlucky Becky's winnings.

Pitt stooped and picked them up, amazed at so much

wealth. "Not that," Rawdon said — "I hope to put a bullet into the man whom that belongs to." He had thought to himself, it would be a fine revenge to wrap a ball in the note, and kill Steyne with it.

After this colloquy the brothers once more shook hands and parted. Lady Jane had heard of the Colonel's arrival and was waiting for her husband in the adjoining dining-room, with female instinct, auguring evil. The door of the dining-room happened to be left open, and the lady of course was issuing from it as the two brothers passed out of the study. She held out her hand to Rawdon, and said she was glad he was come to break-fast; though she could perceive, by his haggard un-shorn face, and the dark looks of her husband, that there was very little question of breakfast between them. Rawdon muttered some excuses about an engagement, squeezing hard the timid little hand which his sister-in-law reached out to him. Her imploring eyes could read nothing but calamity in his face; but he went away without another word. Nor did Sir Pitt vouchsafe her any explanation. The children came up to salute him, and he kissed them in his usual frigid manner. The mother took both of them close to herself, and held a hand of each of them as they knelt down to prayers, which Sir Pitt read to them, and to the servants in their Sunday suits or liveries, ranged upon chairs on the other side of the hissing tea-urn. Breakfast was so late that day, in consequence of the delays which had occurred, that the church-bells began to ring whilst they were sitting over their meal: and Lady Jane was too ill, she said, to go to church, though her thoughts had been entirely astray during the period of family devotion.

Rawdon Crawley meanwhile hurried on from Great Gaunt Street, and knocking at the great bronze Medusa's head which stands on the portal of Gaunt House, brought out the purple Silenus in a red and silver waistcoat, who acts as porter of that palace. The man was scared also by the Colonel's dishevelled appearance, and barred the way as if afraid that the other was going to force it. But Colonel Crawley only took out a card and enjoined him particularly to send it in to Lord Steyne, and to mark the address written on it, and say that Colonel Crawley would be all day after one o'clock at the Regent Club in St. James's Street — not at home. The fat red-faced man looked after him with astonishment as he strode away; so did the people in their Sunday clothes who were out so early; the charity boys with shining faces, the green-grocer lolling at his door, and the publican shutting his shutters in the sunshine, against service commenced. The people joked at the cab-stand about his appearance, as he took a carriage there, and told the driver to drive him to Knightsbridge Barracks.

All the bells were jangling and tolling as he reached that place. He might have seen his old acquaintance Amelia on her way from Brompton to Russell Square had he been looking out. Troops of schools were on their march to church, the shiny pavement and outsides of coaches in the suburbs were thronged with people out upon their Sunday pleasure; but the Colonel was much too busy to take any heed of these phenomena, and, arriving at Knightsbridge, speedily made his way up to the room of his old friend and comrade Captain Macmurdo, who Crawley found, to his satisfaction, was in barracks.

Captain Macmurdo, a veteran officer and Waterloo man, greatly liked by his regiment, in which want of money alone prevented him from attaining the highest ranks, was enjoying the forenoon calmly in bed. He

had been at a fast supper-party, given the night before
by Captain the Honourable George Cinqbars, at his
house in Brompton Square, to several young men of the
regiment, and a number of ladies of the corps de ballet,
and old Mac, who was at home with people of all ages
and ranks, and consorted with generals, dog-fanciers,
opera-dancers, bruisers, and every kind of person, in a
word, was resting himself after the night's labours, and,
not being on duty, was in bed.

His room was hung round with boxing, sporting, and
dancing pictures, presented to him by comrades as they
retired from the regiment, and married and settled into
quiet life. And as he was now nearly fifty years of
age, twenty-four of which he had passed in the corps,
he had a singular museum. He was one of the best
shots in England, and, for a heavy man, one of the
best riders; indeed, he and Crawley had been rivals
when the latter was in the army. To be brief, Mr.
Macmurdo was lying in bed, reading in *Bell's Life* an
account of that very fight between the Tutbury Pet
and the Barking Butcher, which has been before mentioned — a venerable bristly warrior, with a little close-
shaved gray head, with a silk night-cap, a red face and
nose, and a great dyed moustache.

When Rawdon told the Captain he wanted a friend,
the latter knew perfectly well on what duty of friendship
he was called to act, and indeed had conducted scores
of affairs for his acquaintances with the greatest pru-
dence and skill. His Royal Highness the late lamented
Commander-in-Chief had had the greatest regard for
Macmurdo on this account; and he was the common
refuge of gentlemen in trouble.

"What's the row about, Crawley, my boy?" said the
old warrior. "No more gambling business, hay, like
that when we shot Captain Marker?"

"It's about — about my wife," Crawley answered, casting down his eyes and turning very red.

The other gave a whistle. "I always said she'd throw you over," he began: — indeed there were bets in the regiment and at the clubs regarding the probable fate of Colonel Crawley, so lightly was his wife's character esteemed by his comrades and the world; but seeing the savage look with which Rawdon answered the expression of this opinion, Macmurdo did not think fit to enlarge upon it further.

"Is there no way out of it, old boy?" the Captain continued in a grave tone. "Is it only suspicion, you know, or — or what is it? Any letters? Can't you keep it quiet? Best not make any noise about a thing of that sort if you can help it." "Think of his only finding her out now," the Captain thought to himself, and remembered a hundred particular conversations at the mess-table, in which Mrs. Crawley's reputation had been torn to shreds.

"There's no way but one out of it," Rawdon replied — "and there's only a way out of it for one of us, Mac — do you understand? I was put out of the way: arrested: I found 'em alone together. I told him he was a liar and a coward, and knocked him down and thrashed him."

"Serve him right," Macmurdo said. "Who is it?"

Rawdon answered it was Lord Steyne.

"The deuce! a Marquis! they said he — that is, they said you ——"

"What the devil do you mean?" roared out Rawdon; "do you mean that you ever heard a fellow doubt about my wife, and did n't tell me, Mac?"

"The world's very censorious, old boy," the other replied. "What the deuce was the good of my telling you what any tomfools talked about?"

[395]

"It was damned unfriendly, Mac," said Rawdon, quite overcome; and, covering his face with his hands, he gave way to an emotion, the sight of which caused the tough old campaigner opposite him to wince with sympathy. "Hold up, old boy," he said; "great man or not, we'll put a bullet in him, damn him. As for women, they're all so."

"You don't know how fond I was of that one," Rawdon said, half inarticulately. "Damme, I followed her like a footman. I gave up everything I had to her. I'm a beggar because I would marry her. By Jove, Sir, I've pawned my own watch in order to get her anything she fancied: and she — she's been making a purse for herself all the time, and grudged me a hundred pound to get me out of quod." He then fiercely and incoherently, and with an agitation under which his counsellor had never before seen him labour, told Macmurdo the circumstances of the story. His adviser caught at some stray hints in it.

"She may be innocent, after all," he said. "She says so. Steyne has been a hundred times alone with her in the house before."

"It may be so," Rawdon answered sadly; "but this don't look very innocent: " and he showed the Captain the thousand pound note which he had found in Becky's pocket-book. "This is what he gave her, Mac: and she kep it unknown to me: and with this money in the house, she refused to stand by me when I was locked up." The Captain could not but own that the secreting of the money had a very ugly look.

Whilst they were engaged in their conference, Rawdon despatched Captain Macmurdo's servant to Curzon Street, with an order to the domestic there to give up a bag of clothes of which the Colonel had great need. And during the man's absence, and with great labour and a Johnson's Dictionary, which stood them in much stead, Rawdon and his second composed a letter, which the latter was to send to Lord Steyne. Captain Macmurdo had the honour of waiting upon the Marquis of Steyne, on the part of Colonel Rawdon Crawley, and begged to intimate that he was empowered by the Colonel to make any arrangements for the meeting which, he had no doubt, it was his Lordship's intention to demand, and which the circumstances of the morning had rendered inevitable. Captain Macmurdo begged Lord Steyne, in the most polite manner, to appoint a friend, with whom he (Captain M'M.) might communicate, and desired that the meeting might take place with as little delay as possible.

In a postscript the Captain stated that he had in his possession a bank-note for a large amount, which Colonel Crawley had reason to suppose was the property of the Marquis of Steyne. And he was anxious, on the Colonel's behalf, to give up the note to its owner.

By the time this note was composed, the Captain's servant returned from his mission to Colonel Crawley's house in Curzon Street, but without the carpet-bag and portmanteau, for which he had been sent: and with a very puzzled and odd face.

"They won't give 'em up," said the man; "there's a regular shinty in the house; and everything at sixes and sevens. The landlord's come in and took possession. The servants was a drinkin' up in the drawing-room. They said — they said you had gone off with the plate, Colonel" — the man added after a pause: — "One of the servants is off already. And Simpson, the man as was very noisy and drunk indeed, says nothing shall go out of the house until his wages is paid up."

The account of this little revolution in May Fair

astonished and gave a little gaiety to an otherwise very *triste* conversation. The two officers laughed at Rawdon's discomfiture.

"I'm glad the little 'un is n't at home," Rawdon said, biting his nails. "You remember him, Mac, don't you, in the Riding School? How he sat the kicker to be sure! did n't he?"

"That he did, old boy," said the good-natured Captain.

Little Rawdon was then sitting, one of fifty gown boys, in the Chapel of Whitefriars School: thinking, not about the sermon, but about going home next Saturday, when his father would certainly tip him, and perhaps would take him to the play.

"He's a regular trump, that boy," the father went on, still musing about his son. "I say, Mac, if anything goes wrong — if I drop — I should like you to — to go and see him, you know: and say that I was very fond of him, and that. And — dash it — old chap, give him these gold sleeve-buttons: it's all I've got." He covered his face with his black hands: over which the tears rolled and made furrows of white. Mr. Macmurdo had also occasion to take off his silk night-cap and rub it across his eyes.

"Go down and order some breakfast," he said to his man in a loud cheerful voice, — "What'll you have, Crawley? Some devilled kidneys and a herring — let's say — And, Clay, lay out some dressing things for the Colonel: we were always pretty much of a size, Rawdon, my boy, and neither of us ride so light as we did when we first entered the corps." With which, and leaving the Colonel to dress himself, Macmurdo turned round towards the wall, and resumed the perusal of *Bell's Life*, until such time as his friend's toilette was complete, and he was at liberty to commence his own.

This, as he was about to meet a lord, Captain Macmurdo performed with particular care. He waxed his mustachios into a state of brilliant polish, and put on a tight cravat and a trim buff waistcoat: so that all the young officers in the mess-room, whither Crawley had preceded his friend, complimented Mac on his appearance at breakfast, and asked if he was going to be married that Sunday?

PART III

VANITY FAIR

A NOVEL WITHOUT A HERO

CHAPTER I

IN WHICH THE SAME SUBJECT IS PURSUED

BECKY did not rally from the state of stupor and confusion in which the events of the previous night had plunged her intrepid spirit, until the bells of the Curzon Street Chapels were ringing for afternoon service, and rising from her bed she began to ply her own bell, in order to summon the French maid who had left her some hours before.

Mrs. Rawdon Crawley rang many times in vain; and though, on the last occasion, she rang with such vehemence as to pull down the bell-rope, Mademoiselle Fifine did not make her appearance, — no, not though her mistress, in a great pet, and with the bell-rope in her hand, came out to the landing-place with her hair over her shoulders, and screamed out repeatedly for her attendant.

The truth is, she had quitted the premises for many hours, and upon that permission which is called French leave among us. After picking up the trinkets in the drawing-room, Mademoiselle had ascended to her own apartments, packed and corded her own boxes there, tripped out and called a cab for herself, brought down her trunks with her own hand, and without ever so

[1]

much as asking the aid of any of the other servants, who would probably have refused it, as they hated her cordially, and without wishing any one of them good-bye, had made her exit from Curzon Street.

The game, in her opinion, was over in that little domestic establishment. Fifine went off in a cab, as we have known more exalted persons of her nation to do under similar circumstances: but, more provident or lucky than these, she secured not only her own property, but some of her mistress's (if indeed that lady could be said to have any property at all) — and not only carried off the trinkets before alluded to, and some favourite dresses on which she had long kept her eye, but four richly gilt Louis Quatorze candlesticks, six gilt Albums, Keepsakes, and Books of Beauty, a gold enamelled snuff-box which had once belonged to Madame du Barri, and the sweetest little inkstand and mother-of-pearl blotting-book, which Becky used when she composed her charming little pink notes, had vanished from the premises in Curzon Street together with Mademoiselle Fifine, and all the silver laid on the table for the little *festin* which Rawdon interrupted. The plated ware Mademoiselle left behind her was too cumbrous probably, for which reason, no doubt, she also left the fire irons, the chimney-glasses, and the rosewood cottage piano.

A lady very like her subsequently kept a milliner's shop in the Rue du Helder at Paris, where she lived with great credit and enjoyed the patronage of my Lord Steyne. This person always spoke of England as of the most treacherous country in the world, and stated to her young pupils that she had been *affreusement volé* by natives of that island. It was no doubt compassion for her misfortunes which induced the Marquis of Steyne to be so very kind to Madame de Saint Amaranthe. May she flourish as she deserves, — she appears no more in our quarter of Vanity Fair.

Hearing a buzz and a stir below, and indignant at the impudence of those servants who would not answer her summons, Mrs. Crawley flung her morning robe round her, and descended majestically to the drawing-room, whence the noise proceeded.

The cook was there with blackened face, seated on the beautiful chintz sofa by the side of Mrs. Raggles, to whom she was administering Maraschino. The page with the sugar-loaf buttons, who carried about Becky's pink notes, and jumped about her little carriage with such alacrity, was now engaged putting his fingers into a cream dish; the footman was talking to Raggles, who had a face full of perplexity and woe — and yet, though the door was open, and Becky had been screaming a half dozen of times a few feet off, not one of her attendants had obeyed her call. "Have a little drop, do 'ee now Mrs. Raggles," the cook was saying as Becky entered, the white cashmere dressing gown flouncing around her.

"Simpson! Trotter!" the mistress of the house cried in great wrath. "How dare you stay here when you heard me call? How dare you sit down in my presence? Where's my maid?" The page withdrew his fingers from his mouth with a momentary terror: but the cook took off a glass of Maraschino, of which Mrs. Raggles had had enough, staring at Becky over the little gilt glass as she drained its contents. The liquor appeared to give the odious rebel courage.

"*Your* sofy, indeed!" Mrs. Cook said. "I'm a settin' on Mrs. Raggles's sofy. Don't you stir, Mrs. Raggles, Mum. I'm a settin' on Mr. and Mrs. Raggles's sofy, which they bought with honest money, and very dear it cost 'em, too. And I'm thinkin' if I set here until I'm paid

[3]

my wages, I shall set a precious long time, Mrs. Raggles; and set I will, too — ha! ha!" and with this she filled herself another glass of the liquor, and drank it with a more hideously satirical air.

"Trotter! Simpson! turn that drunken wretch out," screamed Mrs. Crawley.

"I shawn't," said Trotter the footman; "turn out yourself. Pay our selleries, and turn me out too. *We'll* go fast enough."

"Are you all here to insult me?" cried Becky in a fury; "when Colonel Crawley comes home I'll —"

At this the servants burst into a horse haw-haw, in which, however, Raggles, who still kept a most melancholy countenance, did not join. "He ain't a coming back," Mr. Trotter resumed. "He sent for his things, and I would n' let 'em go, although Mr. Raggles would: and I don't b'lieve he's no more a Colonel than I am. He's hoff: and I suppose you're a goin' after him. You're no better than swindlers, both on you. Don't be a bullyin' *me*. I won't stand it. Pay us our selleries, I say. Pay us our selleries." It was evident, from Mr. Trotter's flushed countenance and defective intonation, that he, too, had had recourse to vinous stimulus.

"Mr. Raggles," said Becky, in a passion of vexation, "you will not surely let me be insulted by that drunken man?" "Hold your noise, Trotter; do now," said Simpson the page. He was affected by his mistress's deplorable situation, and succeeded in preventing an outrageous denial of the epithet "drunken" on the footman's part.

"O Mam," said Raggles, "I never thought to live to see this year day. I've known the Crawley family ever since I was born. I lived butler with Miss Crawley for thirty years; and I little thought one of that family was a goin' to ruing me — yes, ruing me" — said the poor

fellow with tears in his eyes. " Har you a goin' to pay
me ? You 've lived in this 'ouse four year. You 've
'ad my substance : my plate and linning. You ho me a
milk and butter bill of two 'undred pound, you must
'ave noo laid heggs for your homlets, and cream for
your spanil dog."

" She did n't care what her own flesh and blood had,"
interposed the cook. " Many 's the time, he 'd have
starved but for me."

" He 's a charaty boy now, Cooky," said Mr. Trotter,
with a drunken " ha ! ha ! " — and honest Raggles continued, in a lamentable tone, an enumeration of his
griefs. All he said was true. Becky and her husband
had ruined him. He had bills coming due next week
and no means to meet them. He would be sold up
and turned out of his shop and his house, because he
had trusted to the Crawley family. His tears and
lamentations made Becky more peevish than ever.

" You all seem to be against me," she said, bitterly.
"What do you want? I can't pay you on Sunday.
Come back to-morrow and I 'll pay you everything.
I thought Colonel Crawley had settled with you. He
will to-morrow. I declare to you upon my honour that
he left home this morning with fifteen hundred pounds
in his pocket-book. He has left me nothing. Apply
to him. Give me a bonnet and shawl and let me go
out and find him. There was a difference between us
this morning. You all seem to know it. I promise
you upon my word that you shall all be paid. He has
got a good appointment. Let me go out and find him."

This audacious statement caused Raggles and the
other personages present to look at one another with
a wild surprise, and with it Rebecca left them. She
went upstairs and dressed herself this time without the
aid of her French maid. She went into Rawdon's

room, and there saw that a trunk and bag were packed ready for removal, with a pencil direction that they should be given when called for; then she went into the Frenchwoman's garret; everything was clean, and all the drawers emptied there. She bethought herself of the trinkets which had been left on the ground, and felt certain that the woman had fled. "Good Heavens! was ever such ill luck as mine?" she said; "to be so near, and to lose all. Is it all too late? No; there was one chance more."

She dressed herself, and went away unmolested this time, but alone. It was four o'clock. She went swiftly down the streets (she had no money to pay for a carriage), and never stopped until she came to Sir Pitt Crawley's door, in Great Gaunt Street. Where was Lady Jane Crawley? She was at church. Becky was not sorry. Sir Pitt was in his study, and had given orders not to be disturbed — she must see him — she slipped by the sentinel in livery at once, and was in Sir Pitt's room before the astonished Baronet had even laid down the paper.

He turned red and started back from her with a look of great alarm and horror.

"Do not look so," she said. "I am not guilty, Pitt, dear Pitt; you were my friend once. Before God, I am not guilty. I seem so. Everything is against me. And O! at such a moment! just when all my hopes were about to be realised: just when happiness was in store for us."

"Is this true, what I see in the paper then?" Sir Pitt said — a paragraph in which had greatly surprised him.

"It is true. Lord Steyne told me on Friday night, the night of that fatal ball. He has been promised an appointment any time these six months. Mr. Martyr, the Colonial Secretary, told him yesterday that it was

[6]

made out. That unlucky arrest ensued; that horrible meeting. I was only guilty of too much devotedness to Rawdon's service. I have received Lord Steyne alone a hundred times before. I confess I had money of which Rawdon knew nothing. Don't you know how careless he is of it, and could I dare to confide it to him?" And so she went on with a perfectly connected story, which she poured into the ears of her perplexed kinsman.

It was to the following effect. Becky owned, and with perfect frankness, but deep contrition, that having remarked Lord Steyne's partiality for her (at the mention of which Pitt blushed), and being secure of her own virtue, she had determined to turn the great peer's attachment to the advantage of herself and her family. "I looked for a peerage for you, Pitt," she said (the brother-in-law again turned red). "We have talked about it. Your genius and Lord Steyne's interest made it more than probable, had not this dreadful calamity come to put an end to all our hopes. But, first, I own that it was my object to rescue my dear husband, — him whom I love in spite of all his ill usage and suspicions of me, — to remove him from the poverty and ruin which was impending over us. I saw Lord Steyne's partiality for me," she said, casting down her eyes. "I own that I did everything in my power to make myself pleasing to him, and as far as an honest woman may, to secure his — his esteem. It was only on Friday morning that the news arrived of the death of the Governor of Coventry Island, and my Lord instantly secured the appointment for my dear husband. It was intended as a surprise for him, — he was to see it in the papers to-day. Even after that horrid arrest took place (the expenses of which Lord Steyne generously said he would settle, so that I was in a manner prevented from coming to my husband's assistance), my Lord was laughing with me, and saying that my dearest Rawdon would be consoled when he read of his appointment in the paper, in that shocking spun — bailiff's house. And then — then he came home. His suspicions were excited, — the dreadful scene took place between my Lord and my cruel, cruel Rawdon — and, O my God, what will happen next? Pitt, dear Pitt! pity me, and reconcile us!" And as she spoke she flung herself down on her knees, and bursting into tears, seized hold of Pitt's hand, which she kissed passionately.

It was in this very attitude that Lady Jane, who, returning from church, ran to her husband's room directly she heard Mrs. Rawdon Crawley was closeted there, found the Baronet and his sister-in-law.

"I am surprised that woman has the audacity to enter this house," Lady Jane said, trembling in every limb, and turning quite pale. (Her Ladyship had sent out her maid directly after breakfast, who had communicated with Raggles and Rawdon Crawley's household, who had told her all, and a great deal more than they knew, of that story, and many others besides.) "How dare Mrs. Crawley to enter the house of — of an honest family?"

Sir Pitt started back, amazed at his wife's display of vigour. Becky still kept her kneeling posture, and clung to Sir Pitt's hand.

"Tell her that she does not know all. Tell her that I am innocent, dear Pitt," she whimpered out.

"Upon my word, my love, I think you do Mrs. Crawley injustice," Sir Pitt said; at which speech Rebecca was vastly relieved. "Indeed I believe her to be —— "

"To be what?" cried out Lady Jane, her clear voice thrilling, and her heart beating violently as she spoke. "To be a wicked woman — a heartless mother, a false wife? She never loved her dear little boy, who used to fly here and tell me of her cruelty to him. She never came into a family but she strove to bring misery with her, and to weaken the most sacred affections with her wicked flattery and falsehoods. She has deceived her husband, as she has deceived everybody; her soul is black with vanity, worldliness, and all sorts of crime. I tremble when I touch her. I keep my children out of her sight. I —— "

"Lady Jane!" cried Sir Pitt, starting up, "this is really language —— "

" I have been a true and faithful wife to you, Sir Pitt," Lady Jane continued, intrepidly; "I have kept my marriage vow as I made it to God, and have been obedient and gentle as a wife should. But righteous obedience has its limits, and I declare that I will not bear that — that woman again under my roof: if she enters it, I and my children will leave it. She is not worthy to sit down with Christian people. You — you must choose, sir, between her and me; " and with this my Lady swept out of the room, fluttering with her own audacity, and leaving Rebecca and Sir Pitt not a little astonished at it.

As for Becky, she was not hurt; nay, she was pleased. "It was the diamond-clasp you gave me," she said to Sir Pitt, reaching him out her hand; and before she left him (for which event you may be sure my Lady Jane was looking out from her dressing-room window in the upper story) the Baronet had promised to go and seek out his brother, and endeavour to bring about a reconciliation.

Rawdon found some of the young fellows of the regiment seated in the mess-room at breakfast, and was induced without much difficulty to partake of that meal, and of the devilled legs of fowls and soda-water with which these young gentlemen fortified themselves. Then they had a conversation befitting the day and their time of life : about the next pigeon-match at Battersea, with relative bets upon Ross and Osbaldiston : about Mademoiselle Ariane of the French Opera, and who had left her, and how she was consoled by Panther Carr ; and about the fight between the Butcher and the Pet, and the probabilities that it was a cross. Young Tandyman, a hero of seventeen, laboriously endeavouring to get up a pair of mustachios, had seen the fight, and spoke in the most scientific manner about the battle, and the condition of the men. It was he who had driven the Butcher on to the ground in his drag, and passed the whole of the previous night with him. Had there not been foul play he must have won it. All the old files of the Ring were in it : and Tandyman would n't pay ; no, dammy, he would n't pay. — It was but a year since the young Cornet, now so knowing a hand in Cribb's parlour, had a still lingering liking for toffy, and used to be birched at Eton.

So they went on talking about dancers, fights, drinking, demireps, until Macmurdo came down and joined the boys and the conversation. He did not appear to think that any especial reverence was due to their boyhood ; the old fellow cut in with stories, to the full as choice as any the youngest rake present had to tell ; — nor did his own gray hairs, nor their smooth faces detain him. Old Mac was famous for his good stories. He was not exactly a lady's man ; that is, men asked him to dine rather at the houses of their mistresses than of their mothers. There can scarcely be a life lower, perhaps, than his ; but he was quite contented with it, such as it was, and led it in perfect good nature, simplicity, and modesty of demeanour.

By the time Mac had finished a copious breakfast,

most of the others had concluded their meal. Young
Lord Varinas was smoking an immense Meerschaum
pipe, while Captain Hugues was employed with a cigar:
that violent little devil Tandyman, with his little bull-
terrier between his legs, was tossing for shillings with
all his might (that fellow was always at some game or
other) against Captain Deuceace; and Mac and Rawdon
walked off to the Club, neither, of course, having given
any hint of the business which was occupying their
minds. Both, on the other hand, had joined pretty
gaily in the conversation; for why should they interrupt
it? Feasting, drinking, ribaldry, laughter, go on along-
side of all sorts of other occupations in Vanity Fair, —
the crowds were pouring out of church as Rawdon and
his friend passed down St. James's Street and entered
into their Club.

The old bucks and habitués, who ordinarily stand
gaping and grinning out of the great front window of
the Club, had not arrived at their posts as yet, — the
newspaper-room was almost empty. One man was
present whom Rawdon did not know; another to whom
he owed a little score for whist, and whom, in consequence, he did not care to meet; a third was reading
the *Royalist* (a periodical famous for its scandal and its
attachment to Church and King) Sunday paper at the
table, and, looking up at Crawley with some interest,
said, " Crawley, I congratulate you."

" What do you mean?" said the Colonel.

" It's in the *Observer* and the *Royalist* too," said
Mr. Smith.

" What?" Rawdon cried, turning very red. He
thought that the affair with Lord Steyne was already in
the public prints. Smith looked up wondering and
smiling at the agitation which the Colonel exhibited as
he took up the paper, and trembling, began to read.

[11]

Mr. Smith and Mr. Brown (the gentleman with whom Rawdon had the outstanding whist account) had been talking about the Colonel just before he came in.

" It is come just in the nick of time," said Smith. " I suppose Crawley had not a shilling in the world."

" It 's a wind that blows everybody good," Mr. Brown said. " He can 't go away without paying me a pony he owes me."

" What 's the salary? " asked Smith.

" Two or three thousand," answered the other. " But the climate 's so infernal, they don't enjoy it long. Liverseege died after eighteen months of it: and the man before went off in six weeks, I hear."

" Some people say his brother is a very clever man."

" I always found him a d——bore," Smith ejaculated. " He must have good interest, though. He must have got the Colonel the place."

" *He!* " said Brown, with a sneer — " Pooh. — It was Lord Steyne got it."

" How do you mean? "

" A virtuous woman is a crown to her husband," answered the other, enigmatically, and went to read his papers.

Rawdon, for his part, read in the *Royalist* the following astonishing paragraph : —

" GOVERNORSHIP OF COVENTRY ISLAND. — H.M.S. Yellowjack, Commander Jaunders, has brought letters and papers from Coventry Island. H. E. Sir Thomas Liverseege had fallen a victim to the prevailing fever at Swampton. His loss is deeply felt in the flourishing colony. We hear that the Governorship has been offered to Colonel Rawdon Crawley, C. B., a distinguished Waterloo officer. We need not only men of acknowledged bravery, but men of administrative talents to superintend the affairs of our colonies ; and we have no doubt that the gentleman selected by the Colonial Office to fill the lamented vacancy which has occurred at Coventry Island is admirably calculated for the post which he is about to occupy."

" Coventry Island! where was it? who had appointed him to the government? You must take me out as your secretary, old boy," Captain Macmurdo said laughing; and as Crawley and his friend sat wondering and perplexed over the announcement, the Club waiter brought in to the Colonel a card, on which the name of Mr. Wenham was engraved, who begged to see Colonel Crawley.

The Colonel and his aide-de-camp went out to meet the gentleman, rightly conjecturing that he was an emissary of Lord Steyne. "How d' ye do, Crawley? I am glad to see you," said Mr. Wenham, with a bland smile, and grasping Crawley's hand with great cordiality.

" You come, I suppose, from ——"

" Exactly," said Mr. Wenham.

" Then this is my friend Captain Macmurdo, of the Life Guards Green."

" Delighted to know Captain Macmurdo, I'm sure," Mr. Wenham said, and tendered another smile and shake of the hand to the second, as he had done to the principal. Mac put out one finger, armed with a buckskin glove, and made a very frigid bow to Mr. Wenham over his tight cravat. He was, perhaps, discontented at being put in communication with a *pékin*, and thought that Lord Steyne should have sent him a Colonel at the very least.

" As Macmurdo acts for me, and knows what I mean," Crawley said; " I had better retire and leave you together."

" Of course," said Macmurdo.

[13]

"By no means, my dear Colonel," Mr. Wenham said; "the interview which I had the honour of requesting was with you personally, though the company of Captain Macmurdo cannot fail to be also most pleasing. In fact, Captain, I hope that our conversation will lead to none but the most agreeable results, very different from those which my friend Colonel Crawley appears to anticipate."

"Humph!" said Captain Macmurdo.—Be hanged to these civilians, he thought to himself, they are always for arranging and speechifying. Mr. Wenham took a chair which was not offered to him — took a paper from his pocket, and resumed —

"You have seen this gratifying announcement in the papers this morning, Colonel? Government has secured a most valuable servant, and you, if you accept office, as I presume you will, an excellent appointment. Three thousand a year, delightful climate, excellent government-house, all your own way in the Colony, and a certain promotion. I congratulate you with all my heart. I presume you know, gentlemen, to whom my friend is indebted for this piece of patronage?"

"Hanged if I know," the Captain said: his principal turned very red.

"To one of the most generous and kindest men in the world, as he is one of the greatest — to my excellent friend, the Marquis of Steyne."

"I'll see him d—— before I take his place," growled out Rawdon.

"You are irritated against my noble friend," Mr. Wenham calmly resumed: "and now, in the name of common sense and justice, tell me why?"

"*Why?*" cried Rawdon in surprise.

"Why? Dammy!" said the Captain, ringing his stick on the ground.

"Dammy, indeed," said Mr. Wenham, with the most agreeable smile; "still, look at the matter as a man of the world — as an honest man, and see if you have not been in the wrong. You come home from a journey, and find — what? — my Lord Steyne supping at your house in Curzon Street with Mrs. Crawley. Is the circumstance strange or novel? Has he not been a hundred times before in the same position? Upon my honour and word as a gentleman," (Mr. Wenham here put his hand on his waistcoat with a parliamentary air,) "I declare I think that your suspicions are monstrous and utterly unfounded, and that they injure an honourable gentleman who has proved his good will towards you by a thousand benefactions — and a most spotless and innocent lady."

"You don't mean to say that — that Crawley's mistaken?" said Mr. Macmurdo.

"I believe that Mrs. Crawley is as innocent as my wife, Mrs. Wenham," Mr. Wenham said, with great energy. "I believe that, misled by an infernal jealousy, my friend here strikes a blow against not only an infirm and old man of high station, his constant friend and benefactor, but against his wife, his own dearest honour, his son's future reputation, and his own prospects in life.

"I will tell you what happened," Mr. Wenham continued with great solemnity; "I was sent for this morning by my Lord Steyne, and found him in a pitiable state, as, I need hardly inform Colonel Crawley, any man of age and infirmity would be after a personal conflict with a man of your strength. I say to your face; it was a cruel advantage you took of that strength, Colonel Crawley. It was not only the body of my noble and excellent friend which was wounded — his heart, sir, was bleeding. A man whom he had loaded with benefits and regarded with affection, had subjected him to the foulest indignity. What was this very appointment, which appears in the journals of to-day, but a proof of his kindness to you? When I saw his Lordship this morning I found him in a state pitiable indeed to see: and as anxious as you are to revenge the outrage committed upon him, by blood. You know he has given his proofs, I presume, Colonel Crawley?"

"He has plenty of pluck," said the Colonel. "Nobody ever said he had n't."

"His first order to me was to write a letter of challenge, and to carry it to Colonel Crawley. One or other of us," he said, "must not survive the outrage of last night."

Crawley nodded. "You're coming to the point, Wenham," he said.

"I tried my utmost to calm Lord Steyne. Good God! sir," I said, "how I regret that Mrs. Wenham and myself had not accepted Mrs. Crawley's invitation to sup with her!"

"She asked you to sup with her?" Captain Macmurdo said.

"After the Opera. Here's the note of invitation — stop — no, this is another paper — I thought I had it, but it's of no consequence, and I pledge you my word to the fact. If we had come — and it was only one of Mrs. Wenham's headaches which prevented us — she suffers under them a good deal, especially in the spring — if we had come, and you had returned home, there would have been no quarrel, no insult, no suspicion — and so it is positively because my poor wife has a headache that you are to bring death down upon two men of honour, and plunge two of the most excellent and ancient families in the kingdom into disgrace and sorrow."

Mr. Macmurdo looked at his principal with the air of

a man profoundly puzzled; and Rawdon felt with a kind
of rage that his prey was escaping him. He did not
believe a word of the story, and yet, how discredit or
disprove it?

Mr. Wenham continued with the same fluent oratory,
which in his place in parliament he had so often practised
— " I sate for an hour or more by Lord Steyne's bed-
side, beseeching, imploring Lord Steyne to forego his
intention of demanding a meeting. I pointed out to
him that the circumstances were after all suspicious —
they were suspicious. I acknowledge it, — any man in
your position might have been taken in — I said that
a man furious with jealousy is to all intents and purposes a madman, and should be as such regarded —
that a duel between you must lead to the disgrace of
all parties concerned — that a man of his Lordship's
exalted station had no right in these days, when the
most atrocious revolutionary principles, and the most
dangerous levelling doctrines are preached among the
vulgar, to create a public scandal; and that, however
innocent, the common people would insist that he
was guilty. In fine, I implored him not to send the
challenge."

" I don't believe one word of the whole story," said
Rawdon, grinding his teeth. " I believe it a d——lie,
and that you 're in it, Mr. Wenham. If the challenge
don't come from him, by Jove it shall come from me."

Mr. Wenham turned deadly pale at this savage inter-
ruption of the Colonel, and looked towards the door.

But he found a champion in Captain Macmurdo.
That gentleman rose up with an oath, and rebuked
Rawdon for his language. " You put the affair into my
hands, and you shall act as I think fit, by Jove, and not
as you do. You have no right to insult Mr. Wenham
with this sort of language; and dammy, Mr. Wenham,

you deserve an apology. And as for a challenge
to Lord Steyne, you may get somebody else to carry
it, I won't. If my lord, after being thrashed, chooses to
sit still, dammy let him. And as for the affair with —
with Mrs. Crawley, my belief is, there's nothing proved
at all: that your wife's innocent, as innocent as Mr.
Wenham says she is; and at any rate, that you would
be a d—fool not to take the place and hold your
tongue."

"Captain Macmurdo, you speak like a man of sense,"
Mr. Wenham cried out, immensely relieved — "I forget
any words that Colonel Crawley has used in the irritation
of the moment."

"I thought you would," Rawdon said, with a sneer.

"Shut your mouth, you old stoopid," the Captain
said, good-naturedly. "Mr. Wenham ain't a fighting
man; and quite right, too."

"This matter, in my belief," the Steyne emissary cried,
"ought to be buried in the most profound oblivion.
A word concerning it should never pass these doors. I
speak in the interest of my friend, as well as of Colonel
Crawley, who persists in considering me his enemy."

"I suppose Lord Steyne won't talk about it very
much," said Captain Macmurdo; "and I don't see why
our side should. The affair ain't a very pretty one, any
way you take it; and the less said about it the better.
It's you are thrashed, and not us; and if you are
satisfied, why, I think, we should be."

Mr. Wenham took his hat, upon this, and Captain
Macmurdo following him to the door, shut it upon himself and Lord Steyne's agent, leaving Rawdon chafing
within. When the two were on the other side, Macmurdo looked hard at the other ambassador, and with
an expression of anything but respect on his round jolly
face.

[18]

"You don't stick at a trifle, Mr. Wenham," he said.

"You flatter me, Captain Macmurdo," answered the other, with a smile. "Upon my honour and conscience now, Mrs. Crawley did ask us to sup after the Opera."

"Of course; and Mrs. Wenham had one of her headaches. I say, I've got a thousand-pound note here, which I will give you if you will give me a receipt, please; and I will put the note up in an envelope for Lord Steyne. My man shan't fight him. But we had rather not take his money."

"It was all a mistake,—all a mistake, my dear sir," the other said, with the utmost innocence of manner; and was bowed down the Club steps by Captain Macmurdo, just as Sir Pitt Crawley ascended them. There was a slight acquaintance between these two gentlemen; and the Captain, going back with the Baronet to the room where the latter's brother was, told Sir Pitt, in confidence, that he had made the affair all right between Lord Steyne and the Colonel.

Sir Pitt was well pleased, of course, at this intelligence; and congratulated his brother warmly upon the peaceful issue of the affair, making appropriate moral remarks upon the evils of duelling, and the unsatisfactory nature of that sort of settlement of disputes.

And after this preface, he tried with all his eloquence to effect a reconciliation between Rawdon and his wife. He recapitulated the statements which Becky had made, pointed out the probabilities of their truth, and asserted his own firm belief in her innocence.

But Rawdon would not hear of it. "She has kept money concealed from me these ten years," he said. "She swore, last night only, she had none from Steyne. She knew it was all up, directly I found it. If she's not guilty, Pitt, she's as bad as guilty; and I'll never see

her again, — never." His head sank down on his chest
as he spoke the words; and he looked quite broken and
sad.

"Poor old boy," Macmurdo said, shaking his head.

Rawdon Crawley resisted for some time the idea of
taking the place which had been procured for him by so
odious a patron: and was also for removing the boy
from the school where Lord Steyne's interest had
placed him. He was induced, however, to acquiesce in
these benefits by the entreaties of his brother and Macmurdo: but mainly by the latter pointing out to him
what a fury Steyne would be in, to think that his
enemy's fortune was made through his means.

When the Marquis of Steyne came abroad after his
accident, the Colonial Secretary bowed up to him and
congratulated himself and the Service upon having made
so excellent an appointment. These congratulations
were received with a degree of gratitude which may be
imagined on the part of Lord Steyne.

The secret of the *rencontre* between him and Colonel
Crawley was buried in the profoundest oblivion, as
Wenham said; that is by the seconds and the principals.
But before that evening was over it was talked of at
fifty dinner-tables in Vanity Fair. Little Cackleby himself went to seven evening parties, and told the story
with comments and emendations at each place. How
Mrs. Washington White revelled in it! The Bishopess
of Ealing was shocked beyond expression: the Bishop
went and wrote his name down in the visiting-book
at Gaunt House that very day. Little Southdown was
sorry: so you may be sure was his sister Lady Jane,
very sorry. Lady Southdown wrote it off to her other
daughter at the Cape of Good Hope. It was town-talk
for at least three days, and was only kept out of the

newspapers by the exertions of Mr. Wagg, acting upon a hint from Mr. Wenham.

The bailiffs and brokers seized upon poor Raggles in Curzon Street, and the late fair tenant of that poor little mansion was in the meanwhile — where? Who cared? Who asked after a day or two? Was she guilty or not? We all know how charitable the world is, and how the verdict of Vanity Fair goes when there is a doubt. Some people said she had gone to Naples in pursuit of Lord Steyne; whilst others averred that his lordship quitted that city, and fled to Palermo on hearing of Becky's arrival; some said she was living in Bierstadt, and had become a *dame d'honneur* to the Queen of Bulgaria; some that she was at Boulogne; and others, at a boarding-house at Cheltenham.

Rawdon made her a tolerable annuity; and we may be sure that she was a woman who could make a little money go a great way, as the saying is. He would have paid his debts on leaving England, could he have got any Insurance Office to take his life; but the climate of Coventry Island was so bad that he could borrow no money on the strength of his salary. He remitted, however, to his brother punctually, and wrote to his little boy regularly every mail. He kept Macmurdo in cigars; and sent over quantities of shells, cayenne pepper, hot pickles, guava jelly, and colonial produce to Lady Jane. He sent his brother home the *Swamp Town Gazette*, in which the new Governor was praised with immense enthusiasm; whereas the *Swamp Town Sentinel*, whose wife was not asked to Government House, declared that his Excellency was a tyrant, compared to whom Nero was an enlightened philanthropist. Little Rawdon used to like to get the papers and read about his Excellency.

His mother never made any movement to see the

child. He went home to his aunt for Sundays and holidays; he soon knew every bird's nest about Queen's
Crawley, and rode out with Sir Huddlestone's hounds,
which he admired so on his first well-remembered visit
to Hampshire.

CHAPTER II

GEORGY IS MADE A GENTLEMAN

GEORGY OSBORNE was now fairly established in his grandfather's mansion in Russell Square: occupant of his father's room in the house, and heir-apparent of all the splendours there. The good looks, gallant bearing, and gentlemanlike appearance of the boy won the grandsire's heart for him. Mr. Osborne was as proud of him as ever he had been of the elder George.

The child had many more luxuries and indulgences than had been awarded to his father. Osborne's commerce had prospered greatly of late years. His wealth and importance in the City had very much increased. He had been glad enough in former days to put the elder George to a good private school; and a commission in the army for his son had been a source of no small pride to him: for little George and his future prospects the old man looked much higher. He would make a gentleman of the little chap, was Mr. Osborne's constant saying regarding little Georgy. He saw him in his mind's eye, a collegian, a parliament-man, — a Baronet, perhaps. The old man thought he would die contented if he could see his grandson in a fair way to such honours. He would have none but a tip-top college man to educate him, — none of your quacks and pretenders, — no, no. A few years before, he used to be savage, and inveigh against all parsons, scholars,

[23]

and the like, — declaring that they were a pack of humbugs, and quacks, that were n't fit to get their living but by grinding Latin and Greek, and a set of supercilious dogs, that pretended to look down upon British merchants and gentlemen, who could buy up half a hundred of 'em. He would mourn now, in a very solemn manner, that his own education had been neglected, and repeatedly point out, in pompous orations to Georgy, the necessity and excellence of classical acquirements.

When they met at dinner the grandsire used to ask the lad what he had been reading during the day, and was greatly interested at the report the boy gave of his own studies; pretending to understand little George when he spoke regarding them. He made a hundred blunders, and showed his ignorance many a time. It did not increase the respect which the child had for his senior. A quick brain and a better education elsewhere showed the boy very soon that his grandsire was a dullard; and he began accordingly to command him and to look down upon him; for his previous education, humble and contracted as it had been, had made a much better gentleman of Georgy than any plans of his grandfather could make him. He had been brought up by a kind, weak, and tender woman, who had no pride about anything, but about him, and whose heart was so pure and whose bearing was so meek and humble, that she could not but needs be a true lady. She busied herself in gentle offices and quiet duties; if she never said brilliant things, she never spoke or thought unkind ones: guileless and artless, loving and pure, indeed how could our poor little Amelia be other than a real gentlewoman.

Young Georgy lorded over this soft and yielding nature: and the contrast of its simplicity and delicacy with the coarse pomposity of the dull old man with whom he next came in contact, made him lord over the latter too. If he had been a Prince Royal he could not have been better brought up to think well of himself.

Whilst his mother was yearning after him at home, and I do believe every hour of the day, and during most hours of the sad lonely nights, thinking of him, this young gentleman had a number of pleasures and consolations administered to him, which made him for his part bear the separation from Amelia very easily. Little boys who cry when they are going to school — cry because they are going to a very uncomfortable place. It is only a very few who weep from sheer affection. When you think that the eyes of your childhood dried at the sight of a piece of gingerbread, and that a plum-cake was a compensation for the agony of parting with your mamma and sisters; O my friend and brother, you need not be too confident of your own fine feelings.

Well, then, Master George Osborne had every comfort and luxury that a wealthy and lavish old grandfather thought fit to provide. The coachman was instructed to purchase for him the handsomest pony which could be bought for money; and on this George was taught to ride, first at a riding-school, whence, after having performed satisfactorily without stirrups, and over the leaping-bar, he was conducted through the New Road to Regent's Park, and then to Hyde Park, where he rode in state with Martin the coachman behind him. Old Osborne, who took matters more easily in the City now, where he left his affairs to his junior partners, would often ride out with Miss O. in the same fashionable direction. As little Georgy came cantering up with his dandyfied air, and his heels down, his grandfather would nudge the lad's aunt, and say, "Look, Miss O." And he would laugh, and his face would grow red with pleasure, as he nodded out of the window to the boy, as the groom saluted the carriage, and the footman saluted Master George. Here too his aunt, Mrs. Frederick Bullock, (whose chariot might daily be seen in the Ring, with bullocks *or* emblazoned on the panels and harness, and three pasty-faced little Bullocks, covered with cockades and feathers, staring from the windows), — Mrs. Frederick Bullock, I say, flung glances of the bitterest hatred at the little upstart as he rode by with his hand on his side and his hat on one ear, as proud as a lord.

Though he was scarcely eleven years of age, Master George wore straps and the most beautiful little boots like a man. He had gilt spurs, and a gold-headed whip, and a fine pin in his handkerchief; and the neatest little kid gloves which Lamb's Conduit Street could furnish. His mother had given him a couple of neckcloths, and carefully hemmed and made some little shirts for him; but when her Samuel came to see the widow, they were replaced by much finer linen. He had little jewelled buttons in the lawn shirt-fronts. Her humble presents had been put aside — I believe Miss Osborne had given them to the coachman's boy. Amelia tried to think she was pleased at the change. Indeed, she was happy and charmed to see the boy looking so beautiful.

She had had a little black profile of him done for a shilling: and this was hung up by the side of another portrait over her bed. One day the boy came on his accustomed visit, galloping down the little street at Brompton, and bringing, as usual, all the inhabitants to the windows to admire his splendour, and with great eagerness, and a look of triumph in his face, he pulled a case out of his great-coat — (it

[26]

was a natty white great-coat, with a cape and a velvet collar) — pulled out a red morocco case, which he gave her.

"I bought it with my own money, Mamma," he said. "I thought you 'd like it."

Amelia opened the case, and giving a little cry of delighted affection, seized the boy and embraced him a hundred times. It was a miniature of himself, very prettily done (though not half handsome enough, we may be sure, the widow thought). His grandfather had wished to have a picture of him by an artist whose works, exhibited in a shop-window, in Southampton Row, had caught the old gentleman's eyes; and George, who had plenty of money, bethought him of asking the painter how much a copy of the little portrait would cost, saying that he would pay for it out of his own money, and that he wanted to give it to his mother. The pleased painter executed it for a small price; and old Osborne himself, when he heard of the incident, growled out his satisfaction, and gave the boy twice as many sovereigns as he paid for the miniature.

But what was the grandfather's pleasure compared to Amelia's ecstacy? That proof of the boy's affection charmed her so, that she thought no child in the world was like hers for goodness. For long weeks after, the thought of his love made her happy. She slept better with the picture under her pillow; and how many many times did she kiss it, and weep and pray over it! A small kindness from those she loved made that timid heart grateful. Since her parting with George she had had no such joy and consolation.

At his new home Master George ruled like a lord: at dinner he invited the ladies to drink wine with the utmost coolness, and took off his champagne in a way which charmed his old grandfather. "Look at him," the old man would say, nudging his neighbour with a delighted purple face, " did you ever see such a chap? Lord, Lord ! he 'll be ordering a dressing-case next, and razors to shave with; I 'm blessed if he won't."

The antics of the lad did not, however, delight Mr. Osborne's friends so much as they pleased the old gentleman. It gave Mr. Justice Coffin no pleasure to hear Georgy cut into the conversation and spoil his stories. Colonel Fogey was not interested in seeing the little boy half tipsy. Mr. Serjeant Toffy's lady felt no particular gratitude when, with a twist of his elbow, he tilted a glass of port-wine over her yellow satin, and laughed at the disaster: nor was she better pleased, although old Osborne was highly delighted, when Georgy "whopped" her third boy (a young gentle-man a year older than Georgy, and by chance home for the holidays from Dr. Tickleus's at Ealing School) in Russell Square. George's grandfather gave the boy a couple of sovereigns for that feat, and promised to reward him further for every boy above his own size and age whom he whopped in a similar manner. It is difficult to say what good the old man saw in these combats; he had a vague notion that quarrelling made boys hardy, and that tyranny was a useful accomplish-ment for them to learn. English youth have been so educated time out of mind, and we have hundreds of thousands of apologists and admirers of injustice, misery, and brutality, as perpetrated among children. Flushed with praise and victory over Master Toffy, George wished naturally to pursue his conquests further, and one day as he was strutting about in prodigiously dandyfied new clothes, near St. Pancras, and a young baker's boy made sarcastic comments upon his appear-ance, the youthful patrician pulled off his dandy jacket with great spirit, and giving it in charge to the friend who accompanied him (Master Todd, of Great Coram Street, Russell Square, son of the junior partner of the house of Osborne and Co.) — George tried to whop the little baker. But the chances of war were unfavourable this time, and the little baker whopped Georgy: who came home with a rueful black eye and all his fine shirt frill dabbled with the claret drawn from his own little nose. He told his grandfather that he had been in combat with a giant; and frightened his poor mother at Brompton with long, and by no means authentic, accounts of the battle.

This young Todd, of Coram Street, Russell Square, was Master George's great friend and admirer. They both had a taste for painting theatrical characters; for hard-bake and raspberry tarts; for sliding and skating in the Regent's Park and the Serpentine, when the weather permitted; for going to the play, whither they were often conducted, by Mr. Osborne's orders, by Rowson, Master George's appointed body-servant; with whom they sate in great comfort in the pit.

In the company of this gentleman they visited all the principal theatres of the metropolis — knew the names of all the actors from Drury Lane to Sadler's Wells; and performed, indeed, many of the plays to the Todd family and their youthful friends, with West's famous characters, on their pasteboard theatre. Rowson, the footman, who was of a generous disposition, would not unfrequently, when in cash, treat his young master to oysters after the play, and to a glass of rum-shrub for a night-cap. We may be pretty certain that Mr. Rowson profited in his turn, by his young master's liberality and gratitude for the pleasures to which the footman inducted him.

A famous tailor from the West End of the town, — Mr. Osborne would have none of your City or Holborn bunglers, he said, for the boy (though a City tailor was good enough for *him*), — was summoned to ornament little George's person, and was told to spare no expense in so doing. So, Mr. Woolsey, of Conduit-street, gave a loose to his imagination, and sent the child home fancy trowsers, fancy waistcoats, and fancy jackets enough to furnish a school of little dandies. Georgy had little white waistcoats for evening parties and little cut velvet waistcoats for dinners, and a dear little darling shawl dressing-gown, for all the world like a little man. He dressed for dinner every day, "like a regular West End Swell," as his grandfather remarked; one of the domestics was affected to his special service, attended him at his toilette, answered his bell, and brought him his letters always on a silver tray.

Georgy, after breakfast, would sit in the arm-chair in the dining-room, and read the *Morning Post*, just like a grown-up man. "How he *du* dam and swear," the servants would cry, delighted at his precocity. Those who remembered the Captain his father, declared Master George was his Pa every inch of him. He made the house lively by his activity, his imperiousness, his scolding, and his good-nature.

George's education was confided to a neighbouring scholar and private pedagogue who "prepared young noblemen and gentlemen for the Universities, the senate, and the learned professions: whose system did not embrace the degrading corporal severities still practised at the ancient places of education, and in whose family the pupils would find the elegances of refined society and the confidence and affection of a home." It was in this way that the Reverend Lawrence Veal of Hart Street, Bloomsbury, and domestic Chaplain to the Earl of Bareacres, strove with Mrs. Veal his wife to entice pupils.

By thus advertising and pushing sedulously, the domestic Chaplain and his Lady generally succeeded in
having one or two scholars by them: who paid a high
figure: and were thought to be in uncommonly comfortable quarters. There was a large West Indian, whom
nobody came to see, with a mahogany complexion, a
woolly head, and an exceedingly dandyfied appearance;
there was another hulking boy of three-and-twenty
whose education had been neglected, and whom Mr.
and Mrs. Veal were to introduce into the polite world:
there were two sons of Colonel Bangles of the East India
Company's Service: these four sate down to dinner at
Mrs. Veal's genteel board, when Georgy was introduced
to her establishment.

Georgy was, like some dozen other pupils, only a day
boy; he arrived in the morning under the guardianship
of his friend Mr. Rowson, and if it was fine, would ride
away in the afternoon on his pony, followed by the
groom. The wealth of his grandfather was reported in
the school to be prodigious. The Rev. Mr. Veal used
to compliment Georgy upon it personally, warning him
that he was destined for a high station; that it became
him to prepare, by sedulity and docility in youth, for
the lofty duties to which he would be called in mature
age; that obedience in the child was the best preparation for command in the man; and that he therefore
begged George would not bring toffy into the school,
and ruin the health of the Masters Bangles, who had
everything they wanted at the elegant and abundant
table of Mrs. Veal.

With respect to learning, "the Curriculum," as Mr.
Veal loved to call it, was of prodigious extent: and the
young gentlemen in Hart Street might learn a something of every known science. The Rev. Mr. Veal had
an orrery, an electrifying machine, a turning lathe, a

theatre (in the wash-house), a chemical apparatus, and what he called a select library of all the works of the best authors of ancient and modern times and languages. He took the boys to the British Museum, and descanted upon the antiquities and the specimens of natural history there, so that audiences would gather round him as he spoke, and all Bloomsbury highly admired him as a prodigiously well-informed man. And whenever he spoke (which he did almost always), he took care to produce the very finest and longest words of which the vocabulary gave him the use; rightly judging, that it was as cheap to employ a handsome, large, and sonorous epithet, as to use a little stingy one.

Thus he would say to George in school, " I observed on my return home from taking the indulgence of an evening's scientific conversation with my excellent friend Doctor Bulders — a true archæologian, gentlemen, a true archæologian — that the windows of your venerated grandfather's almost princely mansion in Russell Square were illuminated as if for the purposes of festivity. Am I right in my conjecture, that Mr. Osborne entertained a society of chosen spirits round his sumptuous board last night? "

Little Georgy, who had considerable humour, and used to mimic Mr. Veal to his face with great spirit and dexterity, would reply, that Mr. V. was quite correct in his surmise.

" Then those friends who had the honour of partaking of Mr. Osborne's hospitality, gentlemen, had no reason, I will lay any wager, to complain of their repast. I myself have been more than once so favoured. (By the way, Master Osborne, you came a little late this morning, and have been a defaulter in this respect more than once.) I myself, I say, gentlemen, humble as I am, have been found not unworthy to share Mr. Osborne's

elegant hospitality. And though I have feasted with
the great and noble of the world—for I presume that I
may call my excellent friend and patron, the Right
Honourable George Earl of Bareacres, one of the
number—yet I assure you that the board of the British
merchant was to the full as richly served, and his reception as gratifying and noble. Mr. Bluck, sir, we will resume, if you please, that passage of Eutropius, which
was interrupted by the late arrival of Master Osborne."

To this great man George's education was for some
time entrusted. Amelia was bewildered by his phrases,
but thought him a prodigy of learning. That poor
widow made friends of Mrs. Veal, for reasons of her
own. She liked to be in the house, and see Georgy
coming to school there. She liked to be asked to Mrs.
Veal's *conversazioni*, which took place once a month
(as you were informed on pink cards, with AΘHNH engraved on them), and where the professor welcomed
his pupils and their friends to weak tea and scientific
conversation. Poor little Amelia never missed one of
these entertainments, and thought them delicious so
long as she might have Georgy sitting by her. And
she would walk from Brompton in any weather, and
embrace Mrs. Veal with tearful gratitude for the delightful evening she had passed, when, the company
having retired and Georgy gone off with Mr. Rowson,
his attendant, poor Mrs. Osborne put on her cloaks and
her shawls preparatory to walking home.

As for the learning which Georgy imbibed under this
valuable master of a hundred sciences, to judge from the
weekly reports which the lad took home to his grandfather, his progress was remarkable. The names of a
score or more of desirable branches of knowledge were
printed in a table, and the pupil's progress in each was
marked by the professor. In Greek Georgy was pro-

nounced aristos, in Latin optimus, in French *très bien*, and
so forth ; and everybody had prizes for everything at the
end of the year. Even Mr. Swartz, the woolly-headed
young gentleman, and half-brother to the Honourable
Mrs. Mac Mull and Mr. Bluck, the neglected young pupil
of three-and-twenty from the agricultural districts, and
that idle young scapegrace of a Master Todd before
mentioned, received little eighteen-penny books, with
" Athene " engraved on them, and a pompous Latin
inscription from the Professor to his young friends.

The family of this Master Todd were hangers-on of
the house of Osborne. The old gentleman had advanced Todd from being a clerk to be a junior partner
in his establishment.

Mr. Osborne was the godfather of young Master Todd
(who in subsequent life wrote Mr. Osborne Todd on his
cards, and became a man of decided fashion), while
Miss Osborne had accompanied Miss Maria Todd to
the font, and gave her *protégée* a prayer-book, a collec-
tion of tracts, a volume of very low church poetry, or
some such memento of her goodness every year. Miss
O. drove the Todds out in her carriage now and then:
when they were ill, her footman, in large plush smalls
and waistcoat, brought jellies and delicacies from
Russell Square to Coram Street. Coram Street trembled
and looked up to Russell Square indeed; and Mrs.
Todd, who had a pretty hand at cutting out paper trim-
mings for haunches of mutton, and could make flowers,
ducks, &c. out of turnips and carrots in a very creditable
manner, would go to " the Square," as it was called, and
assist in the preparations incident to a great dinner,
without even so much as thinking of sitting down to the
banquet. If any guest failed at the eleventh hour, Todd
was asked to dine. Mrs. Todd and Maria came across
in the evening, slipped in with a muffled knock, and were

in the drawing-room by the time Miss Osborne and the ladies under her convoy reached that apartment; and ready to fire off duets and sing until the gentlemen came up. Poor Maria Todd; poor young lady! How she had to work and thrum at these duets and sonatas in the Street, before they appeared in public in the Square!

Thus it seemed to be decreed by fate, that Georgy was to domineer over everybody with whom he came in contact, and that friends, relatives, and domestics were all to bow the knee before the little fellow. It must be owned that he accommodated himself very willingly to this arrangement. Most people do so. And Georgy liked to play the part of master, and perhaps had a natural aptitude for it.

In Russell Square everybody was afraid of Mr. Osborne, and Mr. Osborne was afraid of Georgy. The boy's dashing manners, and off-hand rattle about books and learning, his likeness to his father (dead unreconciled in Brussels yonder), awed the old gentleman, and gave the young boy the mastery. The old man would start at some hereditary feature or tone unconsciously used by the little lad, and fancy that George's father was again before him. He tried by indulgence to the grandson to make up for harshness to the elder George. People were surprised at his gentleness to the boy. He growled and swore at Miss Osborne as usual: and would smile when George came down late for breakfast.

Miss Osborne, George's aunt, was a faded old spinster, broken down by more than forty years of dulness and coarse usage. It was easy for a lad of spirit to master *her*. And whenever George wanted anything from her, from the jam-pots in her cupboards, to the cracked and dry old colours in her paint-box (the old paint-box which she had had when she was a pupil of Mr. Smee, and was still almost young and blooming),

Georgy took possession of the object of his desire, which obtained, he took no further notice of his aunt.

For his friends and cronies, he had a pompous old schoolmaster, who flattered him, and a toady, his senior, whom he could thrash. It was dear Mrs. Todd's delight to leave him with her youngest daughter, Rosa Jemima, a darling child of eight years old. The little pair looked so well together, she would say (but not to the folks in " the Square," we may be sure), — " Who knows what might happen? Don't they make a pretty little couple?" the fond mother thought.

The broken-spirited, old, maternal grandfather was likewise subject to the little tyrant. He could not help respecting a lad who had such fine clothes, and rode with a groom behind him. Georgy, on his side, was in the constant habit of hearing coarse abuse and vulgar satire levelled at John Sedley, by his pitiless old enemy, Mr. Osborne. Osborne used to call the other the old pauper, the old coal-man, the old bankrupt, and by many other such names of brutal contumely. How was little George to respect a man so prostrate? A few months after he was with his paternal grandfather, Mrs. Sedley died. There had been little love between her and the child. He did not care to show much grief. He came down to visit his mother in a fine new suit of mourning, and was very angry that he could not go to a play upon which he had set his heart.

The illness of that old lady had been the occupation and perhaps the safeguard of Amelia. What do men know about women's martyrdoms? We should go mad had we to endure the hundredth part of those daily pains which are meekly borne by many women. Ceaseless slavery meeting with no reward; constant gentleness and kindness met by cruelty as constant; love, labour, patience, watchfulness, without even so much as the acknowledgment of a good word; all this, how many of them have to bear in quiet, and appear abroad with cheerful faces as if they felt nothing. Tender slaves that they are, they must needs be hypocrites and weak.

From her chair Amelia's mother had taken to her bed, which she had never left: and from which Mrs. Osborne herself was never absent except when she ran to see George. The old lady grudged her even those rare visits; she, who had been a kind, smiling, good-natured mother once, in the days of her prosperity, but whom poverty and infirmities had broken down. Her illness or estrangement did not affect Amelia. They rather enabled her to support the other calamity under which she was suffering, and from the thoughts of which she was kept by the ceaseless calls of the invalid. Amelia bore her harshness quite gently; smoothed the uneasy pillow; was always ready with a soft answer to the watchful, querulous voice; soothed the sufferer with words of hope, such as her pious simple heart could best feel and utter, and closed the eyes that had once looked so tenderly upon her.

Then all her time and tenderness were devoted to the consolation and comfort of the bereaved old father, who was stunned by the blow which had befallen him, and stood utterly alone in the world. His wife, his honour, his fortune, everything he loved best had fallen away from him. There was only Amelia to stand by and support with her gentle arms the tottering, heart-broken, old man. We are not going to write the history: it would be too dreary and stupid. I can see Vanity Fair yawning over it *d'avance*.

One day as the young gentlemen were assembled in the study at the Rev. Mr. Veal's, and the domestic chaplain to the Right Honourable the Earl of Bareacres was spouting away as usual — a smart carriage drove up to the door decorated with the statue of Athene, and two gentlemen stepped out. The young Masters Bangles rushed to the window, with a vague notion that their father might have arrived from Bombay. The great hulking scholar of three-and-twenty, who was crying secretly over a passage of Eutropius, flattened his neglected nose against the panes, and looked at the drag, as the *laquais de place* sprang from the box and let out the persons in the carriage.

"It's a fat one and a thin one," Mr. Bluck said, as a thundering knock came to the door.

Everybody was interested, from the domestic chaplain himself, who hoped he saw the fathers of some future pupils, down to Master Georgy, glad of any pretext for laying his book down.

The boy in the shabby livery, with the faded copper-buttons, who always thrust himself into the tight coat to open the door, came into the study and said, "Two gentlemen want to see Master Osborne." The Professor had had a trifling altercation in the morning with that young gentleman, owing to a difference about the introduction of crackers in school-time; but his face resumed its habitual expression of bland courtesy, as he said, "Master Osborne, I give you full permission to go and see your carriage friends, — to whom I beg you to convey the respectful compliments of myself and Mrs. Veal."

Georgy went into the reception-room, and saw two strangers, whom he looked at with his head up, in his usual haughty manner. One was fat, with mustachios, and the other was lean and long, in a blue frock-coat, with a brown face, and a grizzled head.

"My God, how like he is!" said the long gentle-

[38]

man, with a start. "Can you guess who we are, George?"

The boy's face flushed up, as it did usually when he was moved, and his eyes brightened. "I don't know the other," he said, "but I should think you must be Major Dobbin."

Indeed it was our old friend. His voice trembled with pleasure as he greeted the boy, and taking both the other's hands in his own, drew the lad to him.

"Your mother has talked to you about me — has she?" he said.

"That she has," Georgy answered, "hundreds and hundreds of times."

CHAPTER III

EOTHEN

IT was one of the many causes for personal pride with which old Osborne chose to recreate himself, that Sedley, his ancient rival, enemy, and benefactor, was in his last days so utterly defeated and humiliated, as to be forced to accept pecuniary obligations at the hands of the man who had most injured and insulted him. The successful man of the world cursed the old pauper, and relieved him from time to time. As he furnished George with money for his mother, he gave the boy to understand by hints, delivered in his brutal, coarse way, that George's maternal grandfather was but a wretched old bankrupt and dependant, and that John Sedley might thank the man to whom he already owed ever so much money, for the aid which his generosity now chose to administer. George carried the pompous supplies to his mother and the shattered old widower whom it was now the main business of her life to tend and comfort. The little fellow patronised the feeble and disappointed old man.

It may have shown a want of " proper pride " in Amelia that she chose to accept these money benefits at the hands of her father's enemy. But proper pride and this poor lady had never had much acquaintance together. A disposition naturally simple and demanding protection; a long course of poverty and humility, of daily privations, and hard words, of kind offices and no returns, had been her lot ever since womanhood almost, or since her luckless marriage with George Osborne. You who see your betters, bearing up under this shame every day, meekly suffering under the slights of fortune, gentle and unpitied, poor, and rather despised for their poverty, do you ever step down from your prosperity and wash the feet of these poor wearied beggars? The very thought of them is odious and low. "There must be classes — there must be rich and poor," Dives says, smacking his claret — (It is well if he even sends the broken meat out to Lazarus sitting under the window.) Very true; but think how mysterious and often unaccountable it is — that lottery of life which gives to this man the purple and fine linen, and sends to the other rags for garments and dogs for comforters.

So I must own, that without much repining, on the contrary with something akin to gratitude, Amelia took the crumbs that her father-in-law let drop now and then and with them fed her own parent. Directly she understood it to be her duty, it was this young woman's nature (ladies, she is but thirty still, and we choose to call her a young woman even at that age) — it was, I say, her nature to sacrifice herself and to fling all that she had at the feet of the beloved object. During what long thankless nights had she worked out her fingers for little Georgy whilst at home with her; what buffets, scorns, privations, poverties had she endured for father and mother! And in the midst of all these solitary resignations and unseen sacrifices, she did not respect herself any more than the world respected her; but I believe thought in her heart that she was a poor-spirited, despicable little creature, whose luck in life was only too good for her merits. O you poor women! O you

[41]

poor secret martyrs and victims, whose life is a torture, who are stretched on racks in your bedrooms, and who lay your heads down on the block daily at the drawing-room table; every man who watches your pains, or peers into those dark places where the torture is administered to you, must pity you — and — and thank God that he has a beard. I recollect seeing, years ago, at the prisons for idiots and madmen at Bicêtre, near Paris, a poor wretch bent down under the bondage of his imprisonment and his personal infirmity, to whom one of our party gave a halfpennyworth of snuff in a *cornet* or "screw" of paper. The kindness was too much for the poor epileptic creature. He cried in an anguish of delight and gratitude: if anybody gave you and me a thousand a year, or saved our lives, we could not be so affected. And so, if you properly tyrannise over a woman, you will find a halfp'orth of kindness act upon her, and bring tears into her eyes, as though you were an angel benefiting her.

Some such boons as these were the best which Fortune allotted to poor little Amelia. Her life, begun not unprosperously, had come down to this — to a mean prison and a long, ignoble bondage. Little George visited her captivity sometimes, and consoled it with feeble gleams of encouragement. Russell Square was the boundary of her prison: she might walk thither occasionally, but was always back to sleep in her cell at night; to perform cheerless duties; to watch by thankless sick-beds; to suffer the harassment and tyranny of querulous disappointed old age. How many thousands of people are there, women for the most part, who are doomed to endure this long slavery? — who are hospital nurses without wages, — sisters of Charity, if you like, without the romance and the sentiment of sacrifice, — who strive, fast, watch, and suffer, unpitied; and fade

away ignobly and unknown. The hidden and awful
Wisdom which apportions the destinies of mankind is
pleased so to humiliate and cast down the tender, good,
and wise; and to set up the selfish, the foolish, or the
wicked. Oh, be humble, my brother, in your prosperity! Be gentle with those who are less lucky, if not
more deserving. Think, what right have you to be
scornful, whose virtue is a deficiency of temptation,
whose success may be a chance, whose rank may be an
ancestor's accident, whose prosperity is very likely a
satire.

They buried Amelia's mother in the church-yard at
Brompton; upon just such a rainy, dark day, as Amelia
recollected when first she had been there to marry
George. Her little boy sate by her side in pompous
new sables. She remembered the old pew-woman and
clerk. Her thoughts were away in other times as the
parson read. But that she held George's hand in her
own, perhaps she would have liked to change places
with . . . Then, as usual, she felt ashamed of her selfish thoughts, and prayed inwardly to be strengthened
to do her duty.

So she determined with all her might and strength to
try and make her old father happy. She slaved, toiled,
patched, and mended, sang and played backgammon,
read out the newspaper, cooked dishes, for old Sedley,
walked him out sedulously into Kensington Gardens or
the Brompton Lanes, listened to his stories with untir-
ing smiles and affectionate hypocrisy, or sate musing by
his side and communing with her own thoughts and
reminiscences, as the old man, feeble and querulous,
sunned himself on the garden benches and prattled
about his wrongs or his sorrows. What sad, unsatisfactory thoughts those of the widow were! The chil-

dren running up and down the slopes and broad paths in the gardens, reminded her of George who was taken from her: the first George was taken from her: her selfish, guilty love, in both instances, had been rebuked and bitterly chastised. She strove to think it was right that she should be so punished. She was such a miserable wicked sinner. She was quite alone in the world.

I know that the account of this kind of solitary imprisonment is insufferably tedious, unless there is some cheerful or humorous incident to enliven it, — a tender gaoler, for instance, or a waggish commandant of the fortress, or a mouse to come out and play about Latude's beard and whiskers, or a subterranean passage under the castle, dug by Trenck with his nails and a toothpick: the historian has no such enlivening incident to relate in the narrative of Amelia's captivity. Fancy her, if you please, during this period, very sad, but always ready to smile when spoken to; in a very mean, poor, not to say vulgar position of life; singing songs, making puddings, playing cards, mending stockings, for her old father's benefit. So, never mind, whether she be a heroine or no; or you and I, however old, scolding, and bankrupt; — may we have in our last days a kind soft shoulder on which to lean, and a gentle hand to soothe our gouty old pillows.

Old Sedley grew very fond of his daughter after his wife's death; and Amelia had her consolation in doing her duty by the old man.

But we are not going to leave these two people long in such a low and ungenteel station of life. Better days, as far as worldly prosperity went, were in store for both. Perhaps the ingenious reader has guessed who was the stout gentleman who called upon Georgy at his school in company with our old friend Major Dobbin. It was another old acquaintance returned to England, and at a time when his presence was likely to be of great comfort to his relatives there.

Major Dobbin having easily succeeded in getting leave from his good-natured commandant to proceed to Madras, and thence probably to Europe, on urgent private affairs, never ceased travelling night and day until he reached his journey's end, and had directed his march with such celerity, that he arrived at Madras in a high fever. His servants who accompanied him, brought him to the house of the friend with whom he had resolved to stay until his departure for Europe in a state of delirium: and it was thought for many, many days that he would never travel farther than the burying-ground of the church of St. George's, where the troops should fire a salvo over his grave, and where many a gallant officer lies far away from his home.

Here, as the poor fellow lay tossing in his fever, the people who watched him might have heard him raving about Amelia. The idea that he should never see her again depressed him in his lucid hours. He thought his last day was come; and he made his solemn preparations for departure: setting his affairs in this world in order, and leaving the little property of which he was possessed to those whom he most desired to benefit. The friend in whose house he was located witnessed his testament. He desired to be buried with a little brown hair-chain which he wore round his neck, and which, if the truth must be known, he had got from Amelia's maid at Brussels, when the young widow's hair was cut off, during the fever which prostrated her after the death of George Osborne on the plateau at Mount St. John.

He recovered, rallied, relapsed again, having undergone such a process of blood-letting and calomel as showed the strength of his original constitution. He was almost a skeleton when they put him on board the

Ramchunder East Indiaman, Captain Bragg, from Calcutta, touching at Madras; and so weak and prostrate, that his friend who had tended him through his illness, prophesied that the honest Major would never survive the voyage, and that he would pass some morning, shrouded in flag and hammock, over the ship's side, and carrying down to the sea with him the relic that he wore at his heart. But whether it was the sea air, or the hope which sprung up in him afresh, from the day that the ship spread her canvas and stood out of the roads towards *home*, our friend began to amend, and he was quite well (though as gaunt as a greyhound) before they reached the Cape. " Kirk will be disappointed of his majority this time," he said, with a smile : " he will expect to find himself gazetted by the time the regiment reaches home." For it must be premised that while the Major was lying ill at Madras, having made such prodigious haste to go thither, the gallant —th, which had passed many years abroad, which after its return from the West Indies had been baulked of its stay at home by the Waterloo campaign, and had been ordered from Flanders to India, had received orders home; and the Major might have accompanied his comrades, had he chosen to wait for their arrival at Madras.

Perhaps he was not inclined to put himself in his exhausted state again under the guardianship of Glorvina. " I think Miss O'Dowd would have done for me," he said, laughingly, to a fellow-passenger, " if we had had her on board, and when she had sunk me, she would have fallen upon you, depend upon it, and carried you in as a prize to Southampton, Jos, my boy."

For indeed it was no other than our stout friend who was also a passenger on board the Ramchunder. He had passed ten years in Bengal. — Constant dinners, tiffins, pale ale and claret, the prodigious labour of cutcherry, and the refreshment of brandy-pawnee which he was forced to take there, had their effect upon Waterloo Sedley. A voyage to Europe was pronounced necessary for him — and having served his full time in India, and had fine appointments which had enabled him to lay by a considerable sum of money, he was free to come home and stay with a good pension, or to return and resume that rank in the service to which his seniority and his vast talents entitled him.

He was rather thinner than when we last saw him, but had gained in majesty and solemnity of demeanour. He had resumed the mustachios to which his services at Waterloo entitled him, and swaggered about on deck in a magnificent velvet cap with a gold band, and a profuse ornamentation of pins and jewellery about his person. He took breakfast in his cabin, and dressed as solemnly to appear on the quarter-deck, as if he were going to turn out for Bond Street, or the Course at Calcutta. He brought a native servant with him, who was his valet and pipe-bearer; and who wore the Sedley crest in silver on his turban. That oriental menial had a wretched life under the tyranny of Jos Sedley. Jos was as vain of his person as a woman, and took as long a time at his toilette as any fading beauty. The youngsters among the passengers, Young Chaffers of the 150th, and poor little Ricketts, coming home after his third fever, used to draw out Sedley at the cuddy-table, and make him tell prodigious stories about himself and his exploits against tigers and Napoleon. He was great when he visited the Emperor's tomb at Longwood, when to these gentlemen and the young officers of the ship, Major Dobbin not being by, he described the whole battle of Waterloo, and all but announced that Napoleon never would have gone to Saint Helena at all but for him, Jos Sedley.

After leaving St. Helena he became very generous, disposing of a great quantity of ship stores, claret, preserved meats, and great casks packed with soda-water, brought out for his private delectation. There were no ladies on board: the Major gave the pas of precedency to the civilian, so that he was the first dignitary at table; and treated by Captain Bragg, and the officers of the Ramchunder, with the respect which his rank warranted. He disappeared rather in a panic during a two-days' gale, in which he had the portholes of his cabin battened down; and remained in his cot reading the "Washerwoman of Finchley Common," left on board the Ramchunder by the Right Honourable the Lady Emily Hornblower, wife of the Rev. Silas Hornblower, when on their passage out to the Cape, where the Reverend gentleman was a missionary: but, for common reading, he had brought a stock of novels and plays which he lent to the rest of the ship, and rendered himself agreeable to all by his kindness and condescension.

Many and many a night as the ship was cutting through the roaring dark sea, the moon and stars shining over head, and the bell singing out the watch, Mr. Sedley and the Major would sit on the quarter-deck of the vessel talking about home, as the Major smoked his cheroot, and the civilian puffed at the hookah which his servant prepared for him.

In these conversations it was wonderful with what perseverance and ingenuity Major Dobbin would manage to bring the talk round to the subject of Amelia and her little boy. Jos, a little testy about his father's misfortunes and unceremonious applications to him, was soothed down by the Major, who pointed out the

elder's ill fortunes and old age. He would not perhaps like to live with the old couple: whose ways
and hours might not agree with those of a younger
man, accustomed to different society, (Jos bowed at
this compliment): but, the Major pointed out, how
advantageous it would be for Jos Sedley to have a
house of his own in London, and not a mere bachelor's establishment as before: how his sister Amelia
would be the very person to preside over it; how
elegant, how gentle she was, and of what refined good
manners. He recounted stories of the success which
Mrs. George Osborne had had in former days at Brussels, and in London, where she was much admired
by people of very great fashion: and he then hinted
how becoming it would be for Jos to send Georgy
to a good school and make a man of him; for his
mother and her parents would be sure to spoil him.
In a word, this artful Major made the civilian promise
to take charge of Amelia and her unprotected child.
He did not know as yet what events had happened
in the little Sedley family: and how death had removed
the mother, and riches had carried off George from
Amelia. But the fact is, that every day and always,
this love-smitten and middle-aged gentleman was thinking about Mrs. Osborne, and his whole heart was bent
upon doing her good. He coaxed, wheedled, cajoled,
and complimented Jos Sedley with a perseverance and
cordiality of which he was not aware himself, very
likely; but some men who have unmarried sisters or
daughters even, may remember how uncommonly
agreeable gentlemen are to the male relations when
they are courting the females; and perhaps this rogue
of a Dobbin was urged by a similar hypocrisy.

The truth is, when Major Dobbin came on board
the Ramchunder, very sick, and for the three days

she lay in the Madras Roads, he did not begin to rally,
nor did even the appearance and recognition of his
old acquaintance, Mr. Sedley, on board much cheer
him, until after a conversation which they had one
day, as the Major was laid languidly on the deck.
He said then he thought he was doomed; he had
left a little something to his godson in his will; and
he trusted Mrs. Osborne would remember him kindly,
and be happy in the marriage she was about to make.
"Married? not the least," Jos answered: "he had
heard from her: she made no mention of the marriage,
and by the way, it was curious, she wrote to say that
Major Dobbin was going to be married, and hoped
that *he* would be happy." What were the dates of
Sedley's letters from Europe? The civilian fetched
them. They were two months later than the Major's;
and the ship's surgeon congratulated himself upon the
treatment adopted by him towards his new patient,
who had been consigned to ship-board by the Madras
practitioner with very small hopes indeed; for, from
that day, the very day that he changed the draught,
Major Dobbin began to mend. And thus it was that
deserving officer, Captain Kirk, was disappointed of
his majority.

After they passed St. Helena, Major Dobbin's gaiety
and strength was such as to astonish all his fellow-
passengers. He larked with the midshipmen, played
single-stick with the mates, ran up the shrouds like
a boy, sang a comic song one night to the amusement of the whole party assembled over their grog
after supper, and rendered himself so gay, lively, and
amiable, that even Captain Bragg, who thought there
was nothing in his passenger, and considered he was
a poor-spirited feller at first, was constrained to own
that the Major was a reserved but well-informed and

meritorious officer. "He ain't got distangy manners, dammy," Bragg observed to his first mate; "he would n't do at Government House, Roper, where his Lordship and Lady William was as kind to me, and shook hands with me before the whole company, and asking me at dinner to take beer with him, before the Commander-in-Chief himself; he ain't got manners, but there's something about him —" And thus Captain Bragg showed that he possessed discrimination as a man, as well as ability as a commander.

But a calm taking place when the Ramchunder was within ten days' sail of England, Dobbin became so impatient and ill-humoured as to surprise those comrades who had before admired his vivacity and good temper. He did not recover until the breeze sprang up again, and was in a highly excited state when the pilot came on board. Good God, how his heart beat as the two friendly spires of Southampton came in sight.

CHAPTER IV

OUR FRIEND THE MAJOR

OUR Major had rendered himself so popular on board the Ramchunder, that when he and Mr. Sedley descended into the welcome shore-boat which was to take them from the ship, the whole crew, men and officers, the great Captain Bragg himself leading off, gave three cheers for Major Dobbin, who blushed very much, and ducked his head in token of thanks. Jos, who very likely thought the cheers were for himself, took off his gold-laced cap and waved it majestically to his friends, and they were pulled to shore and landed with great dignity at the pier, whence they proceeded to the Royal George Hotel.

Although the sight of that magnificent round of beef, and the silver tankard suggestive of real British home-brewed ale and porter, which perennially greet the eyes of the traveller returning from foreign parts, who enters the coffee-room of the George, are so invigorating and delightful, that a man entering such a comfortable snug homely English inn, might well like to stop some days there, yet Dobbin began to talk about a post-chaise instantly, and was no sooner at Southampton than he wished to be on the road to London. Jos, however, would not hear of moving that evening. Why was he to pass a night in a post-chaise instead of a great large undulating downy feather bed which was there ready to replace the horrid little

narrow crib in which the portly Bengal gentleman had
been confined during the voyage? He could not think
of moving till his baggage was cleared, or of travelling
until he could do so with his chillum. So the Major
was forced to wait over that night, and despatched
a letter to his family announcing his arrival; entreating from Jos a promise to write to his own friends.
Jos promised, but did n't keep his promise. The Captain, the surgeon, and one or two passengers came
and dined with our two gentlemen at the inn; Jos
exerting himself in a sumptuous way in ordering the
dinner: and promising to go to town the next day
with the Major. The landlord said it did his eyes
good to see Mr. Sedley take off his first pint of porter.
If I had time and dared to enter into digressions,
I would write a chapter about that first pint of porter
drunk upon English ground. Ah, how good it is!
It is worth while to leave home for a year, just to
enjoy that one draught.

Major Dobbin made his appearance the next morning very neatly shaved and dressed, according to his
wont. Indeed, it was so early in the morning, that
nobody was up in the house except that wonderful
Boots of an inn who never seems to want sleep: and
the Major could hear the snores of the various inmates
of the house roaring through the corridors as he
creaked about in those dim passages. Then the sleep-
less Boots went shirking round from door to door,
gathering up at each the Bluchers, Wellingtons, Oxoni-
ans, which stood outside. Then Jos's native servant
arose and began to get ready his master's ponderous
dressing apparatus, and prepare his hookah: then the
maid servants got up, and meeting the dark man in
the passages, shrieked, and mistook him for the devil.
He and Dobbin stumbled over their pails in the pas-

sages as they were scouring the decks of the Royal George. When the first unshorn waiter appeared and unbarred the door of the inn, the Major thought that the time for departure was arrived, and ordered a post-chaise to be fetched instantly, that they might set off.

He then directed his steps to Mr. Sedley's room, and opened the curtains of the great large family bed wherein Mr. Jos was snoring. "Come, up! Sedley," the Major said, "it's time to be off; the chaise will be at the door in half an hour."

Jos growled from under the counterpane to know what the time was; but when he at last extorted from the blushing Major (who never told fibs, however they might be to his advantage) what was the real hour of the morning, he broke out into a volley of bad language, which we will not repeat here, but by which he gave Dobbin to understand that he would jeopardy his soul if he got up at that moment, that the Major might go and be hanged, that he would not travel with Dobbin, and that it was most unkind and ungentle-manlike to disturb a man out of his sleep in that way; on which the discomfited Major was obliged to retreat, leaving Jos to resume his interrupted slumbers.

The chaise came up presently, and the Major would wait no longer.

If he had been an English nobleman travelling on a pleasure tour, or a newspaper courier bearing des-patches (government messages are generally carried much more quietly), he could not have travelled more quickly. The post-boys wondered at the fees he flung amongst them. How happy and green the country looked as the chaise whirled rapidly from mile-stone to mile-stone, through neat country towns where land-lords came out to welcome him with smiles and bows; by pretty road-side inns, where the signs hung on the elms, and horses and waggoners were drinking under the chequered shadow of the trees; by old halls and parks; rustic hamlets clustered round ancient gray churches — and through the charming friendly English landscape. Is there any in the world like it? To a traveller returning home it looks so kind — it seems to shake hands with you as you pass through it. Well, Major Dobbin passed through all this from Southampton to London, and without noting much beyond the mile-stones along the road. You see he was so eager to see his parents at Camberwell.

He grudged the time lost between Piccadilly and his old haunt at the Slaughters,' whither he drove faithfully. Long years had passed since he saw it last, since he and George, as young men, had enjoyed many a feast, and held many a revel there. He had now passed into the stage of old-fellow-hood. His hair was grizzled, and many a passion and feeling of his youth had grown gray in that interval. There, however, stood the old waiter at the door, in the same greasy black suit, with the same double chin and flaccid face, with the same huge bunch of seals at his fob, rattling his money in his pockets as before, and receiving the Major as if he had gone away only a week ago. "Put the Major's things in twenty-three, that's his room," John said, exhibiting not the least surprise. "Roast fowl for your dinner, I suppose. You ain't got married? They said you was married — the Scotch surgeon of yours was here. No, it was Captain Humby of the thirty-third, as was quartered with the —th in Injee. Like any warm water? What do you come in a chay for — ain't the coach good enough?" And with this, the faithful waiter, who knew and remembered every officer who used the house, and with whom ten years were but as yester-

day, led the way up to Dobbin's old room, where
stood the great moreen bed, and the shabby carpet,
a thought more dingy, and all the old black furniture
covered with faded chintz, just as the Major recollected
them in his youth.

He remembered George pacing up and down the
room, and biting his nails, and swearing that the Governor must come round, and that if he did n't, he
did n't care a straw, on the day before he was married.
He could fancy him walking in, banging the door of
Dobbin's room, and his own hard by —

" You ain't got young," John said, calmly surveying
his friend of former days.

Dobbin laughed. " Ten years and a fever don't make
a man young, John," he said. "It is you that are
always young: — No, you are always old."

" What became of Captain Osborne's widow?" John
said. "Fine young fellow that. Lord, how he used to
spend his money. He never came back after that day
he was married from here. He owes me three pound
at this minute. Look here, I have it in my book.
'April 10, 1815, Captain Osborne: 3*l*.' I wonder
whether his father would pay me," and so saying, John
of the Slaughters' pulled out the very morocco pocket-
book in which he had noted his loan to the Captain,
upon a greasy faded page still extant, with many other
scrawled memoranda regarding the bygone frequenters
of the house.

Having inducted his customer into the room, John
retired with perfect calmness; and Major Dobbin, not
without a blush and a grin at his own absurdity, chose
out of his kit the very smartest and most becoming civil
costume he possessed, and laughed at his own tanned
face and gray hair, as he surveyed them in the dreary
little toilet-glass on the dressing-table.

"I'm glad old John didn't forget me," he thought. "She'll know me, too, I hope." And he sallied out of the inn, bending his steps once more in the direction of Brompton.

Every minute incident of his last meeting with Amelia was present to the constant man's mind as he walked towards her house. The arch and the Achilles statue were up since he had last been in Piccadilly; a hundred changes had occurred which his eye and mind vaguely noted. He began to tremble as he walked up the lane from Brompton, that well-remembered lane leading to the street where she lived. Was she going to be married or not? If he were to meet her with the little boy — Good God, what should he do? He saw a woman coming to him with a child of five years old — was that she? He began to shake at the mere possibility. When he came up to the row of houses, at last, where she lived, and to the gate, he caught hold of it and paused. He might have heard the thumping of his own heart. "May God Almighty bless her, whatever has happened," he thought to himself. "Psha! she may be gone from here," he said, and went in through the gate.

The window of the parlour which she used to occupy was open, and there were no inmates in the room. The Major thought he recognised the piano, though, with the picture over it, as it used to be in former days, and his perturbations were renewed. Mr. Clapp's brass plate was still on the door, at the knocker of which Dobbin performed a summons.

A buxom-looking lass of sixteen, with bright eyes and purple cheeks, came to answer the knock, and looked hard at the Major as he leant back against the little porch.

He was as pale as a ghost, and could hardly falter out the words — "Does Mrs. Osborne live here?"

She looked him hard in the face for a moment — and then turning white too — said, "Lord bless me — it's Major Dobbin." She held out both her hands shaking — "Don't you remember me?" she said. "I used to call you Major Sugarplums." On which, and I believe it was for the first time that he ever so conducted himself in his life, the Major took the girl in his arms and kissed her. She began to laugh and cry hysterically, and calling out "Ma, Pa!" with all her voice, brought up those worthy people, who had already been surveying the Major from the casement of the ornamental kitchen, and were astonished to find their daughter in the little passage in the embrace of a great tall man in a blue frock-coat and white duck trowsers.

"I'm an old friend," he said — not without blushing though. "Don't you remember me, Mrs. Clapp, and those good cakes you used to make for tea? — Don't you recollect me, Clapp? I'm George's godfather, and just come back from India!" A great shaking of hands ensued — Mrs. Clapp was greatly affected and delighted; she called upon heaven to interpose a vast many times in that passage.

The landlord and landlady of the house led the worthy Major into the Sedleys' room (whereof he remembered every single article of furniture, from the old brass ornamented piano, once a natty little instrument, Stothard maker, to the screens and the alabaster miniature tombstone, in the midst of which ticked Mr. Sedley's gold watch), and there as he sat down in the lodger's vacant arm-chair, the father, the mother, and the daughter, with a thousand ejaculatory breaks in the narrative, informed Major Dobbin of what we know already, but of particulars in Amelia's history of which he was not aware — namely of Mrs. Sedley's death, of George's reconcilement with his grandfather Osborne, of the way in which the widow took on at leaving him, and of other particulars of her life. Twice or thrice he was going to ask about the marriage question, but his heart failed him. He did not care to lay it bare to these people. Finally, he was informed that Mrs. O. was gone to walk with her Pa in Kensington Gardens, whither she always went with the old gentleman (who was very weak and peevish now, and led her a sad life, though she behaved to him like an angel, to be sure,) of a fine afternoon after dinner.

"I'm very much pressed for time," the Major said, "and have business to-night of importance. I should like to see Mrs. Osborne tho'. Suppose Miss Polly would come with me and show me the way."

Miss Polly was charmed and astonished at this proposal. She knew the way. She would show Major Dobbin. She had often been with Mr. Sedley when Mrs. O. was gone — was gone Russell Square way: and knew the bench where he liked to sit. She bounced away to her apartment, and appeared presently in her best bonnet and her mamma's yellow shawl and large pebble brooch, of which she assumed the loan in order to make herself a worthy companion for the Major.

That officer, then, in his blue frock-coat and buckskin gloves, gave the young lady his arm, and they walked away very gaily. He was glad to have a friend at hand for the scene which he dreaded somehow. He asked a thousand more questions from his companion about Amelia: his kind heart grieved to think that she should have had to part with her son. How did she bear it? Did she see him often? Was Mr. Sedley pretty comfortable now in a worldly point of view? Polly answered all these questions of Major Sugarplums to the very best of her power.

And in the midst of their walk an incident occurred

which, though very simple in its nature, was productive of the greatest delight to Major Dobbin. A pale young man with feeble whiskers and a stiff white neckcloth came walking down the lane, *en sandwich* : — having a lady, that is, on each arm. One was a tall and commanding middle-aged female, with features and a complexion similar to those of the clergyman of the Church of England by whose side she marched, and the other a stunted little woman with a dark face, ornamented by a fine new bonnet and white ribbons, and in a smart pelisse with a rich gold watch in the midst of her person. The gentleman, pinioned as he was by these two ladies, carried further a parasol, shawl, and basket, so that his arms were entirely engaged, and of course he was unable to touch his hat in acknowledgment of the curtsey with which Miss Mary Clapp greeted him.

He merely bowed his head in reply to her salutation, which the two ladies returned with a patronising air, and at the same time looking severely at the individual in the blue coat and bamboo cane, who accompanied Miss Polly.

"Who's that?" asked the Major, amused by the group, and after he had made way for the three to pass up the lane. Mary looked at him rather roguishly.

"That is our curate, the Reverend Mr. Binny (a twitch from Major Dobbin), and his sister Miss B. Lord bless us, how she did use to worret us at Sunday-school; and the other lady, the little one with a cast in her eye, and the handsome watch, is Mrs. Binny — Miss Grits that was; her Pa was a grocer, and kept the Little Original Gold Tea Pot in Kensington Gravel Pits. They were married last month, and are just come back from Margate. She's five thousand pound to her fortune; but her and Miss B., who made the match, have quarrelled already."

If the Major had twitched before, he started now, and slapped the bamboo on the ground with an emphasis which made Miss Clapp cry, " Law," and laugh too. He stood for a moment silent with open mouth looking after the retreating young couple, while Miss Mary told their history; but he did not hear beyond the announcement of the reverend gentleman's marriage; his head was swimming with felicity. After this rencontre he began to walk double quick towards the place of his destination; and yet they were too soon (for he was in a great tremor at the idea of a meeting for which he had been longing any time these ten years) — through the Brompton lanes, and entering at the little old portal in Kensington Garden wall.

" There they are," said Miss Polly, and she felt him again start back on her arm. She was a confidante at once of the whole business. She knew the story as well as if she had read it in one of her favourite novel-books — " Fatherless Fanny," or the " Scottish Chiefs."

"Suppose you were to run on and tell her," the Major said. Polly ran forward, her yellow shawl streaming in the breeze.

Old Sedley was seated on a bench, his handkerchief placed over his knees, prattling away according to his wont, with some old story about old times, to which Amelia had listened, and awarded a patient smile many a time before. She could of late think of her own affairs, and smile or make other marks of recognition of her father's stories, scarcely hearing a word of the old man's tales. As Mary came bouncing along, and Amelia caught sight of her, she started up from her bench. Her first thought was, that something had happened to Georgy; but the sight of the messenger's eager and happy face dissipated that fear in the timorous mother's bosom.

"News! news!" cried the emissary of Major Dobbin. "He's come! He's come!"

"Who is come?" said Emmy, still thinking of her son.

"Look there," answered Miss Clapp, turning round and pointing; in which direction Amelia looking, saw Dobbin's lean figure and long shadow stalking across the grass. Amelia started in her turn, blushed up, and, of course, began to cry. At all this simple little creature's fêtes, the *grandes eaux* were accustomed to play.

He looked at her — oh, how fondly — as she came running towards him, her hands before her, ready to give them to him. She was n't changed. She was a little pale: a little stouter in figure. Her eyes were the same, the kind trustful eyes. There were scarce three lines of silver in her soft brown hair. She gave him both her hands as she looked up flushing and smiling through her tears into his honest homely face. He took the two little hands between his two, and held them there. He was speechless for a moment. Why did he not take her in his arms, and swear that he would never leave her? She must have yielded: she could not but have obeyed him.

"I — I 've another arrival to announce," he said, after a pause.

"Mrs. Dobbin?" Amelia said, making a movement back — Why did n't he speak?

"No," he said, letting her hands go: "Who has told you those lies? — I mean, your brother Jos came in the same ship with me, and is come home to make you all happy."

"Papa, papa!" Emmy cried out, "here are news! My brother is in England. He is come to take care of you. — Here is Major Dobbin."

Mr. Sedley started up, shaking a great deal, and gathering up his thoughts. Then he stepped forward and made an old-fashioned bow to the Major, whom he called Mr. Dobbin, and hoped his worthy father, Sir William, was quite well. He proposed to call upon Sir William, who had done him the honour of a visit a short time ago. Sir William had not called upon the old gentleman for eight years — it was that visit he was thinking of returning.

" He is very much shaken," Emmy whispered, as Dobbin went up and cordially shook hands with the old man.

Although he had such particular business in London that evening, the Major consented to forego it upon Mr. Sedley's invitation to him to come home and partake of tea. Amelia put her arm under that of her young friend with the yellow shawl, and headed the party on their return homewards, so that Mr. Sedley fell to Dobbin's share. The old man walked very slowly, and told a number of ancient histories about himself and his poor Bessy, his former prosperity, and his bankruptcy. His thoughts, as is usual with failing old men, were quite in former times. The present, with the exception of the one catastrophe which he felt, he knew little about. The Major was glad to let him talk on. His eyes were fixed upon the figure in front of him — the dear little figure always present to his imagination and in his prayers, and visiting his dreams wakeful or slumbering.

Amelia was very happy, smiling, and active all that evening; performing her duties as hostess of the little entertainment with the utmost grace and propriety, as Dobbin thought. His eyes followed her about as they sate in the twilight. How many a time had he longed for that moment, and thought of her far away

under hot winds and in weary marches, gentle and
happy, kindly ministering to the wants of old age, and
decorating poverty with sweet submission — as he saw
her now. I do not say that his taste was the highest,
or that it is the duty of great intellects to be content
with a bread-and-butter paradise, such as sufficed our
simple old friend; but his desires were of this sort
whether for good or bad; and, with Amelia to help
him, he was as ready to drink as many cups of tea
as Doctor Johnson.

Amelia seeing this propensity, laughingly encouraged
it; and looked exceedingly roguish as she administered
to him cup after cup. It is true she did not know that
the Major had had no dinner, and that the cloth was
laid for him at the Slaughters', and a plate laid thereon
to mark that the table was retained, in that very box
in which the Major and George had sate many a time
carousing, when she was a child just come home from
Miss Pinkerton's school.

The first thing Mrs. Osborne showed the Major was
Georgy's miniature, for which she ran upstairs on
her arrival at home. It was not half handsome enough
of course for the boy, but was n't it noble of him to
think of bringing it to his mother? Whilst her papa
was awake she did not talk much about Georgy. To
hear about Mr. Osborne and Russell Square was not
agreeable to the old man, who very likely was unconscious that he had been living for some months past
mainly on the bounty of his richer rival; and lost
his temper if allusion was made to the other.

Dobbin told him all, and a little more perhaps than
all, that had happened on board the Ramchunder; and
exaggerated Jos's benevolent dispositions towards his
father, and resolution to make him comfortable in his
old days. The truth is, that during the voyage the

Major had impressed this duty most strongly upon his fellow-passenger and extorted promises from him that he would take charge of his sister and her child. He soothed Jos's irritation with regard to the bills which the old gentleman had drawn upon him, gave a laughing account of his own sufferings on the same score, and of the famous consignment of wine with which the old man had favoured him: and brought Mr. Jos, who was by no means an ill-natured person when well pleased and moderately flattered, to a very good state of feeling regarding his relatives in Europe.

And in fine I am ashamed to say that the Major stretched the truth so far as to tell old Mr. Sedley that it was mainly a desire to see his parent which brought Jos once more to Europe.

At his accustomed hour Mr. Sedley began to doze in his chair, and then it was Amelia's opportunity to commence her conversation, which she did with great eagerness; — it related exclusively to Georgy. She did not talk at all about her own sufferings at breaking from him, for indeed this worthy woman, though she was half-killed by the separation from the child, yet thought it was very wicked in her to repine at losing him; but everything concerning him, his virtues, talents, and prospects, she poured out. She described his angelic beauty; narrated a hundred instances of his generosity and greatness of mind whilst living with her: how a Royal Duchess had stopped and admired him in Kensington Gardens; how splendidly he was cared for now. and how he had a groom and a pony; what quickness and cleverness he had, and what a prodigiously well-read and delightful person the Reverend Lawrence Veal was, George's master. "He knows *everything*," Amelia said. "He has the most delightful parties. You who are so learned yourself, and

[65]

have read so much, and are so clever and accomplished — don't shake your head and say no — *He* always used to say you were — you will be charmed with Mr. Veal's parties. The last Tuesday in every month. He says there is no place in the bar or the senate that Georgy may not aspire to. Look here," and she went to the piano-drawer and drew out a theme of Georgy's composition. This great effort of genius, which is still in the possession of George's mother, is as follows:

On Selfishness. — Of all the vices which degrade the human character, Selfishness is the most odious and contemptible. An undue love of Self leads to the most monstrous crimes; and occasions the greatest misfortunes both in *States and Families.* As a selfish man will impoverish his family and often bring them to ruin: so a selfish king brings ruin on his people and often plunges them into war.

Example: The selfishness of Achilles, as remarked by the poet Homer, occasioned a thousand woes to the Greeks — μυρί᾽ Ἀχαιοῖς ἄλγε ἔθηκε — (Hom. Il. A. 2). The selfishness of the late Napoleon Bonaparte occasioned innumerable wars in Europe, and caused him to perish, himself, in a miserable island — that of Saint Helena in the Atlantic Ocean.

We see by these examples that we are not to consult our own interest and ambition, but that we are to consider the interests of others as well as our own.

GEORGE S. OSBORNE.

Athenè House, 24 April, 1827.

"Think of him writing such a hand, and quoting Greek too, at his age," the delighted mother said. "O William," she added, holding out her hand to the Major — "what a treasure Heaven has given me in that boy! He is the comfort of my life — and he is the image of — of him that's gone!"

"Ought I to be angry with her for being faithful to him?" William thought. "Ought I to be jealous of my friend in the grave, or hurt that such a heart as Amelia's can love only once and for ever? Oh, George, George, how little you knew the prize you had, though." This sentiment passed rapidly through William's mind, as he was holding Amelia's hand, whilst the handkerchief was veiling her eyes.

"Dear friend," she said, pressing the hand which held hers, "how good, how kind you always have been to me! See! Papa is stirring. You will go and see Georgy to-morrow, won't you?"

"Not to-morrow," said poor old Dobbin. "I have business." He did not like to own that he had not as yet been to his parents' and his dear sister Anne — a remissness for which I am sure every well-regulated person will blame the Major. And presently he took his leave, leaving his address behind him for Jos, against the latter's arrival. And so the first day was over, and he had seen her.

When he got back to the Slaughters', the roast fowl was of course cold, in which condition he ate it for supper. And knowing what early hours his family kept, and that it would be needless to disturb their slumbers at so late an hour, it is on record, that Major Dobbin treated himself to half-price at the Haymarket Theatre that evening, where let us hope he enjoyed himself.

CHAPTER V

THE OLD PIANO

THE Major's visit left old John Sedley in a great state of agitation and excitement. His daughter could not induce him to settle down to his customary occupations or amusements that night. He passed the evening fumbling amongst his boxes and desks, untying his papers with trembling hands, and sorting and arranging them against Jos's arrival. He had them in the greatest order — his tapes and his files, his receipts, and his letters with lawyers and correspondents; the documents relative to the Wine Project (which failed from a most unaccountable accident, after commencing with the most splendid prospects), the Coal Project (which only a want of capital prevented from becoming the most successful scheme ever put before the public), the Patent Saw-mills and Sawdust Consolidation Project, &c. &c. — All night, until a very late hour, he passed in the preparation of these documents, trembling about from one room to another, with a quivering candle and shaky hands. — Here 's the wine papers, here 's the sawdust, here 's the coals; here 's my letters to Calcutta and Madras, and replies from Major Dobbin, C.B., and Mr. Joseph Sedley to the same. "He shall find no irregularity about *me*, Emmy," the old gentleman said.

Emmy smiled. "I don't think Jos will care about seeing those papers, Papa," she said.

"You don't know anything about business, my dear," answered the sire, shaking his head with an important air. And it must be confessed, that on this point Emmy was very ignorant, and that is a pity, some people are so knowing. All these twopenny documents arranged on a side table, old Sedley covered them carefully over with a clean bandanna handkerchief (one out of Major Dobbin's lot), and enjoined the maid and landlady of the house, in the most solemn way, not to disturb those papers, which were arranged for the arrival of Mr. Joseph Sedley the next morning, " Mr. Joseph Sedley of the Honourable East India Company's Bengal Civil Service."

Amelia found him up very early the next morning, more eager, more hectic, and more shaky than ever. " I did n't sleep much, Emmy my dear," he said. " I was thinking of my poor Bessy. I wish she was alive, to ride in Jos's carriage once again. She kept her own, and became it very well." And his eyes filled with tears, which trickled down his furrowed old face. Amelia wiped them away, and smilingly kissed him, and tied the old man's neckcloth in a smart bow, and put his brooch into his best shirt frill, in which, in his Sunday suit of mourning, he sat from six o'clock in the morning awaiting the arrival of his son.

There are some splendid tailors' shops in the High Street of Southampton, in the fine plate-glass windows of which hang gorgeous waistcoats of all sorts, of silk and velvet, and gold and crimson, and pictures of the last new fashions in which those wonderful gentlemen with quizzing glasses, and holding on to little boys with the exceeding large eyes and curly hair, ogle ladies in riding habits prancing by the Statue of Achilles at Apsley House. Jos, although provided with some of the most splendid vests that Calcutta could furnish, thought he could not go to town until he was supplied with one or two of these garments, and selected a crimson satin, embroidered with gold butterflies, and a black and red velvet tartan with white stripes and a rolling collar, with which, and a rich blue satin stock and a gold pin, consisting of a five-barred gate with a horseman in pink enamel jumping over it, he thought he might make his entry into London with some dignity. For Jos's former shyness and blundering blushing timidity had given way to a more candid and courageous self-assertion of his worth. " I don't care about owning it," Waterloo Sedley would say to his friends, " I am a dressy man : " and though rather uneasy if the ladies looked at him at the Government House balls, and though he blushed and turned away alarmed under their glances, it was chiefly from a dread lest they should make love to him, that he avoided them, being averse to marriage altogether. But there was no such swell in Calcutta as Waterloo Sedley, I have heard say : and he had the handsomest turn-out, gave the best bachelor dinners, and had the finest plate in the whole place.

To make these waistcoats for a man of his size and dignity took at least a day, part of which he employed in hiring a servant to wait upon him and his native ; and in instructing the agent who cleared his baggage, his boxes, his books, which he never read ; his chests of mangoes, chutney, and currie-powders ; his shawls for presents to people whom he did n't know as yet ; and the rest of his *Persicos apparatus.*

At length, he drove leisurely to London on the third day, and in the new waistcoat : the native, with chattering teeth, shuddering in a shawl on the box by the side of the new European servant ; Jos puffing his pipe at intervals within, and looking so majestic, that the little boys cried Hooray, and many people thought he must be a Governor-General. *He*, I promise, did not decline the obsequious invitation of the landlords to alight and refresh himself in the neat country towns. Having partaken of a copious breakfast, with fish, and rice, and hard eggs, at Southampton, he had so far rallied at Winchester as to think a glass of sherry necessary. At Alton he stepped out of the carriage, at his servant's request, and imbibed some of the ale for which the place is famous. At Farnham he stopped to view the Bishop's Castle, and to partake of a light dinner of stewed eels, veal cutlets, and French beans, with a bottle of claret. He was cold over Bagshot Heath, where the native chattered more and more, and Jos Sahib took some brandy-and-water; in fact, when he drove into town, he was as full of wine, beer, meat, pickles, cherry-brandy, and tobacco, as the steward's cabin of a steam-packet. It was evening when his carriage thundered up to the little door in Brompton, whither the affectionate fellow drove first, and before hieing to the apartments secured for him by Mr. Dobbin at the Slaughters'.

All the faces in the street were in the windows; the little maid-servant flew to the wicket-gate, the Mesdames Clapp looked out from the casement of the ornamented kitchen; Emmy, in a great flutter, was in the passage among the hats and coats, and old Sedley in the parlour inside, shaking all over. Jos descended from the post-chaise and down the creaking swaying steps in awful state, supported by the new valet from Southampton and the shuddering native, whose brown face was now livid with cold, and of the colour of a turkey's gizzard. He created an immense sensation in the passage presently, where Mrs. and Miss Clapp, coming perhaps to listen at the parlour door, found Loll Jewab shaking upon the hall-bench under the coats,

[71]

moaning in a strange piteous way, and showing his yellow eyeballs and white teeth.

For, you see, we have adroitly shut the door upon the meeting between Jos and the old father, and the poor little gentle sister inside. The old man was very much affected: so, of course, was his daughter: nor was Jos without feeling. In that long absence of ten years, the most selfish will think about home and early ties. Distance sanctifies both. Long brooding over those lost pleasures exaggerates their charm and sweetness. Jos was unaffectedly glad to see and shake the hand of his father, between whom and himself there had been a coolness — glad to see his little sister, whom he remembered so pretty and smiling, and pained at the alteration which time, grief, and misfortune had made in the shattered old man. Emmy had come out to the door in her black clothes and whispered to him of her mother's death, and not to speak of it to their father. There was no need of this caution, for the elder Sedley himself began immediately to speak of the event, and prattled about it, and wept over it plenteously. It shocked the Indian not a little, and made him think of himself less than the poor fellow was accustomed to do.

The result of the interview must have been very satisfactory, for when Jos had reascended his post-chaise, and had driven away to his hotel, Emmy embraced her father tenderly, appealing to him with an air of triumph, and asking the old man whether she did not always say that her brother had a good heart?

Indeed, Joseph Sedley, affected by the humble position in which he found his relations, and in the expansiveness and overflowing of heart occasioned by the first meeting, declared that they should never suffer want or discomfort any more, that he was at home for some time at any rate, during which his house and everything he had should be theirs: and that Amelia would look very pretty at the head of his table — until she would accept one of her own.

She shook her head sadly, and had, as usual, recourse to the water-works. She knew what he meant. She and her young confidante, Miss Mary, had talked over the matter most fully, the very night of the Major's visit: beyond which time the impetuous Polly could not refrain from talking of the discovery which she had made, and describing the start and tremor of joy by which Major Dobbin betrayed himself when Mr. Binny passed with his bride, and the Major learned that he had no longer a rival to fear. " Did n't you see how he shook all over when you asked if he was married, and he said, ' Who told you those lies? ' O Ma'am," Polly said, " he never kept his eyes off you ; and I 'm sure he 's grown gray a-thinking of you."

But Amelia, looking up at her bed, over which hung the portraits of her husband and son, told her young *protégée*, never, never, to speak on that subject again ; that Major Dobbin had been her husband's dearest friend, and her own and George's most kind and affectionate guardian ; that she loved him as a brother — but that a woman who had been married to such an angel as that, and she pointed to the wall, could never think of any other union. Poor Polly sighed : she thought what she should do if young Mr. Tomkins, at the surgery, who always looked at her so at church, and who, by those mere aggressive glances had put her timorous little heart into such a flutter that she was ready to surrender at once, — what she should do if he were to die? She knew he was consumptive, his cheeks were so red, and he was so uncommon thin in the waist.

Not that Emmy, being made aware of the honest

Major's passion, rebuffed him in any way, or felt dis-
pleased with him. Such an attachment from so true
and loyal a gentleman could make no woman angry.
Desdemona was not angry with Cassio, though there is
very little doubt she saw the Lieutenant's partiality for
her (and I for my part believe that many more things
took place in that sad affair than the worthy Moorish
officer ever knew of); why, Miranda was even very
kind to Caliban, and we may be pretty sure for the same
reason. Not that she would encourage him in the least,
— the poor uncouth monster — of course not. No
more would Emmy by any means encourage her admirer, the Major. She would give him that friendly
regard, which so much excellence and fidelity merited;
she would treat him with perfect cordiality and frankness until he made his proposals; and *then* it would be
time enough for her to speak, and to put an end to
hopes which never could be realised.

She slept, therefore, very soundly that evening, after
the conversation with Miss Polly, and was more than
ordinarily happy, in spite of Jos's delaying. "I am
glad he is not going to marry that Miss O'Dowd," she
thought. "Colonel O'Dowd never could have a sister
fit for such an accomplished man as Major William."
Who was there amongst her little circle, who would
make him a good wife? Not Miss Binny, she was too
old and ill-tempered; Miss Osborne? — too old too.
Little Polly was too young. Mrs. Osborne could not
find anybody to suit the Major before she went to sleep.

However, when the postman made his appearance,
the little party were put out of suspense by the receipt
of a letter from Jos to his sister, who announced, that he
felt a little fatigued after his voyage, and should not be
able to move on that day, but that he would leave
Southampton early the next morning, and be with his

father and mother at evening. Amelia, as she read out the letter to her father, paused over the latter word; her brother, it was clear, did not know what had happened in the family. Nor could he: for the fact is that though the Major rightly suspected that his travelling companion never would be got into motion in so short a space as twenty-four hours, and would find some excuse for delaying, yet Dobbin had not written to Jos to inform him of the calamity which had befallen the Sedley family: being occupied in talking with Amelia until long after post-hour.

The same morning brought Major Dobbin a letter to the Slaughters' Coffee House from his friend at Southampton; begging dear Dob to excuse Jos for being in a rage when awakened the day before (he had a confounded headache, and was just in his first sleep), and entreating Dob to engage comfortable rooms at the Slaughters' for Mr. Sedley and his servants. The Major had become necessary to Jos during the voyage. He was attached to him, and hung upon him. The other passengers were away to London. Young Ricketts and little Chaffers went away on the coach that day — Ricketts on the box, and taking the reins from Botley; the Doctor was off to his family at Portsea; Bragg gone to town to his co-partners: and the first mate busy in the unloading of the Ramchunder. Mr. Jos was very lonely at Southampton, and got the landlord of the George to take a glass of wine with him that day; at the very hour at which Major Dobbin was seated at the table of his father, Sir William, where his sister found out (for it was impossible for the Major to tell fibs) that he had been to see Mrs. George Osborne.

Jos was so comfortably situated in St. Martin's Lane, he could enjoy his hookah there with such perfect ease, and could swagger down to the theatres, when minded, so agreeably, that, perhaps, he would have remained altogether at the Slaughters' had not his friend, the Major, been at his elbow. The gentleman would not let the Bengalee rest until he had executed his promise of having a home for Amelia and his father. Jos was a soft fellow in anybody's hands; Dobbin most active in anybody's concerns but his own; the civilian was, therefore, an easy victim to the guileless arts of this good-natured diplomatist, and was ready to do, to purchase, hire, or relinquish whatever his friend thought fit. Loll Jewab, of whom the boys about St. Martin's Lane used to make cruel fun whenever he showed his dusky countenance in the street, was sent back to Calcutta in the Lady Kicklebury East Indiaman, in which Sir William Dobbin had a share; having previously taught Jos's European the art of preparing curries, pilaus, and pipes. It was a matter of great delight and occupation to Jos to superintend the building of a smart chariot, which he and the Major ordered in the neighbouring Long Acre: and a pair of handsome horses were jobbed, with which Jos drove about in state in the Park, or to call upon his Indian friends. Amelia was not seldom by his side on these excursions, when also Major Dobbin would be seen in the back seat of the carriage. At other times old Sedley and his daughter took advantage of it: and Miss Clapp, who frequently accompanied her friend, had great pleasure in being recognised as she sate in the carriage, dressed in the famous yellow shawl, by the young gentleman at the surgery, whose face might commonly be seen over the window-blinds as she passed.

Shortly after Jos's first appearance at Brompton, a dismal scene, indeed, took place at that humble cottage, at which the Sedleys had passed the last ten years of

their life. Jos's carriage (the temporary one, not the
chariot under construction) arrived one day and carried
off old Sedley and his daughter — to return no more.
The tears that were shed by the landlady and the landlady's daughter at that event were as genuine tears
of sorrow as any that have been outpoured in the
course of this history. In their long acquaintanceship
and intimacy they could not recall a harsh word that
had been uttered by Amelia. She had been all sweetness and kindness, always thankful, always gentle, even
when Mrs. Clapp lost her own temper, and pressed for
the rent. When the kind creature was going away for
good and all, the landlady reproached herself bitterly
for ever having used a rough expression to her — how
she wept, as they stuck up with wafers on the window,
a paper notifying that the little rooms so long occupied
were to let! They never would have such lodgers
again, that was quite clear. After-life proved the
truth of this melancholy prophecy: and Mrs. Clapp
revenged herself for the deterioration of mankind by
levying the most savage contributions upon the tea-
caddies and legs of mutton of her *locataires*. Most of
them scolded and grumbled; some of them did not
pay: none of them stayed. The landlady might well
regret those old, old friends, who had left her.

As for Miss Mary, her sorrow at Amelia's departure
was such as I shall not attempt to depict. From childhood upwards she had been with her daily, and had
attached herself so passionately to that dear good lady,
that when the grand barouche came to carry her off
into splendour, she fainted in the arms of her friend,
who was indeed scarcely less affected than the good-
natured girl. Amelia loved her like a daughter. During eleven years the girl had been her constant friend
and associate. The separation was a very painful one

indeed to her. But it was of course arranged that
Mary was to come and stay often at the grand new
house whither Mrs. Osborne was going; and where
Mary was sure she would never be so happy as she
had been in their humble cot, as Miss Clapp called
it, in the language of the novels which she loved.

Let us hope she was wrong in her judgment. Poor
Emmy's days of happiness had been very few in that
humble cot. A gloomy Fate had oppressed her there.
She never liked to come back to the house after she
had left it, or to face the landlady who had tyrannised
over her when ill-humoured and unpaid, or when pleased
had treated her with a coarse familiarity scarcely less
odious. Her servility and fulsome compliments when
Emmy was in prosperity were not more to that lady's
liking. She cast about notes of admiration all over
the new house, extolling every article of furniture or
ornament; she fingered Mrs. Osborne's dresses, and
calculated their price. Nothing could be too good
for that sweet lady, she vowed and protested. But in
the vulgar sycophant who now paid court to her
Emmy always remembered the coarse tyrant who had
made her miserable many a time, to whom she had
been forced to put up petitions for time, when the
rent was overdue; who cried out at her extravagance
if she bought delicacies for her ailing mother or
father; who had seen her humble and trampled upon
her.

Nobody ever heard of these griefs, which had been
part of our poor little woman's lot in life. She kept
them secret from her father, whose improvidence was
the cause of much of her misery. She had to bear
all the blame of his misdoings, and indeed was so
utterly gentle and humble as to be made by nature for
a victim.

I hope she is not to suffer much more of that hard usage. And, as in all griefs there is said to be some consolation, I may mention that poor Mary, when left at her friend's departure in a hysterical condition, was placed under the medical treatment of the young fellow from the surgery, under whose care she rallied after a short period. Emmy, when she went away from Brompton, endowed Mary with every article of furniture that the house contained: only taking away her pictures (the two pictures over the bed) and her piano — that little old piano which had now passed into a plaintive jingling old age, but which she loved for reasons of her own. She was a child when first she played on it: and her parents gave it her. It had been given to her again since, as the reader may remember, when her father's house was gone to ruin, and the instrument was recovered out of the wreck.

Major Dobbin was exceedingly pleased when, as he was superintending the arrangements of Jos's new house, which the Major insisted should be very handsome and comfortable; the cart arrived from Brompton, bringing the trunks and band-boxes of the emigrants from that village, and with them the old piano. Amelia would have it up in her sitting-room, a neat little apartment on the second floor, adjoining her father's chamber: and where the old gentleman sate commonly of evenings.

When the men appeared then bearing this old music-box, and Amelia gave orders that it should be placed in the chamber aforesaid, Dobbin was quite elated. "I'm glad you've kept it," he said in a very sentimental manner. "I was afraid you didn't care about it."

"I value it more than anything I have in the world," said Amelia.

" *Do* you, Amelia? " cried the Major. The fact was, as he had bought it himself, though he never said anything about it, it never entered into his head to suppose that Emmy should think anybody else was the purchaser, and as a matter of course he fancied that she knew the gift came from him. " Do you, Amelia? " he said; and the question, the great question of all, was trembling on his lips, when Emmy replied —

" Can I do otherwise? — did not *he* give it me? "

" I did not know," said poor old Dob, and his countenance fell.

Emmy did not note the circumstance at the time, nor take immediate heed of the very dismal expression which honest Dobbin's countenance assumed; but she thought of it afterwards. And then it struck her, with inexpressible pain and mortification too, that it was William who was the giver of the piano; and not George, as she had fancied. It was not George's gift; the only one which she had received from her lover, as she thought — the thing she had cherished beyond all others — her dearest relic and prize. She had spoken to it about George; played his favourite airs upon it: sate for long evening hours, touching, to the best of her simple art, melancholy harmonies on the keys, and weeping over them in silence. It was not George's relic. It was valueless now. The next time that old Sedley asked her to play, she said it was shockingly out of tune, that she had a headache, that she could n't play.

Then, according to her custom, she rebuked herself for her pettishness and ingratitude, and determined to make a reparation to honest William for the slight she had not expressed to him, but had felt for his piano. A few days afterwards, as they were seated in the drawing-room, where Jos had fallen asleep with

great comfort after dinner, Amelia said with rather
a faltering voice to Major Dobbin, —

"I have to beg your pardon for something."

"About what?" said he.

"About — about that little square piano. I never
thanked you for it when you gave it me; many, many
years ago, before I was married. I thought somebody
else had given it. Thank you, William." She held
out her hand; but the poor little woman's heart was
bleeding; and as for her eyes, of course they were
at their work.

But William could hold no more. "Amelia, Amelia,"
he said, "I did buy it for you. I loved you then as
I do now. I must tell you. I think I loved you from
the first minute that I saw you, when George brought
me to your house, to show me the Amelia whom he
was engaged to. You were but a girl, in white, with
large ringlets; you came down singing — do you
remember? — and we went to Vauxhall. Since then
I have thought of but one woman in the world, and
that was you. I think there is no hour in the day
has passed for twelve years that I haven't thought
of you. I came to tell you this before I went to India,
but you did not care, and I hadn't the heart to speak.
You did not care whether I stayed or went."

"I was very ungrateful," Amelia said.

"No; only indifferent," Dobbin continued, desper-
ately. "I have nothing to make a woman to be otherwise. I know what you are feeling now. You are
hurt in your heart at the discovery about the piano;
and that it came from me and not from George. I
forgot, or I should never have spoken of it so. It
is for me to ask your pardon for being a fool for
a moment, and thinking that years of constancy and
devotion might have pleaded with you."

[81]

"It is you who are cruel now," Amelia said with some spirit. "George is my husband, here and in heaven. How could I love any other but him? I am his now as when you first saw me, dear William. It was he who told me how good and generous you were, and who taught me to love you as a brother. Have you not been everything to me and my boy? Our dearest, truest, kindest friend and protector? Had you come a few months sooner perhaps you might have spared me that — that dreadful parting. O, it nearly killed me, William — but you did n't come, though I wished and prayed for you to come, and they took him too away from me. Is n't he a noble boy, William? Be his friend still and mine" — and here her voice broke, and she hid her face on his shoulder.

The Major folded his arms round her, holding her to him as if she was a child, and kissed her head. "I will not change, dear Amelia," he said. "I ask for no more than your love. I think I would not have it otherwise. Only let me stay near you, and see you often."

"Yes, often," Amelia said. And so William was at liberty to look and long: as the poor boy at school who has no money may sigh after the contents of the tart-woman's tray.

CHAPTER VI

RETURNS TO THE GENTEEL WORLD

GOOD fortune now begins to smile upon Amelia. We are glad to get her out of that low sphere in which she has been creeping hitherto, and introduce her into a polite circle; not so grand and refined as that in which our other female friend, Mrs. Becky, has appeared, but still having no small pretensions to gentility and fashion. Jos's friends were all from the three presidencies, and his new house was in the comfortable Anglo-Indian district of which Moira Place is the centre. Minto Square, Great Clive Street, Warren Street, Hastings Street, Ochterlony Place, Plassy Square, Assaye Terrace, ("Gardens" was a felicitous word not applied to stucco houses with asphalte terraces in front, so early as 1827)—who does not know these respectable abodes of the retired Indian aristocracy, and the quarter which Mr. Wenham calls the Black Hole, in a word? Jos's position in life was not grand enough to entitle him to a house in Moira Place, where none can live but retired Members of Council, and partners of Indian firms (who break after having settled a hundred thousand pounds on their wives, and retire into comparative penury to a country place and four thousand a year): he engaged a comfortable house of a second or third-rate order in Gillespie Street, purchasing the carpets, costly mirrors, and handsome and appropriate planned furniture by Seddons, from the assignees of

Mr. Scape, lately admitted partner into the great Calcutta House of Fogle, Fake, and Cracksman, in which poor Scape had embarked seventy thousand pounds, the earnings of a long and honourable life, taking Fake's place, who retired to a princely Park in Sussex, (the Fogles have been long out of the firm, and Sir Horace Fogle is about to be raised to the peerage as Baron Bandanna) — admitted, I say, partner into the great agency house of Fogle and Fake two years before it failed for a million, and plunged half the Indian public into misery and ruin.

Scape, ruined, honest, and broken-hearted at sixty-five years of age, went out to Calcutta to wind up the affairs of the house. Walter Scape was withdrawn from Eton, and put into a merchant's house. Florence Scape, Fanny Scape, and their mother faded away to Boulogne, and will be heard of no more. To be brief, Jos stepped in and bought their carpets and sideboards, and admired himself in the mirrors which had reflected their kind handsome faces. The Scape tradesmen, all honourably paid, left their cards, and were eager to supply the new household. The large men in white waistcoats, who waited at Scape's dinners, green-grocers, bank-porters, and milkmen in their private capacity, left their addresses, and ingratiated themselves with the butler. Mr. Chummy, the chimney-purifier, who had swep the last three families, tried to coax the butler and the boy under him, whose duty it was to go out covered with buttons and with stripes down his trowsers, for the protection of Mrs. Amelia whenever she chose to walk abroad.

It was a modest establishment. The butler was Jos's valet also, and never was more drunk than a butler in a small family should be who has a proper regard for his master's wine. Emmy was supplied with a maid, grown on Sir William Dobbin's suburban estate; a good girl, whose kindness and humility disarmed Mrs. Osborne, who was at first terrified at the idea of having a servant to wait upon herself, who did not in the least know how to use one, and who always spoke to domestics with the most reverential politeness. But this maid was very useful in the family, in dexterously tending old Mr. Sedley, who kept almost entirely to his own quarter of the house, and never mixed in any of the gay doings which took place there.

Numbers of people came to see Mrs. Osborne. Lady Dobbin and daughters were delighted at her change of fortune, and waited upon her. Miss Osborne from Russell Square came in her grand chariot with the flaming hammercloth emblazoned with the Leeds arms. Jos was reported to be immensely rich. Old Osborne had no objection that Georgy should inherit his uncle's property as well as his own. " Damn it, we will make a man of the feller," he said; " and I 'll see him in Parliament before I die. *You* may go and see his mother, Miss O., though I 'll never set eyes on her: " and Miss Osborne came. Emmy, you may be sure, was very glad to see her, and so be brought nearer to George. That young fellow was allowed to come much more frequently than before to visit his mother. He dined once or twice a week in Gillespie Street, and bullied the servants and his relations there, just as he did in Russell Square.

He was always respectful to Major Dobbin, however, and more modest in his demeanour when that gentleman was present. He was a clever lad, and afraid of the Major. George could not help admiring his friend's simplicity, his good-humour, his various learning quietly imparted, his general love of truth and justice. He had met no such man as yet in the course of his experience,

and he had an instinctive liking for a gentleman. He
hung fondly by his godfather's side; and it was his
delight to walk in the Parks and hear Dobbin talk.
William told George about his father, about India and
Waterloo, about everything but himself. When George
was more than usually pert and conceited, the Major
made jokes at him, which Mrs. Osborne thought very
cruel. One day, taking him to the play, and the boy
declining to go into the pit because it was vulgar, the
Major took him to the boxes, left him there, and went
down himself to the pit. He had not been seated there
very long, before he felt an arm thrust under his, and a
dandy little hand in a kid-glove squeezing his arm.
George had seen the absurdity of his ways, and come
down from the upper region. A tender laugh of benevolence lighted up old Dobbin's face and eyes as he
looked at the repentant little prodigal. He loved the
boy, as he did everything that belonged to Amelia.
How charmed she was when she heard of this instance
of George's goodness! Her eyes looked more kindly
on Dobbin than they ever had done. She blushed, he
thought, after looking at him so.

Georgy never tired of his praises of the Major to his
mother. "I like him, Mamma, because he knows such
lots of things; and he ain't like old Veal, who is always
bragging and using such long words, don't you know?
The chaps call him 'Longtail' at school. I gave him
the name; ain't it capital? But Dob reads Latin like
English, and French and that; and when we go out
together he tells me stories about my Papa, and never
about himself; though I heard Colonel Buckler, at
Grandpapa's, say that he was one of the bravest
officers in the army, and had distinguished himself
ever so much. Grandpapa was quite surprised, and
said, ' *That* feller! why, I did n't think he could say

Bo to a goose' — but *I* know he could, could n't he, Mamma?"

Emmy laughed: she thought it was very likely the Major could do thus much.

If there was a sincere liking between George and the Major, it must be confessed that between the boy and his uncle no great love existed. George had got a way of blowing out his cheeks, and putting his hands in his waistcoat pockets, and saying, "God bless my soul, you don't say so," so exactly after the fashion of old Jos, that it was impossible to refrain from laughter. The servants would explode at dinner if the lad, asking for something which was n't at table, put on that countenance and used that favourite phrase. Even Dobbin would shoot out a sudden peal at the boy's mimicry. If George did not mimic his uncle to his face, it was only by Dobbin's rebukes and Amelia's terrified entreaties that the little scapegrace was induced to resist. And the worthy civilian being haunted by a dim consciousness that the lad thought him an ass, and was inclined to turn him into ridicule, used to be extremely timorous and, of course, doubly pompous and dignified in the presence of Master Georgy. When it was announced that the young gentleman was expected in Gillespie Street to dine with his mother, Mr. Jos commonly found that he had an engagement at the Club. Perhaps nobody was much grieved at his absence. On those days Mr. Sedley would commonly be induced to come out from his place of refuge in the upper storeys; and there would be a small family party, whereof Major Dobbin pretty generally formed one. He was the *ami de la maison;* old Sedley's friend, Emmy's friend, Georgy's friend, Jos's counsel and adviser. "He might almost as well be at Madras for anything *we* see of him," Miss Ann Dobbin remarked, at Camberwell. Ah! Miss

Ann, did it not strike you that it was not *you* whom the Major wanted to marry?

Joseph Sedley then led a life of dignified otiosity such as became a person of his eminence. His very first point, of course, was to become a member of the Oriental Club: where he spent his mornings in the company of his brother Indians, where he dined, or whence he brought home men to dine.

Amelia had to receive and entertain these gentlemen and their ladies. From these she heard how soon Smith would be in Council; how many lacs Jones had brought home with him, how Thomson's House in London had refused the bills drawn by Thomson, Kibobjee, and Co., the Bombay House, and how it was thought the Calcutta House must go too: how very imprudent, to say the least of it, Mrs. Brown's conduct (wife of Brown of the Ahmednuggur Irregulars) had been with young Swankey of the Body Guard, sitting up with him on deck until all hours, and losing themselves as they were riding out at the Cape; how Mrs. Hardyman had had out her thirteen sisters, daughters of a country curate, the Rev. Felix Rabbits, and married eleven of them, seven high up in the service: how Hornby was wild because his wife would stay in Europe, and Trotter was appointed Collector at Ummerapoora. This and similar talk took place, at the grand dinners all round. They had the same conversation; the same silver dishes; the same saddles of mutton, boiled turkeys, and entrées. Politics set in a short time after dessert, when the ladies retired upstairs and talked about their complaints and their children.

Mutato nomine, it is all the same. Don't the barristers' wives talk about Circuit? — Don't the soldiers' ladies gossip about the Regiment? — don't the clergymen's ladies discourse about Sunday Schools, and who

takes whose duty? — don't the very greatest ladies of all talk about that small clique of persons to whom they belong, and why should our Indian friends not have their own conversation? — only I admit it is slow for the laymen whose fate it sometimes is to sit by and listen.

Before long Emmy had a visiting-book, and was driving about regularly in a carriage, calling upon Lady Bludyer (wife of Major-General Sir Roger Bludyer, K.C.B., Bengal Army); Lady Huff, wife of Sir G. Huff, Bombay ditto; Mrs. Pice, the Lady of Pice the Director, &c. We are not long in using ourselves to changes in life. That carriage came round to Gillespie Street every day: that buttony boy sprang up and down from the box with Emmy's and Jos's visiting cards; at stated hours Emmy and the carriage went for Jos to the Club, and took him an airing; or, putting old Sedley into the vehicle, she drove the old man round the Regent's Park. The lady's maid and the chariot, the visiting-book and the buttony page, became soon as familiar to Amelia as the humble routine of Brompton. She accommodated herself to one as to the other. If Fate had ordained that she should be a duchess, she would even have done that duty too. She was voted, in Jos's female society, rather a pleasing young person — not much in her, but pleasing, and that sort of thing.

The men, as usual, liked her artless kindness and simple refined demeanour. The gallant young Indian dandies at home on furlough — immense dandies these — chained and moustached — driving in tearing cabs, the pillars of the theatres, living at West End Hotels, — nevertheless admired Mrs. Osborne, liked to bow to her carriage in the Park, and to be admitted to have the honour of paying her a morning visit. Swankey of the Body Guard himself, that dangerous youth, and the greatest buck of all the Indian army now on leave, was one day discovered by Major Dobbin *tête-à-tête* with Amelia, and describing the sport of pig-sticking to her with great humour and eloquence : and he spoke afterwards of a d—d king's officer that's always hanging about the house — a long, thin, queer-looking oldish fellow — a dry fellow though, that took the shine out of a man in the talking line.

Had the Major possessed a little more personal vanity he would have been jealous of so dangerous a young buck as that fascinating Bengal Captain. But Dobbin was of too simple and generous a nature to have any doubts about Amelia. He was glad that the young men should pay her respect; and that others should admire her. Ever since her womanhood almost, had she not been persecuted and undervalued? It pleased him to see how kindness brought out her good qualities, and how her spirits gently rose with her prosperity. Any person who appreciated her paid a compliment to the Major's good judgment — that is, if a man may be said to have good judgment who is under the influence of Love's delusion.

After Jos went to Court, which we may be sure he did as a loyal subject of his Sovereign (showing himself in his full court suit at the Club, whither Dobbin came to fetch him in a very shabby old uniform,) he who had always been a staunch Loyalist and admirer of George IV., became such a tremendous Tory and pillar of the State, that he was for having Amelia to go to a Drawing-room, too. He somehow had worked himself up to believe that he was implicated in the maintenance of the public welfare, and that the Sovereign would not be happy unless Jos Sedley and his family appeared to rally round him at St. James's.

Emmy laughed. "Shall I wear the family diamonds, Jos?" she said.

"I wish you would let me buy you some," thought the Major. "I should like to see any that were too good for you."

CHAPTER VII

IN WHICH TWO LIGHTS ARE PUT OUT

THERE came a day when the round of decorous pleasures and solemn gaieties in which Mr. Jos Sedley's family indulged, was interrupted by an event which happens in most houses. As you ascend the staircase of your house from the drawing towards the bed-room floors, you may have remarked a little arch in the wall right before you, which at once gives light to the stair which leads from the second story to the third (where the nursery and servants' chambers commonly are) and serves for another purpose of utility, of which the undertaker's men can give you a notion. They rest the coffins upon that arch, or pass them through it so as not to disturb in any unseemly manner the cold tenant slumbering within the black arch.

That second-floor arch in a London house, looking up and down the well of the staircase, and commanding the main thoroughfare by which the inhabitants are passing; by which cook lurks down before daylight to scour her pots and pans in the kitchen; by which young master stealthily ascends, having left his boots in the hall, and let himself in after dawn from a jolly night at the Club; down which miss comes rustling in fresh ribbons and spreading muslins, brilliant and beautiful, and prepared for conquest and the ball; or master Tommy slides, preferring the bannisters for a mode of conveyance, and disdaining danger and the stair; down

which the mother is fondly carried smiling in her strong
husband's arms, as he steps steadily step by step, and
followed by the monthly nurse, on the day when the
medical man has pronounced that the charming patient
may go downstairs; up which John lurks to bed, yawning with a sputtering tallow candle, and to gather up
before sunrise the boots which are awaiting him in the
passages; — that stair, up or down which babies are
carried, old people are helped, guests are marshalled to
the ball, the parson walks to the christening, the doctor
to the sick room, and the undertaker's men to the upper
floor — what a memento of Life, Death, and Vanity it is
— that arch and stair — if you choose to consider it,
and sit on the landing, looking up and down the well!
The doctor will come up to us too for the last time
there, my friend in motley. The nurse will look in at
the curtains, and you take no notice — and then she
will fling open the windows for a little, and let in the
air. Then they will pull down all the front blinds of
the house and live in the back rooms — then they will
send for the lawyer and other men in black, &c. — Your
comedy and mine will have been played then, and we
shall be removed, O how far, from the trumpets, and
the shouting, and the posture-making. If we are gentlefolks they will put hatchments over our late domicile,
with gilt cherubim, and mottoes stating that there is
" Quiet in Heaven." Your son will new furnish the
house, or perhaps let it, and go into a more modern
quarter; your name will be among the " Members
Deceased," in the lists of your clubs next year. However much you may be mourned, your widow will like
to have her weeds neatly made — the cook will send or
come up to ask about dinner — the survivor will soon
bear to look at your picture over the mantel-piece,
which will presently be deposed from the place of

honour, to make way for the portrait of the son who reigns.

Which of the dead are most tenderly and passionately deplored? Those who love the survivors the least, I believe. The death of a child occasions a passion of grief and frantic tears, such as your end, brother reader, will never inspire. The death of an infant which scarce knew you, which a week's absence from you would have caused to forget you, will strike you down more than the loss of your closest friend, or your first-born son — a man grown like yourself, with children of his own. We may be harsh and stern with Judah and Simeon — our love and pity gush out for Benjamin, the little one. And if you are old, as some reader of this may be or shall be — old and rich, or old and poor — you may one day be thinking for yourself — " These people are very good round about me; but they won't grieve too much when I am gone. I am very rich, and they want my inheritance — or very poor, and they are tired of supporting me."

The period of mourning for Mrs. Sedley's death was only just concluded, and Jos scarcely had had time to cast off his black and appear in the splendid waistcoats which he loved, when it became evident to those about Mr. Sedley, that another event was at hand, and that the old man was about to go seek for his wife in the dark land whither she had preceded him. " The state of my father's health," Jos Sedley solemnly remarked at the Club, " prevents me from giving any *large* parties this season: but if you will come in quietly at half-past six, Chutney, my boy, and take a homely dinner with one or two of the old set — I shall be always glad to see you." So Jos and his acquaintances dined and drank their claret among themselves in silence; whilst the sands of life were running out in the old man's glass

upstairs. The velvet-footed butler brought them their wine; and they composed themselves to a rubber after dinner: at which Major Dobbin would sometimes come and take a hand: and Mrs. Osborne would occasionally descend, when her patient above was settled for the night, and had commenced one of those lightly troubled slumbers which visit the pillow of old age.

The old man clung to his daughter during this sickness. He would take his broths and medicines from scarcely any other hand. To tend him became almost the sole business of her life. Her bed was placed close by the door which opened into his chamber, and she was alive at the slightest noise or disturbance from the couch of the querulous invalid. Though, to do him justice, he lay awake many an hour, silent and without stirring, unwilling to awaken his kind and vigilant nurse.

He loved his daughter with more fondness now, perhaps, than ever he had done since the days of her childhood. In the discharge of gentle offices and kind filial duties, this simple creature shone most especially. " She walks into the room as silently as a sunbeam," Mr. Dobbin thought, as he saw her passing in and out from her father's room; a cheerful sweetness lighting up her face as she moved to and fro, graceful and noiseless. When women are brooding over their children, or busied in a sick room, who has not seen in their faces those sweet angelic beams of love and pity?

A secret feud of some years standing was thus healed: and with a tacit reconciliation. In these last hours, and touched by her love and goodness, the old man forgot all his grief against her, and wrongs which he and his wife had many a long night debated: how she had given up everything for her boy: how she was careless of her parents in their old age and misfortune, and only thought of the child: how absurdly and foolishly, impiously indeed, she took on, when George was removed from her. Old Sedley forgot these charges as he was making up his last account, and did justice to the gentle and uncomplaining little martyr. One night when she stole into his room, she found him awake, when the broken old man made his confession. " O, Emmy, I 've been thinking we were very unkind and unjust to you," he said, and put out his cold and feeble hand to her. She knelt down and prayed by his bedside, as he did too, having still hold of her hand. When our turn comes, friend, may we have such company in our prayers.

Perhaps as he was lying awake then, his life may have passed before him — his early hopeful struggles, his manly successes and prosperity, his downfall in his declining years, and his present helpless condition — no chance of revenge against Fortune, which had had the better of him — neither name nor money to bequeath — a spent-out, bootless life of defeat and disappointment, and the end here! Which, I wonder, brother reader, is the better lot, to die prosperous and famous, or poor and disappointed? To have, and to be forced to yield; or to sink out of life, having played and lost the game? That must be a strange feeling, when a day of our life comes and we say, " *To-morrow*, success or failure won't matter much : and the sun will rise, and all the myriads of mankind go to their work or their pleasure as usual, but I shall be out of the turmoil."

So there came one morning and sunrise, when all the world got up and set about its various works and pleasures, with the exception of old John Sedley, who was not to fight with fortune, or to hope or scheme any more : but to go and take up a quiet and utterly unknown residence in a churchyard at Brompton by the side of his old wife.

Major Dobbin, Jos, and Georgy followed his remains

to the grave, in a black cloth coach. Jos came on purpose from the Star and Garter at Richmond, whither he retreated after the deplorable event. He did not care to remain in the house, with the — under the circumstances, you understand. But Emmy stayed and did her duty as usual. She was bowed down by no especial grief, and rather solemn than sorrowful. She prayed that her own end might be as calm and painless, and thought with trust and reverence of the words which she had heard from her father during his illness, indicative of his faith, his resignation, and his future hope.

Yes, I think that will be the better ending of the two, after all. Suppose you are particularly rich and well to do, and say on that last day, " I am very rich; I am tolerably well known; I have lived all my life in the best society, and thank Heaven, come of a most respectable family. I have served my King and country with honour. I was in Parliament for several years, where, I may say, my speeches were listened to, and pretty well received. I don't owe any man a shilling: on the contrary, I lent my old college friend, Jack Lazarus, fifty pounds, for which my executors will not press him. I leave my daughters with ten thousand pounds a-piece — very good portions for girls: I bequeath my plate and furniture, my house in Baker Street, with a handsome jointure, to my widow for her life; and my landed property, besides money in the funds, and my cellar of well-selected wine in Baker Street, to my son. I leave twenty pound a-year to my valet; and I defy any man after I am gone to find anything against my character." Or suppose, on the other hand, your swan sings quite a different sort of dirge, and you say, " I am a poor blighted, disappointed old fellow, and have made an utter failure through life. I was not endowed either with brains or with good fortune: and confess that I have committed a hundred mistakes and blunders. I own to having forgotten my duty many a time. I can't pay what I owe. On my last bed I lie utterly helpless and humble: and I pray forgiveness for my weakness, and throw myself with a contrite heart, at the feet of the Divine Mercy." Which of these two speeches, think you, would be the best oration for your own funeral? Old Sedley made the last; and in that humble frame of mind, and holding by the hand of his daughter, life and disappointment and vanity sank away from under him.

"You see," said old Osborne to George, "what comes of merit and industry, and judicious speculations, and that. Look at me and my banker's account. Look at your poor grandfather, Sedley, and his failure. And yet he was a better man than I was, this day twenty years — a better man, I should say, by ten thousand pound."

Beyond these people and Mr. Clapp's family, who came over from Brompton to pay a visit of condolence, not a single soul alive ever cared a penny piece about old John Sedley, or remembered the existence of such a person.

When old Osborne first heard from his friend Colonel Buckler (as little Georgy has already informed us) how distinguished an officer Major Dobbin was, he exhibited a great deal of scornful incredulity, and expressed his surprise how ever such a feller as that should possess either brains or reputation. But he heard of the Major's fame from various members of his society. Sir William Dobbin had a great opinion of his son, and narrated many stories illustrative of the Major's learning, valour, and estimation in the world's opinion. Finally, his name appeared in the lists of one or two great parties of the nobility; and this circumstance had a prodigious effect upon the old aristocrat of Russell Square.

The Major's position, as guardian to Georgy, whose possession had been ceded to his grandfather, rendered some meetings between the two gentlemen inevitable; and it was in one of these that old Osborne, a keen man of business, looking into the Major's accounts with his ward and the boy's mother, got a hint which staggered him very much, and at once pained and pleased him, that it was out of William Dobbin's own pocket that a part of the fund had been supplied upon which the poor widow and the child had subsisted.

When pressed upon the point, Dobbin, who could not tell lies, blushed and stammered a good deal, and finally confessed. "The marriage," he said, (at which his interlocutor's face grew dark,) "was very much my doing. I thought my poor friend had gone so far, that retreat from his engagement would have been dishonour to him, and death to Mrs. Osborne; and I could do no less, when she was left without resources, than give what money I could spare to maintain her."

"Major D.," Mr. Osborne said, looking hard at him, and turning very red too — "you did me a great injury; but give me leave to tell you, sir, you are an honest feller. There's my hand, sir, though I little thought that my flesh and blood was living on you — " and the pair shook hands, with great confusion on Major Dobbin's part, thus found out in his act of charitable hypocrisy.

He strove to soften the old man, and reconcile him towards his son's memory. "He was such a noble fellow," he said, "that all of us loved him, and would have done anything for him. I, as a young man in those days, was flattered beyond measure by his preference for me; and was more pleased to be seen in his company than in that of the Commander-in-Chief. I never saw his equal for pluck and daring, and all the

qualities of a soldier ; " and Dobbin told the old father
as many stories as he could remember regarding the
gallantry and achievements of his son. " And Georgy
is so like him," the Major added.

" He 's so like him that he makes me tremble sometimes," the grandfather said.

On one or two evenings the Major came to dine with
Mr. Osborne (it was during the time of the sickness
of Mr. Sedley), and as the two sate together in the
evening after dinner all their talk was about the departed hero. The father boasted about him according
to his wont, glorifying himself in recounting his son's
feats and gallantry, but his mood was at any rate better
and more charitable than that in which he had been
disposed until now to regard the poor fellow; and the
Christian heart of the kind Major was pleased at these
symptoms of returning peace and good will. On the
second evening old Osborne called Dobbin, William,
just as he used to do at the time when Dobbin and
George were boys together : and the honest gentleman
was pleased by that mark of reconciliation.

On the next day at breakfast when Miss Osborne,
with the asperity of her age and character, ventured
to make some remark reflecting slightingly upon the
Major's appearance or behaviour — the master of the
house interrupted her. " You 'd have been glad enough
to git him for yourself, Miss O. But them grapes are
sour. Ha! ha! Major William is a fine feller."

" That he is, Grandpapa," said Georgy, approvingly :
and going up close to the old gentleman he took
a hold of his large gray whiskers, and laughed in his
face good-humouredly and kissed him. And he told
the story at night to his mother: who fully agreed
with the boy. " Indeed he is," she said. " Your dear
father always said so. He is one of the best and most

upright of men." Dobbin happened to drop in very
soon after this conversation, which made Amelia blush
perhaps: and the young scapegrace increased the
confusion by telling Dobbin the other part of the
story. "I say, Dob," he said, "there's such an uncommon nice girl wants to marry you. She's plenty
of tin: she wears a front: and she scolds the servants from morning till night." "Who is it?" asked
Dobbin.

"It's aunt O.," the boy answered. "Grandpapa
said so. And I say, Dob, how prime it would be to
have you for my uncle." Old Sedley's quavering voice
from the next room at this moment weakly called for
Amelia and the laughing ended.

That old Osborne's mind was changing, was pretty
clear. He asked George about his uncle sometimes,
and laughed at the boy's imitation of the way in which
Jos said, "God-bless-my-soul," and gobbled his soup.
Then he said, "It's not respectful, sir, of you younkers
to be imitating of your relations. Miss O., when you
go out a-driving to-day, leave my card upon Mr.
Sedley, do you hear? There's no quarrel betwigst
me and him anyhow."

The card was returned, and Jos and the Major were
asked to dinner, — to a dinner the most splendid and
stupid that perhaps ever Mr. Osborne gave; every
inch of the family plate was exhibited, and the best
company was asked. Mr. Sedley took down Miss O.
to dinner, and she was very gracious to him; whereas
she hardly spoke to the Major, who sat apart from
her, and by the side of Mr. Osborne, very timid. Jos
said, with great solemnity, it was the best turtle soup
he had ever tasted in his life; and asked Mr. Osborne
where he got his Madeira?

"It is some of Sedley's wine," whispered the butler

to his master. "I've had it a long time, and paid a good figure for it, too," Mr. Osborne said aloud to his guest; and then whispered to his right-hand neighbour how he had got it " at the old chap's sale."

More than once he asked the Major about — about Mrs. George Osborne — a theme on which the Major could be very eloquent when he chose. He told Mr. Osborne of her sufferings — of her passionate attachment to her husband, whose memory she worshipped still — of the tender and dutiful manner in which she had supported her parents, and given up her boy, when it seemed to her her duty to do so. "You don't know what she endured, sir," said honest Dobbin with a tremor in his voice; "and I hope and trust you will be reconciled to her. If she took your son away from you, she gave hers to you; and however much you loved your George, depend on it, she loved hers ten times more."

"By God, you are a good feller, sir," was all Mr. Osborne said. It had never struck him that the widow would feel any pain at parting from the boy, or that his having a fine fortune could grieve her. A reconciliation was announced as speedy and inevitable; and Amelia's heart already began to beat at the notion of the awful meeting with George's father.

It was never, however, destined to take place. Old Sedley's lingering illness and death supervened, after which a meeting was for some time impossible. That catastrophe and other events may have worked upon Mr. Osborne. He was much shaken of late, and aged, and his mind was working inwardly. He had sent for his lawyers, and probably changed something in his will. The medical man who looked in, pronounced him shaky, agitated, and talked of a little blood and the sea-side; but he took neither of these remedies.

One day when he should have come down to breakfast, his servant missing him, went into his dressing-room, and found him lying at the foot of the dressing-table in a fit. Miss Osborne was apprised; the doctors were sent for, Georgy stopped away from school; the bleeders and cuppers came. Osborne partially regained cognisance; but never could speak again, though he tried dreadfully once or twice, and in four days he died. The doctors went down, and the undertaker's men went up the stairs; and all the shutters were shut towards the garden in Russell Square. Bullock rushed from the City in a hurry. "How much money had he left to that boy?—not half, surely? Surely share and share alike between the three?" It was an agitating moment.

What was it that poor old man tried once or twice in vain to say? I hope it was that he wanted to see Amelia, and be reconciled before he left the world to the dear and faithful wife of his son: it was most likely that; for his will showed that the hatred which he had so long cherished had gone out of his heart.

They found in the pocket of his dressing-gown the letter with the great red seal, which George had written him from Waterloo. He had looked at the other papers too, relative to his son, for the key of the box in which he kept them was also in his pocket, and it was found the seals and envelopes had been broken—very likely on the night before the seizure—when the butler had taken him tea into his study, and found him reading in the great red family Bible.

When the will was opened, it was found that half the property was left to George, and the remainder between the two sisters. Mr. Bullock to continue, for their joint benefit, the affairs of the commercial house, or to go out, as he thought fit. An annuity of five hundred pounds, chargeable on George's property, was left to his mother, "the widow of my beloved son, George Osborne," who was to resume the guardianship of the boy.

"Major William Dobbin, my beloved son's friend," was appointed executor; "and as out of his kindness and bounty, and with his own private funds, he maintained my grandson and my son's widow, when they were otherwise without means of support," (the testator went on to say,) "I hereby thank him heartily for his love and regard for them: and beseech him to accept such a sum as may be sufficient to purchase his commission as a Lieutenant-Colonel, or to be disposed of in any way he may think fit."

When Amelia heard that her father-in-law was reconciled to her, her heart melted, and she was grateful for the fortune left to her. But when she heard how Georgy was restored to her, and knew how and by whom, and how it was William's bounty that supported her in poverty, how it was William who gave her her husband and her son — O, then she sank on her knees, and prayed for blessings on that constant and kind heart: she bowed down and humbled herself, and kissed the feet, as it were, of that beautiful and generous affection.

And gratitude was all that she had to pay back for such admirable devotion and benefits — only gratitude! If she thought of any other return, the image of George stood up out of the grave, and said, "You are mine, and mine only, now and for ever."

William knew her feelings: had he not passed his whole life in divining them?

When the nature of Mr. Osborne's will became known to the world, it was edifying to remark how

Mrs. George Osborne rose in the estimation of the people forming her circle of acquaintance. The servants of Jos's establishment, who used to question her humble orders, and say they would "ask Master," whether or not they could obey, never thought now of that sort of appeal. The cook forgot to sneer at her shabby old gowns (which, indeed, were quite eclipsed by that lady's finery when she was dressed to go to church of a Sunday evening), the others no longer grumbled at the sound of her bell, or delayed to answer that summons. The coachman, who grumbled that his 'osses should be brought out, and his carriage made into an hospital for that old feller and Mrs. O., drove her with the utmost alacrity now, and trembling lest he should be superseded by Mr. Osborne's coachman, asked "what them there Russell Square coachmen knew about town, and whether *they* was fit to sit on a box before a lady?" Jos's friends, male and female, suddenly became interested about Emmy, and cards of condolence multiplied on her hall table. Jos himself, who had looked on her as a good-natured harmless pauper, to whom it was his duty to give victuals and shelter, paid her and the rich little boy, his nephew, the greatest respect — was anxious that she should have change and amusement after her troubles and trials, "poor dear girl" — and began to appear at the breakfast-table, and most particularly to ask how she would like to dispose of the day.

In her capacity of guardian to Georgy, she, with the consent of the Major, her fellow-trustee, begged Miss Osborne to live in the Russell Square house as long as ever she chose to dwell there; but that lady, with thanks, declared that she never could think of remaining alone in that melancholy mansion, and departed in deep mourning to Cheltenham, with a couple of her old

domestics. The rest were liberally paid and dismissed;
the faithful old butler, whom Mrs. Osborne proposed to
retain, resigning and preferring to invest his savings in
a public-house, where, let us hope, he was not unpros-
perous. Miss Osborne not choosing to live in Russell
Square, Mrs. Osborne also, after consultation, declined
to occupy the gloomy old mansion there. The house
was dismantled; the rich furniture and effects, the awful
chandeliers and dreary blank mirrors packed away and
hidden, the rich rosewood drawing-room suite was
muffled in straw, the carpets were rolled up and corded,
the small select library of well-bound books was stowed
into two wine-chests, and the whole paraphernalia
rolled away in several enormous vans to the Pantechni-
con, where they were to lie until Georgy's majority. And
the great heavy dark plate-chests went off to Messrs.
Stumpy and Rowdy, to lie in the cellars of those
eminent bankers until the same period should arrive.

One day Emmy with George in her hand and clad in
deep sables went to visit the deserted mansion which
she had not entered since she was a girl. The place in
front was littered with straw where the vans had been
laden and rolled off. They went into the great blank
rooms, the walls of which bore the marks where the
pictures and mirrors had hung. Then they went up the
great blank stone-staircases into the upper rooms, into
that where grandpapa died, as George said in a whisper,
and then higher still into George's own room. The boy
was still clinging by her side, but she thought of another
besides him. She knew that it had been his father's
room as well as his own.

She went up to one of the open windows (one of
those at which she used to gaze with a sick heart when
the child was first taken from her), and thence as she
looked out she could see, over the trees of Russell

Square, the old house in which she herself was born, and where she had passed so many happy days of sacred youth. They all came back to her, the pleasant holidays, the kind faces, the careless, joyful past times : and the long pains and trials that had since cast her down. She thought of these and of the man who had been her constant protector, her good genius, her sole benefactor, her tender and generous friend.

" Look here, mother," said Georgy, " here's a G. O. scratched on the glass with a diamond; I never saw it before, *I* never did it."

" It was your father's room long before you were born, George," she said, and she blushed as she kissed the boy.

She was very silent as they drove back to Richmond where they had taken a temporary house: where the smiling lawyers used to come bustling over to see her (and we may be sure noted the visit in the bill): and where of course there was a room for Major Dobbin too, who rode over frequently, having much business to transact on behalf of his little ward.

Georgy at this time was removed from Mr. Veal's on an unlimited holiday, and that gentleman was engaged to prepare an inscription for a fine marble slab, to be placed up in the Foundling under the monument of Captain George Osborne.

The female Bullock, aunt of Georgy, although de-spoiled by that little monster of one-half of the sum which she expected from her father, nevertheless showed her charitableness of spirit by being reconciled to the mother and the boy. Roehampton is not far from Richmond, and one day the chariot, with the golden bullocks emblazoned on the panels, and the flaccid children within, drove to Amelia's house at Richmond ;

and the Bullock family made an irruption into the garden, where Amelia was reading a book, Jos was in an arbour placidly dipping strawberries into wine, and the Major in one of his Indian jackets was giving a back to Georgy, who chose to jump over him. He went over his head, and bounded into the little advance of Bullocks, with immense black bows in their hats, and huge black sashes, accompanying their mourning mamma.

"He is just of the age for Rosa," the fond parent thought, and glanced towards that dear child, an unwholesome little Miss of seven years of age.

"Rosa, go and kiss your dear cousin," Mrs. Frederick said. "Don't you know me, George? — I am your aunt."

"*I* know you well enough," George said; "but I don't like kissing, please; " and he retreated from the obedient caresses of his cousin.

"Take me to your dear mamma, you droll child," Mrs. Frederick said; and those ladies accordingly met, after an absence of more than fifteen years. During Emmy's cares and poverty the other had never once thought about coming to see her; but now that she was decently prosperous in the world, her sister-in-law came to her as a matter of course.

So did numbers more. Our old friend, Miss Swartz, and her husband came thundering over from Hampton Court, with flaming yellow liveries, and was as impetuously fond of Amelia as ever. Miss Swartz would have liked her always if she could have seen her. One must do her that justice. But, *que voulez-vous ?* — in this vast town one has not the time to go and seek one's friends; if they drop out of the rank they disappear, and we march on without them. Who is ever missed in Vanity Fair?

But so, in a word, and before the period of grief for Mr. Osborne's death had subsided, Emmy found herself in the centre of a very genteel circle indeed; the members of which could not conceive that anybody belonging to it was not very lucky. There was scarce one of the ladies that had n't a relation a peer, though the husband might be a drysalter in the City. Some of the ladies were very blue and well informed; reading Mrs. Somerville, and frequenting the Royal Institution; others were severe and Evangelical, and held by Exeter Hall. Emmy, it must be owned, found herself entirely at a loss in the midst of their clavers, and suffered wofully on the one or two occasions on which she was compelled to accept Mrs. Frederick Bullock's hospitalities. That lady persisted in patronising her, and determined most graciousiy to form her. She found Amelia's milliners for her, and regulated her household and her manners. She drove over constantly from Roehampton, and entertained her friend with faint fashionable fiddlefaddle and feeble Court slipslop. Jos liked to hear it, but the Major used to go off growling at the appearance of this woman, with her twopenny gentility. He went to sleep under Frederick Bullock's bald head, after dinner, at one of the banker's best parties, (Fred was still anxious that the balance of the Osborne property should be transferred from Stumpy and Rowdy's to them), and whilst Amelia, who did not know Latin, or who wrote the last crack article in the Edinburgh, and did not in the least deplore, or otherwise, Mr. Peel's late extraordinary tergiversation on the fatal Catholic Relief Bill, sate dumb amongst the ladies in the grand drawing-room, looking out upon velvet lawns, trim gravel walks, and glistening hot-houses.

"She seems good-natured but insipid," said Mrs. Rowdy; "that Major seems to be particularly *épris.*"

"She wants *ton* sadly," said Mrs. Hollyock. "My dear creature, you never will be able to form her."

"She is dreadfully ignorant or indifferent," said Mrs. Glowry, with a voice as if from the grave, and a sad shake of the head and turban. — "I asked her if she thought that it was in 1836, according to Mr. Jowls, or in 1839, according to Mr. Wapshot, that the Pope was to fall: and she said — 'Poor Pope! I hope not — What has he done?'"

"She is my brother's widow, my dear friends," Mrs. Frederick replied, "and as such I think we're all bound to give her every attention and instruction on entering into the world. You may fancy there can be no *mercenary* motives in those whose *disappointments* are well known."

"That poor dear Mrs. Bullock," said Rowdy to Hollyock, as they drove away together — "she is always scheming and managing. She wants Mrs. Osborne's account to be taken from our house to hers — and the way in which she coaxes that boy, and makes him sit by that blear-eyed little Rosa, is perfectly ridiculous."

"I wish Glowry was choked with her Man of Sin and her Battle of Armageddon," cried the other; and the carriage rolled away over Putney Bridge.

But this sort of society was too cruelly genteel for Emmy: and all jumped for joy when a foreign tour was proposed.

CHAPTER VIII

AM RHEIN

THE above every-day events had occurred, and a few weeks had passed, when, on one fine morning, Parliament being over, the summer advanced, and all the good company in London about to quit that city for their annual tour in search of pleasure or health, the Batavier steamboat left the Tower-stairs laden with a goodly company of English fugitives. The quarter-deck awnings were up, and the benches and gangways crowded with scores of rosy children, bustling nursemaids, ladies in the prettiest pink bonnets and summer dresses, gentlemen in travelling caps and linen jackets, whose mustachios had just begun to sprout for the ensuing tour; and the stout trim old veterans with starched neckcloths and neat-brushed hats, such as have invaded Europe any time since the conclusion of the war, and carry the national Goddem into every city of the Continent. The congregation of hat-boxes, and Bramah desks, and dressing-cases was prodigious. There were jaunty young Cambridge-men travelling with their tutor, and going for a reading excursion to Nonnenwerth or Königswinter: there were Irish gentlemen, with the most dashing whiskers and jewellery, talking about horses incessantly, and prodigiously polite to the young ladies on board, whom, on the contrary, the Cambridge lads and their pale-faced tutor avoided with maiden coyness: there were old Pall Mall

[111]

loungers bound for Ems and Wiesbaden, and a course of waters to clear off the dinners of the season, and a little roulette and *trente-et-quarante* to keep the excitement going : there was old Methuselah, who had married his young wife, with Captain Papillon of the Guards holding her parasol and guide-books : there was young May who was carrying off his bride on a pleasure tour (Mrs. Winter that was, and who had been at school with May's grandmother) ; there was Sir John and my Lady with a dozen children, and corresponding nurse-maids ; and the great grandee Bareacres family that sate by themselves near the wheel, stared at everybody, and spoke to no one. Their carriages, emblazoned with coronets, and heaped with shining imperials, were on the foredeck ; locked in with a dozen more such vehicles : it was difficult to pass in and out amongst them : and the poor inmates of the fore-cabin had scarcely any space for locomotion. These consisted of a few magnificently attired gentlemen from Houndsditch, who brought their own provisions, and could have bought half the gay people in the grand saloon ; a few honest fellows with mustachios and portfolios, who set to sketching before they had been half-an-hour on board ; one or two French *femmes de chambre* who began to be dreadfully ill by the time the boat had passed Greenwich ; a groom or two who lounged in the neighbourhood of the horse-boxes under their charge, or leaned over the side by the paddle-wheels, and talked about who was good for the Leger, and what they stood to win or lose for the Goodwood cup.

All the couriers, when they had done plunging about the ship, and had settled their various masters in the cabins or on the deck, congregated together and began to chatter and smoke ; the Hebrew gentlemen joining them and looking at the carriages. There was Sir

John's great carriage that would hold thirteen people; my Lord Methuselah's carriage, my Lord Bareacres' chariot, britska, and fourgon, that anybody might pay for who liked. It was a wonder how my Lord got the ready money to pay for the expenses of the journey. The Hebrew gentlemen knew how he got it. They knew what money his Lordship had in his pocket at that instant, and what interest he paid for it, and who gave it him. Finally there was a very neat, handsome travelling carriage, about which the gentlemen speculated.

"*A qui cette voiture là?*" said one gentleman-courier with a large morocco money-bag and ear-rings, to another with ear-rings and a large morocco money-bag.

"*C'est à Kirsch je bense — je l'ai vu toute à l'heure — qui brenoit des sangviches dans la voiture,*" said the courier in a fine German French.

Kirsch emerging presently from the neighbourhood of the hold, where he had been bellowing instructions intermingled with polyglot oaths to the ship's men engaged in secreting the passengers' luggage, came to give an account of himself to his brother interpreters. He informed them that the carriage belonged to a Nabob from Calcutta and Jamaica, enormously rich, and with whom he was engaged to travel; and at this moment a young gentleman who had been warned off the bridge between the paddle-boxes, and who had dropped thence on to the roof of Lord Methuselah's carriage, from which he made his way over other carriages and imperials until he had clambered on to his own, descended thence and through the window into the body of the carriage to the applause of the couriers looking on.

"*Nous allons avoir une belle traversée,* Monsieur George," said the courier with a grin, as he lifted his gold-laced cap.

"D— your French," said the young gentleman, "where's the biscuits, ay?" Whereupon, Kirsch answered him in the English language or in such an imitation of it as he could command, — for though he was familiar with all languages, Mr. Kirsch was not acquainted with a single one, and spoke all with indifferent volubility and incorrectness.

The imperious young gentleman who gobbled the biscuits (and indeed it was time to refresh himself, for he had breakfasted at Richmond full three hours before), was our young friend George Osborne. Uncle Jos and his mamma were on the quarter-deck with a gentleman of whom they used to see a good deal, and the four were about to make a summer tour.

Jos was seated at that moment on deck under the awning, and pretty nearly opposite to the Earl of Bareacres and his family, whose proceedings absorbed the Bengalee almost entirely. Both the noble couple looked rather younger than in the eventful year '15, when Jos remembered to have seen them at Brussels (indeed he always gave out in India that he was intimately acquainted with them). Lady Bareacres' hair which was then dark was now a beautiful golden auburn, whereas Lord Bareacres' whiskers, formerly red, were at present of a rich black with purple and green reflections in the light. But changed as they were, the movements of the noble pair occupied Jos's mind entirely. The presence of a lord fascinated him, and he could look at nothing else.

"Those people seem to interest you a good deal," said Dobbin, laughing and watching him. Amelia too laughed. She was in a straw bonnet with black ribbons, and otherwise dressed in mourning: but the little bustle and holiday of the journey pleased and excited her, and she looked particularly happy.

[114]

"What a heavenly day!" Emmy said, and added, with great originality, "I hope we shall have a calm passage."

Jos waved his hand, scornfully glancing at the same time under his eyelids at the great folks opposite. "If you had made the voyages we have," he said, "you would n't much care about the weather." But nevertheless, traveller as he was, he passed the night direfully sick in his carriage, where his courier tended him with brandy-and-water and every luxury.

In due time this happy party landed at the quays of Rotterdam, whence they were transported by another steamer to the city of Cologne. Here the carriage and the family took to the shore, and Jos was not a little gratified to see his arrival announced in the Cologne newspapers as "Herr Graf Lord von Sedley nebst Begleitung aus London." He had his court dress with him: he had insisted that Dobbin should bring his regimental paraphernalia: he announced that it was his intention to be presented at some foreign courts, and pay his respects to the Sovereigns of the countries which he honoured with a visit.

Wherever the party stopped, and an opportunity was offered, Mr. Jos left his own card and the Major's upon "Our Minister." It was with great difficulty that he could be restrained from putting on his cocked hat and tights to wait upon the English consul at the Free City of Judenstadt, when that hospitable functionary asked our travellers to dinner. He kept a journal of his voyage, and noted elaborately the defects or excellences of the various inns at which he put up, and of the wines and dishes of which he partook.

As for Emmy, she was very happy and pleased. Dobbin used to carry about for her her stool and sketchbook, and admired the drawings of the good-natured little artist, as they never had been admired before. She sate upon steamers' decks and drew crags and castles, or she mounted upon donkeys and ascended to ancient robber-towers, attended by her two aides-de-camp, Georgy and Dobbin. She laughed, and the Major did too, at his droll figure on donkey-back, with his long legs touching the ground. He was the interpreter for the party, having a good military knowledge of the German language; and he and the delighted George fought the campaigns of the Rhine and the Palatinate. In the course of a few weeks, and by assiduously conversing with Herr Kirsch on the box of the carriage, Georgy made prodigious advance in the knowledge of High Dutch, and could talk to hotel waiters and postilions in a way that charmed his mother, and amused his guardian.

Mr. Jos did not much engage in the afternoon excursions of his fellow-travellers. He slept a good deal after dinner, or basked in the arbours of the pleasant inn-gardens. Pleasant Rhine gardens! Fair scenes of peace and sunshine — noble purple mountains, whose crests are reflected in the magnificent stream — who has ever seen you, that has not a grateful memory of those scenes of friendly repose and beauty? To lay down the pen, and even to think of that beautiful Rhineland makes one happy. At this time of summer evening, the cows are trooping down from the hills, lowing and with their bells tinkling, to the old town, with its old moats, and gates, and spires, and chestnut-trees, with long blue shadows stretching over the grass; the sky and the river below flame in crimson and gold; and the moon is already out, looking pale towards the sunset. The sun sinks behind the great castle-crested mountains, the night falls suddenly, the river grows darker and darker, lights quiver in it from the windows in the old ramparts, and twinkle peacefully in the villages under the hills on the opposite shore.

So Jos used to go to sleep a good deal with his bandanna over his face and be very comfortable, and read all the English news, and every word of Galignani's admirable newspaper (may the blessings of all Englishmen who have ever been abroad rest on the founders and proprietors of that piratical print!) and whether he woke or slept his friends did not very much miss him. Yes, they were very happy. They went to the Opera often of evenings — to those snug, unassuming, dear old operas in the German towns, where the noblesse sits and cries, and knits stockings on the one side, over against the bourgeoise on the other; and his Transparency the Duke and his Transparent family, all very fat and good-natured, come and occupy the great box in the middle; and the pit is full of the most elegant slim-waisted officers with straw-coloured mustachios, and twopence a-day on full pay. Here it was that Emmy found her delight, and was introduced for the first time to the wonders of Mozart and Cimarosa. The Major's musical taste has been before alluded to, and his performances on the flute commended. But perhaps the chief pleasure he had in these operas was in watching Emmy's rapture while listening to them. A new world of love and beauty broke upon her when she was introduced to those divine compositions: this lady had the keenest and finest sensibility, and how could she be indifferent when she heard Mozart? The tender parts of " Don Juan " awakened in her raptures so exquisite that she would ask herself when she went to say her prayers of a night, whether it was not wicked to feel so much delight as that with which " Vedrai Carino " and " Batti Batti " filled her gentle little bosom? But the Major, whom she consulted upon this head, as her theological adviser (and who himself had a pious and reverent soul), said that for his part, every beauty of art or nature made him thankful as well as happy; and that the pleasure to be had in listening to fine music, as in looking at the stars in the sky, or at a beautiful landscape or picture, was a benefit for which we might thank Heaven as sincerely as for any other worldly blessing. And in reply to some faint objections of Mrs. Amelia's (taken from certain theological works like the "Washerwoman of Finchley Common" and others of that school, with which Mrs. Osborne had been furnished during her life at Brompton) he told her an Eastern fable of the Owl who thought that the sunshine was unbearable for the eyes, and that the Nightingale was a most overrated bird. "It is one's nature to sing and the other's to hoot," he said, laughing, "and with such a sweet voice as you have yourself, you must belong to the Bulbul faction."

I like to dwell upon this period of her life, and to think that she was cheerful and happy. You see she has not had too much of that sort of existence as yet, and has not fallen in the way of means to educate her tastes or her intelligence. She has been domineered over hitherto by vulgar intellects. It is the lot of many a woman. And as every one of the dear sex is the rival of the rest of her kind, timidity passes for folly in their charitable judgments; and gentleness for dulness; and silence — which is but timid denial of the unwelcome assertion of ruling folks, and tacit protestantism — above all, finds no mercy at the hands of the female Inquisition. Thus, my dear and civilised reader, if you and I were to find ourselves this evening in a society of green-grocers, let us say; it is probable that our conversation would not be brilliant; if, on the other hand, a green-grocer should find himself at your refined and polite tea-table, where everybody was saying witty things, and everybody of fashion and repute tearing her friends to pieces in the most delightful manner, it is possible that the stranger would not be very talkative, and by no means interesting or interested.

And it must be remembered, that this poor lady had never met a gentleman in her life until this present moment. Perhaps these are rarer personages than some of us think for. Which of us can point out many such in his circle — men whose aims are generous, whose truth is constant, and not only constant in its kind but elevated in its degree; whose want of meanness makes them simple: who can look the world honestly in the face with an equal manly sympathy for the great and the small? We all know a hundred whose coats are very well made, and a score who have excellent manners, and one or two happy beings who are what they call, in the inner circles, and have shot into the very centre and bull's eye of the fashion; but of gentlemen how many? Let us take a little scrap of paper and each make out his list.

My friend the Major I write, without any doubt, in mine. He had very long legs, a yellow face, and a slight lisp, which at first was rather ridiculous. But his thoughts were just, his brains were fairly good, his life was honest and pure, and his heart warm and humble. He certainly had very large hands and feet, which the two George Osbornes used to caricature and laugh at; and their jeers and laughter perhaps led poor little Emmy astray as to his worth. But have we not all been misled about our heroes, and changed our opinions a hundred times? Emmy, in this happy time, found that hers underwent a very great change in respect of the merits of the Major.

Perhaps it was the happiest time of both their lives indeed, if they did but know it — and who does? Which

of us can point out and say that was the culmination —
that was the summit of human joy?   But at all events,
this couple were very decently contented, and enjoyed
as pleasant a summer tour as any pair that left England
that year.   Georgy was always present at the play, but
it was the Major who put Emmy's shawl on after the
entertainment; and in the walks and excursions the
young lad would be on a-head, and up a tower-stair or
a tree, whilst the soberer couple were below, the Major
smoking his cigar with great placidity and constancy,
whilst Emmy sketched the site or the ruin.   It was on
this very tour that I, the present writer of a history of
which every word is true, had the pleasure to see them
first, and to make their acquaintance.

It was at the little comfortable Ducal town of Pumpernickel (that very place where Sir Pitt Crawley had been
so distinguished as an *attaché;* but that was in early
early days, and before the news of the battle of Auster-
litz sent all the English diplomatists in Germany to the
right about) that I first saw Colonel Dobbin and his
party.   They had arrived with the carriage and courier
at the Erbprinz Hotel, the best of the town, and the
whole party dined at the *table d'hôte*.   Everybody remarked the majesty of Jos, and the knowing way in
which he sipped, or rather sucked, the Johannisberger,
which he ordered for dinner.   The little boy, too, we observed, had a famous appetite, and consumed schinken,
and braten, and kartoffeln, and cranberry jam, and salad,
and pudding, and roast fowls, and sweetmeats, with a
gallantry that did honour to his nation.   After about
fifteen dishes, he concluded the repast with dessert,
some of which he even carried out of doors; for some
young gentlemen at table, amused with his coolness and
gallant free and easy manner, induced him to pocket a

handful of macaroons, which he discussed on his way to the theatre, whither everybody went in the cheery social little German place. The lady in black, the boy's mamma, laughed and blushed, and looked exceedingly pleased and shy as the dinner went on, and at the various feats and instances of *espièglerie* on the part of her son. The Colonel — for so he became very soon afterwards — I remember joked the boy with a great deal of grave fun, pointing out dishes which he *had n't* tried, and entreating him not to baulk his appetite, but to have a second supply of this or that.

It was what they call a *gast-rolle* night at the Royal Grand Ducal Pumpernickelisch Hof, — or Court theatre; and Madame Schroeder Devrient, then in the bloom of her beauty and genius, performed the part of the heroine in the wonderful opera of "Fidelio." From our places in the stalls we could see our four friends of the *table d'hôte*, in the loge which Schwendler of the Erbprinz kept for his best guests: and I could not help remarking the effect which the magnificent actress and music produced upon Mrs. Osborne, for so we heard the stout gentleman in the mustachios call her. During the astonishing Chorus of the Prisoners, over which the delightful voice of the actress rose and soared in the most ravishing harmony, the English lady's face wore such an expression of wonder and delight that it struck even little Fipps, the *blasé* attaché, who drawled out, as he fixed his glass upon her, "Gayd, it really does one good to see a woman caypable of that stayt of excaytement." And in the Prison Scene where Fidelio, rushing to her husband, cries, "Nichts nichts mein Florestan," she fairly lost herself and covered her face with her handkerchief. Every woman in the house was snivelling at the time: but I suppose it was because it was predestined that I was to write this particular lady's memoirs that I remarked her.

The next day they gave another piece of Beethoven. "Die Schlacht bei Vittoria." Malbrook is introduced at the beginning of the performance, as indicative of the brisk advance of the French Army. Then come drums, trumpets, thunders of artillery, and groans of the dying, and at last in a grand triumphant swell, "God save the King" is performed.

There may have been a score of Englishmen in the house, but at the burst of that beloved and well-known music, everyone of them, we young fellows in the stalls, Sir John and Lady Bullminster (who had taken a house at Pumpernickel for the education of their nine children), the fat gentleman with the mustachios, the long Major in white duck trowsers, and the lady with the little boy upon whom he was so sweet: even Kirsch, the courier in the gallery, stood bolt upright in their places, and proclaimed themselves to be members of the dear old British nation. As for Tapeworm, the Chargé d'Affaires, he rose up in his box and bowed and simpered, as if he would represent the whole empire. Tapeworm was nephew and heir of old Marshal Tiptoff, who has been introduced in this story as General Tiptoff, just before Waterloo, who was Colonel of the —th regiment in which Major Dobbin served, and who died in this year full of honours, and of an aspic of plovers' eggs; when the regiment was graciously given by his Majesty to Colonel Sir Michael O'Dowd, K.C.B., who had commanded it in many glorious fields.

Tapeworm must have met with Colonel Dobbin at the house of the Colonel's Colonel, the Marshal, for he recognised him on this night at the theatre; and with the utmost condescension, his Majesty's minister

came over from his own box, and publicly shook hands
with his new-found friend.

"Look at that infernal sly-boots of a Tapeworm,"
Fipps whispered, examining his chief from the stalls.
"Wherever there's a pretty woman he always twists
himself in." And I wonder what were diplomatists
made for but for that?

"Have I the honour of addressing myself to Mrs.
Dobbin?" asked the Secretary, with a most insinuating
grin.

Georgy burst out laughing, and said, "By Jove, that
is a good 'un." — Emmy and the Major blushed: we
saw them from the stalls.

"This lady is Mrs. George Osborne," said the Major,
"and this is her brother, Mr. Sedley, a distinguished
officer of the Bengal Civil Service: permit me to introduce him to your lordship."

My lord nearly sent Jos off his legs, with the most
fascinating smile. "Are you going to stop in Pumpernickel?" he said. "It is a dull place: but we want
some nice people, and we would try and make it *so*
agreeable to you. Mr. — Ahum — Mrs. — Oho. I
shall do myself the honour of calling upon you to-
morrow at your inn." — And he went away with a
Parthian grin and glance, which he thought must finish
Mrs. Osborne completely.

The performance over, the young fellows lounged
about the lobbies, and we saw the society take its
departure. The Duchess Dowager went off in her
jingling old coach, attended by two faithful and withered old maids of honour, and a little snuffy spindle-
shanked gentleman in waiting, in a brown jasey and
a green coat covered with orders — of which the star
and the grand yellow cordon of the order of St. Michael
of Pumpernickel were most conspicuous. The drums

rolled, the guards saluted, and the old carriage drove away.

Then came his Transparency the Duke and Transparent family, with his great officers of state and household. He bowed serenely to everybody. And amid the saluting of the guards, and the flaring of the torches of the running footmen, clad in scarlet, the Transparent carriages drove away to the old Ducal Schloss, with its towers and pinnacles standing on the Schlossberg. Everybody in Pumpernickel knew everybody. No sooner was a foreigner seen there, than the Minister of Foreign Affairs, or some other great or small officer of state, went round to the Erbprinz, and found out the name of the new arrivals.

We watched them, too, out of the theatre. Tapeworm had just walked off, enveloped in his cloak, with which his gigantic chasseur was always in attendance, and looking as much as possible like Don Juan. The Prime Minister's lady had just squeezed herself into her sedan, and her daughter, the charming Ida, had put on her calash and clogs: when the English party came out, the boy yawning drearily, the Major taking great pains in keeping the shawl over Mrs. Osborne's head, and Mr. Sedley looking grand, with a crush opera-hat on one side of his head, and his hand in the stomach of a voluminous white waistcoat. We took off our hats to our acquaintances of the *table d'hôte*, and the lady, in return, presented us with a little smile and a curtsey, for which everybody might be thankful.

The carriage from the inn, under the superintendence of the bustling Mr. Kirsch, was in waiting to convey the party; but the fat man said he would walk, and smoke his cigar on his way homewards; so the other three, with nods and smiles to us, went without Mr.

Sedley; Kirsch, with the cigar-case, following in his master's wake.

We all walked together, and talked to the stout gentleman about the *agrémens* of the place. It was very agreeable for the English. There were shooting-parties and battues; there was a plenty of balls and entertainments at the hospitable Court; the society was generally good; the theatre excellent, and the living cheap.

"And our Minister seems a most delightful and affable person," our new friend said. "With such a represent-ative, and — and a good medical man, I can fancy the place to be most eligible. Good night, gentlemen." And Jos creaked up the stairs to bedward, followed by Kirsch with a flambeau. We rather hoped that nice-looking woman would be induced to stay some time in the town.

CHAPTER IX

IN WHICH WE MEET AN OLD ACQUAINTANCE

SUCH polite behaviour as that of Lord Tapeworm did not fail to have the most favourable effect upon Mr. Sedley's mind, and the very next morning, at breakfast, he pronounced his opinion that Pumpernickel was the pleasantest little place of any which he had visited on their tour. Jos's motives and artifices were not very difficult of comprehension : and Dobbin laughed in his sleeve, like a hypocrite as he was, when he found by the knowing air of the Civilian and the off-hand manner in which the latter talked about Tapeworm Castle, and the other members of the family, that Jos had been up already in the morning, consulting his travelling Peerage. Yes, he had seen the Right Honourable the Earl of Bagwig, his lordship's father; he was sure he had, he had met him at—at the Levee—did n't Dob remember? and when the Diplomatist called on the party, faithful to his promise, Jos received him with such a salute and honours as were seldom accorded to the little Envoy. He winked at Kirsch on his Excellency's arrival, and that emissary instructed beforehand, went out and superintended an entertainment of cold meats, jellies, and other delicacies, brought in upon trays, and of which Mr. Jos absolutely insisted that his noble guest should partake.

Tapeworm, so long as he could have an opportunity of admiring the bright eyes of Mrs. Osborne (whose freshness of complexion bore daylight remarkably well)

[126]

was not ill pleased to accept any invitation to stay in Mr. Sedley's lodgings; he put one or two dexterous questions to him about India and the dancing-girls there; asked Amelia about that beautiful boy who had been with her, and complimented the astonished little woman upon the prodigious sensation which she had made in the house; and tried to fascinate Dobbin by talking of the late war, and the exploits of the Pumpernickel contingent under the command of the Hereditary Prince, now Duke of Pumpernickel.

Lord Tapeworm inherited no little portion of the family gallantry, and it was his happy belief, that almost every woman upon whom he himself cast friendly eyes, was in love with him. He left Emmy under the persuasion that she was slain by his wit and attractions, and went home to his lodgings to write a pretty little note to her. She was not fascinated; only puzzled by his grinning, his simpering, his scented cambric handkerchief, and his high-heeled lacquered boots. She did not understand one half the compliments which he paid; she had never, in her small experience of mankind, met a professional ladies' man as yet, and looked upon my lord as something curious rather than pleasant; and if she did not admire, certainly wondered at him. Jos, on the contrary, was delighted. "How very affable his Lordship is," he said; "How very kind of his Lordship to say he would send his medical man! Kirsch, you will carry our cards to the Count de Schlüsselback directly: the Major and I will have the greatest pleasure in paying our respects at Court as soon as possible. Put out my uniform, Kirsch, — both our uniforms. It is a mark of politeness which every English gentleman ought to show to the countries which he visits, to pay his respects to the sovereigns of those countries as to the representatives of his own."

When Tapeworm's doctor came, Doctor von Glauber, Body Physician to H. S. H. the Duke, he speedily convinced Jos that the Pumpernickel mineral springs and the Doctor's particular treatment would infallibly restore the Bengalee to youth and slimness. " Dere came here last year," he said, " Sheneral Bulkeley, an English Sheneral, tvice so pic as you, Sir. I sent him back qvite tin after tree months, and he danced vid Baroness Glauber at the end of two."

Jos's mind was made up, the springs, the Doctor, the Court, and the Chargé d'Affaires convinced him, and he proposed to spend the autumn in these delightful quarters. — And punctual to his word, on the next day the Chargé d'Affaires presented Jos and the Major to Victor Aurelius XVII., being conducted to their audience with that sovereign by the Count de Schlüsselback, Marshal of the Court.

They were straightway invited to dinner at Court, and their intention of staying in the town being announced, the politest ladies of the whole town instantly called upon Mrs. Osborne; and as not one of these, however poor they might be, was under the rank of a Baroness, Jos's delight was beyond expression. He wrote off to Chutney at the Club to say that the Service was highly appreciated in Germany, that he was going to show his friend, the Count de Schlüsselback, how to stick a pig in the Indian fashion, and that his august friends, the Duke and Duchess, were everything that was kind and civil.

Emmy, too, was presented to the august family, and as mourning is not admitted in Court on certain days, she appeared in a pink crape dress, with a diamond ornament in the corsage, presented to her by her brother, and she looked so pretty in this costume that the Duke and Court (putting out of the question the Major, who

had scarcely ever seen her before in an evening dress,
and vowed that she did not look five-and-twenty) all
admired her excessively.

In this dress she walked a Polonaise with Major Dobbin at a Court-ball, in which easy dance Mr. Jos had the
honour of leading out the Countess of Schlüsselback, an
old lady with a hump back, but with sixteen good quarters of nobility, and related to half the royal houses of
Germany.

Pumpernickel stands in the midst of a happy valley,
through which sparkles — to mingle with the Rhine some-
where, but I have not the map at hand to say exactly
at what point — the fertilising stream of the Pump. In
some places the river is big enough to support a ferry-
boat, in others to turn a mill; in Pumpernickel itself,
the last Transparency but three, the great and renowned
Victor Aurelius XIV. built a magnificent bridge, on
which his own statue rises, surrounded by water-nymphs
and emblems of victory, peace, and plenty; he has his
foot on the neck of a prostrate Turk — history says he
engaged and ran a Janissary through the body at the
relief of Vienna by Sobieski, — but, quite undisturbed by
the agonies of that prostrate Mahometan, who writhes
at his feet in the most ghastly manner, the Prince smiles
blandly, and points with his truncheon in the direction
of the Aurelius Platz, where he began to erect a new
palace that would have been the wonder of his age, had
the great-souled Prince but had funds to complete it.
But the completion of Monplaisir (*Monblaisir* the honest
German folks call it) was stopped for lack of ready
money, and it and its park and garden are now in
rather a faded condition, and not more than ten times
big enough to accommodate the Court of the reigning
Sovereign.

The gardens were arranged to emulate those of Versailles, and amidst the terraces and groves there are some huge allegorical waterworks still, which spout and froth stupendously upon fête-days, and frighten one with their enormous aquatic insurrections. There is the Trophonius' cave in which, by some artifice, the leaden Tritons are made not only to spout water, but to play the most dreadful groans out of their lead conchs — there is the Nymph-bath and the Niagara cataract, which the people of the neighbourhood admire beyond expression, when they come to the yearly fair at the opening of the Chamber, or to the fêtes with which the happy little nation still celebrates the birth-days and marriage-days of its princely governors.

Then from all the towns of the Duchy which stretches for nearly ten miles, — from Bolkum, which lies on its western frontier bidding defiance to Prussia, from Grogwitz where the Prince has a hunting-lodge, and where his dominions are separated by the Pump river from those of the neighbouring Prince of Potzenthal; from all the little villages, which besides these three great cities, dot over the happy Principality — from the farms and the mills along the Pump, come troops of people in red petticoats and velvet head-dresses, or with three-cornered hats and pipes in their mouths, who flock to the Residenz and share in the pleasures of the fair and the festivities there. Then the theatre is open for nothing, then the waters of Monblaisir begin to play (it is lucky that there is company to behold them, for one would be afraid to see them alone) — then there come mountebanks and riding troops (the way in which his Transparency was fascinated by one of the horse-riders, is well known, and it is believed that *La Petite Vivandière*, as she was called, was a spy in the French interest), and the delighted people are permitted to march through room after room of the Grand Ducal palace, and admire the slippery floor, the rich hangings, and the spittoons at the doors of all the innumerable chambers. There is one Pavilion at Monblaisir which Aurelius Victor XV. had arranged — a great Prince but too fond of pleasure — and which I am told is a perfect wonder of licentious elegance. It is painted with the story of Bacchus and Ariadne, and the table works in and out of the room by means of a windlass so that the company was served without any intervention of domestics. But the place was shut up by Barbara, Aurelius XV.'s widow, a severe and devout Princess of the House of Bolkum and Regent of the Duchy during her son's glorious minority, and after the death of her husband, cut off in the pride of his pleasures.

The theatre of Pumpernickel is known and famous in that quarter of Germany. It languished a little when the present Duke in his youth insisted upon having his own operas played there, and it is said one day, in a fury, from his place in the orchestra, when he attended a rehearsal, broke a bassoon on the head of the Chapel Master, who was conducting, and led too slow; and during which time the Duchess Sophia wrote domestic comedies which must have been very dreary to witness. But the Prince executes his music in private now, and the Duchess only gives away her plays to the foreigners of distinction who visit her kind little Court.

It is conducted with no small comfort and splendour. When there are balls, though there may be four hundred people at supper, there is a servant in scarlet and lace to attend upon every four, and every one is served on silver. There are festivals and entertainments going continually on; and the Duke has his chamberlains and equerries, and the Duchess her mistress of the wardrobe and ladies of honour just like any other and more potent potentates.

The Constitution is or was a moderate despotism, tempered by a Chamber that might or might not be elected. I never certainly could hear of its sitting in my time at Pumpernickel. The Prime Minister had lodgings in a second floor; and the Foreign Secretary occupied the comfortable lodgings over Zwieback's Conditorey. The army consisted of a magnificent band that also did duty on the stage, where it was quite pleasant to see the worthy fellows marching in Turkish dresses with rouge on and wooden scimitars, or as Roman warriors with ophicleides and trombones, — to see them again, I say, at night, after one had listened to them all the morning in the Aurelius Platz, where they performed opposite the Café where we breakfasted. Besides the band, there was a rich and numerous staff of officers, and, I believe, a few men. Besides the regular sentries, three or four men, habited as hussars, used to do duty at the Palace, but I never saw them on horseback, and *au fait*, what was the use of cavalry in a time of profound peace? — and whither the deuce should the hussars ride?

Everybody — everybody that was noble of course, for as for the Bourgeois we could not quite be expected to take notice of *them* —visited his neighbour. H. E. Madame de Burst received once a week, H. E. Madame de Schnurrbart had her night — the theatre was open twice a week, the Court graciously received once, so that a man's life might in fact be a perfect round of pleasure in the unpretending Pumpernickel way.

That there were feuds in the place, no one can deny. Politics ran very high at Pumpernickel, and parties were very bitter. There was the Strumpff faction and the Lederlung party, the one supported by our Envoy and the other by the French Chargé d'Affaires, M. de Macabau. Indeed it sufficed for our Minister to stand up for Madame Strumpff, who was clearly the greater singer of the two, and had three more notes in her voice than Madame Lederlung her rival — it sufficed, I say, for our Minister to advance *any* opinion to have it instantly contradicted by the French diplomatist.

Everybody in the town was ranged in one or other of these factions. The Lederlung was a prettyish little creature certainly, and her voice (what there was of it,) was very sweet, and there is no doubt that the Strumpff was not in her first youth and beauty, and certainly too stout; when she came on in the last scene of the " Sonnambula" for instance in her night-chemise with a lamp in her hand, and had to go out of the window, and pass over the plank of the mill, it was all she could do to squeeze out of the window, and the plank used to bend and creak again under her weight — but how she poured out the finale of the opera! and with what a burst of feeling she rushed into Elvino's arms — almost fit to smother him! Whereas the little Lederlung — but a truce to this gossip — the fact is, that these two women were the two flags of the French and the English party at Pumpernickel, and the society was divided in its allegiance to those two great nations.

We had on our side the Home Minister, the Master of the Horse, the Duke's Private Secretary, and the Prince's Tutor: whereas of the French party were the Foreign Minister, the Commander-in-Chief's Lady, who had served under Napoleon, and the Hof-Marschall and his wife, who was glad enough to get the fashions from Paris, and always had them and her caps by M. de Macabau's courier. The Secretary of his Chancery was little Grignac, a young fellow, as malicious as Satan, and who made caricatures of Tapeworm in all the albums of the place.

Their head-quarters and table d'hôte were established at the Pariser Hof, the other inn of the town; and though, of course, these gentlemen were obliged to be civil in public, yet they cut at each other with epigrams that were as sharp as razors, as I have seen a couple of wrestlers in Devonshire, lashing at each other's shins, and never showing their agony upon a muscle of their faces. Neither Tapeworm nor Macabau ever sent home a despatch to his government, without a most savage series of attacks upon his rival. For instance, on our side we would write, "The interests of Great Britain in this place, and throughout the whole of Germany, are perilled by the continuance in office of the present French envoy; this man is of a character so infamous that he will stick at no falsehood, or hesitate at no crime, to attain his ends. He poisons the mind of the Court against the English minister, represents the conduct of Great Britain in the most odious and atrocious light, and is unhappily backed by a minister whose ignorance and necessities are as notorious as his influence is fatal." On their side they would say, "M. de Tapeworm continues his system of stupid insular arrogance and vulgar falsehood against the greatest nation in the world. Yesterday he was heard to speak lightly of Her Royal Highness Madame the Duchess of Berri: on a former occasion he insulted the heroic Duke of Angoulême, and dared to insinuate that H. R. H. the Duke of Orleans was conspiring against the august throne of the lilies. His gold is prodigated in every direction which his stupid menaces fail to frighten. By one and the other, he has won over creatures of the Court here, — and, in fine, Pumpernickel will not be quiet, Germany tranquil, France respected, or Europe content, until this poisonous viper be crushed under heel:" and so on. When one side or the other had written any particularly spicy despatch, news of it was sure to slip out.

Before the winter was far advanced it is actually on record that Emmy took a night and received company with great propriety and modesty. She had a French master who complimented her upon the purity of her accent and her facility of learning; the fact is she had learned long ago, and grounded herself subsequently in the grammar so as to be able to teach it to George; and Madame Strumpff came to give her lessons in singing, which she performed so well and with such a true voice that the Major's windows, who had lodgings opposite under the Prime Minister, were always open to hear the lesson. Some of the German ladies, who are very sentimental and simple in their tastes, fell in love with her and began to call her *du* at once. These are trivial details, but they relate to happy times. The Major made himself George's tutor, and read Cæsar and mathematics with him, and they had a German master and rode out of evenings by the side of Emmy's carriage — she was always too timid, and made a dreadful outcry at the slightest disturbance on horseback. So she drove about with one of her dear German friends, and Jos asleep on the back-seat of the barouche.

He was becoming very sweet upon the Gräfinn Fanny de Butterbrod, a very gentle tender-hearted and unassuming young creature, a Canoness and Countess in her own right, but with scarcely ten pounds per year to her fortune, and Fanny for her part declared that to be Amelia's sister was the greatest delight that heaven could bestow on her, and Jos might have put a Countess's shield and coronet by the side of his own arms on his carriage and forks; when — when events occurred, and those grand fêtes given upon the marriage of the He-

reditary Prince of Pumpernickel with the lovely Princess
Amelia of Humbourg-Schlippenschloppen took place.

At this festival the magnificence displayed was such
as had not been known in the little German place since
the days of the prodigal Victor XIV. All the neighbouring Princes, Princesses, and Grandees were invited to
the feast. Beds rose to half-a-crown per night in Pumpernickel, and the army was exhausted in providing
guards of honour for the Highnesses, Serenities, and Excellencies, who arrived from all quarters. The Princess
was married by proxy, at her father's residence, by the
Count de Schlüsselback. Snuff-boxes were given away
in profusion (as we learned from the Court jeweller, who
sold and afterwards bought them again), and bushels of
the Order of Saint Michael of Pumpernickel were sent
to the nobles of the Court, while hampers of the cordons
and decorations of the Wheel of St. Catherine of Schlip-
penschloppen were brought to ours. The French envoy got both. " He is covered with ribbons like a prize
cart-horse," Tapeworm said, who was not allowed by
the rules of his service to take any decorations: " Let
him have the cordons; but with whom is the victory?"
The fact is, it was a triumph of British diplomacy: the
French party having proposed and tried their utmost to
carry a marriage with a Princess of the house of Potz-
tausend-Donnerwetter, whom, as a matter of course, we
opposed.

Everybody was asked to the fêtes of the marriage.
Garlands and triumphal arches were hung across the
road to welcome the young bride. The great Saint
Michael's Fountain ran with uncommonly sour wine,
while that in the Artillery Place frothed with beer. The
great waters played; and poles were put up in the park
and gardens for the happy peasantry, which they might
climb at their leisure, carrying off watches, silver forks,

prize sausages hung with pink ribbon, &c., at the top. Georgy got one, wrenching it off, having swarmed up the pole to the delight of the spectators, and sliding down with the rapidity of a fall of water. But it was for the glory's sake merely. The boy gave the sausage to a peasant, who had very nearly seized it, and stood at the foot of the mast, blubbering, because he was unsuccessful.

At the French Chancellerie they had six more lampions in their illumination than ours had; but our transparency, which represented the young Couple advancing, and Discord flying away, with the most ludicrous likeness to the French ambassador, beat the French picture hollow; and I have no doubt got Tapeworm the advancement and the Cross of the Bath, which he subsequently attained.

Crowds of foreigners arrived for the fêtes: and of English of course. Besides the Court balls, public balls were given at the Town Hall and the Redoute, and in the former place there was a room for *trente-et-quarante* and *roulette* established, for the week of the festivities only, and by one of the great German companies from Ems or Aix-la-Chapelle. The officers or inhabitants of the town were not allowed to play at these games, but strangers, peasants, ladies were admitted, and any one who chose to lose or win money.

That little scapegrace Georgy Osborne amongst others, whose pockets were always full of dollars, and whose relations were away at the grand festival of the Court, came to the Stadthaus ball in company of his uncle's courier, Mr. Kirsch, and having only peeped into a play-room at Baden Baden when he hung on Dobbin's arm, and where, of course, he was not permitted to gamble, came eagerly to this part of the entertainment, and hankered round the tables where the croupiers and the punters were at work. Women were playing; they were masked, some of them; this license was allowed in these wild times of carnival.

A woman with light hair, in a low dress, by no means so fresh as it had been, and with a black mask on, through the eyelets of which her eyes twinkled strangely, was seated at one of the roulette-tables with a card and a pin, and a couple of florins before her. As the croupier called out the colour and number, she pricked on the card with great care and regularity, and only ventured her money on the colours after the red or black had come up a certain number of times. It was strange to look at her.

But in spite of her care and assiduity she guessed wrong, and the last two florins followed each other under the croupier's rake, as he cried out with his inexorable voice, the winning colour and number. She gave a sigh, a shrug with her shoulders, which were already too much out of her gown, and dashing the pin through the card on to the table, sat thrumming it for a while. Then she looked round her, and saw Georgy's honest face staring at the scene. The little scamp! what business had he to be there?

When she saw the boy, at whose face she looked hard through her shining eyes and mask, she said, "*Monsieur n'est pas joueur?*"

"*Non, Madame*," said the boy: but she must have known, from his accent, of what country he was, for she answered him with a slight foreign tone. "You have nevare played — will you do me a littl' favor?"

"What is it?" said Georgy, blushing again. Mr. Kirsch was at work for his part at the *rouge et noir*, and did not see his young master.

"Play this for me, if you please, put it on any number, any number." And she took from her bosom a purse, and out of it a gold piece, the only coin there, and she put it into George's hand. The boy laughed, and did as he was bid.

The number came up sure enough. There is a power that arranges that, they say, for beginners.

"Thank you," said she, pulling the money towards her; "thank you. What is your name?"

"My name's Osborne," said Georgy, and was fingering in his own pockets for dollars, and just about to make a trial, when the Major, in his uniform, and Jos, *en Marquis*, from the Court ball, made their appearance. Other people finding the entertainment stupid, and preferring the fun at the Stadthaus, had quitted the Palace ball earlier; but it is probable the Major and Jos had gone home and found the boy's absence, for the former instantly went up to him, and taking him by the shoulder, pulled him briskly back from the place of temptation. Then, looking round the room, he saw Kirsch employed as we have said, and going up to him, asked how he dared to bring Mr. George to such a place.

"*Laissez-moi tranquille*," said Mr. Kirsch, very much excited by play and wine. "*Il faut s'amuser, parbleu. Je ne suis pas au service de Monsieur.*"

Seeing his condition the Major did not choose to argue with the man; but contented himself with drawing away George, and asking Jos if he would come away. He was standing close by the lady in the mask, who was playing with pretty good luck now; and looking on much interested at the game.

"Hadn't you better come, Jos," the Major said, "with George and me?"

"I'll stop and go home with that rascal, Kirsch," Jos said; and for the same reason of modesty, which he thought ought to be preserved before the boy, Dobbin did not care to remonstrate with Jos, but left him and walked home with Georgy.

"Did you play?" asked the Major, when they were out, and on their way home.

The boy said "No."

"Give me your word of honour as a gentleman, that you never will."

"Why?" said the boy: "It seems very good fun." And, in a very eloquent and impressive manner, the Major showed him why he shouldn't, and would have enforced his precepts by the example of Georgy's own father, had he liked to say anything that should reflect on the other's memory. When he had housed him he went to bed, and saw his light, in the little room outside of Amelia's, presently disappear. Amelia's followed half an hour afterwards. I don't know what made the Major note it so accurately.

Jos, however, remained behind over the play-table; he was no gambler, but not averse to the little excitement of the sport now and then; and he had some Napoleons chinking in the embroidered pockets of his court waistcoat. He put down one over the fair shoulder of the little gambler before him, and they won. She made a little movement to make room for him by her side, and just took the skirt of her gown from a vacant chair there.

"Come and give me good luck," she said, still in a foreign accent, quite different from that frank and perfectly English "Thank you," with which she had saluted George's *coup* in her favour. The portly gentleman, looking round to see that nobody of rank observed him, sat down; he muttered — "Ah, really, well now, God bless my soul. I'm very fortunate; I'm sure to give you good fortune, and other words of compliment and confusion."

"Do you play much?" the foreign mask said.

"I put a Nap or two down," said Jos, with a superb air, flinging down a gold piece.

"Yes; ay nap after dinner," said the mask, archly. But Jos looking frightened, she continued, in her pretty French accent, "You do not play to win. No more do I. I play to forget, but I cannot. I cannot forget old times, Monsieur. Your little nephew is the image of his father; and you—you are not changed—but yes, you are. Everybody changes, everybody forgets; nobody has any heart."

"Good God, who is it?" asked Jos in a flutter.

"Can't you guess, Joseph Sedley?" said the little woman, in a sad voice, and undoing her mask, she looked at him. "You have forgotten me."

"Good Heavens! Mrs. Crawley!" gasped out Jos.

"Rebecca," said the other, putting her hand on his; but she followed the game still, all the time she was looking at him.

"I am stopping at the Elephant," she continued. "Ask for Madame de Raudon. I saw my dear Amelia to-day; how pretty she looked, and how happy! So do you! Everybody but me, who am wretched, Joseph Sedley." And she put her money over from the red to the black, as if by a chance movement of her hand, and while she was wiping her eyes with a pocket-handkerchief fringed with torn lace.

The red came up again, and she lost the whole of that stake. "Come away," she said. "Come with me a little—we are old friends, are we not, dear Mr. Sedley?"

And Mr. Kirsch having lost all his money by this time, followed his master out into the moonlight, where the illuminations were winking out, and the transparency over our mission was scarcely visible.

CHAPTER X

A VAGABOND CHAPTER

WE must pass over a part of Mrs. Rebecca Crawley's biography with that lightness and delicacy which the world demands — the moral world, that has, perhaps, no particular objection to vice, but an insuperable repugnance to hearing vice called by its proper name. There are things we do and know perfectly well in Vanity Fair, though we never speak of them: as the Ahrimanians worship the devil, but don't mention him: and a polite public will no more bear to read an authentic description of vice than a truly-refined English or American female will permit the word breeches to be pronounced in her chaste hearing. And yet, Madam, both are walking the world before our faces every day, without much shocking us. If you were to blush every time they went by, what complexions you would have! It is only when their naughty names are called out that your modesty has any occasion to show alarm or sense of outrage, and it has been the wish of the present writer, all through this story, deferentially to submit to the fashion at present prevailing, and only to hint at the existence of wickedness in a light, easy, and agreeable manner, so that nobody's fine feelings may be offended. I defy any one to say that our Becky, who has certainly some vices, has not been presented to the public in a perfectly genteel and inoffensive manner. In describing this syren, sing-

ing and smiling, coaxing and cajoling, the author, with
modest pride, asks his readers all round, has he once
forgotten the laws of politeness, and showed the monster's hideous tail above water? No! Those who like
may peep down under waves that are pretty transparent, and see it writhing and twirling, diabolically hideous and slimy, flapping amongst bones, or curling round
corpses; but above the water-line, I ask, has not everything been proper, agreeable, and decorous, and has any
the most squeamish immoralist in Vanity Fair a right to
cry fie? When, however, the syren disappears and dives
below, down among the dead men, the water of course
grows turbid over her, and it is labour lost to look into
it ever so curiously. They look pretty enough when
they sit upon a rock, twanging their harps and combing
their hair, and sing, and beckon to you to come and
hold the looking-glass; but when they sink into their
native element, depend on it those mermaids are about
no good, and we had best not examine the fiendish ma-
rine cannibals, revelling and feasting on their wretched
pickled victims. And so, when Becky is out of the
way, be sure that she is not particularly well employed,
and that the less that is said about her doings is in fact
the better.

If we were to give a full account of her proceedings
during a couple of years that followed after the Curzon
Street catastrophe, there might be some reason for people to say this book was improper. The actions of very
vain, heartless, pleasure-seeking people are very often
improper (as are many of yours, my friend with the
grave face and spotless reputation; — but that is merely
by the way); and what are those of a woman without
faith — or love — or character? And I am inclined to
think that there was a period in Mrs. Becky's life, when
she was seized, not by remorse, but by a kind of de-

spair, and absolutely neglected her person, and did not even care for her reputation.

This *abattement* and degradation did not take place all at once: it was brought about by degrees, after her calamity, and after many struggles to keep up — as a man who goes overboard hangs on to a spar whilst any hope is left, and then flings it away and goes down, when he finds that struggling is in vain.

She lingered about London whilst her husband was making preparations for his departure to his seat of government: and it is believed made more than one attempt to see her brother-in-law, Sir Pitt Crawley, and to work upon his feelings, which she had almost enlisted in her favour. As Sir Pitt and Mr. Wenham were walking down to the House of Commons, the latter spied Mrs. Rawdon in a black veil, and lurking near the palace of the legislature. She sneaked away when her eyes met those of Wenham, and indeed never succeeded in her designs upon the Baronet.

Probably Lady Jane interposed. I have heard that she quite astonished her husband by the spirit which she exhibited in this quarrel, and her determination to disown Mrs. Becky. Of her own movement, she invited Rawdon to come and stop in Gaunt Street until his departure for Coventry Island, knowing that with him for a guard Mrs. Becky would not try to force her door: and she looked curiously at the superscriptions of all the letters which arrived for Sir Pitt, lest he and his sister-in-law should be corresponding. Not but that Rebecca could have written had she a mind: but she did not try to see or to write to Pitt at his own house, and after one or two attempts consented to his demand that the correspondence regarding her conjugal differences should be carried on by lawyers only.

The fact was, that Pitt's mind had been poisoned

against her. A short time after Lord Steyne's accident
Wenham had been with the Baronet; and given him
such a biography of Mrs. Becky as had astonished the
member for Queen's Crawley. He knew everything
regarding her: who her father was; in what year her
mother danced at the Opera; what had been her previous history, and what her conduct during her married
life: — as I have no doubt that the greater part of the
story was false and dictated by interested malevolence,
it shall not be repeated here. But Becky was left with a
sad sad reputation in the esteem of a country gentleman
and relative who had been once rather partial to her.

The revenues of the Governor of Coventry Island are
not large. A part of them were set aside by his Excellency for the payment of certain outstanding debts and
liabilities, the charges incident on his high situation
required considerable expense; finally, it was found
that he could not spare to his wife more than three
hundred pounds a year, which he proposed to pay
to her on an undertaking that she would never trouble
him. Otherwise: scandal, separation, Doctors' Commons would ensue. But it was Mr. Wenham's business,
Lord Steyne's business, Rawdon's, everybody's—to get
her out of the country, and hush up a most disagreeable
affair.

She was probably so much occupied in arranging
these affairs of business with her husband's lawyers, that
she forgot to take any step whatever about her son, the
little Rawdon, and did not even once propose to go and
see him. That young gentleman was consigned to the
entire guardianship of his aunt and uncle, the former of
whom had always possessed a great share of the child's
affection. His mamma wrote him a neat letter from
Boulogne when she quitted England, in which she re-
quested him to mind his book, and said she was going

to take a Continental tour, during which she would have the pleasure of writing to him again. But she never did for a year afterwards, and not, indeed, until Sir Pitt's only boy, always sickly, died of hooping-cough and measles; — then Rawdon's mamma wrote the most affectionate composition to her darling son, who was made heir of Queen's Crawley by this accident, and drawn more closely than ever to the kind lady, whose tender heart had already adopted him. Rawdon Crawley, then grown a tall, fine lad, blushed when he got the letter. "Oh, Aunt Jane, you are my mother!" he said; "and not — and not that one." But he wrote back a kind and respectful letter to Mrs. Rebecca, then living at a boarding-house at Florence. But we are advancing matters.

Our darling Becky's first flight was not very far. She perched upon the French coast at Boulogne, that refuge of so much exiled English innocence; and there lived in rather a genteel, widowed manner, with a *femme de chambre* and a couple of rooms, at an hotel. She dined at the *table d'hôte*, where people thought her very pleasant, and where she entertained her neighbours by stories of her brother, Sir Pitt, and her great London acquaintance; talking that easy, fashionable slipslop, which has so much effect upon certain folks of small breeding. She passed with many of them for a person of importance; she gave little tea-parties in her private room, and shared in the innocent amusements of the place, — in sea-bathing, and in jaunts in open carriages, in strolls on the sands, and in visits to the play. Mrs. Burjoice, the printer's lady, who was boarding with her family at the hotel for the summer, and to whom her Burjoice came of a Saturday and Sunday, voted her charming, until that little rogue of a Burjoice began to pay her too much attention. But there was nothing in the story, only that Becky was always affable, easy, and good-natured — and with men especially.

Numbers of people were going abroad as usual at the end of the season, and Becky had plenty of opportunities of finding out by the behaviour of her acquaintances of the great London world the opinion of "society" as regarded her conduct. One day it was Lady Partlet and her daughters whom Becky confronted as she was walking modestly on Boulogne pier, the cliffs of Albion shining in the distance across the deep blue sea. Lady Partlet marshalled all her daughters round her with a sweep of her parasol, and retreated from the pier darting savage glances at poor little Becky who stood alone there.

On another day the packet came in. It had been blowing fresh, and it always suited Becky's humour to see the droll woe-begone faces of the people as they emerged from the boat. Lady Slingstone happened to be on board this day. Her ladyship had been exceedingly ill in her carriage, and was greatly exhausted and scarcely fit to walk up the plank from the ship to the pier. But all her energies rallied the instant she saw Becky smiling roguishly under a pink bonnet: and giving her a glance of scorn, such as would have shrivelled up most women, she walked into the Custom House quite unsupported. Becky only laughed: but I don't think she liked it. She felt she was alone, quite alone: and the far-off shining cliffs of England were impassable to her.

The behaviour of the men had undergone too I don't know what change. Grinstone showed his teeth and laughed in her face with a familiarity that was not pleasant. Little Bob Suckling, who was cap in hand to her three months before, and would walk a mile in the rain to see for her carriage in the line at Gaunt House, was

talking to Fitzoof of the Guards (Lord Heehaw's son)
one day upon the jetty, as Becky took her walk there.
Little Bobby nodded to her over his shoulder without
moving his hat, and continued his conversation with the
heir of Heehaw. Tom Raikes tried to walk into her sitting-room at the inn with a cigar in his mouth; but she
closed the door upon him and would have locked it
only that his fingers were inside. She began to feel
that she was very lonely indeed. "If *he'd* been here,"
she said, "those cowards would never have dared to insult me." She thought about "him" with great sadness, and perhaps longing — about his honest, stupid,
constant kindness and fidelity: his never-ceasing obedience; his good humour; his bravery and courage.
Very likely she cried, for she was particularly lively,
and had put on a little extra rouge when she came
down to dinner.

She rouged regularly now: and — and her maid got
Cognac for her besides that which was charged in the
hotel bill.

Perhaps the insults of the men were not, however, so
intolerable to her as the sympathy of certain women.
Mrs. Crackenbury and Mrs. Washington White passed
through Boulogne on their way to Switzerland. (The
party were protected by Colonel Horner, young Beaumoris, and of course old Crackenbury, and Mrs. White's
little girl.) *They* did not avoid her. They giggled,
cackled, tattled, condoled, consoled, and patronised her
until they drove her almost wild with rage. To be patronised by *them!* she thought, as they went away simpering after kissing her. And she heard Beaumoris's
laugh ringing on the stair, and knew quite well how to
interpret his hilarity.

It was after this visit that Becky, who had paid her
weekly bills, Becky who had made herself agreeable to

every body in the house, who smiled at the landlady, called the waiters "Monsieur," and paid the chambermaids in politeness and apologies, what far more than compensated for a little niggardliness in point of money (of which Becky never was free), that Becky, we say, received a notice to quit from the landlord, who had been told by some one that she was quite an unfit person to have at his hotel, where English ladies would not sit down with her. And she was forced to fly into lodgings, of which the dulness and solitude were most wearisome to her.

Still she held up, in spite of these rebuffs, and tried to make a character for herself, and conquer scandal. She went to church very regularly, and sang louder than anybody there. She took up the cause of the widows of the shipwrecked fishermen, and gave work and drawings for the Quashyboo Mission; she subscribed to the Assembly and *would n't* waltz. In a word, she did everything that was respectable, and that is why we dwell upon this part of her career with more fondness than upon subsequent parts of her history, which are not so pleasant. She saw people avoiding her, and still laboriously smiled upon them; you never could suppose from her countenance what pangs of humiliation she might be enduring inwardly.

Her history was after all a mystery. Parties were divided about her. Some people, who took the trouble to busy themselves in the matter, said that she was the criminal; whilst others vowed that she was as innocent as a lamb, and that her odious husband was in fault. She won over a good many by bursting into tears about her boy, and exhibiting the most frantic grief when his name was mentioned, or she saw anybody like him. She gained good Mrs. Alderney's heart in that way, who was rather the Queen of British Boulogne, and gave the most dinners and balls of all the residents there, by weeping when Master Alderney came from Dr. Swishtail's academy to pass his holidays with his mother. " He and her Rawdon were of the same age, and *so* like," Becky said, in a voice choking with agony; whereas there was five years' difference between the boys' ages, and no more likeness between them than between, my respected reader and his humble servant. Wenham, when he was going abroad, on his way to Kissengen to join Lord Steyne, enlightened Mrs. Alderney on this point, and told her how he was much more able to describe little Rawdon than his mamma, who notoriously hated him, and never saw him; how he was thirteen years old, while little Alderney was but nine; fair, while the other darling was dark, — in a word, caused the lady in question to repent of her good humour.

Whenever Becky made a little circle for herself with incredible toils and labour, somebody came and swept it down rudely, and she had all her work to begin over again. It was very hard: very hard; lonely and disheartening.

There was Mrs. Newbright, who took her up for some time, attracted by the sweetness of her singing at church, and by her proper views upon serious subjects, concerning which in former days, at Queen's Crawley, Mrs. Becky had had a good deal of instruction. — Well, she not only took tracts, but she read them. She worked flannel petticoats for the Quashyboos — cotton nightcaps for the Cocoanut Indians — painted handscreens for the conversion of the Pope and the Jews — sate under Mr. Rowls on Wednesdays, Mr. Huggleton on Thursdays, attended two Sunday services at church, besides Mr. Bawler, the Darbyite, in the evening, and all in vain. Mrs. Newbright had occasion to correspond with the Countess of Southdown about the Warmingpan

Fund for the Feejee Islanders (for the management of which admirable charity both these ladies formed part of a female committee), and having mentioned her "sweet friend," Mrs. Rawdon Crawley, the Dowager Countess wrote back such a letter regarding Becky, with such particulars, hints, facts, falsehoods, and general comminations, that intimacy between Mrs. Newbright and Mrs. Crawley ceased forthwith : and all the serious world of Tours, where this misfortune took place, immediately parted company with the reprobate. Those who know the English Colonies abroad know that we carry with us our pride, pills, prejudices, Harvey-sauces, cayenne-peppers, and other Lares, making a little Britain wherever we settle down.

From one colony to another Becky fled uneasily. From Boulogne to Dieppe, from Dieppe to Caen, from Caen to Tours — trying with all her might to be respectable, and alas! always found out some day or other, and pecked out of the cage by the real daws.

Mrs. Hook Eagles took her up at one of these places : — a woman without a blemish in her character, and a house in Portman-square. She was staying at the hotel at Dieppe, whither Becky fled, and they made each other's acquaintance first at sea, where they were swimming together, and subsequently at the *table d'hôte* of the hotel. Mrs. Eagles had heard, — who indeed had not? — some of the scandal of the Steyne affair; but after a conversation with Becky, she pronounced that Mrs. Crawley was an angel, her husband a ruffian, Lord Steyne an unprincipled wretch, as everybody knew, and the whole case against Mrs. Crawley, an infamous and wicked conspiracy of that rascal Wenham. "If you were a man of any spirit, Mr. Eagles, you would box the wretch's ears the next time you see him at the Club," she said to her husband. But Eagles was only a quiet old gentleman, husband to Mrs. Eagles, with a taste for geology, and not tall enough to reach anybody's ears.

The Eagles then patronised Mrs. Rawdon, took her to live with her at her own house at Paris, quarrelled with the ambassador's wife because she would not receive her *protégée*, and did all that lay in woman's power to keep Becky straight in the paths of virtue and good repute.

Becky was very respectable and orderly at first, but the life of humdrum virtue grew utterly tedious to her before long. It was the same routine every day, the same dulness and comfort, the same drive over the same stupid Bois de Boulogne, the same company of an evening, the same Blair's Sermon of a Sunday night — the same opera always being acted over and over again : Becky was dying of weariness, when, luckily for her, young Mr. Eagles came from Cambridge, and his mother, seeing the impression which her little friend made upon him, straightway gave Becky warning.

Then she tried keeping house with a female friend; then the double *ménage* began to quarrel and get into debt. Then she determined upon a boarding-house existence, and lived for some time at that famous mansion kept by Madame de Saint Amour, in the Rue Royale, at Paris, where she began exercising her graces and fascinations upon the shabby dandies and fly-blown beauties who frequented her landlady's *salons*. Becky loved society, and, indeed, could no more exist without it than an opium-eater without his dram, and she was happy enough at the period of her boarding-house life. " The women here are as amusing as those in May Fair," she told an old London friend who met her — " only, their dresses are not quite so fresh. The men wear cleaned gloves, and are sad rogues, certainly, but they are not worse than Jack This, and Tom That. The mistress of the house is a little vulgar, but I don't think she is so vulgar as Lady —— " and here she named the name of a great leader of fashion that I would die rather than reveal. In fact, when you saw Madame de Saint Amour's rooms lighted up of a night, men with *plaques* and *cordons* at the *écarté* tables, and the women at a little distance, you might fancy yourself for a while in good society, and that Madame was a real Countess. Many people did so fancy: and Becky was for a while one of the most dashing ladies of the Countess's *salons*.

But it is probable that her old creditors of 1815 found her out and caused her to leave Paris, for the poor little woman was forced to fly from the city rather suddenly; and went thence to Brussels.

How well she remembered the place! She grinned as she looked up at the little *entresol* which she had occupied, and thought of the Bareacres family, bawling for horses and flight, as their carriage stood in the *porte-cochère* of the hotel. She went to Waterloo and to Lacken, where George Osborne's monument much struck her. She made a little sketch of it. " That poor Cupid!" she said; "how dreadfully he was in love with me, and what a fool he was! I wonder whether little Emmy is alive. It was a good little creature: and that fat brother of hers. I have his funny fat picture still among my papers. They were kind simple people."

At Brussels Becky arrived, recommended by Madame de Saint Amour to her friend, Madame la Comtesse de Borodino, widow of Napoleon's General, the famous Count de Borodino, who was left with no resource by the deceased hero but that of a *table-d'hôte* and an *écarté* table. Second-rate dandies and *roués*, widow-ladies who always have a law-suit, and very simple English folks, who fancy they see "Continental society" at these houses, put down their money, or ate their meals, at Madame de Borodino's tables. The gallant young fellows treated the company round to champagne at the *table-d'hôte*, rode out with the women, or hired horses on country excursions, clubbed money to take boxes at the play or the Opera, betted over the fair shoulders of the ladies at the *écarté* tables, and wrote home to their parents, in Devonshire, about their felicitous introduction to foreign society.

Here, as at Paris, Becky was a boarding-house queen: and ruled in select *pensions*. She never refused the champagne, or the bouquets, or the drives into the country, or the private boxes; but what she preferred was the *écarté* at night, — and she played audaciously. First she played only for a little, then for five-franc pieces, then for Napoleons, then for notes: then she would not be able to pay her month's *pension:* then she borrowed from the young gentlemen: then she got into cash again, and bullied Madame de Borodino, whom she had coaxed and wheedled before: then she was playing for ten sous at a time, and in a dire state of poverty: then her quarter's allowance would come in, and she would pay off Madame de Borodino's score: and would once more take the cards against Monsieur de Rossignol, or the Chevalier de Raff.

When Becky left Brussels, the sad truth is, that she owed three months' *pension* to Madame de Borodino, of which fact, and of the gambling, and of the drinking, and of the going down on her knees to the Reverend Mr. Muff, Ministre Anglican, and borrowing money of him, and of her coaxing and flirting with Milor Noodle, son of Sir Noodle, pupil of the Rev. Mr. Muff, whom she used to take into her private room, and of whom she

won large sums at *écarté* — of which fact, I say, and of a
hundred of her other knaveries, the Countess de Borodino informs every English person who stops at her
establishment, and announces that Madame Rawdon
was no better than a *vipère*.

So our little wanderer went about setting up her tent
in various cities of Europe, as restless as Ulysses or
Bampfylde Moore Carew. Her taste for disrespecta-
bility grew more and more remarkable. She became a
perfect Bohemian ere long, herding with people whom
it would make your hair stand on end to meet.

There is no town of any mark in Europe but it has
its little colony of English raffs — men whose names
Mr. Hemp the officer reads out periodically at the
Sheriffs' Court — young gentlemen of very good family
often, only that the latter disowns them; frequenters of
billiard-rooms and estaminets, patrons of foreign races
and gaming-tables. They people the debtors' prisons
— they drink and swagger — they fight and brawl —
they run away without paying — they have duels with
French and German officers — they cheat Mr. Spooney
at *écarté* — they get the money, and drive off to Baden
in magnificent britzkas — they try their infallible martin-
gale, and lurk about the tables with empty pockets,
shabby bullies, penniless bucks, until they can swindle a
Jew banker with a sham bill of exchange, or find another
Mr. Spooney to rob. The alternations of splendour
and misery which these people undergo are very queer
to view. Their life must be one of great excitement.
Becky — must it be owned? — took to this life, and
took to it not unkindly. She went about from town to
town among these Bohemians. The lucky Mrs. Rawdon
was known at every play-table in Germany. She and
Madame de Cruchecassée kept house at Florence
together. It is said she was ordered out of Munich;

and my friend Mr. Frederick Pigeon avers that it was at her house at Lausanne that he was hocussed at supper and lost eight hundred pounds to Major Loder and the Honourable Mr. Deuceace. We are bound, you see, to give some account of Becky's biography; but of this part, the less, perhaps, that is said the better.

They say, that when Mrs. Crawley was particularly down on her luck, she gave concerts and lessons in music here and there. There was a Madame de Raudon, who certainly had a *matinée musicale* at Wildbad, accompanied by Herr Spoff, premier pianist to the Hospodar of Wallachia, and my little friend Mr. Eaves, who knew everybody, and had travelled everywhere, always used to declare that he was at Strasburg in the year 1830, when a certain Madame Rebecque made her appearance in the opera of the "Dame Blanche," giving occasion to a furious row in the theatre there. She was hissed off the stage by the audience, partly from her own incompetency, but chiefly from the ill-advised sympathy of some persons in the *parquet*, (where the officers of the garrison had their admissions); and Eaves was certain that the unfortunate *débutante* in question was no other than Mrs. Rawdon Crawley.

She was, in fact, no better than a vagabond upon this earth. When she got her money she gambled; when she had gambled it she was put to shifts to live; who knows how or by what means she succeeded? It is said that she was once seen at St. Petersburg, but was summarily dismissed from that capital by the police, so that there cannot be any possibility of truth in the report that she was a Russian spy at Töplitz and Vienna afterwards. I have even been informed, that at Paris she discovered a relation of her own, no less a person than her maternal grandmother, who was not by any means a Montmorenci, but a hideous old box-opener at a theatre on the Boulevards. The meeting between them, of which other persons, as it is hinted elsewhere, seem to have been acquainted, must have been a very affecting interview. The present historian can give no certain details regarding the event.

It happened at Rome once, that Mrs. de Rawdon's half-year's salary had just been paid into the principal bankers there, and, as everybody who had a balance of above five hundred scudi was invited to the balls which this prince of merchants gave during the winter, Becky had the honour of a card, and appeared at one of the Prince and Princess Polonia's splendid evening entertainments. The Princess was of the family of Pompili, lineally descended from the second king of Rome, and Egeria of the house of Olympus, while the Prince's grandfather, Alessandro Polonia, sold wash-balls, essences, tobacco, and pocket-handkerchiefs, ran errands for gentlemen, and lent money in a small way. All the great company in Rome thronged to his saloons — Princes, Dukes, Ambassadors, artists, fiddlers, monsignori, young bears with their leaders — every rank and condition of man. His halls blazed with light and magnificence; were resplendent with gilt frames (containing pictures), and dubious antiques: and the enormous gilt crown and arms of the princely owner, a gold mushroom on a crimson field (the colour of the pocket-handkerchiefs which he sold), and the silver fountain of the Pompili family shone all over the roof, doors, and panels of the house, and over the grand velvet baldaquins prepared to receive Popes and Emperors.

So Becky, who had arrived in the diligence from Florence, and was lodged at an inn in a very modest way, got a card for Prince Polonia's entertainment, and her maid dressed her with unusual care, and she went to this fine ball leaning on the arm of Major Loder, with whom she happened to be travelling at the time — (the same man who shot Prince Ravoli at Naples the next year, and was caned by Sir John Buckskin for carrying four kings in his hat besides those which he used in playing at *écarté*) — and this pair went into the rooms together, and Becky saw a number of old faces which she remembered in happier days, when she was not innocent, but not found out. Major Loder knew a great number of foreigners, keen-looking whiskered men with dirty striped ribbons in their button-holes, and a very small display of linen; but his own countrymen, it might be remarked, eschewed the Major. Becky, too, knew some ladies here and there — French widows, dubious Italian countesses, whose husbands had treated them ill — faugh — what shall we say, we who have moved among some of the finest company of Vanity Fair, of this refuse and sediment of rascals? If we play, let it be with clean cards, and not with this dirty pack. But every man who has formed one of the innumerable army of travellers has seen these marauding irregulars hanging on, like Nym and Pistol, to the main force; wearing the king's colours, and boasting of his commission, but pillaging for themselves, and occasionally gibbeted by the road-side.

Well, she was hanging on the arm of Major Loder and they went through the rooms together, and drank a great quantity of champagne at the buffet, where the people, and especially the Major's irregular corps, struggled furiously for refreshments, of which when the pair had had enough, they pushed on until they reached the Duchess's own pink velvet saloon, at the end of the suite of apartments (where the statue of the Venus is, and the great Venice looking-glasses, framed in silver,) and where the princely family were entertaining their most distinguished guests at a round table at supper.

It was just such a little select banquet as that of which
Becky recollected that she had partaken at Lord Steyne's
— and there he sat at Polonia's table, and she saw him.

The scar cut by the diamond on his white, bald,
shining forehead, made a burning red mark; his red
whiskers were dyed of a purple hue, which made his
pale face look still paler. He wore his collar and orders,
his blue ribbon and garter. He was a greater prince
than any there, though there was a reigning duke and a
royal highness, with their princesses, and near his lordship was seated the beautiful Countess of Belladonna,
née de Glandier, whose husband (the Count Paolo della
Belladonna) so well known for his brilliant entomological
collections, had been long absent on a mission to the
Emperor of Morocco.

When Becky beheld that familiar and illustrious face,
how vulgar all of a sudden did Major Loder appear to
her, and how that odious Captain Rook did smell of
tobacco! In one instant she reassumed her fine-lady-
ship, and tried to look and feel as if she was in May
Fair once more. "That woman looks stupid and ill-
humoured," she thought; "I am sure she can't amuse
him. No, he must be bored by her — he never was by
me." A hundred such touching hopes, fears, and memories palpitated in her little heart, as she looked with her
brightest eyes (the rouge which she wore up to her eyelids made them twinkle) towards the great nobleman.
Of a Star and Garter night Lord Steyne used also to
put on his grandest manner, and to look and speak like
a great prince, as he was. Becky admired him smiling
sumptuously, easy, lofty, and stately. Ah, *bon dieu*,
what a pleasant companion he was, what a brilliant wit,
what a rich fund of talk, what a grand manner! — and
she had exchanged this for Major Loder, reeking of
cigars and brandy-and-water, and Captain Rook with

his horse-jockey jokes and prize-ring slang, and their
like. "I wonder whether he will know me," she
thought. Lord Steyne was talking and laughing with
a great and illustrious lady at his side, when he looked
up and saw Becky.

She was all over in a flutter as their eyes met, and
she put on the very best smile she could muster, and
dropped him a little, timid, imploring curtsey. He
stared aghast at her for a minute, as Macbeth might
on beholding Banquo's sudden appearance at his ball-
supper; and remained looking at her with open mouth,
when that horrid Major Loder pulled her away.

"Come away into the supper-room, Mrs. R.," was that
gentleman's remark: "seeing these nobs grubbing away
has made me peckish too. Let's go and try the old
governor's champagne." Becky thought the Major had
had a great deal too much already.

The day after she went to walk on the Pincian Hill —
the Hyde Park of the Roman idlers — possibly in hopes
to have another sight of Lord Steyne. But she met
another acquaintance there: it was Mr. Fiche, his lordship's confidential man, who came up nodding to her
rather familiarly, and putting a finger to his hat. "I
knew that Madame was here," he said; "I followed her
from her hotel. I have some advice to give Madame."

"From the Marquis of Steyne?" Becky asked, resum-
ing as much of her dignity as she could muster, and not
a little agitated by hope and expectation.

"No," said the valet; "it is from me. Rome is very
unwholesome."

"Not at this season, Monsieur Fiche, — not till after
Easter."

"I tell Madame it is unwholesome now. There is always malaria for some people. That cursed marsh wind
kills many at all seasons. Look, Madame Crawley, you

were always *bon enfant*, and I have an interest in you
parole d'honneur. Be warned. Go away from Rome, I
tell you — or you will be ill and die."

Becky laughed, though in rage and fury. "What!
assassinate poor little me?" she said. "How romantic.
Does my lord carry bravos for couriers, and stilettos in
the fourgons? Bah! I will stay, if but to plague him.
I have those who will defend me whilst I am here."

It was Monsieur Fiche's turn to laugh now. "Defend
you," he said, "and who? The Major, the Captain, any
one of those gambling men whom Madame sees, would
take her life for a hundred Louis. We know things
about Major Loder (he is no more a Major than I am
my Lord the Marquis) which would send him to the
galleys or worse. We know everything, and have friends
everywhere. We know whom you saw at Paris, and
what relations you found there. Yes, Madame may
stare, but we do. How was it that no minister on the
Continent would receive Madame? She has offended
somebody: who never forgives — whose rage redoubled
when he saw you. He was like a madman last night
when he came home. Madame de Belladonna made
him a scene about you, and fired off in one of her
furies."

"O, it was Madame de Belladonna, was it?" Becky
said, relieved a little, for the information she had just
got had scared her.

"No — she does not matter — she is always jealous.
I tell you it was Monseigneur. You did wrong to show
yourself to him. And if you stay here you will repent
it. Mark my words. Go. Here is my lord's carriage"
— and seizing Becky's arm, he rushed down an alley of
the garden as Lord Steyne's barouche, blazing with
heraldic devices, came whirling along the avenue, borne
by the almost priceless horses, and bearing Madame de

Belladonna lolling on the cushions, dark, sulky, and blooming, a King Charles in her lap, a white parasol swaying over her head, and old Steyne stretched at her side with a livid face and ghastly eyes. Hate, or anger, or desire, caused them to brighten now and then still; but ordinarily, they gave no light, and seemed tired of looking out on a world of which almost all the pleasure and all the best beauty had palled upon the worn-out wicked old man.

"Monseigneur has never recovered the shock of that night, never," Monsieur Fiche whispered to Mrs. Crawley as the carriage flashed by, and she peeped out at it from behind the shrubs that hid her. "That was a consolation at any rate," Becky thought.

Whether my lord really had murderous intentions towards Mrs. Becky as Monsieur Fiche said — (since Monseigneur's death he has returned to his native country, where he lives much respected, and has purchased from his Prince the title of Baron Ficci), — and the factotum objected to have to do with assassination; or whether he simply had a commission to frighten Mrs. Crawley out of a city where his lordship proposed to pass the winter, and the sight of her would be eminently disagreeable to the great nobleman, is a point which has never been ascertained: but the threat had its effect upon the little woman, and she sought no more to intrude herself upon the presence of her old patron.

Everybody knows the melancholy end of that nobleman, which befell at Naples two months after the French Revolution of 1830: when the Most Honourable George Gustavus, Marquis of Steyne, Earl of Gaunt and of Gaunt Castle, in the Peerage of Ireland, Viscount Hellborough, Baron Pitchley and Grillsby, a Knight of the Most Noble Order of the Garter, of the Golden Fleece of Spain, of the Russian Order of Saint Nicholas of the First Class, of the Turkish Order of the Crescent, First Lord of the Powder Closet and Groom of the Back Stairs, Colonel of the Gaunt or Regent's Own Regiment of Militia, a Trustee of the British Museum, an elder Brother of the Trinity House, a Governor of the White Friars, and D.C.L., — died after a series of fits, brought on, as the papers said, by the shock occasioned to his lordship's sensibilities by the downfall of the ancient French monarchy.

An eloquent catalogue appeared in a weekly print, describing his virtues, his magnificence, his talents, and his good actions. His sensibility, his attachment to the illustrious House of Bourbon, with which he claimed an alliance, were such that he could not survive the misfortunes of his august kinsmen. His body was buried at Naples, and his heart — that heart which always beat with every generous and noble emotion — was brought back to Castle Gaunt in a silver urn. "In him," Mr. Wagg said, "the poor and the Fine Arts have lost a beneficent patron, society one of its most brilliant ornaments, and England one of her loftiest patriots and statesmen," &c., &c.

His will was a good deal disputed, and an attempt was made to force from Madame de Belladonna the celebrated jewel called the "Jew's-eye" diamond, which his lordship always wore on his forefinger, and which it was said that she removed from it after his lamented demise. But his confidential friend and attendant, Monsieur Fiche, proved that the ring had been presented to the said Madame de Belladonna two days before the Marquis's death; as were the bank-notes, jewels, Neapolitan and French bonds, &c., found in his lordship's secretaire, and claimed by his heirs from that injured woman.

CHAPTER XI

FULL OF BUSINESS AND PLEASURE

THE day after the meeting at the play-table, Jos had himself arrayed with unusual care and splendour, and without thinking it necessary to say a word to any member of his family regarding the occurrences of the previous night, or asking for their company in his walk, he sallied forth at an early hour, and was presently seen making inquiries at the door of the Elephant Hotel. In consequence of the *fêtes* the house was full of company, the tables in the street were already surrounded by persons smoking and drinking the national small-beer, the public rooms were in a cloud of smoke, and Mr. Jos having, in his pompous way, and with his clumsy German, made inquiries for the person of whom he was in search, was directed to the very top of the house, above the first-floor rooms where some travelling pedlars had lived, and were exhibiting their jewellery and brocades; above the second-floor apartments occupied by the *état major* of the gambling firm; above the third-floor rooms, tenanted by the band of renowned Bohemian vaulters and tumblers; and so on to the little cabins of the roof, where, among students, bag-men, small tradesmen, and country-folks, come in for the festival, Becky had found a little nest; — as dirty a little refuge as ever beauty lay hid in.

Becky liked the life. She was at home with everybody in the place, pedlars, punters, tumblers, students
and all. She was of a wild, roving nature, inherited
from father and mother, who were both Bohemians, by
taste and circumstance; if a lord was not by, she would
talk to his courier with the greatest pleasure; the din,
the stir, the drink, the smoke, the tattle of the Hebrew
pedlars, the solemn, braggart ways of the poor tumblers,
the *sournois* talk of the gambling-table officials, the songs
and swagger of the students, and the general buzz and
hum of the place had pleased and tickled the little
woman, even when her luck was down, and she had not
wherewithal to pay her bill. How pleasant was all the
bustle to her now that her purse was full of the money
which little Georgy had won for her the night before!

As Jos came creaking and puffing up the final stairs,
and was speechless when he got to the landing, and
began to wipe his face and then to look for No. 92, the
room where he was directed to seek for the person he
wanted, the door of the opposite chamber, No. 90, was
open, and a student, in jack-boots and a dirty schlafrock,
was lying on the bed smoking a long pipe; whilst
another student in long yellow hair and a braided coat,
exceeding smart and dirty too, was actually on his knees
at No. 92, bawling through the keyhole supplications to
the person within.

" Go away," said a well-known voice, which made Jos
thrill, " I expect somebody; I expect my grandpapa.
He must n't see you there."

" Angel Engländerinn ! " bellowed the kneeling student with the whity-brown ringlets and the large
finger-ring, " do take compassion upon us. Make an
appointment. Dine with me and Fritz at the inn in
the park. We will have roast pheasants and porter, plum-
pudding and French wine. We shall die if you don't."

"That we will," said the young nobleman on the bed; and this colloquy Jos overheard, though he did not comprehend it, for the reason that he had never studied the language in which it was carried on.

"*Newmero kattervang dooze, si vous plait,*" Jos said in his grandest manner, when he was able to speak.

"*Quater fang tooce!*" said the student, starting up, and he bounced into his own room, where he locked the door, and where Jos heard him laughing with his comrade on the bed.

The gentleman from Bengal was standing disconcerted by this incident, when the door of the 92 opened of itself, and Becky's little head peeped out full of archness and mischief. She lighted on Jos. "It's you," she said, coming out. "How I have been waiting for you! Stop! not yet — in one minute you shall come in." In that instant she put a rouge-pot, a brandy bottle, and a plate of broken meat into the bed, gave one smooth to her hair, and finally let in her visitor.

She had, by way of morning robe, a pink domino, a trifle faded and soiled, and marked here and there with pomatum; but her arms shone out from the loose sleeves of the dress very white and fair, and it was tied round her little waist, so as not ill to set off the trim little figure of the wearer. She led Jos by the hand into her garret. "Come in," she said. "Come, and talk to me. Sit yonder on the chair;" and she gave the civilian's hand a little squeeze, and laughingly placed him upon it. As for herself, she placed herself on the bed — not on the bottle and plate, you may be sure — on which Jos might have reposed, had he chosen that seat; and so there she sate and talked with her old admirer.

"How little years have changed you," she said, with a look of tender interest. "I should have known you anywhere. What a comfort it is amongst strangers to see once more the frank honest face of an old friend!"

The frank honest face, to tell the truth, at this moment bore any expression but one of openness and honesty: it was, on the contrary, much perturbed and puzzled in look. Jos was surveying the queer little apartment in which he found his old flame. One of her gowns hung over the bed, another depending from a hook of the door: her bonnet obscured half the looking-glass, on which, too, lay the prettiest little pair of bronze boots; a French novel was on the table by the bedside, with a candle, not of wax. Becky thought of popping that into the bed too, but she only put in the little paper night-cap with which she had put the candle out on going to sleep.

"I should have known you anywhere," she continued; "a woman never forgets some things. And you were the first man I ever — I ever saw."

"Was I, really?" said Jos. "God bless my soul, you — you don't say so."

"When I came with your sister from Chiswick, I was scarcely more than a child," Becky said. "How is that dear love? Oh, her husband was a sad wicked man, and of course it was of me that the poor dear was jealous. As if I cared about him, heigho! when there was somebody — but no — don't let us talk of old times;" and she passed her handkerchief with the tattered lace across her eyelids.

"Is not this a strange place," she continued, "for a woman, who has lived in a very different world too, to be found in? I have had so many griefs and wrongs, Joseph Sedley, I have been made to suffer so cruelly, that I am almost made mad sometimes. I can't stay still in any place, but wander about always restless and unhappy. All my friends have been false to me — all.

There is no such thing as an honest man in the world. I was the truest wife that ever lived, though I married my husband out of pique, because somebody else — but never mind that. I was true, and he trampled upon me, and deserted me. I was the fondest mother. I had but one child, one darling, one hope, one joy, which I held to my heart with a mother's affection, which was my life, my prayer, my — my blessing; and they — they tore it from me — tore it from me; " and she put her hand to her heart with a passionate gesture of despair, burying her face for a moment on the bed.

The brandy-bottle inside clinked up against the plate which held the cold sausage. Both were moved, no doubt, by the exhibition of so much grief. Max and Fritz were at the door listening with wonder to Mrs. Becky's sobs and cries. Jos, too, was a good deal frightened and affected at seeing his old flame in this condition. And she began, forthwith, to tell her story — a tale so neat, simple, and artless, that it was quite evident from hearing her, that if ever there was a white-robed angel escaped from heaven to be subject to the infernal machinations and villany of fiends here below, that spotless being — that miserable unsullied martyr, was present on the bed before Jos — on the bed, sitting on the brandy-bottle.

They had a very long, amicable, and confidential talk there; in the course of which, Jos Sedley was some-how made aware (but in a manner that did not in the least scare or offend him) that Becky's heart had first learned to beat at his enchanting presence: that George Osborne had certainly paid an unjustifiable court to *her*, which might account for Amelia's jealousy, and their little rupture; but that Becky never gave the least encouragement to the unfortunate officer, and that she had never ceased to think about Jos from the very first day she had seen him, though, of course, her duties as a married woman were paramount — duties which she had always preserved, and would, to her dying day, or until the proverbially bad climate in which Colonel Crawley was living, should release her from a yoke which his cruelty had rendered odious to her.

Jos went away, convinced that she was the most virtuous, as she was one of the most fascinating of women, and revolving in his mind all sorts of benevolent schemes for her welfare. Her persecutions ought to be ended : she ought to return to the society of which she was an ornament. He would see what ought to be done. She must quit that place, and take a quiet lodging. Amelia must come and see her, and befriend her. He would go and settle about it, and consult with the Major. She wept tears of heartfelt gratitude as she parted from him, and pressed his hand as the gallant stout gentleman stooped down to kiss hers.

So Becky bowed Jos out of her little garret with as much grace as if it was a palace of which she did the honours ; and that heavy gentleman having disappeared down the stairs, Hans and Fritz came out of their hole, pipe in mouth, and she amused herself by mimicking Jos to them as she munched her cold bread and sausage and took draughts of her favourite brandy-and-water.

Jos walked over to Dobbin's lodgings with great solemnity, and there imparted to him the affecting history with which he had just been made acquainted, without, however, mentioning the play-business of the night before. And the two gentlemen were laying their heads together, and consulting as to the best means of being useful to Mrs. Becky, while she was finishing her interrupted *déjeuner à la fourchette*.

How was it that she had come to that little town ? How was it that she had no friends and was wandering about alone? Little boys at school are taught in their earliest Latin book, that the path of Avernus is very easy of descent. Let us skip over the interval in the history of her downward progress. She was not worse now than she had been in the days of her prosperity:— only a little down on her luck.

As for Mrs. Amelia, she was a woman of such a soft and foolish disposition, that when she heard of anybody unhappy, her heart straightway melted towards the sufferer; and as she had never thought or done anything mortally guilty herself, she had not that abhorrence for wickedness which distinguishes moralists much more knowing. If she spoiled everybody who came near her with kindness and compliments, — if she begged pardon of all her servants for troubling them to answer the bell, — if she apologised to a shop-boy who showed her a piece of silk, or made a curtsey to a street-sweeper, with a complimentary remark upon the elegant state of his crossing — and she was almost capable of every one of these follies — the notion that an old acquaintance was miserable was sure to soften her heart; nor would she hear of anybody's being deservedly unhappy. A world under such legislation as hers would not be a very orderly place of abode; but there are not many women, at least not of the rulers, who are of her sort. This lady, I believe, would have abolished all gaols, punishments, handcuffs, whippings, poverty, sickness, hunger, in the world; and was such a mean-spirited creature, that — we are obliged to confess it — she could even forget a mortal injury.

When the Major heard from Jos of the sentimental adventure which had just befallen the latter, he was not, it must be owned, nearly as much interested as the gentleman from Bengal. On the contrary, his excitement was quite the reverse from a pleasurable one; he made use of a brief but improper expression regarding

a poor woman in distress, saying, in fact, — "the little
minx, has she come to light again?" He never had
had the slightest liking for her; but had heartily mis-
trusted her from the very first moment when her green
eyes had looked at, and turned away from, his own.

"That little devil brings mischief wherever she goes,"
the Major said, disrespectfully. "Who knows what sort
of life she has been leading? and what business has she
here abroad and alone? Don't tell me about perse-
cutors and enemies; an honest woman always has
friends, and never is separated from her family. Why
has she left her husband? He may have been disreputable and wicked, as you say. He always was. I remember the confounded blackleg, and the way in which
he used to cheat and hoodwink poor George. Wasn't
there a scandal about their separation? I think I heard
something," cried out Major Dobbin, who did not care
much about gossip; and whom Jos tried in vain to convince that Mrs. Becky was in all respects a most injured
and virtuous female.

"Well, well; let's ask Mrs. George," said that arch-
diplomatist of a Major. "Only let us go and consult
her. I suppose you will allow that *she* is a good judge at
any rate, and knows what is right in such matters."

"Hm! Emmy is very well," said Jos, who did not
happen to be in love with his sister.

"Very well? by Gad, sir, she's the finest lady I ever
met in my life," bounced out the Major. "I say at once,
let us go and ask her if this woman ought to be visited
or not — I will be content with her verdict." Now this
odious, artful rogue of a Major was thinking in his own
mind that he was sure of his case. Emmy, he remembered, was at one time cruelly and deservedly jealous of
Rebecca, never mentioned her name but with a shrinking
and terror — a jealous woman never forgives, thought

[171]

Dobbin: and so the pair went across the street to Mrs. George's house, where she was contentedly warbling at a music-lesson with Madame Strumpff.

When that lady took her leave, Jos opened the business with his usual pomp of words. "Amelia, my dear," said he, "I have just had the most extraordinary — yes — God bless my soul! the most extraordinary adventure — an old friend — yes, a most interesting old friend of yours, and I may say in old times, has just arrived here, and I should like you to see her."

"Her!" said Amelia, "who is it? Major Dobbin, if you please not to break my scissors." The Major was twirling them round by the little chain from which they sometimes hung to their lady's waist, and was thereby endangering his own eye.

"It is a woman whom I dislike very much," said the Major, doggedly; "and whom you have no cause to love."

"It is Rebecca, I'm sure it is Rebecca," Amelia said blushing, and being very much agitated.

"You are right; you always are," Dobbin answered. Brussels, Waterloo, old, old times, griefs, pangs, remembrances, rushed back into Amelia's gentle heart, and caused a cruel agitation there.

"Don't let me see her," Emmy continued. "I couldn't see her."

"I told you so," Dobbin said to Jos.

"She is very unhappy, and — and that sort of thing," Jos urged. "She is very poor and unprotected: and has been ill — exceedingly ill — and that scoundrel of a husband has deserted her."

"Ah!" said Amelia.

"She hasn't a friend in the world," Jos went on, not undexterously; "and she said she thought she might trust in you. She's so miserable, Emmy. She has

been almost mad with grief. Her story quite affected
me : — 'pon my word and honour, it did — never was
such a cruel persecution borne so angelically, I may say.
Her family has been most cruel to her."

" Poor creature ! " Amelia said.

" And if she can get no friend, she says she thinks
she 'll die," Jos proceeded, in a low tremulous voice. —
" God bless my soul ! do you know that she tried to
kill herself? She carries laudanum with her — I saw
the bottle in her room — such a miserable little room —
at a third-rate house, the Elephant, up in the roof at the
top of all. I went there."

This did not seem to affect Emmy. She even smiled
a little. Perhaps she figured Jos to herself panting up
the stair.

" She 's beside herself with grief," he resumed. " The
agonies that woman has endured are quite frightful to
hear of. She had a little boy, of the same age as
Georgy."

" Yes, yes, I think I remember," Emmy remarked.
" Well ? "

" The most beautiful child ever seen," Jos said,
who was very fat, and easily moved, and had been
touched by the story Becky told ; " a perfect angel,
who adored his mother. The ruffians tore him shrieking out of her arms, and have never allowed him to
see her."

" Dear Joseph," Emmy cried out, starting up at once,
" let us go and see her this minute." And she ran into
her adjoining bed-chamber, tied on her bonnet in a
flutter, came out with her shawl on her arm, and ordered
Dobbin to follow.

He went and put her shawl — it was a white Cashmere, consigned to her by the Major himself from India
— over her shoulders. He saw there was nothing for it

but to obey; and she put her hand into his arm, and they went away.

"It is number 92, up four pair of stairs," Jos said, perhaps not very willing to ascend the steps again; but he placed himself in the window of his drawing-room, which commands the place on which the Elephant stands, and saw the pair marching through the market.

It was as well that Becky saw them too from her garret; for she and the two students were chattering and laughing there; they had been joking about the appearance of Becky's grandpapa — whose arrival and departure they had witnessed — but she had time to dismiss them, and have her little room clear before the landlord of the Elephant, who knew that Mrs. Osborne was a great favourite at the Serene Court, and respected her accordingly, led the way up the stairs to the roof-story, encouraging Miladi and the Herr Major as they achieved the ascent.

"Gracious lady, gracious lady!" said the landlord, knocking at Becky's door; he had called her Madame the day before, and was by no means courteous to her.

"Who is it?" Becky said, putting out her head, and she gave a little scream. There stood Emmy in a tremble, and Dobbin, the tall Major, with his cane.

He stood still watching, and very much interested at the scene; but Emmy sprang forward with open arms towards Rebecca, and forgave her at that moment, and embraced her and kissed her with all her heart. Ah, poor wretch, when was your lip pressed before by such pure kisses?

CHAPTER XII

AMANTIUM IRÆ

FRANKNESS and kindness like Amelia's were likely to touch even such a hardened little reprobate as Becky. She returned Emmy's caresses and kind speeches with something very like gratitude, and an emotion which, if it was not lasting, for a moment was almost genuine. That was a lucky stroke of hers about the child "torn from her arms shrieking." It was by that harrowing misfortune that Becky had won her friend back, and it was one of the very first points, we may be certain, upon which our poor simple little Emmy began to talk to her new-found acquaintance.

"And so they took your darling child from you," our simpleton cried out. "Oh, Rebecca, my poor dear suffering friend, I know what it is to lose a boy, and to feel for those who have lost one. But please Heaven yours will be restored to you, as a merciful merciful Providence has brought me back mine."

"The child, my child? Oh, yes, my agonies were frightful," Becky owned, not perhaps without a twinge of conscience. It jarred upon her, to be obliged to commence instantly to tell lies in reply to so much confidence and simplicity. But that is the misfortune of beginning with this kind of forgery. When one fib becomes due as it were, you must forge another to take up the old acceptance; and so the stock of your lies in

[175]

circulation inevitably multiplies, and the danger of detection increases every day.

"My agonies," Becky continued, "were terrible (I hope she won't sit down on the bottle) when they took him away from me; I thought I should die; but I fortunately had a brain fever, during which my doctor gave me up, and — and I recovered, and — and here I am, poor and friendless."

"How old is he?" Emmy asked.

"Eleven," said Becky.

"Eleven!" cried the other. "Why, he was born the same year with Georgy, who is — "

"I know, I know," Becky cried out, who had in fact quite forgotten all about little Rawdon's age. "Grief has made me forget so many things, dearest Amelia. I am very much changed: half wild sometimes. He was eleven when they took him away from me. Bless his sweet face; I have never seen it again."

"Was he fair or dark?" went on that absurd little Emmy. "Show me his hair."

Becky almost laughed at her simplicity. "Not to-day, love, — some other time, when my trunks arrive from Leipzig, whence I came to this place, — and a little drawing of him, which I made in happy days."

"Poor Becky, poor Becky!" said Emmy. "How thankful, how thankful I ought to be!" (though I doubt whether that practice of piety inculcated upon us by our womankind in early youth, namely, to be thankful because we are better off than somebody else, be a very rational religious exercise;) and then she began to think as usual, how her son was the handsomest, the best, and the cleverest boy in the whole world.

"You will see my Georgy," was the best thing Emmy could think of to console Becky. If anything could make her comfortable that would.

[176]

And so the two women continued talking for an hour
or more, during which Becky had the opportunity of
giving her new friend a full and complete version of her
private history. She showed how her marriage with
Rawdon Crawley had always been viewed by the family
with feelings of the utmost hostility; how her sister-in-
law (an artful woman) had poisoned her husband's mind
against her; how he had formed odious connections,
which had estranged his affections from her: how she
had borne everything — poverty, neglect, coldness from
the being whom she most loved — and all for the sake
of her child; how, finally, and by the most flagrant outrage, she had been driven into demanding a separation
from her husband, when the wretch did not scruple to
ask that she should sacrifice her own fair fame so that
he might procure advancement through the means of a
very great and powerful but unprincipled man — the
Marquis of Steyne, indeed. The atrocious monster!

This part of her eventful history Becky gave with the
utmost feminine delicacy, and the most indignant virtue.
Forced to fly her husband's roof by this insult, the
coward had pursued his revenge by taking her child
from her. And thus Becky said she was a wanderer,
poor, unprotected, friendless, and wretched.

Emmy received this story, which was told at some
length, as those persons who are acquainted with her
character may imagine that she would. She quivered
with indignation at the account of the conduct of the
miserable Rawdon and the unprincipled Steyne. Her
eyes made notes of admiration for every one of the sen-
tences in which Becky described the persecutions of her
aristocratic relatives, and the falling away of her husband. (Becky did not abuse him. She spoke rather
in sorrow than in anger. She had loved him only too
fondly: and was he not the father of her boy?) And

as for the separation-scene from the child, while Becky was reciting it, Emmy retired altogether behind her pocket-handkerchief, so that the consummate little tragedian must have been charmed to see the effect which her performance produced on her audience.

Whilst the ladies were carrying on their conversation, Amelia's constant escort, the Major (who, of course, did not wish to interrupt their conference, and found himself rather tired of creaking about the narrow stair passage of which the roof brushed the nap from his hat), descended to the ground-floor of the house and into the great room common to all the frequenters of the Elephant, out of which the stair led. This apartment is always in a fume of smoke, and liberally sprinkled with beer. On a dirty table stand scores of corresponding brass-candlesticks with tallow candles for the lodgers, whose keys hang up in rows over the candles. Emmy had passed blushing through the room anon, where all sorts of people were collected ; Tyrolese glove-sellers and Danubian linen-merchants, with their packs ; students recruiting themselves with butterbrods and meat ; idlers, playing cards or dominoes on the sloppy, beery tables ; tumblers refreshing during the cessation of their performances ; — in a word, all the *fumum* and *strepitus* of a German inn in fair time. The waiter brought the Major a mug of beer, as a matter of course ; and he took out a cigar, and amused himself with that pernicious vegetable and a newspaper until his charge should come down to claim him.

Max and Fritz came presently downstairs, their caps on one side, their spurs jingling, their pipes splendid with coats-of-arms and full-blown tassels, and they hung up the key of No. 90 on the board, and called for the ration of butterbrod and beer. The pair sate down by the Major, and fell into a conversation of which he

could not help hearing somewhat. It was mainly about
" Fuchs " and " Philister," and duels and drinking-bouts
at the neighbouring University of Schoppenhausen, from
which renowned seat of learning they had just come in
the Eilwagen, with Becky, as it appeared, by their
side, and in order to be present at the bridal fêtes at
Pumpernickel.

" The little Engländerinn seems to be *en bays de
gonnoisance*," said Max, who knew the French language,
to Fritz, his comrade. " After the fat grandfather went
away, there came a pretty little compatriot. I heard
them chattering and whimpering together in the little
woman's chamber."

" We must take the tickets for her concert," Fritz
said. " Hast thou any money, Max ? "

" Bah," said the other, " the concert is a concert *in
nubibus*. Hans said that she advertised one at Leipzig:
and the Burschen took many tickets. But she went off
without singing. She said in the coach yesterday that
her pianist had fallen ill at Dresden. She cannot sing,
it is my belief: her voice is as cracked as thine, O thou
beer-soaking Renowner ! "

" It is cracked; *I* hear her trying out of her window
a schrecklich English ballad, called ' De Rose upon de
Balgony.' "

" Saufen and singen go not together," observed Fritz
with the red nose, who evidently preferred the former
amusement. " No, thou shalt take none of her tickets.
She won money at the *trente* and *quarante* last night. I
saw her: she made a little English boy play for her.
We will spend thy money there or at the theatre, or we
will treat her to French wine or Cognac in the Aurelius
Garden, but the tickets we will not buy. What sayest
thou ? Yet, another mug of beer ? " and one and another
successively having buried their blond whiskers in the

mawkish draught, curled them and swaggered off into the fair.

The Major, who had seen the key of No. 90 put up on its hook, and had heard the conversation of the two young university bloods, was not at a loss to understand that their talk related to Becky. "The little devil is at her old tricks," he thought, and he smiled as he recalled old days, when he had witnessed the desperate flirtation with Jos, and the ludicrous end of that adventure. He and George had often laughed over it subsequently, and until a few weeks after George's marriage, when he also was caught in the little Circe's toils, and had an understanding with her which his comrade certainly suspected, but preferred to ignore. William was too much hurt or ashamed to ask to fathom that disgraceful mystery, although once, and evidently with remorse on his mind, George had alluded to it. It was on the morning of Waterloo, as the young men stood together in front of their line, surveying the black masses of Frenchmen who crowned the opposite heights, and as the rain was coming down, "I have been mixing in a foolish intrigue with a woman," George said. "I am glad we were marched away. If I drop, I hope Emmy will never know of that business. I wish to God it had never been begun!" And William was pleased to think, and had more than once soothed poor George's widow with the narrative, that Osborne, after quitting his wife, and after the action of Quatre Bras, on the first day, spoke gravely and affectionately, to his comrade of his father and his wife. On these facts, too, William had insisted very strongly in his conversations with the elder Osborne: and had thus been the means of reconciling the old gentleman to his son's memory, just at the close of the elder man's life.

"And so this devil is still going on with her intrigues," thought William. "I wish she were a hundred miles from here. She brings mischief wherever she goes." And he was pursuing these forebodings and this uncomfortable train of thought, with his head between his hands, and the "Pumpernickel Gazette" of last week unread under his nose, when somebody tapped his shoulder with a parasol, and he looked up and saw Mrs. Amelia.

This woman had a way of tyrannising over Major Dobbin (for the weakest of all people will domineer over somebody), and she ordered him about, and patted him, and made him fetch and carry just as if he was a great Newfoundland dog. He liked, so to speak, to jump into the water if she said "High, Dobbin!" and to trot behind her with her reticule in his mouth. This history has been written to very little purpose if the reader has not perceived that the Major was a spooney.

"Why did you not wait for me, sir, to escort me downstairs?" she said, giving a little toss of her head, and a most sarcastic curtsey.

"I could n't stand up in the passage," he answered, with a comical deprecatory look; and, delighted to give her his arm, and to take her out of the horrid smoky place, he would have walked off without even so much as remembering the waiter, had not the young fellow run after him and stopped him on the threshold of the Elephant, to make him pay for the beer which he had not consumed. Emmy laughed: she called him a naughty man, who wanted to run away in debt: and, in fact, made some jokes suitable to the occasion and the small-beer. She was in high spirits and good humour, and tripped across the market-place very briskly. She wanted to see Jos that instant. The Major laughed at the impetuous affection Mrs. Amelia exhibited; for, in truth, it was not very often that she wanted her brother "that instant."

They found the Civilian in his saloon on the first-floor; he had been pacing the room, and biting his nails, and looking over the market-place towards the Elephant a hundred times at least during the past hour, whilst Emmy was closeted with her friend in the garret, and the Major was beating the tattoo on the sloppy tables of the public room below, and he was, on his side too, very anxious to see Mrs. Osborne.

"Well?" said he.

"The poor dear creature, how she has suffered!" Emmy said.

"God bless my soul, yes," Jos said, wagging his head, so that his cheeks quivered like jellies.

"She may have Payne's room; who can go upstairs," Emmy continued. Payne was a staid English maid and personal attendant upon Mrs. Osborne, to whom the courier, as in duty bound, paid court, and whom Georgy used to "lark" dreadfully with accounts of German robbers and ghosts. She passed her time chiefly in grumbling, in ordering about her mistress, and in stating her intention to return the next morning to her native village of Clapham. "She may have Payne's room," Emmy said.

"Why, you don't mean to say you are going to have that woman into the *house?*" bounced out the Major, jumping up.

"Of course we are," said Amelia in the most innocent way in the world. "Don't be angry, and break the furniture, Major Dobbin. Of course we are going to have her here."

"Of course, my dear," Jos said.

"The poor creature, after all her sufferings," Emmy continued: "her horrid banker broken and run away: her husband — wicked wretch — having deserted her and taken her child away from her (here she doubled her

two little fists and held them in a most menacing attitude before her, so that the Major was charmed to see
such a dauntless virago), the poor dear thing! quite
alone and absolutely forced to give lessons in singing to
get her bread — and not have her here!"

"Take lessons, my dear, Mrs. George," cried the
Major, "but don't have her in the house. I implore
you don't."

"Pooh," said Jos.

"You who are always good and kind: always used to
be at any rate: I'm astonished at you, Major William,"
Amelia cried. "Why, what is the moment to help
her but when she is so miserable? Now is the time to
be of service to her. The oldest friend I ever had, and
not —"

"She was not always your friend, Amelia," the Major
said, for he was quite angry. This allusion was too
much for Emmy, who, looking the Major almost fiercely
in the face, said, "For shame, Major Dobbin!" and
after having fired this shot, she walked out of the room
with a most majestic air, and shut her own door briskly
on herself and her outraged dignity.

"To allude to *that!*" she said, when the door was
closed. "Oh, it was cruel of him to remind me of it,"
and she looked up at George's picture, which hung
there as usual, with the portrait of the boy underneath.
"It was cruel of him. If I had forgiven it, ought he
to have spoken? No. And it is from his own lips
that I know how wicked and groundless my jealousy
was; and that you were pure — Oh yes, you were pure,
my saint in heaven!"

She paced the room trembling and indignant. She
went and leaned on the chest of drawers over which the
picture hung, and gazed and gazed at it. Its eyes
seemed to look down on her with a reproach that deep-

ened as she looked. The early dear, dear memories of that brief prime of love rushed back upon her. The wound which years had scarcely cicatrised bled afresh, and oh, how bitterly! She could not bear the reproaches of the husband there before her. It could n't be. Never, never.

Poor Dobbin; poor old William! That unlucky word had undone the work of many a year — the long laborious edifice of a life of love and constancy — raised too upon what secret and hidden foundations, wherein lay buried passions, uncounted struggles, unknown sacrifices — a little word was spoken, and down fell the fair palace of hope — one word, and away flew the bird which he had been trying all his life to lure!

William, though he saw by Amelia's looks that a great crisis had come, nevertheless continued to implore Sedley, in the most energetic terms, to beware of Rebecca: and he eagerly, almost frantically, adjured Jos not to receive her. He besought Mr. Sedley to inquire at least regarding her: told him how he had heard that she was in the company of gamblers and people of ill repute; pointed out what evil she had done in former days: how she and Crawley had misled poor George into ruin: how she was now parted from her husband, by her own confession, and, perhaps, for good reason. What a dangerous companion she would be for his sister, who knew nothing of the affairs of the world! William implored Jos, with all the eloquence which he could bring to bear, and a great deal more energy than this quiet gentleman was ordinarily in the habit of showing, to keep Rebecca out of his household.

Had he been less violent, or more dexterous, he might have succeeded in his supplications to Jos; but the Civilian was not a little jealous of the airs of superiority which the Major constantly exhibited towards him, as he fancied (indeed, he had imparted his opinions to Mr. Kirsch, the courier, whose bills Major Dobbin checked on this journey, and who sided with his master), and he began a blustering speech about his competency to defend his own honour, his desire not to have his affairs meddled with, his intention, in fine, to rebel against the Major, when the colloquy — rather a long and stormy one — was put an end to in the simplest way possible, namely, by the arrival of Mrs. Becky, with a porter from the Elephant Hotel, in charge of her very meagre baggage.

She greeted her host with affectionate respect, and made a shrinking, but amicable, salutation to Major Dobbin, who, as her instinct assured her at once, was her enemy, and had been speaking against her; and the bustle and clatter consequent upon her arrival brought Amelia out of her room. Emmy went up and embraced her guest with the greatest warmth, and took no notice of the Major, except to fling him an angry look — the most unjust and scornful glance that had perhaps ever appeared in that poor little woman's face since she was born. But she had private reasons of her own, and was bent upon being angry with him. And Dobbin, indignant at the injustice, not at the defeat, went off, making her a bow quite as haughty as the killing curtsey with which the little woman chose to bid him farewell.

He being gone, Emmy was particularly lively and affectionate to Rebecca, and bustled about the apartments and installed her guest in her room with an eagerness and activity seldom exhibited by our placid little friend. But when an act of injustice is to be done, especially by weak people, it is best that it should be down quickly; and Emmy thought she was displaying a great deal of firmness and proper feeling and veneration for the late Captain Osborne in her present behaviour.

Georgy came in from the fêtes for dinner-time, and found four covers laid as usual; but one of the places was occupied by a lady, instead of by Major Dobbin. "Hullo! where's Dob?" the young gentleman asked, with his usual simplicity of language. "Major Dobbin is dining out, I suppose," his mother said; and, drawing the boy to her, kissed him a great deal, and put his hair off his forehead, and introduced him to Mrs. Crawley. "This is my boy, Rebecca," Mrs. Osborne said — as much as to say — can the world produce anything like that? Becky looked at him with rapture, and pressed his hand fondly. "Dear boy!" she said — "he is just like my——" Emotion choked her further utterance; but Amelia understood, as well as if she had spoken, that Becky was thinking of her own blessed child. However, the company of her friend consoled Mrs. Crawley, and she ate a very good dinner.

During the repast, she had occasion to speak several times, when Georgy eyed her and listened to her. At the dessert Emmy was gone out to superintend further domestic arrangements: Jos was in his great chair dozing over *Galignani*: Georgy and the new arrival sat close to each other: he had continued to look at her knowingly more than once, and at last, he laid down the nut-crackers.

"I say," said Georgy.

"What do you say?" Becky said, laughing.

"You're the lady I saw in the mask at the Rouge et Noir."

"Hush! you little sly creature," Becky said, taking up his hand and kissing it. "Your uncle was there too, and mamma must n't know."

"Oh no — not by no means," answered the little fellow.

"You see we are quite good friends already," Becky said to Emmy, who now re-entered; and it must be owned that Mrs. Osborne had introduced a most judicious and amiable companion into her house.

William, in a state of great indignation, though still unaware of all the treason that was in store for him, walked about the town wildly until he fell upon the Secretary of Legation, Tapeworm, who invited him to dinner. As they were discussing that meal, he took occasion to ask the Secretary whether he knew anything about a certain Mrs. Rawdon Crawley, who had, he believed, made some noise in London; and then Tapeworm, who of course knew all the London gossip, and was besides a relative of Lady Gaunt, poured out into the astonished Major's ears such a history about Becky and her husband as astonished the querist, and supplied all the points of this narrative, for it was at that very table years ago that the present writer had the pleasure of hearing the tale. Tufto, Steyne, the Crawleys, and their history — everything connected with Becky and her previous life passed under the record of the bitter diplomatist. He knew everything and a great deal besides, about all the world; — in a word, he made the most astounding revelations to the simple-hearted Major. When Dobbin said that Mrs. Osborne and Mr. Sedley had taken her into their house, Tapeworm burst into a peal of laughter which shocked the Major, and asked if they had not better send into the prison, and take in one or two of the gentlemen in shaved heads and yellow jackets, who swept the streets of Pumpernickel, chained in pairs, to board and lodge, and act as tutor to that little scapegrace Georgy.

This information astonished and horrified the Major not a little. It had been agreed in the morning (before meeting with Rebecca) that Amelia should go to the Court ball that night. There would be the place where he should tell her. The Major went home and dressed himself in his uniform, and repaired to Court, in hopes to see Mrs. Osborne. She never came. When he returned to his lodgings all the lights in the Sedley tenement were put out. He could not see her till the morning. I don't know what sort of a night's rest he had with this frightful secret in bed with him.

At the earliest convenient hour in the morning he sent his servant across the way with a note, saying, that he wished very particularly to speak with her. A message came back to say, that Mrs. Osborne was exceedingly unwell, and was keeping her room.

She too, had been awake all that night. She had been thinking of a thing which had agitated her mind a hundred times before. A hundred times on the point of yielding, she had shrunk back from a sacrifice which she felt was too much for her. She could n't, in spite of his love and constancy, and her own acknowledged regard, respect, and gratitude. What are benefits, what is constancy, or merit? One curl of a girl's ringlet, one hair of a whisker, will turn the scale against them all in a minute. They did not weigh with Emmy more than with other women. She had tried them; wanted to make them pass; could not; and the pitiless little woman had found a pretext, and determined to be free.

When at length, in the afternoon, the Major gained admission to Amelia, instead of the cordial and affectionate greeting, to which he had been accustomed now for many a long day, he received the salutation of a curtsey, and of a little gloved hand, retracted the moment after it was accorded to him.

Rebecca, too, was in the room, and advanced to meet

him with a smile and an extended hand. Dobbin drew back rather confusedly. "I — I beg your pardon, ma'am," he said; "but I am bound to tell you that it is not as your friend that I am come here now."

"Pooh! damn; don't let us have this sort of thing!" Jos cried out, alarmed, and anxious to get rid of a scene.

"I wonder what Major Dobbin has to say against Rebecca?" Amelia said in a low, clear voice with a slight quiver in it, and a very determined look about the eyes.

"I will *not* have this sort of thing in my house," Jos again interposed. "I say I will not have it: and Dobbin, I beg, sir, you 'll stop it." And he looked round trembling and turning very red, and gave a great puff, and made for his door.

"Dear friend!" Rebecca said with angelic sweetness, "do hear what Major Dobbin has to say against me."

"I will *not* hear it, I say," squeaked out Jos at the top of his voice, and, gathering up his dressing-gown, he was gone.

"We are only two women," Amelia said. "You can speak now, sir."

"This manner towards me is one which scarcely becomes you, Amelia," the Major answered haughtily; "nor I believe am I guilty of habitual harshness to women. It is not a pleasure to me to do the duty which I am come to do."

"Pray proceed with it quickly, if you please, Major Dobbin," said Amelia, who was more and more in a pet. The expression of Dobbin's face, as she spoke in this imperious manner, was not pleasant.

"I came to say — and as you stay, Mrs. Crawley, I must say it in your presence — that I think you — you ought not to form a member of the family of my friends.

A lady who is separated from her husband, who travels not under her own name, who frequents public-gaming-tables — "

"It was to the ball I went," cried out Becky.

" — is not a fit companion for Mrs. Osborne and her son," Dobbin went on: "and I may add that there are people here who know you, and who profess to know that regarding your conduct, about which I don't even wish to speak before — before Mrs. Osborne."

"Yours is a very modest and convenient sort of calumny, Major Dobbin," Rebecca said. "You leave me under the weight of an accusation which, after all, is unsaid. What is it? Is it unfaithfulness to my husband? I scorn it, and defy anybody to prove it — I defy you, I say. My honour is as untouched as that of the bitterest enemy who ever maligned me. Is it of being poor, forsaken, wretched, that you accuse me? Yes, I am guilty of those faults, and punished for them every day. Let me go, Emmy. It is only to suppose that I have not met you, and I am no worse to-day than I was yesterday. It is only to suppose that the night is over and the poor wanderer is on her way. Don't you remember the song we used to sing in old, dear old days? I have been wandering ever since then — a poor castaway, scorned for being miserable, and insulted because I am alone. Let me go: my stay here interferes with the plans of this gentleman."

"Indeed it does, madam," said the Major. "If I have any authority in this house — "

"Authority, none!" broke out Amelia. "Rebecca, you stay with me. *I* won't desert you, because you have been persecuted, or insult you, because — because Major Dobbin chooses to do so. Come away, dear." And the two women made towards their door.

William opened it. As they were going out, however,

he took Amelia's hand, and said — "Will you stay a moment and speak to me?"

"He wishes to speak with you away from me," said Becky, looking like a martyr. Amelia griped her hand in reply.

"Upon my honour it is not about you that I am going to speak," Dobbin said. "Come back, Amelia," and she came. Dobbin bowed to Mrs. Crawley, as he shut the door upon her. Amelia looked at him, leaning against the glass: her face and her lips were quite white.

"I was confused when I spoke just now," the Major said, after a pause; "and I misused the word authority."

"You did," said Amelia, with her teeth chattering.

"At least I have claims to be heard," Dobbin continued.

"It is generous to remind me of our obligations to you," the woman answered.

"The claims I mean, are those left me by George's father," William said.

"Yes, and you insulted his memory. You did yesterday. You know you did. And I will never forgive you. Never!" said Amelia. She shot out each little sentence in a tremor of anger and emotion.

"You don't mean that, Amelia?" William said, sadly. "You don't mean that these words, uttered in a hurried moment, are to weigh against a whole life's devotion? I think that George's memory has not been injured by the way in which I have dealt with it, and if we are come to bandying reproaches, I at least merit none from his widow and the mother of his son. Reflect, afterwards when — when you are at leisure, and your con science will withdraw this accusation. It does even now." Amelia held down her head.

"It is not that speech of yesterday," he continued, "which moves you. That is but the pretext, Amelia, or I have loved you and watched you for fifteen years in vain. Have I not learned in that time to read all your feelings, and look into your thoughts? I know what your heart is capable of: it can cling faithfully to a recollection, and cherish a fancy; but it can't feel an attachment as mine deserves to mate with, and such as I would have won from a woman more generous than you. No, you are not worthy of the love which I have devoted to you. I knew all along that the prize I had set my life on was not worth the winning; that I was a fool, with fond fancies, too, bartering away my all of truth and ardour against your little feeble remnant of love. I will bargain no more: I withdraw. I find no fault with you. You are very good-natured, and have done your best; but you could n't — you could n't reach up to the height of the attachment which I bore you, and which a loftier soul than yours might have been proud to share. Good-bye, Amelia! I have watched your struggle. Let it end. We are both weary of it."

Amelia stood scared and silent as William thus suddenly broke the chain by which she held him, and declared his independence and superiority. He had placed himself at her feet so long that the poor little woman had been accustomed to trample upon him. She did n't wish to marry him, but she wished to keep him. She wished to give him nothing, but that he should give her all. It is a bargain not unfrequently levied in love.

William's sally had quite broken and cast her down. *Her* assault was long since over and beaten back.

"Am I to understand then, — that you are going — away, — William?" she said.

He gave a sad laugh. "I went once before," he

said, " and came back after twelve years. We were young then, Amelia. Good-bye. I have spent enough of my life at this play."

Whilst they had been talking, the door into Mrs. Osborne's room had opened ever so little; indeed, Becky had kept a hold of the handle, and had turned it on the instant when Dobbin quitted it; and she heard every word of the conversation that had passed between these two. " What a noble heart that man has," she thought, " and how shamefully that woman plays with it." She admired Dobbin; she bore him no rancour for the part he had taken against her. It was an open move in the game, and played fairly. "Ah!" she thought, " if I could have had such a husband as that— a man with a heart and brains too! I would not have minded his large feet;" and running into her room, she absolutely bethought herself of something, and wrote him a note, beseeching him to stop for a few days— not to think of going—and that she could serve him with A.

The parting was over. Once more poor William walked to the door and was gone; and the little widow, the author of all this work, had her will, and had won her victory, and was left to enjoy it as she best might. Let the ladies envy her triumph.

At the romantic hour of dinner, Mr. Georgy made his appearance, and again remarked the absence of " Old Dob." The meal was eaten in silence by the party. Jos's appetite not being diminished, but Emmy taking nothing at all.

After the meal, Georgy was lolling in the cushions of the old window, a large window, with three sides of glass abutting from the gable, and commanding on one side the Market Place, where the Elephant is, his mother being busy hard by, when he remarked symptoms of movement at the Major's house on the other side of the street.

"Hullo!" said he, "there's Dob's trap — they are bringing it out of the court-yard." The "trap" in question was a carriage which the Major had bought for six pounds sterling, and about which they used to rally him a good deal.

Emmy gave a little start but said nothing.

"Hullo!" Georgy continued, "there's Francis coming out with the portmanteaus, and Kunz, the one-eyed postilion, coming down the market with three schimmels. Look at his boots and yellow jacket, — ain't he a rum one? Why — they're putting the horses to Dob's carriage. Is he going anywhere?"

"Yes," said Emmy, "he is going on a journey."

"Going a journey; and when is he coming back?"

"He is — not coming back," answered Emmy.

"Not coming back!" cried out Georgy, jumping up. "Stay here, sir," roared out Jos. "Stay, Georgy," said his mother, with a very sad face. The boy stopped; kicked about the room; jumped up and down from the window-seat with his knees, and showed every symptom of uneasiness and curiosity.

The horses were put to. The baggage was strapped on. Francis came out with his master's sword, cane, and umbrella tied up together, and laid them in the well, and his desk and old tin-cocked-hat case, which he placed under the seat. Francis brought out the stained old blue cloak lined with red camlet, which had wrapped the owner up any time these fifteen years, and had *manchen Sturm erlebt*, as a favourite song of those days said. It had been new for the campaign of Waterloo, and had covered George and William after the night of Quatre Bras.

Old Burcke, the landlord of the lodgings, came out, then Francis, with more packages — final packages —

then Major William, — Burcke wanted to kiss him. The Major was adored by all people with whom he had to do. It was with difficulty he could escape from this demonstration of attachment.

"By Jove, I *will* go!" screamed out George. "Give him this," said Becky, quite interested, and put a paper into the boy's hand. He had rushed down the stairs and flung across the street in a minute — the yellow postilion was cracking his whip gently.

William had got into the carriage, released from the embraces of his landlord. George bounded in afterwards and flung his arms round the Major's neck (as they saw from the window), and began asking him multiplied questions. Then he felt in his waistcoat-pocket and gave him a note. William seized at it rather eagerly, he opened it trembling, but instantly his countenance changed, and he tore the paper in two, and dropped it out of the carriage. He kissed Georgy on the head, and the boy got out, doubling his fists into his eyes, and with the aid of Francis. He lingered with his hand on the panel. Fort Schwager! The yellow postilion cracked his whip prodigiously, up sprang Francis to the box, away went the schimmels, and Dobbin with his head on his breast. He never looked up as they passed under Amelia's window: and Georgy, left alone in the street, burst out crying in the face of all the crowd.

Emmy's maid heard him howling again during the night, and brought him some preserved apricots to console him. She mingled her lamentations with his. All the poor, all the humble, all honest folks, all good men who knew him, loved that kind-hearted and simple gentleman.

As for Emmy, had she not done her duty? She had her picture of George for a consolation.

CHAPTER XIII

WHICH CONTAINS BIRTHS, MARRIAGES, AND DEATHS

WHATEVER Becky's private plan might be by which Dobbin's true love was to be crowned with success, the little woman thought that the secret might keep, and indeed, being by no means so much interested about anybody's welfare as about her own, she had a great number of things pertaining to herself to consider, and which concerned her a great deal more than Major Dobbin's happiness in this life.

She found herself suddenly and unexpectedly in snug comfortable quarters: surrounded by friends, kindness, and good-natured simple people, such as she had not met with for many a long day; and, wanderer as she was by force and inclination, there were moments when rest was pleasant to her. As the most hardened Arab that ever careered across the Desert over the hump of a dromedary, likes to repose sometimes under the date-trees by the water; or to come into the cities, walk in the bazaars, refresh himself in the baths, and say his prayers in the Mosques, before he goes out again marauding; Jos's tents and pilau were pleasant to this little Ishmaelite. She picketed her steed, hung up her weapons, and warmed herself comfortably by his fire. The halt in that roving, restless life, was inexpressibly soothing and pleasant to her.

So, pleased herself, she tried with all her might to please everybody; and we know that she was eminent

and successful as a practitioner in the art of giving
pleasure. As for Jos, even in that little interview in the
garret at the Elephant Inn, she had found means to win
back a great deal of his good will. In the course of a
week, the civilian was her sworn slave and frantic admirer.
He did n't go to sleep after dinner, as his custom was, in
the much less lively society of Amelia. He drove out
with Becky in his open carriage. He asked little parties
and invented festivities to do her honour.

Tapeworm, the Chargé d'Affaires, who had abused her
so cruelly, came to dine with Jos, and then came every
day to pay his respects to Becky. Poor Emmy, who
was never very talkative, and more glum and silent than
ever after Dobbin's departure, was quite forgotten when
this superior genius made her appearance. The French
Minister was as much charmed with her as his English
rival. The German ladies, never particularly squeamish
as regards morals, especially in English people, were
delighted with the cleverness and wit of Mrs. Osborne's
charming friend; and though she did not ask to go to
Court, yet the most august and Transparent Personages
there heard of her fascinations, and were quite curious
to know her. When it became known that she was
noble, of an ancient English family, that her husband
was a Colonel of the Guard, Excellenz and Governor of
an island, only separated from his lady by one of those
trifling differences which are of little account in a country
where " Werther " is still read, and the " Wahlverwand-
schaften" of Goethe is considered an edifying moral
book, nobody thought of refusing to receive her in the
very highest society of the little Duchy; and the ladies
were even more ready to call her *du*, and to swear
eternal friendship for her, than they had been to bestow
the same inestimable benefits upon Amelia. Love and
Liberty are interpreted by those simple Germans in a

way which honest folks in Yorkshire and Somersetshire little understand; and a lady might, in some philosophic and civilized towns, be divorced ever so many times from her respective husbands, and keep her character in society. Jos's house never was so pleasant since he had a house of his own, as Rebecca caused it to be. She sang, she played, she laughed, she talked in two or three languages; she brought everybody to the house: and she made Jos believe that it was his own great social talents and wit which gathered the society of the place round about him.

As for Emmy, who found herself not in the least mistress of her own house, except when the bills were to be paid, Becky soon discovered the way to soothe and please her. She talked to her perpetually about Major Dobbin sent about his business, and made no scruple of declaring her admiration for that excellent, high-minded gentleman, and of telling Emmy that she had behaved most cruelly regarding him. Emmy defended her conduct, and showed that it was dictated only by the purest religious principles; that a woman once, &c., and to such an angel as him whom she had had the good fortune to marry, was married for ever; but she had no objection to hear the Major praised as much as ever Becky chose to praise him; and indeed brought the conversation round to the Dobbin subject a score of times every day.

Means were easily found to win the favour of Georgy and the servants. Amelia's maid, it has been said, was heart and soul in favour of the generous Major. Having at first disliked Becky for being the means of dismissing him from the presence of her mistress, she was reconciled to Mrs. Crawley subsequently, because the latter became William's most ardent admirer and champion. And in those nightly conclaves in which the two ladies indulged after their parties, and while Miss Payne was "brushing their 'airs," as she called the yellow locks of the one, and the soft brown tresses of the other, this girl always put in her word for that dear good gentleman Major Dobbin. Her advocacy did not make Amelia angry any more than Rebecca's admiration of him. She made George write to him constantly, and persisted in sending Mamma's kind love in a postscript. And as she looked at her husband's portrait of nights, it no longer reproached her — perhaps she reproached it, now William was gone.

Emmy was not very happy after her heroic sacrifice. She was very *distraite*, nervous, silent, and ill to please. The family had never known her so peevish. She grew pale and ill. She used to try and sing certain songs ("Einsam bin ich nicht alleine," was one of them; that tender love-song of Weber's, which, in old-fashioned days, young ladies, and when you were scarcely born, showed that those who lived before you knew too how to love and to sing); — certain songs, I say, to which the Major was partial; and as she warbled them in the twilight in the drawing-room, she would break off in the midst of the song, and walk into her neighbouring apartment, and there, no doubt, take refuge in the miniature of her husband.

Some books still subsisted, after Dobbin's departure, with his name written in them; a German Dictionary, for instance, with "William Dobbin, —th Reg.," in the fly-leaf; a guide-book with his initials, and one or two other volumes which belonged to the Major. Emmy cleared these away, and put them on the drawers, where she placed her work-box, her desk, her Bible, and Prayer-book, under the pictures of the two Georges. And the Major, on going away, having left his gloves behind him, it is a fact that Georgy, rummaging his mother's desk some time afterwards, found the gloves neatly folded up, and put away in what they call the secret drawers of the desk.

Not caring for society, and moping there a great deal, Emmy's chief pleasure in the summer evenings was to take long walks with Georgy (during which Rebecca was left to the society of Mr. Joseph), and then the mother and son used to talk about the Major in a way which even made the boy smile. She told him that she thought Major William was the best man in all the world; the gentlest and the kindest, the bravest and the humblest. Over and over again, she told him how they owed everything which they possessed in the world to that kind friend's benevolent care of them; how he had befriended them all through their poverty and misfortunes; watched over them when nobody cared for them; how all his comrades admired him though he never spoke of his own gallant actions; how Georgy's father trusted him beyond all other men, and had been constantly befriended by the good William. "Why, when your papa was a little boy," she said, "he often told me that it was William who defended him against a tyrant at the school where they were; and their friendship never ceased from that day until the last, when your dear father fell."

"Did Dobbin kill the man who killed papa?" Georgy said. "I'm sure he did, or he would if he could have caught him; wouldn't he, mother? When I'm in the army, won't I hate the French? — that's all."

In such colloquies the mother and the child passed a great deal of their time together. The artless woman had made a confidant of the boy. He was as much William's friend as everybody else who knew him well.

By the way, Mrs. Becky, not to be behind-hand in
sentiment, had got a miniature too hanging up in her
room, to the surprise and amusement of most people,
and the delight of the original, who was no other than
our friend Jos. On her first coming to favour the Sedleys with a visit, the little woman, who had arrived with
a remarkably small shabby kit, was perhaps ashamed of
the meanness of her trunks and band-boxes, and often
spoke with great respect about her baggage left behind
at Leipzig, which she must have from that city. When
a traveller talks to you perpetually about the splendour
of his luggage, which he does not happen to have with
him; my son, beware of that traveller! He is, ten to
one, an impostor.

Neither Jos nor Emmy knew this important maxim.
It seemed to them of no consequence whether Becky
had a quantity of very fine clothes in invisible trunks;
but as her present supply was exceedingly shabby,
Emmy supplied her out of her own stores, or took her
to the best milliner in the town, and there fitted her
out. It was no more torn collars now, I promise you, and
faded silks trailing off at the shoulder. Becky changed
her habits with her situation in life — the rouge-pot was
suspended — another excitement to which she had accustomed herself was also put aside, or at least only
indulged in in privacy; as when she was prevailed on
by Jos of a summer evening, Emmy and the boy being
absent on their walks, to take a little spirit-and-water.
But if she did not indulge — the courier did: that
rascal Kirsch could not be kept from the bottle; nor
could he tell how much he took when he applied to it.
He was sometimes surprised himself at the way in which
Mr. Sedley's Cognac diminished. Well, well; this is a
painful subject. Becky did not very likely indulge so
much as she used before she entered a decorous family.

At last the much-bragged about boxes arrived from Leipzig; — three of them not by any means large or splendid; — nor did Becky appear to take out any sort of dresses or ornaments from the boxes when they did arrive. But out of one, which contained a mass of her papers (it was that very box which Rawdon Crawley had ransacked in his furious hunt for Becky's concealed money), she took a picture with great glee, which she pinned up in her room, and to which she introduced Jos. It was the portrait of a gentleman in pencil, his face having the advantage of being painted up in pink. He was riding on an elephant away from some cocoa-nut trees, and a pagoda: it was an Eastern scene.

"God bless my soul, it is my portrait," Jos cried out. It was he indeed, blooming in youth and beauty, in a nankeen jacket of the cut of 1804. It was the old picture that used to hang up in Russell Square.

"I bought it," said Becky, in a voice trembling with emotion; "I went to see if I could be of any use to my kind friends. I have never parted with that picture — I never will."

"Won't you?" Jos cried, with a look of unutterable rapture and satisfaction. "Did you really now value it for my sake?"

"You know I did, well enough," said Becky; "but why speak, — why think, — why look back! It is too late now!"

That evening's conversation was delicious for Jos. Emmy only came in to go to bed very tired and unwell. Jos and his fair guest had a charming *tête-à-tête*, and his sister could hear, as she lay awake in her adjoining chamber, Rebecca singing over to Jos the old songs of 1815. He did not sleep, for a wonder, that night, any more than Amelia.

It was June, and, by consequence, high season in

London; Jos, who read the incomparable *Galignani* (the exile's best friend) through every day, used to favour the ladies with extracts from his paper during their breakfast. Every week in this paper there is a full account of military movements, in which Jos, as a man who had seen service, was especially interested. On one occasion he read out — " Arrival of the —th regiment.— Gravesend, June 20.—The Ramchunder, East Indiaman, came into the river this morning, having on board 14 officers, and 132 rank and file of this gallant corps. They have been absent from England fourteen years, having been embarked the year after Waterloo, in which glorious conflict they took an active part, and having subsequently distinguished themselves in the Burmese war. The veteran colonel, Sir Michael O'Dowd, K.C.B., with his lady and sister, landed here yesterday, with Captains Posky, Stubble, Macraw, Malony; Lieutenants Smith, Jones, Thompson, F. Thomson; Ensigns Hicks and Grady; the band on the pier playing the national anthem, and the crowd loudly cheering the gallant veterans as they went into Wayte's hotel, where a sumptuous banquet was provided for the defenders of Old England. During the repast, which we need not say was served up in Wayte's best style, the cheering continued so enthusiastically, that Lady O'Dowd and the Colonel came forward to the balcony, and drank the healths of their fellow-countrymen in a bumper of Wayte's best claret."

On a second occasion Jos read a brief announcement — Major Dobbin had joined the —th regiment at Chatham; and subsequently he promulgated accounts of the presentations at the Drawing-room, of Colonel Sir Michael O'Dowd, K.C.B., Lady O'Dowd (by Mrs. Molloy Malony of Ballymalony), and Miss Glorvina O'Dowd (by Lady O'Dowd). Almost directly after this, Dob-

bin's name appeared among the Lieutenant-Colonels:
for old Marshal Tiptoff had died during the passage of
the —th from Madras, and the Sovereign was pleased
to advance Colonel Sir Michael O'Dowd to the rank of
Major-General on his return to England, with an inti-
mation that he should be Colonel of the distinguished
regiment which he had so long commanded.

Amelia had been made aware of some of these movements. The correspondence between George and his
guardian had not ceased by any means: William had
even written once or twice to her since his departure,
but in a manner so unconstrainedly cold, that the poor
woman felt now in her turn that she had lost her power
over him, and that, as he had said, he was free. He
had left her, and she was wretched. The memory of
his almost countless services, and lofty and affectionate
regard, now presented itself to her, and rebuked her
day and night. She brooded over those recollections
according to her wont: saw the purity and beauty of
the affection with which she had trifled, and reproached
herself for having flung away such a treasure.

It was gone indeed. William had spent it all out.
He loved her no more, he thought, as he had loved her.
He never could again. That sort of regard, which he
had proffered to her for so many faithful years, can't be
flung down and shattered, and mended so as to show no
scars. The little heedless tyrant had so destroyed it.
No, William thought again and again, "It was myself
I deluded, and persisted in cajoling; had she been
worthy of the love I gave her, she would have returned it
long ago. It was a fond mistake. Isn't the whole
course of life made up of such? and suppose I had won
her, should I not have been disenchanted the day after
my victory? Why pine, or be ashamed of my defeat?"

The more he thought of this long passage of his life, the more clearly he saw his deception. "I'll go into harness again," he said, "and do my duty in that state of life in which it has pleased Heaven to place me. I will see that the buttons of the recruits are properly bright, and that the sergeants make no mistakes in their accounts. I will dine at mess, and listen to the Scotch surgeon telling his stories. When I am old and broken, I will go on half-pay, and my old sisters shall scold me. I have ' geliebt and gelebet ' as the girl in Wallenstein says. I am done. — Pay the bills, and get me a cigar : find out what there is at the play to-night, Francis ; to-morrow we cross by the ' Batavier.' " He made the above speech, whereof Francis only heard the last two lines, pacing up and down the Boompjes at Rotterdam. The " Batavier " was lying in the basin. He could see the place on the quarter-deck, where he and Emmy had sate on the happy voyage out. What had that little Mrs. Crawley to say to him? Psha! to-morrow we will put to sea, and return to England, home, and duty!

After June all the little Court Society of Pumper-nickel used to separate, according to the German plan, and make for a hundred watering-places, where they drank at the wells ; rode upon donkeys ; gambled at the *redoutes*, if they had money and a mind ; rushed with hundreds of their kind, to gormandise at the *tables d'hôte;* and idled away the summer. The English diplomatists went off to Toeplitz and Kissengen, their French rivals shut up their *chancellerie* and whisked away to their darling Boulevard de Gand. The Transparent reigning family took too to the waters, or retired to their hunting-lodges. Everybody went away having any pretensions to politeness, and, of course, with them,

Doctor von Glauber, the Court Doctor and his Baroness. The seasons for the baths were the most productive periods of the Doctor's practice — he united business with pleasure, and his chief place of resort was Ostend, which is much frequented by Germans, and where the Doctor treated himself and his spouse to what he called a " dib " in the sea.

His interesting patient, Jos, was a regular milch cow to the Doctor, and he easily persuaded the civilian, both for his own health's sake and that of his charming sister, which was really very much shattered, to pass the summer at that hideous seaport town. Emmy did not care where she went much. Georgy jumped at the idea of a move. As for Becky, she came as a matter of course in the fourth place inside of the fine barouche Mr. Jos had bought: the two domestics being on the box in front. She might have some misgivings about the friends whom she should meet at Ostend, and who might be likely to tell ugly stories — but, bah! she was strong enough to hold her own. She had cast such an anchor in Jos now as would require a strong storm to shake. That incident of the picture had finished him. Becky took down her elephant, and put it into the little box which she had had from Amelia ever so many years ago. Emmy also came off with her Lares, — her two pictures, — and the party, finally, were lodged in an exceedingly dear and uncomfortable house at Ostend.

There Amelia began to take baths, and get what good she could from them, and though scores of people of Becky's acquaintance passed her and cut her, yet Mrs. Osborne, who walked about with her, and who knew nobody, was not aware of the treatment experienced by the friend whom she had chosen so judiciously as a companion; indeed, Becky never thought fit to tell her what was passing under her innocent eyes.

Some of Mrs. Rawdon Crawley's acquaintances, however, acknowledged her readily enough, — perhaps more
readily than she would have desired. Among those
were Major Loder (unattached), and Captain Rook (late
of the Rifles), who might be seen any day on the Dyke,
smoking and staring at the women, and who speedily got
an introduction to the hospitable board and select circle
of Mr. Joseph Sedley. In fact, they would take no denial;
they burst into the house whether Becky was at home
or not, walked into Mrs. Osborne's drawing-room, which
they perfumed with their coats and mustachios, called
Jos "Old buck," and invaded his dinner-table, and
laughed and drank for long hours there.

"What can they mean?" asked Georgy, who did not
like these gentlemen. "I heard the Major say to Mrs.
Crawley yesterday, 'No, no, Becky, you shan't keep the
old buck to yourself. We must have the bones in, or,
dammy, I'll split.' What could the Major mean,
Mamma?"

"Major! don't call *him* Major!" Emmy said. "I'm
sure I can't tell what he meant." His presence and that
of his friend inspired the little lady with intolerable terror and aversion. They paid her tipsy compliments;
they leered at her over the dinner-table. And the Captain made her advances that filled her with sickening
dismay, nor would she ever see him unless she had
George by her side.

Rebecca, to do her justice, never would let either
of these men remain alone with Amelia; the Major
was disengaged too, and swore he would be the winner
of her. A couple of ruffians were fighting for this
innocent creature, gambling for her at her own table;
and though she was not aware of the rascals' designs
upon her, yet she felt a horror and uneasiness in their
presence, and longed to fly.

She besought, she entreated Jos to go. Not he. He was slow of movement, tied to his Doctor, and perhaps to some other leading-strings. At least Becky was not anxious to go to England.

At last she took a great resolution — made the great plunge. She wrote off a letter to a friend whom she had on the other side of the water; a letter about which she did not speak a word to anybody, which she carried herself to the post under her shawl, nor was any remark made about it; only that she looked very much flushed and agitated when Georgy met her; and she kissed him and hung over him a great deal that night. She did not come out of her room after her return from her walk. Becky thought it was Major Loder and the Captain who frightened her.

"She must n't stop here," Becky reasoned with herself. "She must go away, the silly little fool. She is still whimpering after that gaby of a husband — dead (and served right!) these fifteen years. She shan't marry either of these men. It's too bad of Loder. No; she shall marry the bamboo-cane, I'll settle it this very night."

So Becky took a cup of tea to Amelia in her private apartment, and found that lady in the company of her miniatures, and in a most melancholy and nervous condition. She laid down the cup of tea.

"Thank you," said Amelia.

"Listen to me, Amelia," said Becky, marching up and down the room before the other, and surveying her with a sort of contemptuous kindness. "I want to talk to you. You must go away from here and from the impertinences of these men. I won't have you harassed by them: and they will insult you if you stay. I tell you they are rascals; men fit to send to the hulks. Never mind how I know them. I know everybody.

Jos can't protect you, he is too weak, and wants a protector himself. You are no more fit to live in the world than a baby in arms. You must marry, or you and your precious boy will go to ruin. You must have a husband, you fool; and one of the best gentlemen I ever saw has offered you a hundred times, and you have rejected him, you silly, heartless, ungrateful little creature!"

"I tried — I tried my best, indeed I did, Rebecca," said Amelia, deprecatingly, "but I couldn't forget — ;" and she finished the sentence by looking up at the portrait.

"Couldn't forget *him!*" cried out Becky, "that selfish humbug, that low-bred cockney-dandy, that padded booby, who had neither wit, nor manners, nor heart, and was no more to be compared to your friend with the bamboo cane than you are to Queen Elizabeth. Why, the man was weary of you, and would have jilted you, but that Dobbin forced him to keep his word. He owned it to me. He never cared for you. He used to sneer about you to me, time after time; and made love to me the week after he married you."

"It's false! It's false! Rebecca," cried out Amelia, starting up.

"Look there, you fool," Becky said, still with provoking good humour, and taking a little paper out of her belt, she opened it and flung it into Emmy's lap. "You know his hand-writing. He wrote that to me — wanted me to run away with him — gave it me under your nose, the day before he was shot — and served him right!" Becky repeated.

Emmy did not hear her; she was looking at the letter. It was that which George had put into the bouquet and given to Becky on the night of the Duchess of Richmond's ball. It was as she said: the foolish young man had asked her to fly.

Emmy's head sank down, and for almost the last time in which she shall be called upon to weep in this history, she commenced that work. Her head fell to her bosom, and her hands went up to her eyes; and there for a while, she gave way to her emotions, as Becky stood on and regarded her. Who shall analyse those tears, and say whether they were sweet or bitter? Was she most grieved, because the idol of her life was tumbled down and shivered at her feet, or indignant that her love had been so despised, or glad because the barrier was removed which modesty had placed between her and a new, a real affection? "There is nothing to forbid me now," she thought. " I may love him with all my heart now. O, I will, I will, if he will but let me, and forgive me." I believe it was this feeling rushed over all the others which agitated that gentle little bosom.

Indeed, she did not cry so much as Becky expected — the other soothed and kissed her — a rare mark of sympathy with Mrs. Becky. She treated Emmy like a child, and patted her head. " And now let us get pen and ink, and write to him to come this minute," she said.

" I — I wrote to him this morning," Emmy said, blushing exceedingly. Becky screamed with laughter — " *Un biglietto*," she sang out with Rosina, " *eccolo quà !* " — the whole house echoed with her shrill singing.

Two mornings after this little scene, although the day was rainy and gusty, and Amelia had had an exceedingly wakeful night, listening to the wind roaring, and pitying all travellers by land and by water, yet she got up early, and insisted upon taking a walk on the Dyke with Georgy; and there she paced as the rain beat into her face, and she looked out westward across the dark sea line, and over the swollen billows which came tumbling and frothing to the shore. Neither spoke much, except now and then, when the boy said a few words to his timid companion, indicative of sympathy and protection.

"I hope he won't cross in such weather," Emmy said.

"I bet ten to one he does," the boy answered. "Look, mother, there's the smoke of the steamer." It was that signal, sure enough.

But though the steamer was under weigh, he might not be on board; he might not have got the letter; he might not choose to come. — A hundred fears poured one over the other into the little heart, as fast as the waves on to the dyke.

The boat followed the smoke into sight. Georgy had a dandy telescope, and got the vessel under view in the most skilful manner. And he made appropriate nautical comments upon the manner of the approach of the steamer as she came nearer and nearer, dipping and rising in the water. The signal of an English steamer in sight went fluttering up to the mast on the pier. I dare say Mrs. Amelia's heart was in a similar flutter.

Emmy tried to look through the telescope over George's shoulder, but she could make nothing of it. She only saw a black eclipse bobbing up and down before her eyes.

George took the glass again and raked the vessel. "How she does pitch!" he said. "There goes a wave slap over her bows. There's only two people on deck besides the steersman. There's a man lying down, and a — chap in a — cloak with a — Hooray! — It's Dob by Jingo!" He clapped to the telescope and flung his arms round his mother. As for that lady: let us say what she did in the words of a favourite poet— Δακρυοεν γελασασα. She was sure it was William. It could be no other. What she had said about hoping that he would not come was all hypocrisy. Of course he would come : what could he do else but come. She knew he would come.

The ship came swiftly nearer and nearer. As they went in to meet her at the landing-place at the Quay, Emmy's knees trembled so that she scarcely could run. She would have liked to kneel down and say her prayers of thanks there. Oh, she thought, she would be all her life saying them !

It was such a bad day that as the vessel came along-side of the Quay there were no idlers abroad ; scarcely even a commissioner on the look-out for the few passengers in the steamer. That young scapegrace George had fled too : and as the gentleman in the old cloak lined with red stuff stepped on to the shore, there was scarcely any one present to see what took place, which was briefly this :

A lady in a dripping white bonnet and shawl, with her two little hands out before her, went up to him, and in the next minute she had altogether disappeared under the folds of the old cloak, and was kissing one of his hands with all her might ; whilst the other, I suppose, was engaged in holding her to his heart (which her head just about reached) and in preventing her from tumbling down. She was murmuring something about — forgive — dear William — dear, dear, dearest friend — kiss, kiss, kiss, and so forth — and in fact went on under the cloak in an absurd manner.

When Emmy emerged from it, she still kept tight hold of one of William's hands, and looked up in his face. It was full of sadness and tender love and pity. She understood its reproach, and hung down her head.

"It was time you sent for me, dear Amelia," he said.

"You will never go again, William."

"No, never," he answered: and pressed the dear little soul once more to his heart.

As they issued out of the Custom-house precincts, Georgy broke out on them, with his telescope up to his eye, and a loud laugh of welcome; he danced round the couple, and performed many facetious antics as he led them up to the house. Jos was n't up yet; Becky not visible (though she looked at them through the blinds). Georgy ran off to see about breakfast. Emmy, whose shawl and bonnet were off in the passage in the hands of Mrs. Payne, now went to undo the clasp of William's cloak, and — we will, if you please, go with George, and look after breakfast for the Colonel. The vessel is in port. He has got the prize he has been trying for all his life. The bird has come in at last. There it is with its head on his shoulder, billing and cooing close up to his heart, with soft outstretched fluttering wings. This is what he has asked for every day and hour for eighteen years. This is what he pined after. Here it is — the summit, the end — the last page of the third volume. Good-bye, Colonel — God bless you, honest William! — Farewell, dear Amelia — Grow green again, tender little parasite, round the rugged old oak to which you cling!

Perhaps it was compunction towards the kind and simple creature, who had been the first in life to defend her, perhaps it was a dislike to all such sentimental scenes,— but Rebecca, satisfied with her part in the transaction, never presented herself before Colonel Dobbin and the lady whom he married. "Particular business," she said, took her to Bruges, whither she went; and only Georgy and his uncle were present at the marriage ceremony. When it was over, and Georgy had rejoined his parents, Mrs. Becky returned (just for a few days) to comfort the solitary bachelor, Joseph Sedley. He preferred a continental life, he said, and declined to join in housekeeping with his sister and her husband.

Emmy was very glad in her heart to think that she had written to her husband before she read or knew of that letter of George's. "I knew it all along," William said; "but could I use that weapon against the poor fellow's memory? It was that which made me suffer so when you —— "

"Never speak of that day again," Emmy cried out, so contrite and humble, that William turned off the conversation, by his account of Glorvina and dear old Peggy O'Dowd, with whom he was sitting when the letter of recall reached him. "If you had n't sent for me," he added with a laugh, "who knows what Glorvina's name might be now?"

At present it is Glorvina Posky (now Mrs. Major Posky), she took him on the death of his first wife; having resolved never to marry out of the regiment. Lady O'Dowd is also so attached to it that, she says, if anything were to happen to Mick, bedad she 'd come back and marry some of 'em. But the Major-General is quite well, and lives in great splendour at O'Dowdstown, with a pack of beagles, and (with the exception of perhaps their neighbour, Hoggarty of Castle Hoggarty) he is the first man of his county. Her Ladyship still dances jigs, and insisted on standing up with the Master of the Horse at the Lord Lieutenant's last ball. Both she and Glorvina declared that Dobbin had used the latter *sheamfully*, but Posky falling in, Glorvina was consoled, and a beautiful turban from Paris appeased the wrath of Lady O'Dowd.

When Colonel Dobbin quitted the service, which he did immediately after his marriage, he rented a pretty little country place in Hampshire, not far from Queen's

Crawley, where, after the passing of the Reform Bill, Sir Pitt and his family constantly resided now. All idea of a peerage was out of the question, the baronet's two seats in Parliament being lost. He was both out of pocket and out of spirits by that catastrophe, failed in his health, and prophesied the speedy ruin of the Empire.

Lady Jane and Mrs. Dobbin became great friends — there was a perpetual crossing of pony-chaises between the Hall and the Evergreens, the Colonel's place (rented of his friend Major Ponto, who was abroad with his family). Her Ladyship was godmother to Mrs. Dobbin's child, which bore her name, and was christened by the Rev. James Crawley, who succeeded his father in the living: and a pretty close friendship subsisted between the two lads, George and Rawdon, who hunted and shot together in the vacations, were both entered of the same College at Cambridge, and quarrelled with each other about Lady Jane's daughter, with whom they were both, of course, in love. A match between George and that young lady was long a favourite scheme of both the matrons, though I have heard that Miss Crawley herself inclined towards her cousin.

Mrs. Rawdon Crawley's name was never mentioned by either family. There were reasons why all should be silent regarding her. For wherever Mr. Joseph Sedley went, she travelled likewise; and that infatuated man seemed to be entirely her slave. The Colonel's lawyers informed him that his brother-in-law had effected a heavy insurance upon his life, whence it was probable that he had been raising money to discharge debts. He procured prolonged leave of absence from the East India House, and indeed his infirmities were daily increasing.

On hearing the news about the insurance, Amelia, in a good deal of alarm, entreated her husband to go to

Brussels, where Jos then was, and inquire into the state of his affairs. The Colonel quitted home with reluctance (for he was deeply immersed in his " History of the Punjaub," which still occupies him, and much alarmed about his little daughter, whom he idolizes, and who was just recovering from the chicken-pox), and went to Brussels and found Jos living at one of the enormous hotels in that city. Mrs. Crawley, who had her carriage, gave entertainments, and lived in a very genteel manner, occupied another suite of apartments in the same hotel.

The Colonel, of course, did not desire to see that lady, or even think proper to notify his arrival at Brussels, except privately to Jos by a message through his valet. Jos begged the Colonel to come and see him that night, when Mrs. Crawley would be at a *soirée*, and when they could meet *alone*. He found his brother-in-law in a condition of pitiable infirmity; and dreadfully afraid of Rebecca, though eager in his praises of her. She tended him through a series of unheard-of illnesses, with a fidelity most admirable. She had been a daughter to him. "But — but — oh for God's sake, do come and live near me, and — and — see me sometimes," whimpered out the unfortunate man.

The Colonel's brow darkened at this. "We can't, Jos," he said. " Considering the circumstances, Amelia can't visit you."

"I swear to you — I swear to you on the Bible," gasped out Joseph, wanting to kiss the book, " that she is as innocent as a child, as spotless as your own wife."

"It may be so," said the Colonel, gloomily; " but Emmy can't come to you. Be a man, Jos: break off this disreputable connection. Come home to your family. We hear your affairs are involved."

"Involved !" cried Jos. " Who has told such calumnies. All my money is placed out most advantageously.

Mrs. Crawley — that is — I mean, — it is laid out to the best interest."

"You are not in debt, then? Why did you insure your life?"

"I thought — a little present to her — in case anything happened; and you know my health is so delicate — common gratitude you know — and I intend to leave all my money to you — and I can spare it out of my income, indeed I can," cried out William's weak brother-in-law.

The Colonel besought Jos to fly at once — to go back to India, whither Mrs. Crawley could not follow him; to do anything to break off a connection which might have the most fatal consequences to him.

Jos clasped his hands, and cried, — "He would go back to India. He would do anything: only he must have time: they must n't say anything to Mrs. Crawley: — she 'd — she 'd kill me if she knew it. You don't know what a terrible woman she is," the poor wretch said.

"Then, why not come away with me?" said Dobbin in reply; but Jos had not the courage. "He would see Dobbin again in the morning; he must on no account say that he had been there. He must go now. Becky might come in." And Dobbin quitted him full of forebodings.

He never saw Jos more. Three months afterwards Joseph Sedley died at Aix-la-Chapelle. It was found that all his property had been muddled away in speculations, and was represented by valueless shares in different bubble companies. All his available assets were the two thousand pounds for which his life was insured, and which were left equally between his beloved "sister Amelia, wife of, &c., and his friend and invaluable attendant during sickness, Rebecca, wife of

Lieutenant-Colonel Rawdon Crawley, C.B.," who was appointed administratrix.

The solicitor of the Insurance Company swore it was the blackest case that ever had come before him; talked of sending a commission to Aix to examine into the death, and the Company refused payment of the policy. But Mrs., or Lady Crawley, as she styled herself, came to town at once (attended with her solicitors, Messrs. Burke, Thurtell, and Hayes, of Thavies Inn), and dared the Company to refuse the payment. They invited examination, they declared that she was the object of an infamous conspiracy, which had been pursuing her all through life, and triumphed finally. The money was paid, and her character established, but Colonel Dobbin sent back his share of the legacy to the Insurance Office, and rigidly declined to hold any communication with Rebecca.

She never was Lady Crawley, though she continued so to call herself. His Excellency Colonel Rawdon Crawley died of yellow fever at Coventry Island, most deeply beloved and deplored, and six weeks before the demise of his brother, Sir Pitt. The estate consequently devolved upon the present Sir Rawdon Crawley, Bart.

He, too, has declined to see his mother, to whom he makes a liberal allowance; and who, besides, appears to be very wealthy. The Baronet lives entirely at Queen's Crawley, with Lady Jane and her daughter; whilst Rebecca, Lady Crawley, chiefly hangs about Bath and Cheltenham, where a very strong party of excellent people consider her to be a most injured woman. She has her enemies. Who has not? Her life is her answer to them. She busies herself in works of piety. She goes to church, and never without a footman. Her name is in all the Charity Lists. The Destitute Orange-girl, the Neglected Washerwoman, the Distressed Muffin-man, find in her a fast and generous friend. She is always having stalls at Fancy Fairs for the benefit of these hapless beings. Emmy, her children, and the Colonel, coming to London some time back, found themselves suddenly before her at one of these fairs. She cast down her eyes demurely and smiled as they started away from her; Emmy skurrying off on the arm of George (now grown a dashing young gentleman), and the Colonel seizing up his little Janey, of whom he is fonder than of anything in the world — fonder even than of his "History of the Punjaub."

"Fonder than he is of me," Emmy thinks, with a sigh. But he never said a word to Amelia that was not kind and gentle; or thought of a want of hers that he did not try to gratify.

Ah! *Vanitas Vanitatum!* which of us is happy in this world? Which of us has his desire? or, having it, is satisfied? — come, children, let us shut up the box and the puppets, for our play is played out.